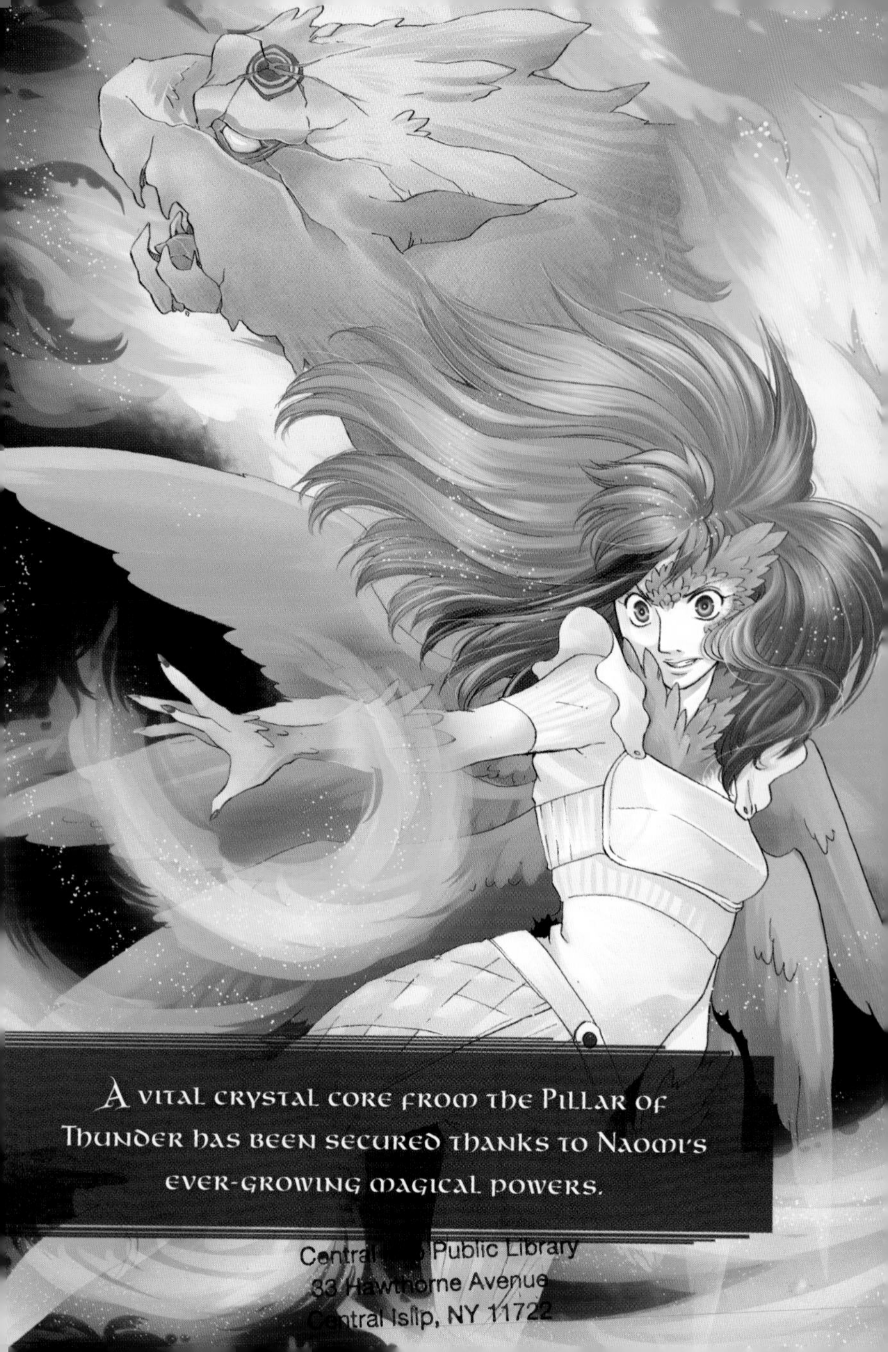
A vital crystal core from the Pillar of Thunder has been secured thanks to Naomi's ever-growing magical powers.

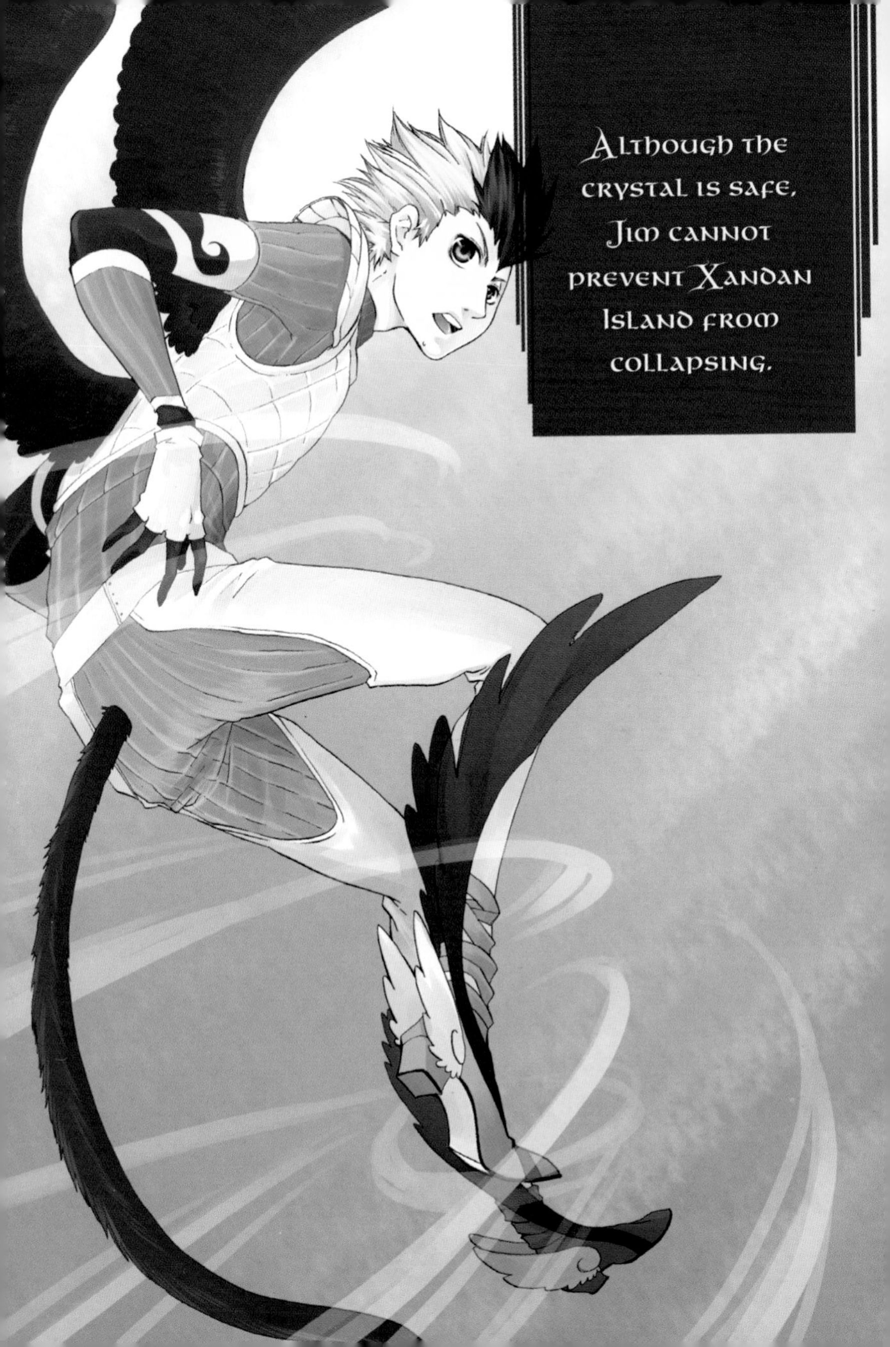
Although the crystal is safe, Jim cannot prevent Xandan Island from collapsing.

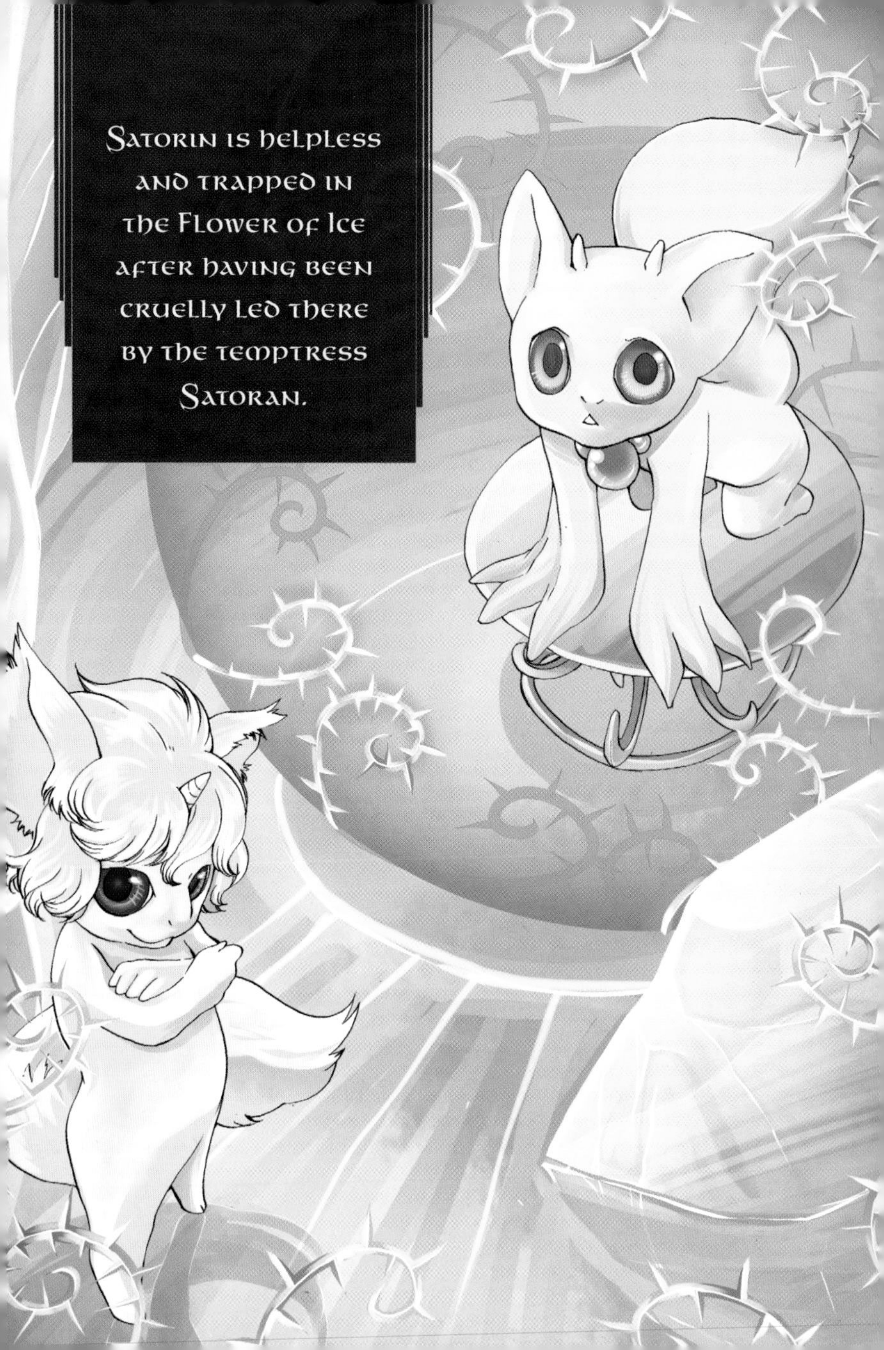
Satorin is helpless and trapped in the Flower of Ice after having been cruelly led there by the temptress Satoran.

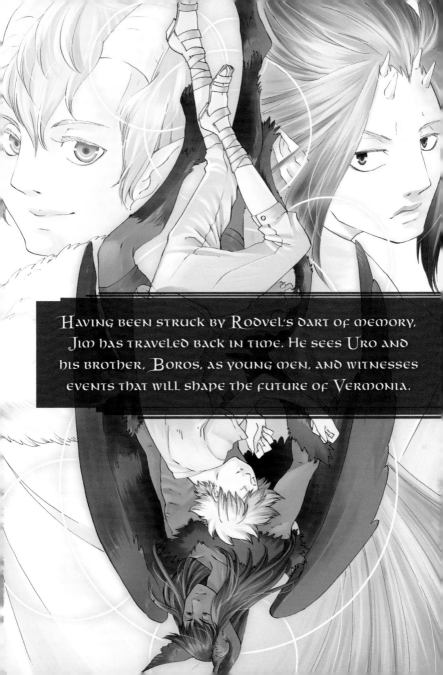

HAVING BEEN STRUCK BY RODVEL'S DART OF MEMORY, JIM HAS TRAVELED BACK IN TIME. HE SEES URO AND HIS BROTHER, BOROS, AS YOUNG MEN, AND WITNESSES EVENTS THAT WILL SHAPE THE FUTURE OF VERMONIA.

VERMONIA

To the Pillar of Wind

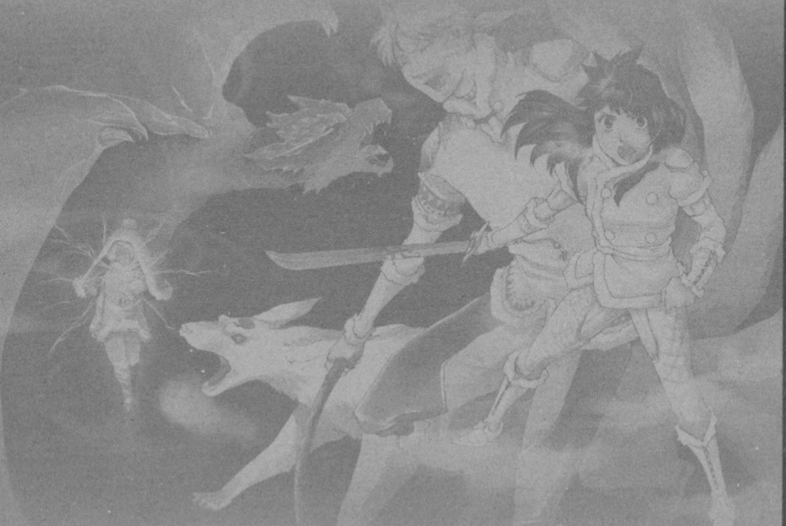

YOYO

ヨーヨー

Candlewick Press

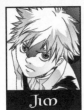

Jim

Bass Player
Blue Star Warrior

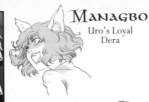

Managbo

Uro's Loyal
Dera

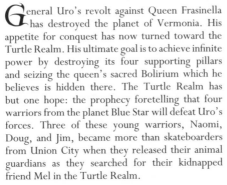

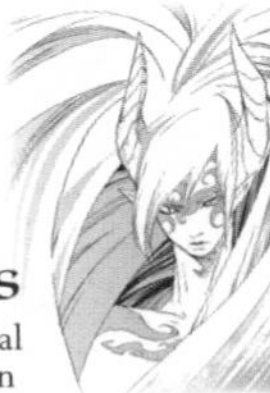

Omus

Uro's Loyal
Henchman

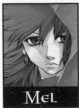

Mel

Lead Vocalist
Blue Star Warrior

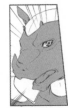

Miranda

Warrior of the Umli

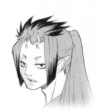

General Uro

Master of Dark
Yami Magic

General Uro's revolt against Queen Frasinella has destroyed the planet of Vermonia. His appetite for conquest has now turned toward the Turtle Realm. His ultimate goal is to achieve infinite power by destroying its four supporting pillars and seizing the queen's sacred Bolirium which he believes is hidden there. The Turtle Realm has but one hope: the prophecy foretelling that four warriors from the planet Blue Star will defeat Uro's forces. Three of these young warriors, Naomi, Doug, and Jim, became more than skateboarders from Union City when they released their animal guardians as they searched for their kidnapped friend Mel in the Turtle Realm.

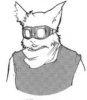

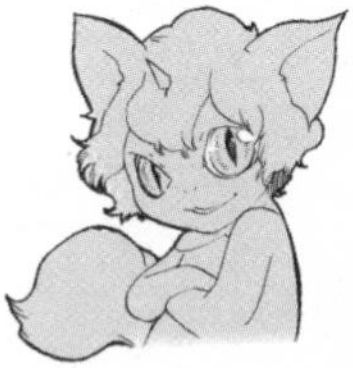

In Volume 5, Jim and Doug save a small crystal core of the Pillar of Thunder, barely escaping with their lives. This rock from Xandan Island is vital to fuel the Vleste, the warship of the Aqami people, which will be used to protect the remaining pillar: the Pillar of Wind. But first, before it's too late, the Blue Star warriors must save Mel and their mysterious guide, the squelp Satorin, from Uro's prison. A magical dart from Uro's lieutenant, Rodvel, has sent Jim inside a memory of Vermonia. Will he find the clues he needs to free his friends and save the last pillar?

Vulka

Blacksmith
Captain of the Vleste

Satoran

Shapeshifting
Monster

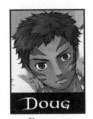

Doug

Drummer
Blue Star Warrior

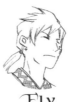

Satorin

Magical Squelp

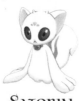

Fly

Potonawi Warrior

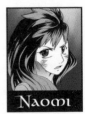

Naomi

Lead Guitarist
Blue Star Warrior

FOR MORE INFORMATION GO TO VERMONIA.COM

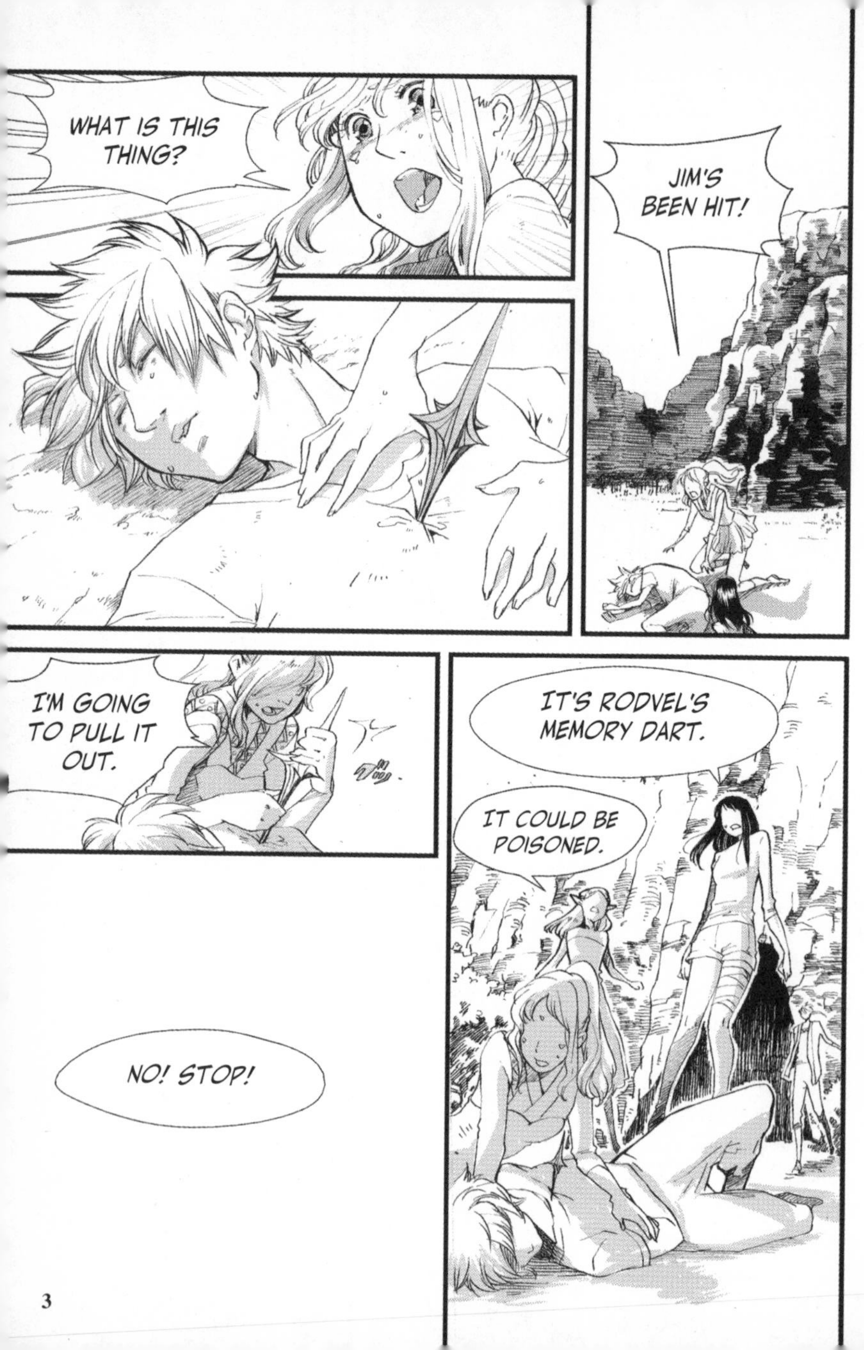
JIM'S BEEN HIT!
WHAT IS THIS THING?
IT'S RODVEL'S MEMORY DART.
IT COULD BE POISONED.
I'M GOING TO PULL IT OUT.
NO! STOP!

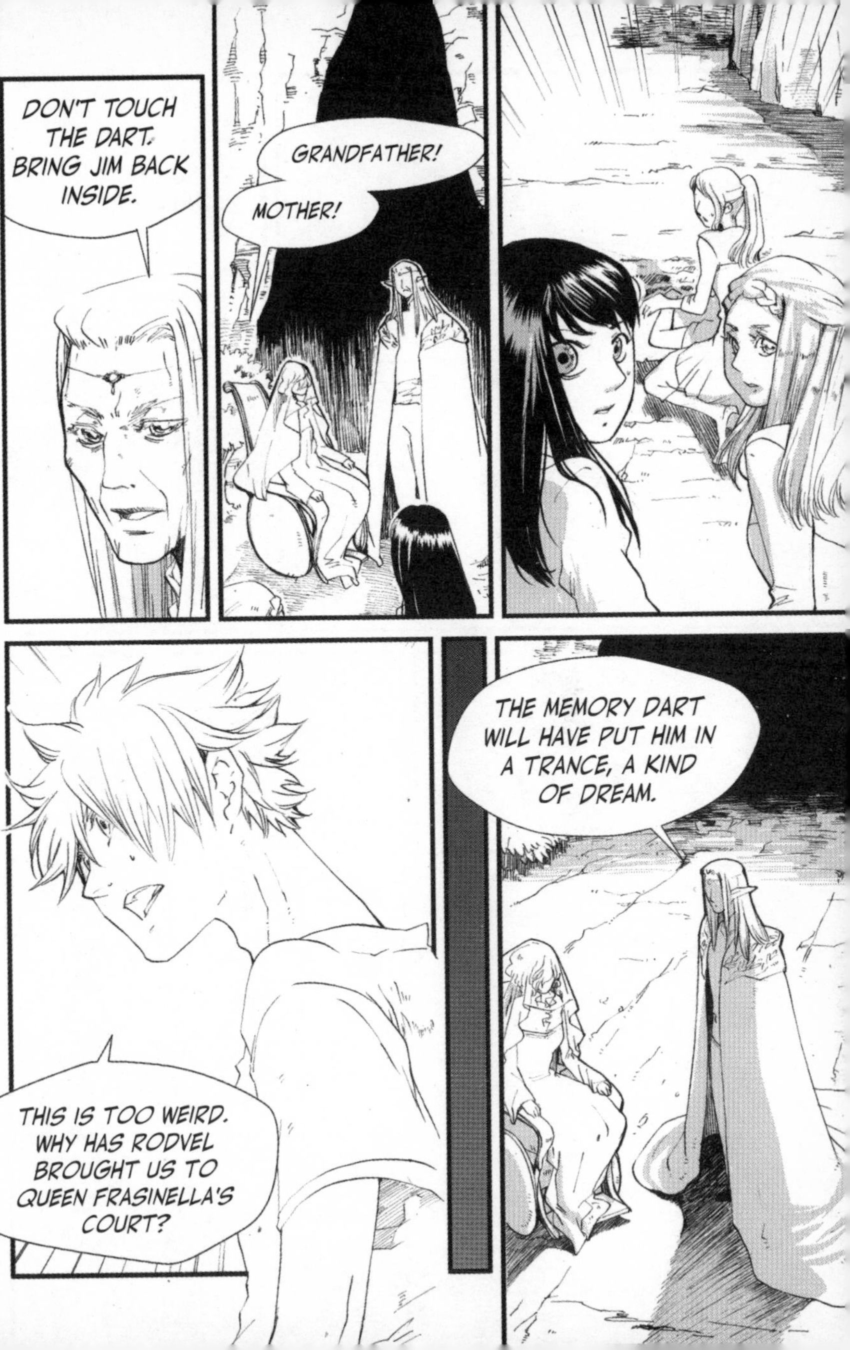
GRANDFATHER!
MOTHER!
DON'T TOUCH THE DART. BRING JIM BACK INSIDE.
THE MEMORY DART WILL HAVE PUT HIM IN A TRANCE, A KIND OF DREAM.
THIS IS TOO WEIRD. WHY HAS RODVEL BROUGHT US TO QUEEN FRASINELLA'S COURT?

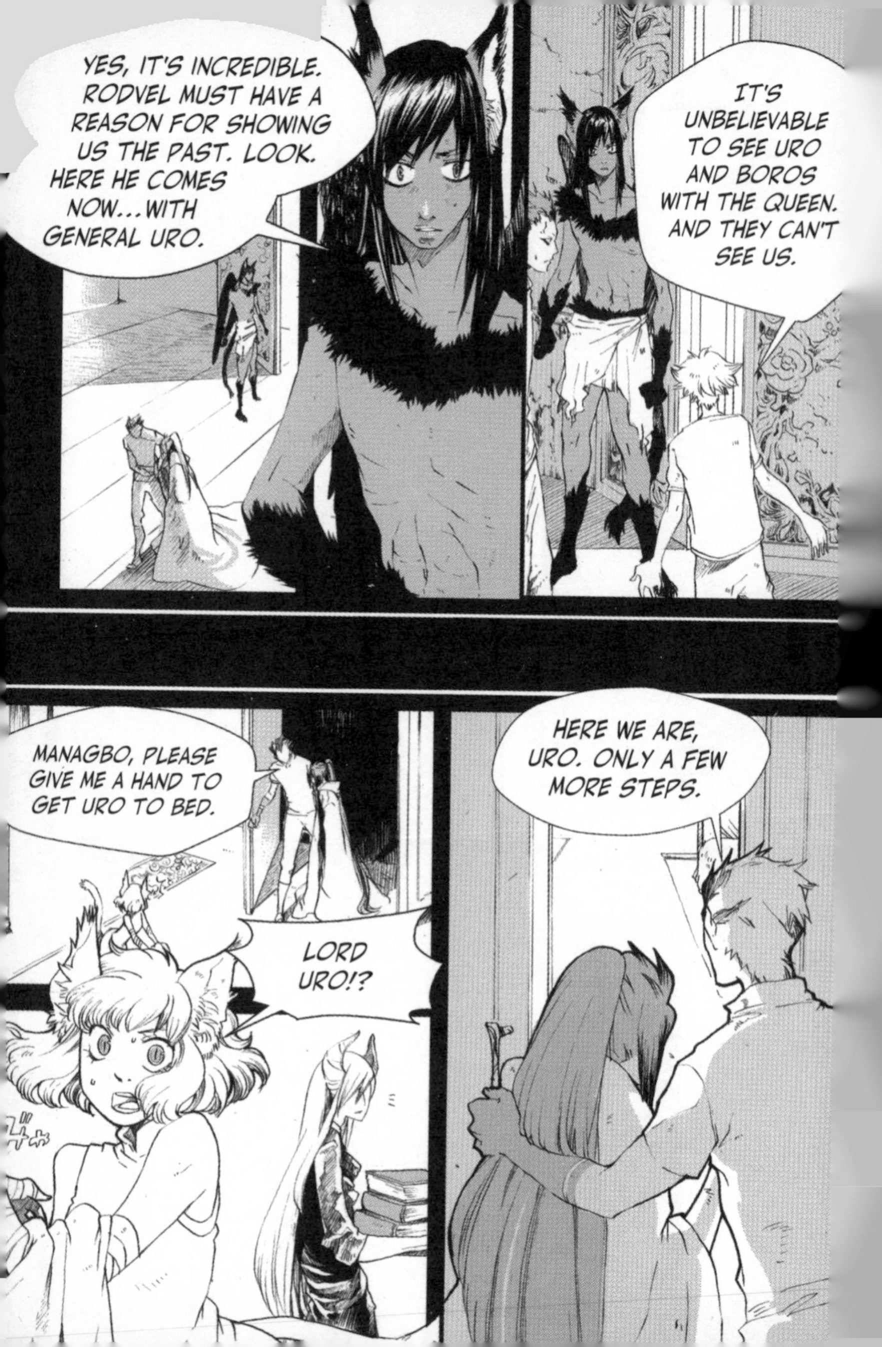
IT'S UNBELIEVABLE TO SEE URO AND BOROS WITH THE QUEEN. AND THEY CAN'T SEE US.
YES, IT'S INCREDIBLE. RODVEL MUST HAVE A REASON FOR SHOWING US THE PAST. LOOK. HERE HE COMES NOW...WITH GENERAL URO.
HERE WE ARE, URO. ONLY A FEW MORE STEPS.
MANAGBO, PLEASE GIVE ME A HAND TO GET URO TO BED.
LORD URO!?

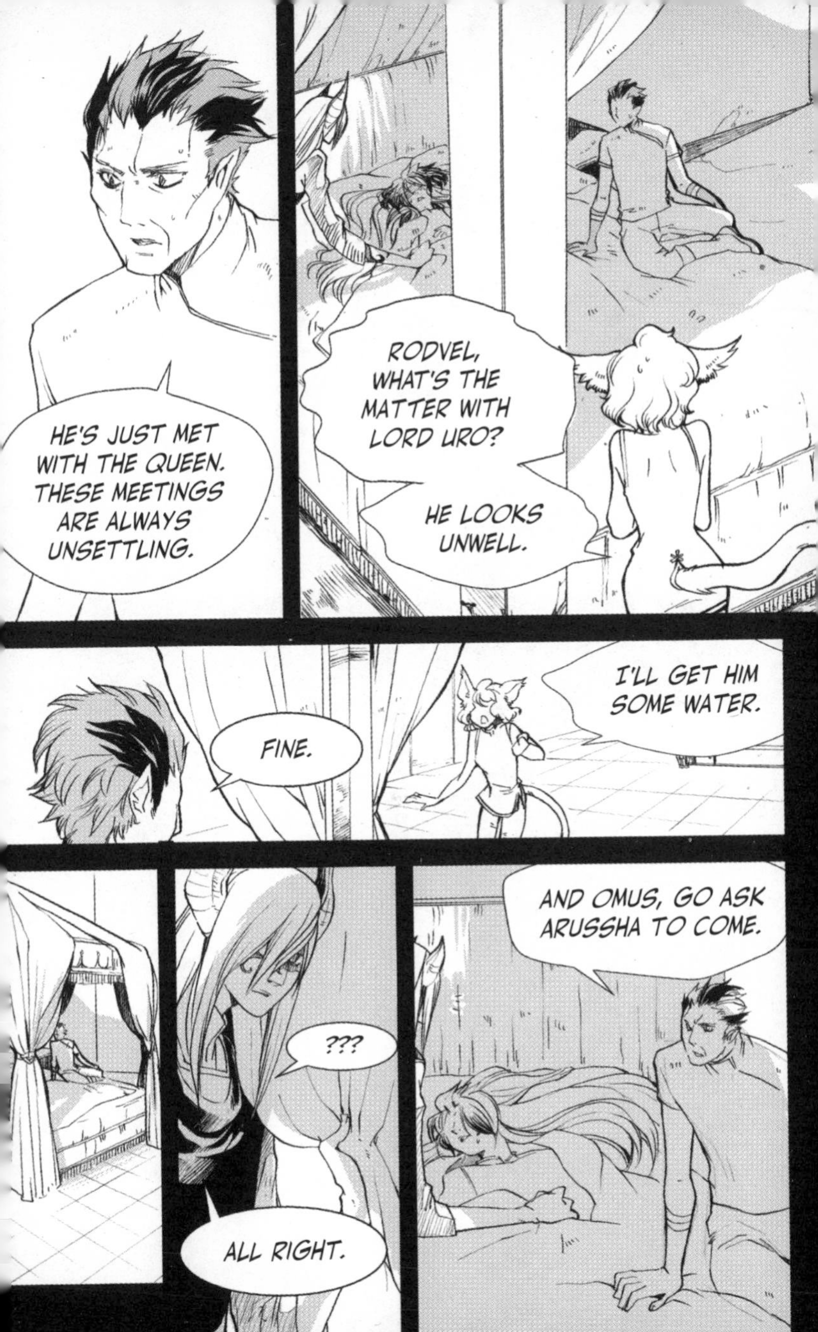
RODVEL, WHAT'S THE MATTER WITH LORD URO?
HE LOOKS UNWELL.
HE'S JUST MET WITH THE QUEEN. THESE MEETINGS ARE ALWAYS UNSETTLING.
I'LL GET HIM SOME WATER.
FINE.
AND OMUS, GO ASK ARUSSHA TO COME.
???
ALL RIGHT.

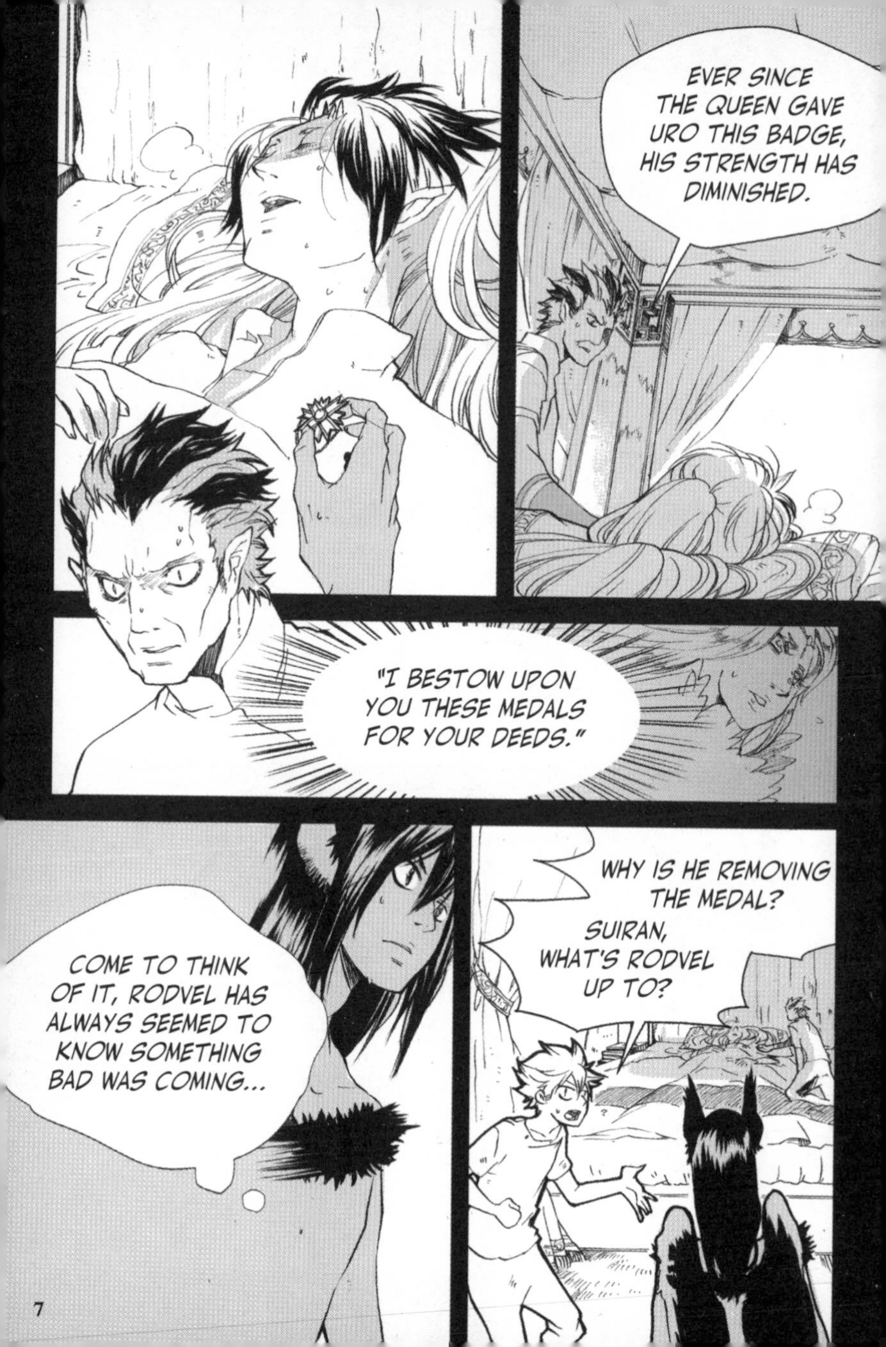
EVER SINCE THE QUEEN GAVE URO THIS BADGE, HIS STRENGTH HAS DIMINISHED.
"I BESTOW UPON YOU THESE MEDALS FOR YOUR DEEDS."
WHY IS HE REMOVING THE MEDAL?
SUIRAN, WHAT'S RODVEL UP TO?
COME TO THINK OF IT, RODVEL HAS ALWAYS SEEMED TO KNOW SOMETHING BAD WAS COMING...

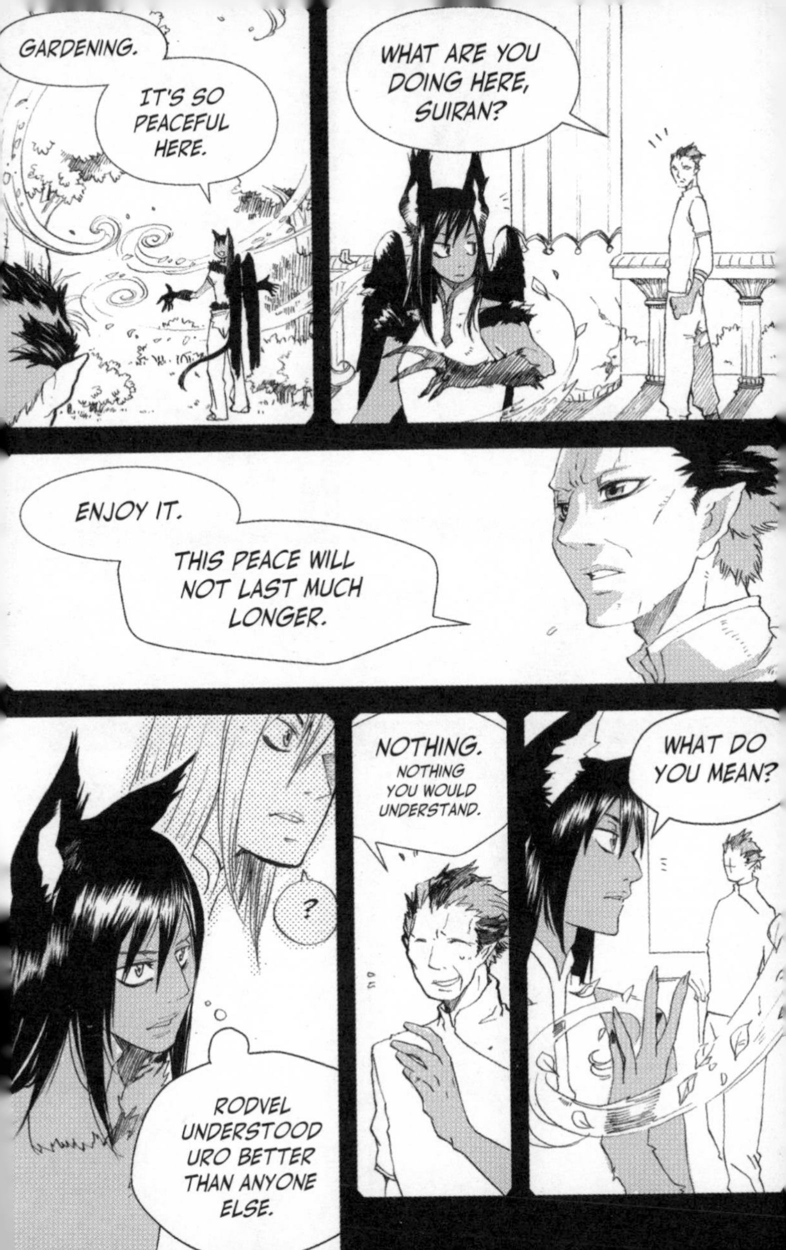
WHAT ARE YOU DOING HERE, SUIRAN?
GARDENING.
IT'S SO PEACEFUL HERE.
ENJOY IT.
THIS PEACE WILL NOT LAST MUCH LONGER.
WHAT DO YOU MEAN?
NOTHING. NOTHING YOU WOULD UNDERSTAND.
?
RODVEL UNDERSTOOD URO BETTER THAN ANYONE ELSE.

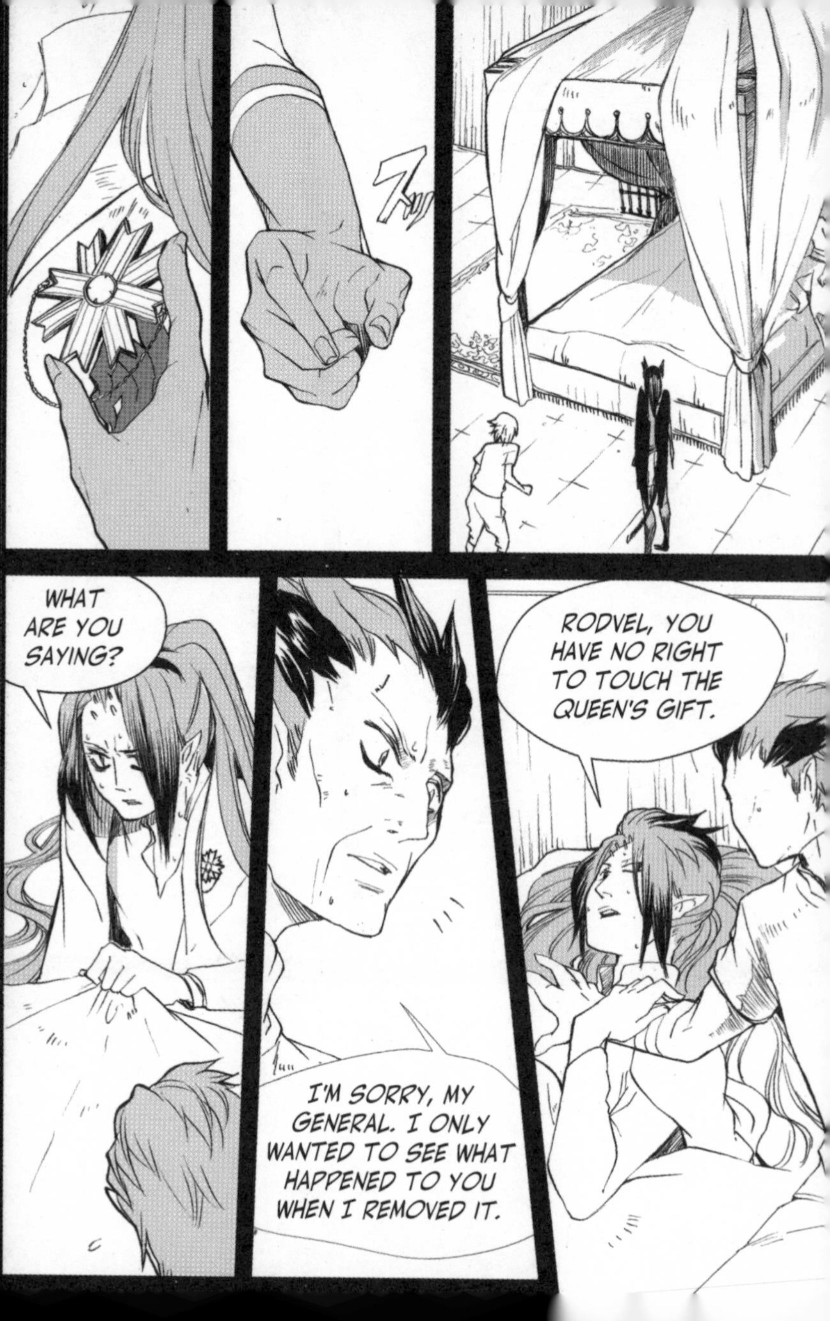
RODVEL, YOU HAVE NO RIGHT TO TOUCH THE QUEEN'S GIFT.
I'M SORRY, MY GENERAL. I ONLY WANTED TO SEE WHAT HAPPENED TO YOU WHEN I REMOVED IT.
WHAT ARE YOU SAYING?

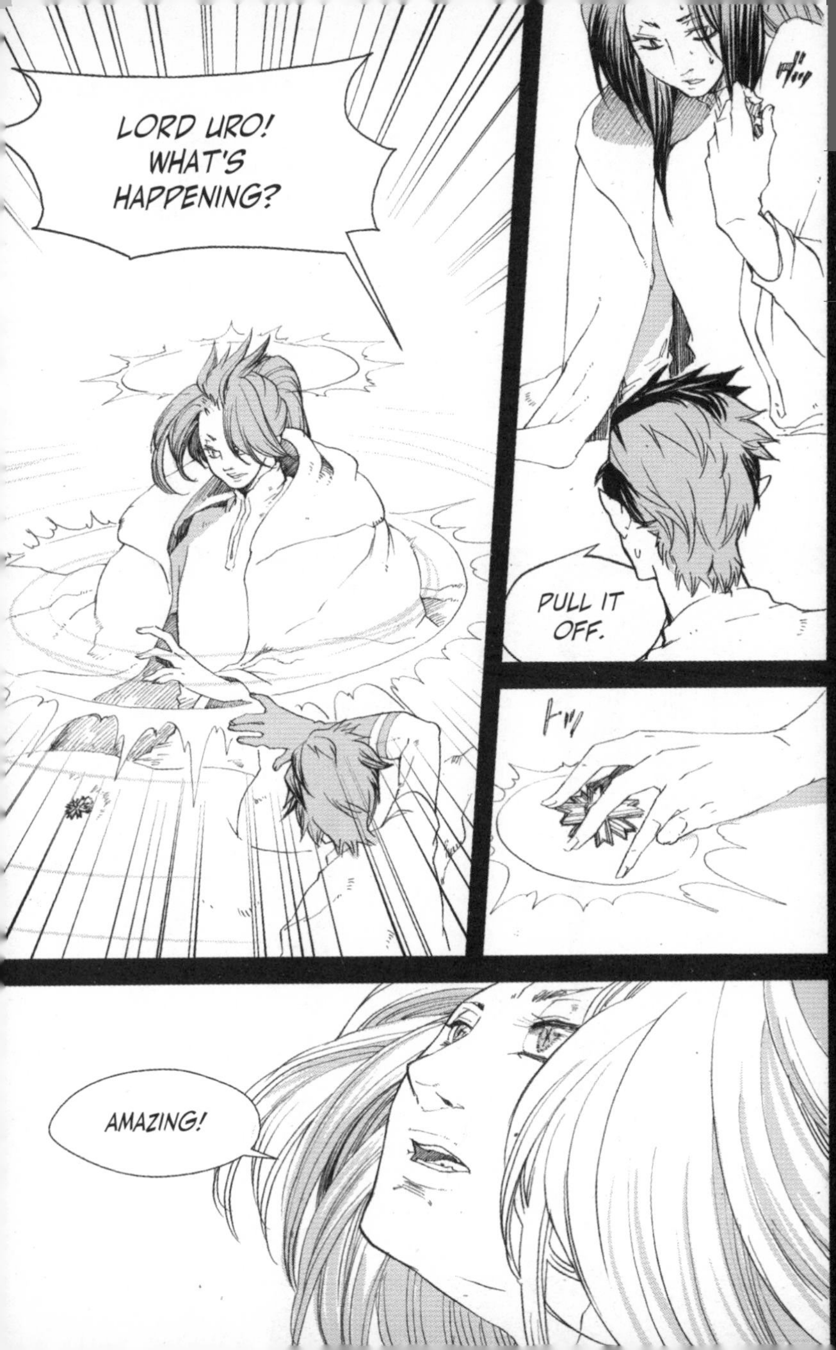
PULL IT OFF.
LORD URO! WHAT'S HAPPENING?
AMAZING!

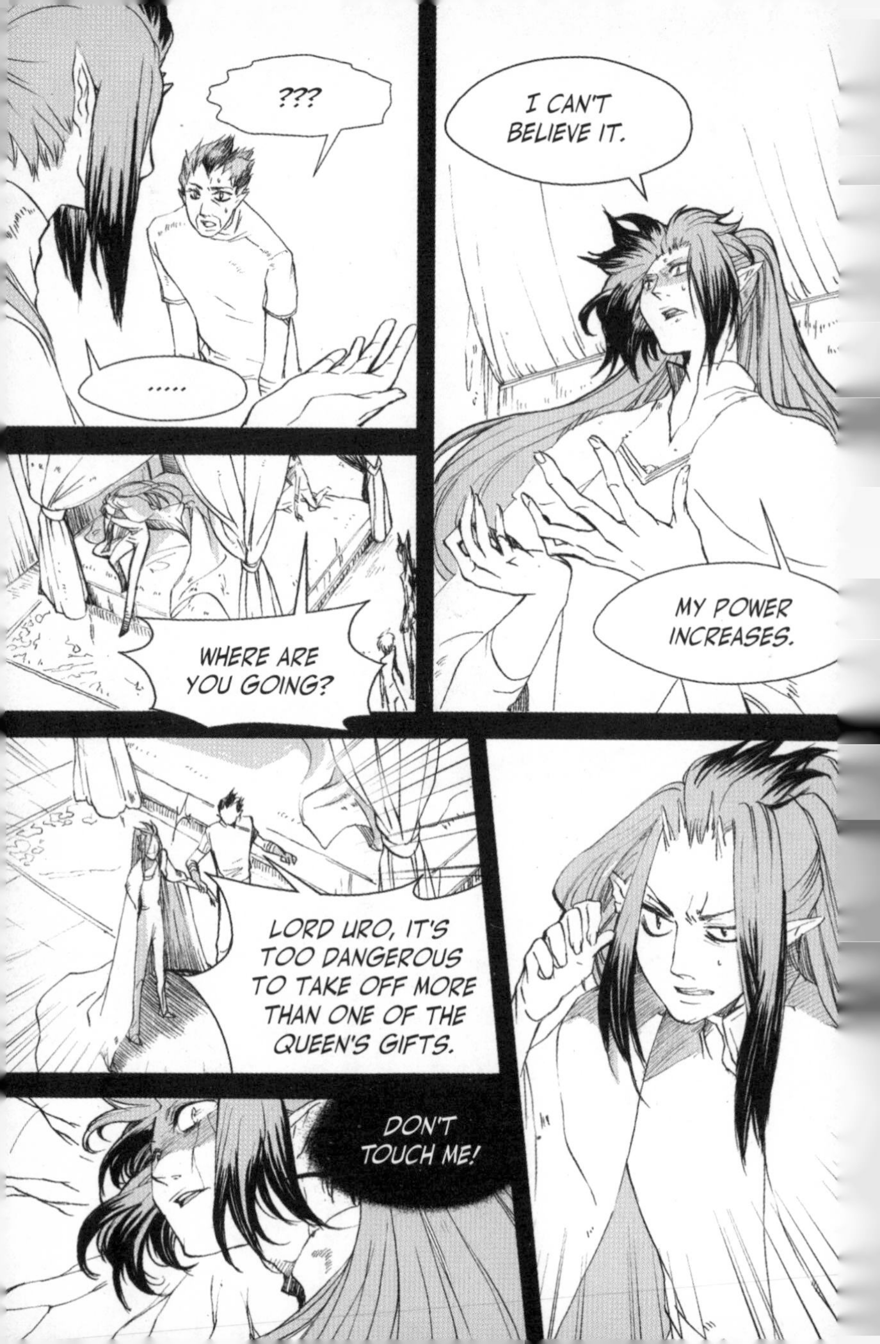
I CAN'T BELIEVE IT.
MY POWER INCREASES.
???
......
WHERE ARE YOU GOING?
LORD URO, IT'S TOO DANGEROUS TO TAKE OFF MORE THAN ONE OF THE QUEEN'S GIFTS.
DON'T TOUCH ME!

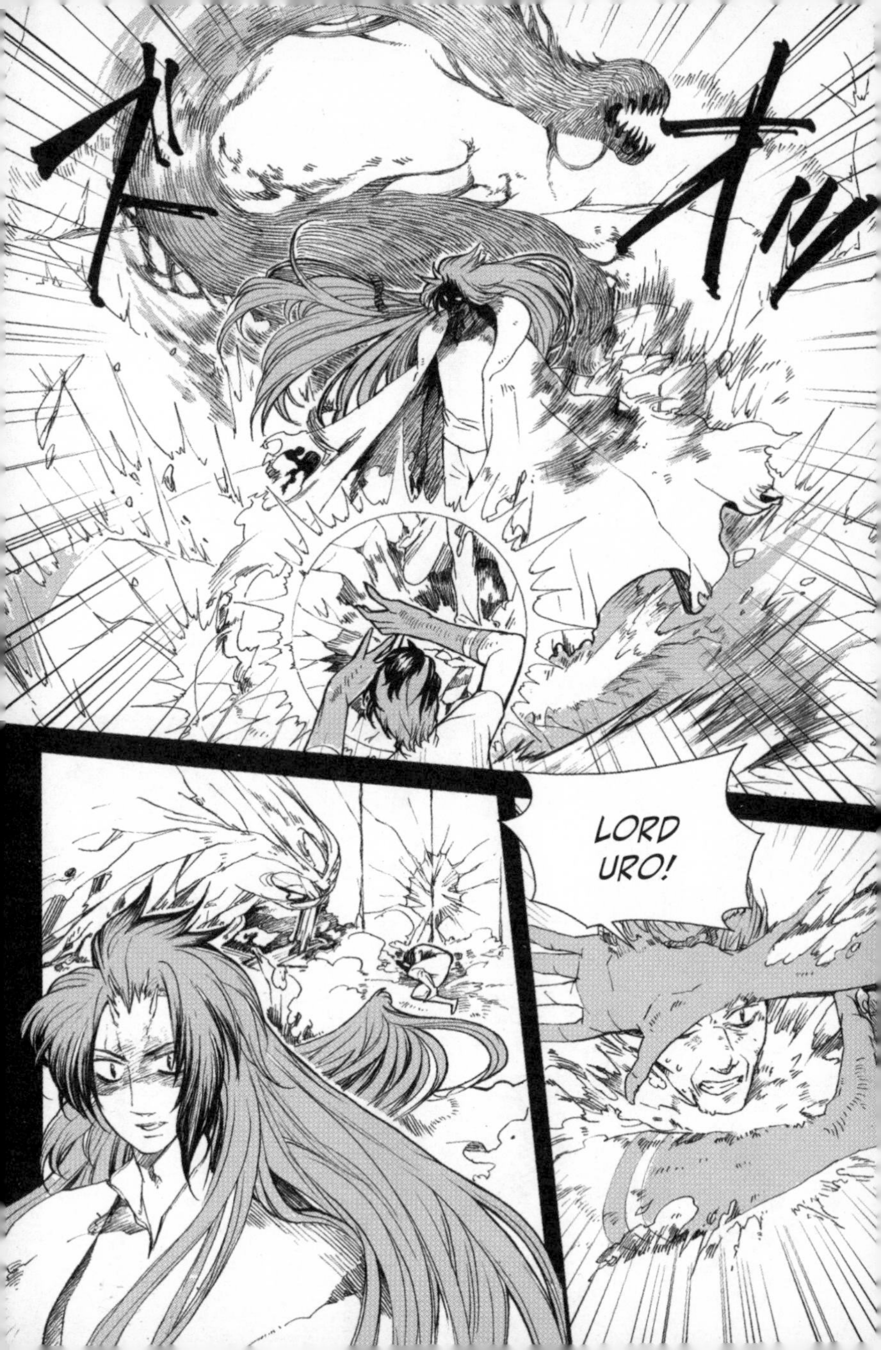
LORD URO!

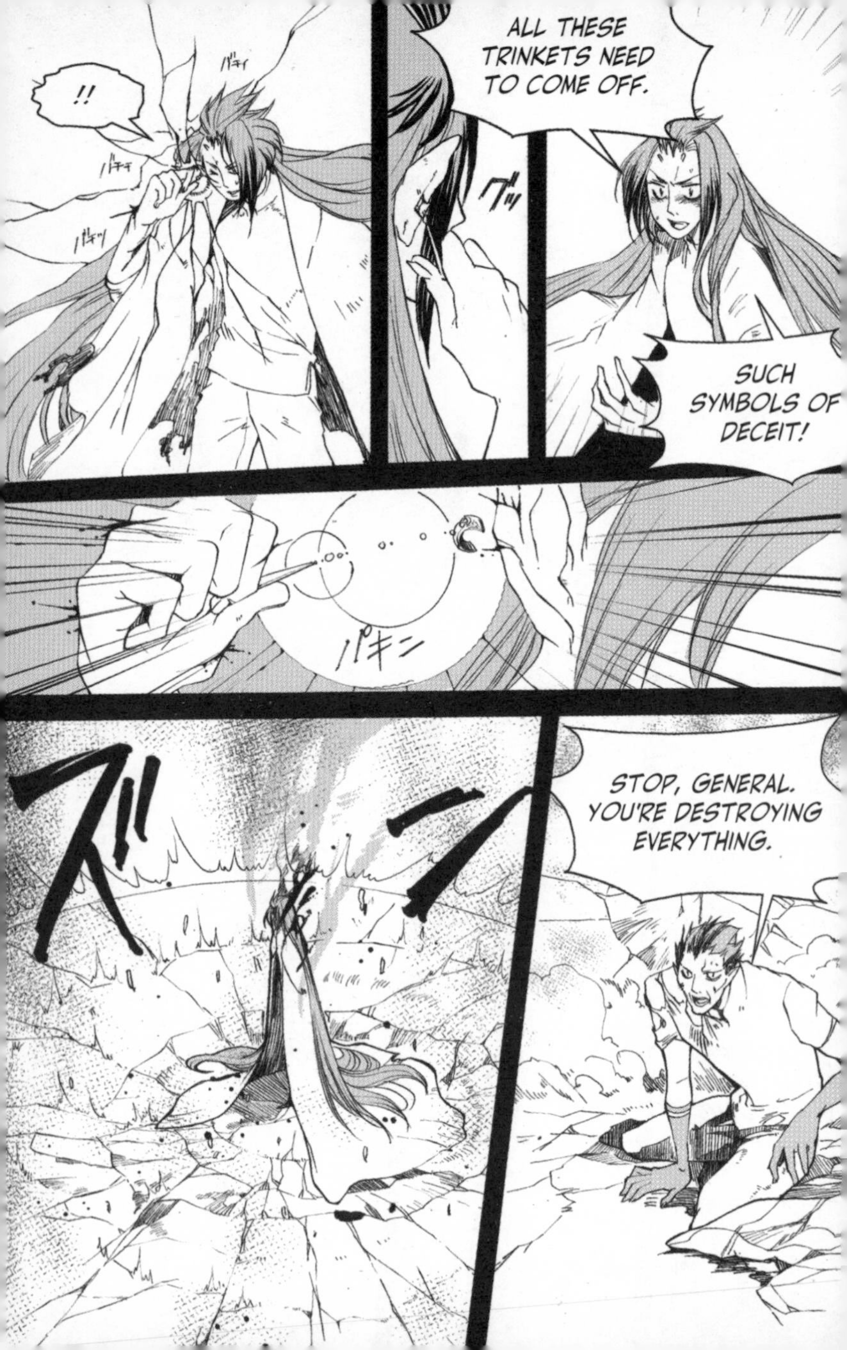
ALL THESE TRINKETS NEED TO COME OFF.
SUCH SYMBOLS OF DECEIT!
グッ
!!
パキン
STOP, GENERAL. YOU'RE DESTROYING EVERYTHING.

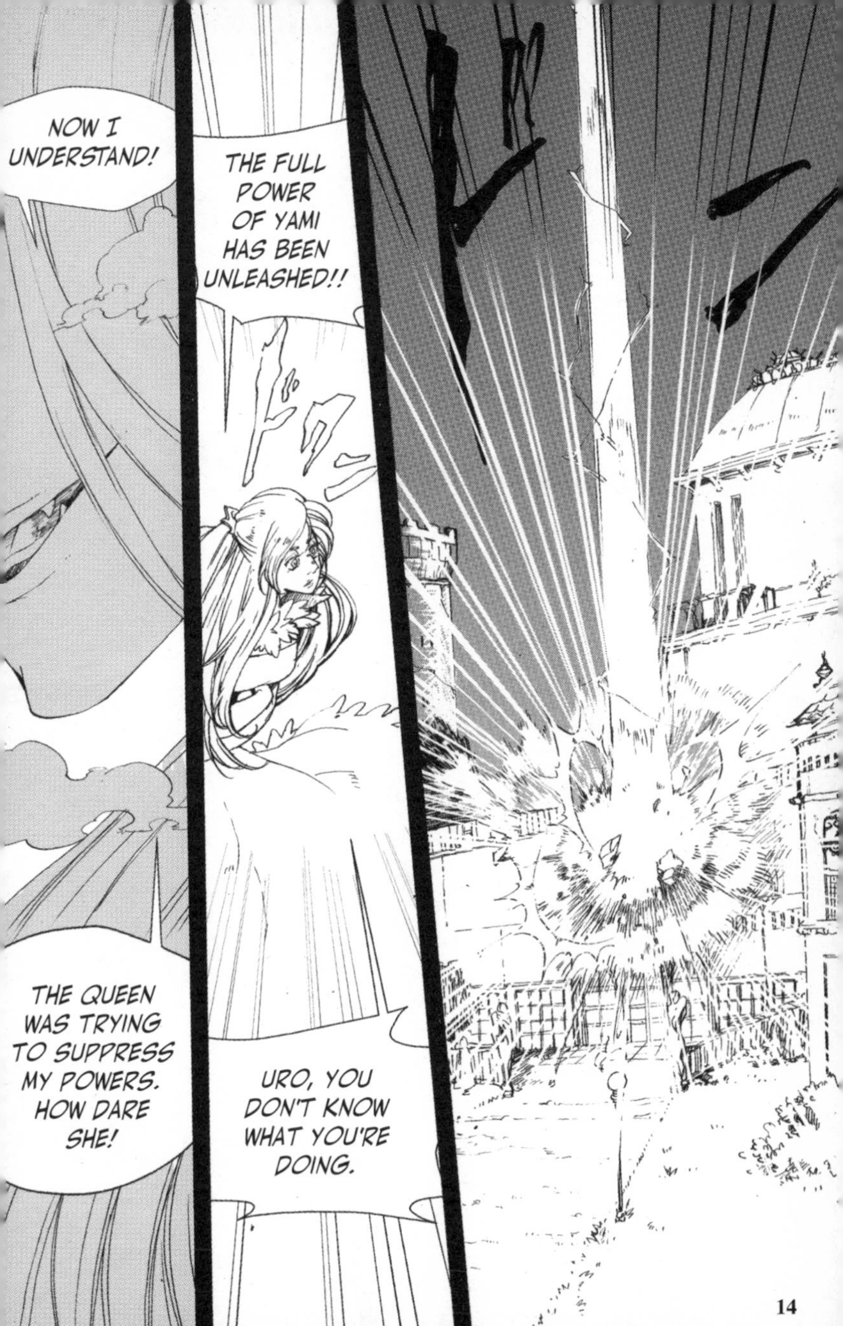
THE FULL POWER OF YAMI HAS BEEN UNLEASHED!!
URO, YOU DON'T KNOW WHAT YOU'RE DOING.
NOW I UNDERSTAND!
THE QUEEN WAS TRYING TO SUPPRESS MY POWERS. HOW DARE SHE!

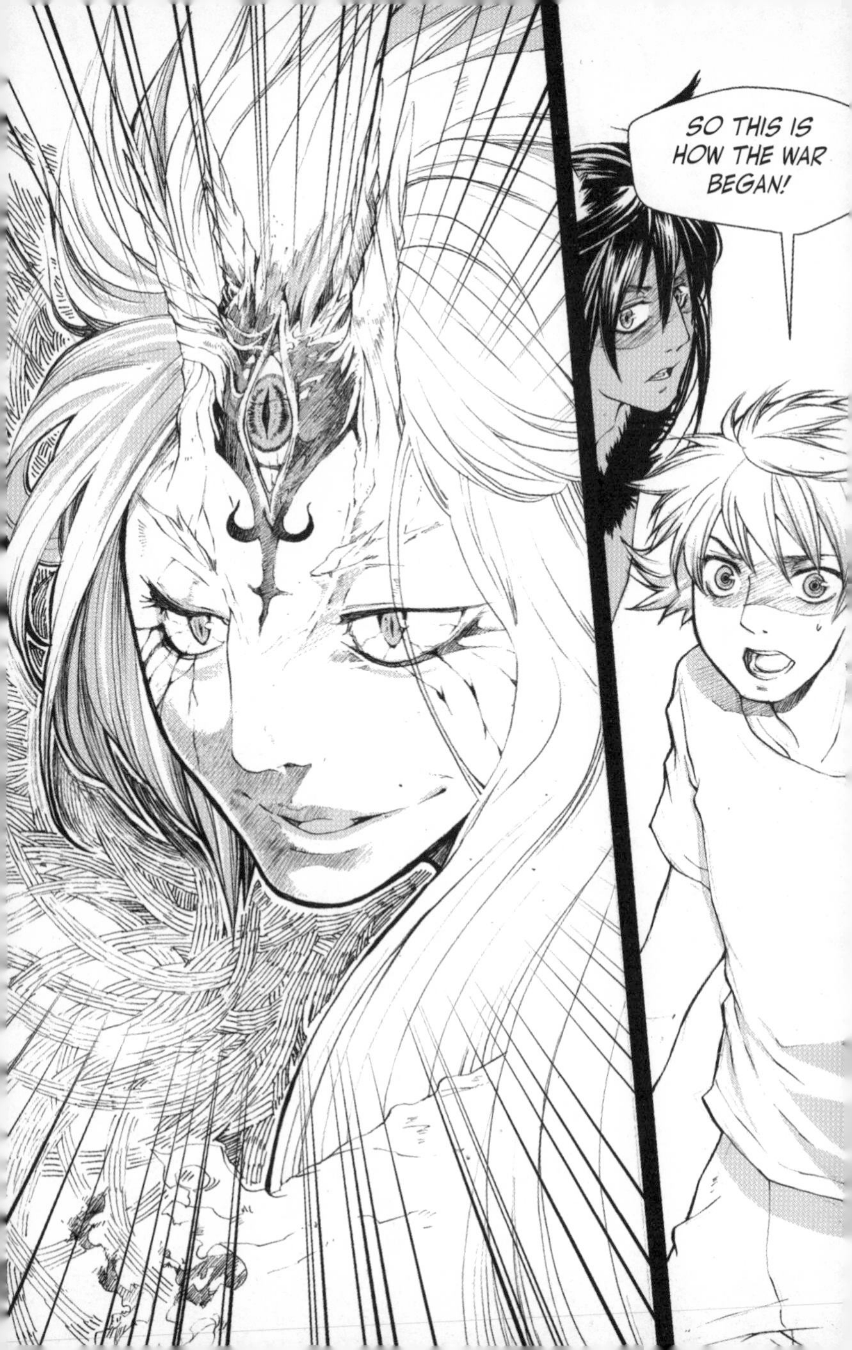
SO THIS IS HOW THE WAR BEGAN!

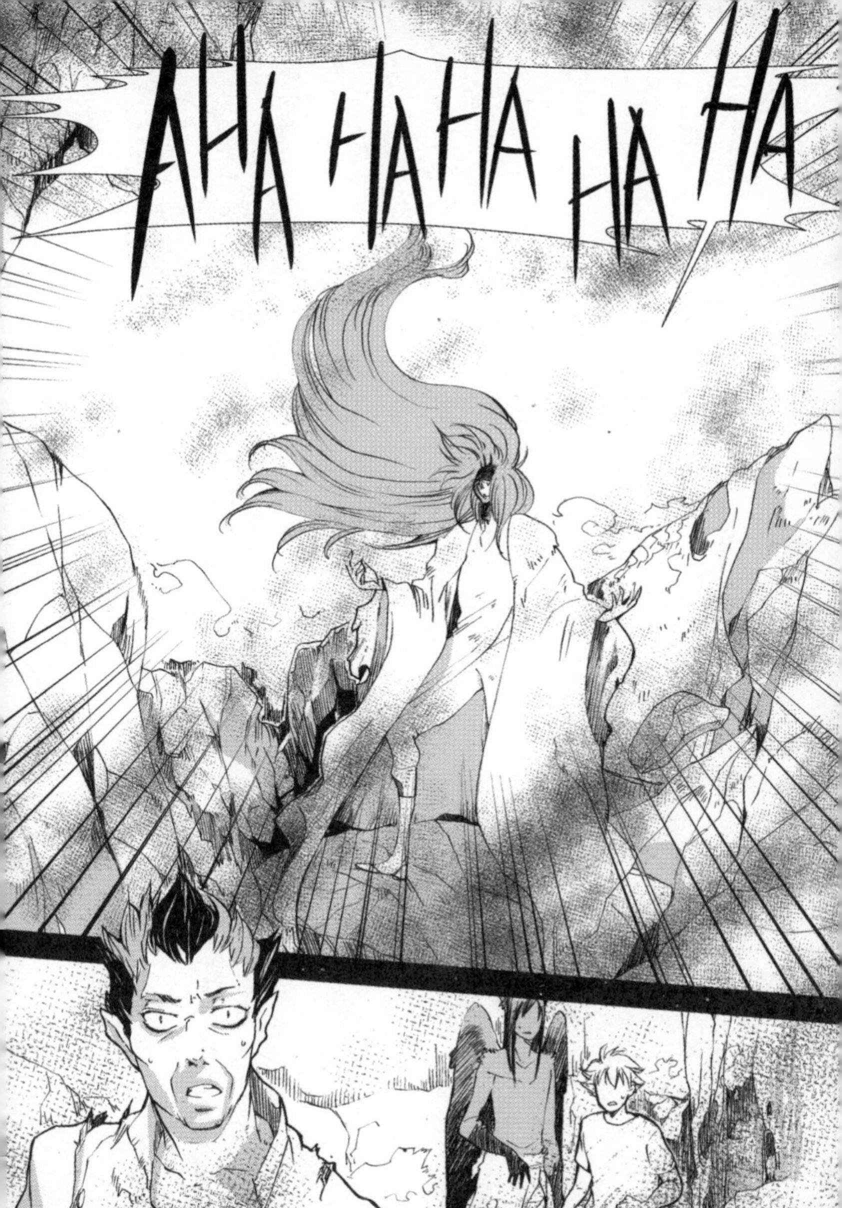
AHA HA HA HA HA HA

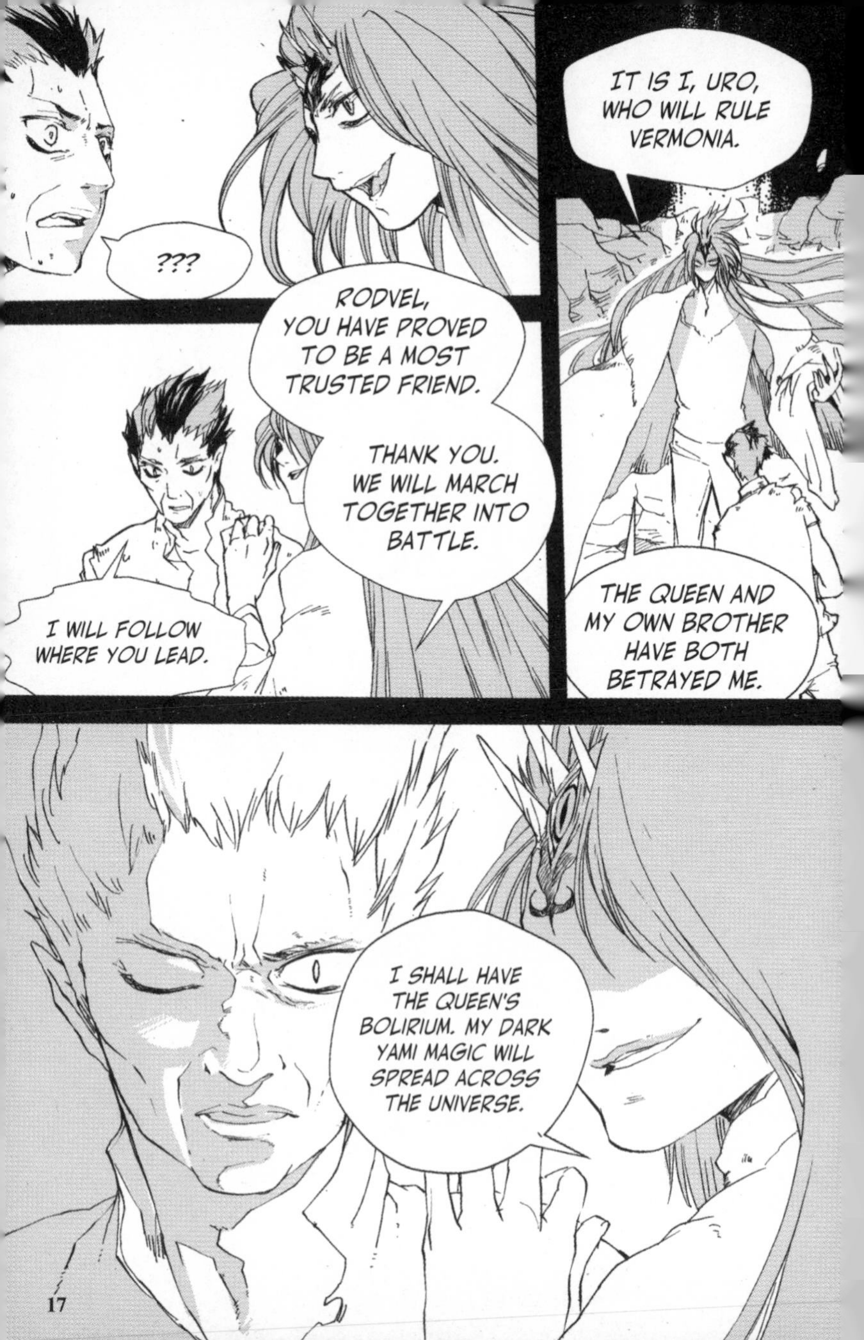
IT IS I, URO, WHO WILL RULE VERMONIA.
THE QUEEN AND MY OWN BROTHER HAVE BOTH BETRAYED ME.
???
RODVEL, YOU HAVE PROVED TO BE A MOST TRUSTED FRIEND.
THANK YOU. WE WILL MARCH TOGETHER INTO BATTLE.
I WILL FOLLOW WHERE YOU LEAD.
I SHALL HAVE THE QUEEN'S BOLIRIUM. MY DARK YAMI MAGIC WILL SPREAD ACROSS THE UNIVERSE.

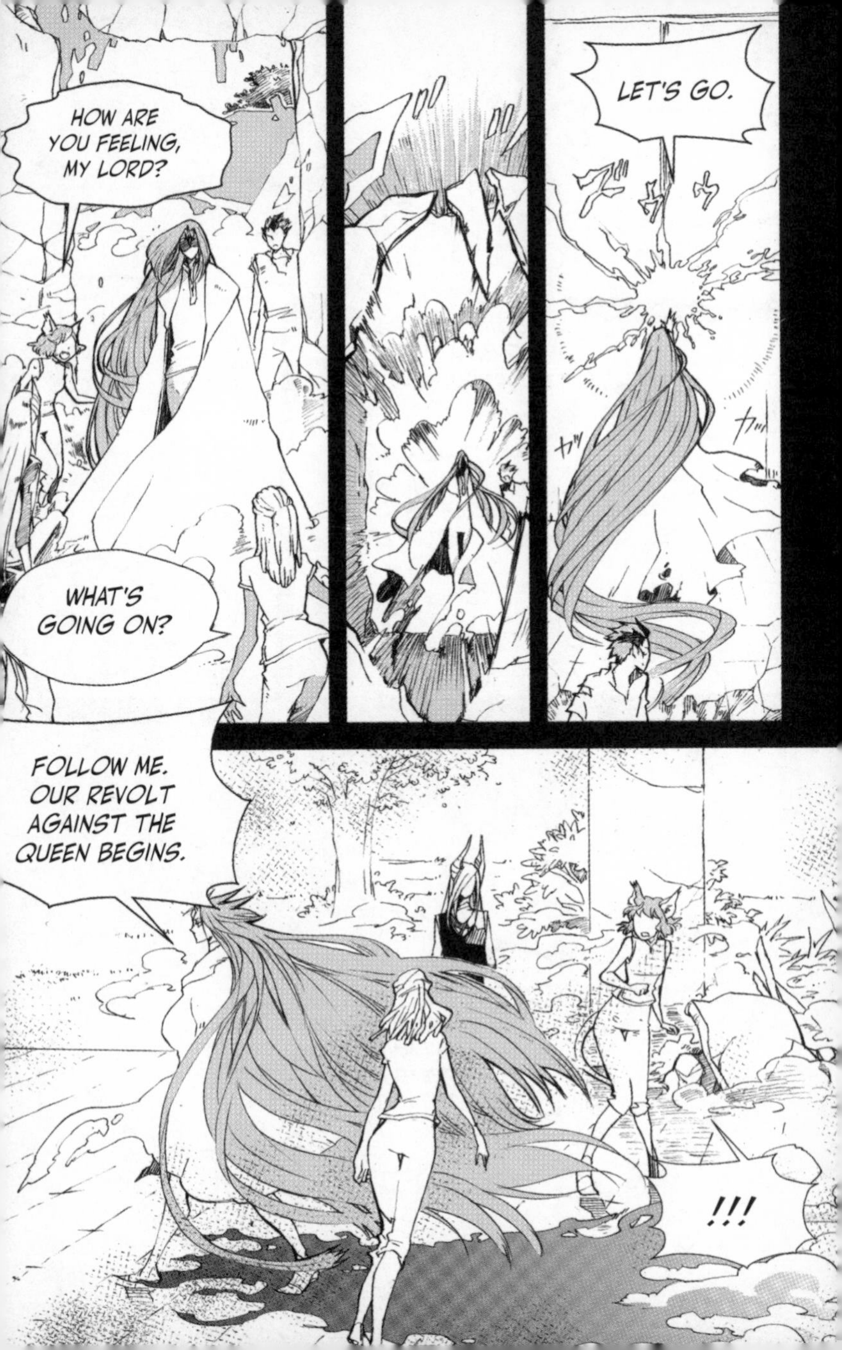

LET'S GO.
HOW ARE YOU FEELING, MY LORD?
WHAT'S GOING ON?
FOLLOW ME. OUR REVOLT AGAINST THE QUEEN BEGINS.
!!!

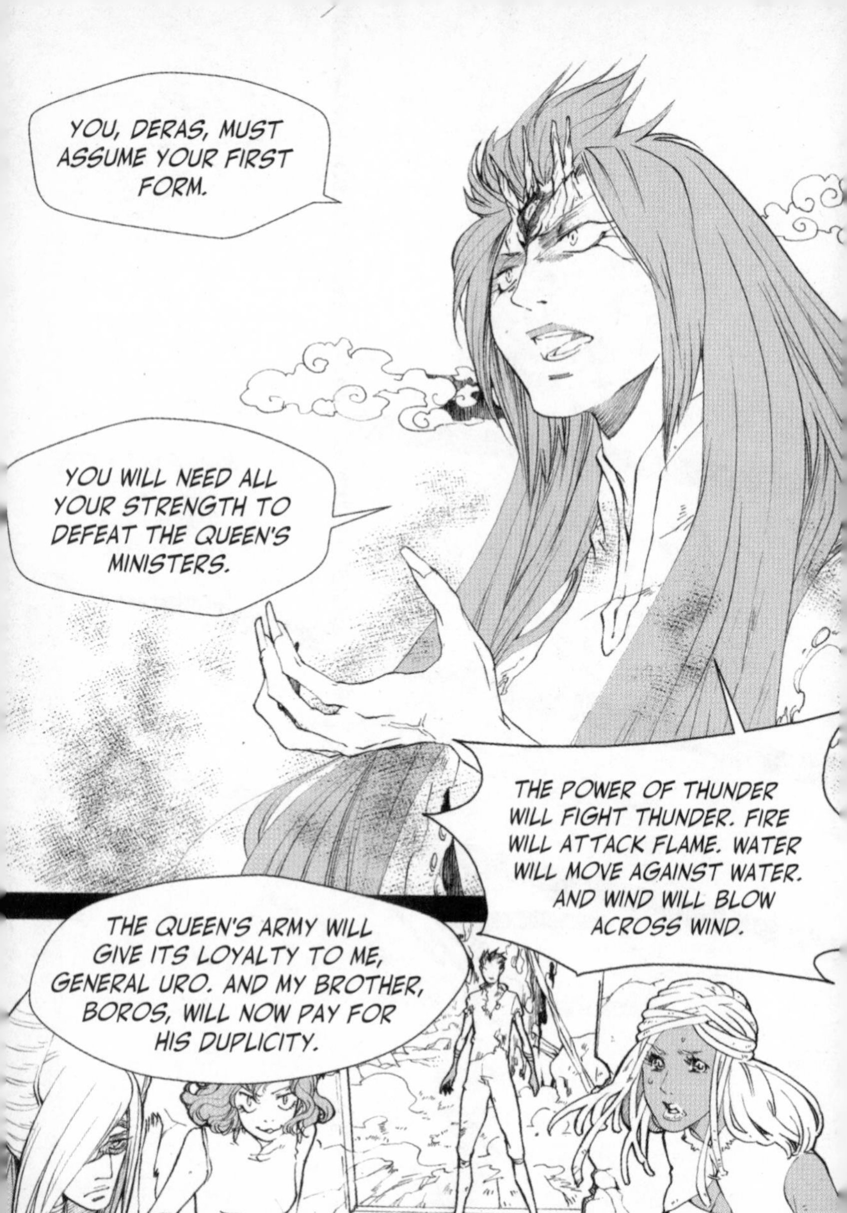
YOU, DERAS, MUST ASSUME YOUR FIRST FORM.
YOU WILL NEED ALL YOUR STRENGTH TO DEFEAT THE QUEEN'S MINISTERS.
THE POWER OF THUNDER WILL FIGHT THUNDER. FIRE WILL ATTACK FLAME. WATER WILL MOVE AGAINST WATER. AND WIND WILL BLOW ACROSS WIND.
THE QUEEN'S ARMY WILL GIVE ITS LOYALTY TO ME, GENERAL URO. AND MY BROTHER, BOROS, WILL NOW PAY FOR HIS DUPLICITY.

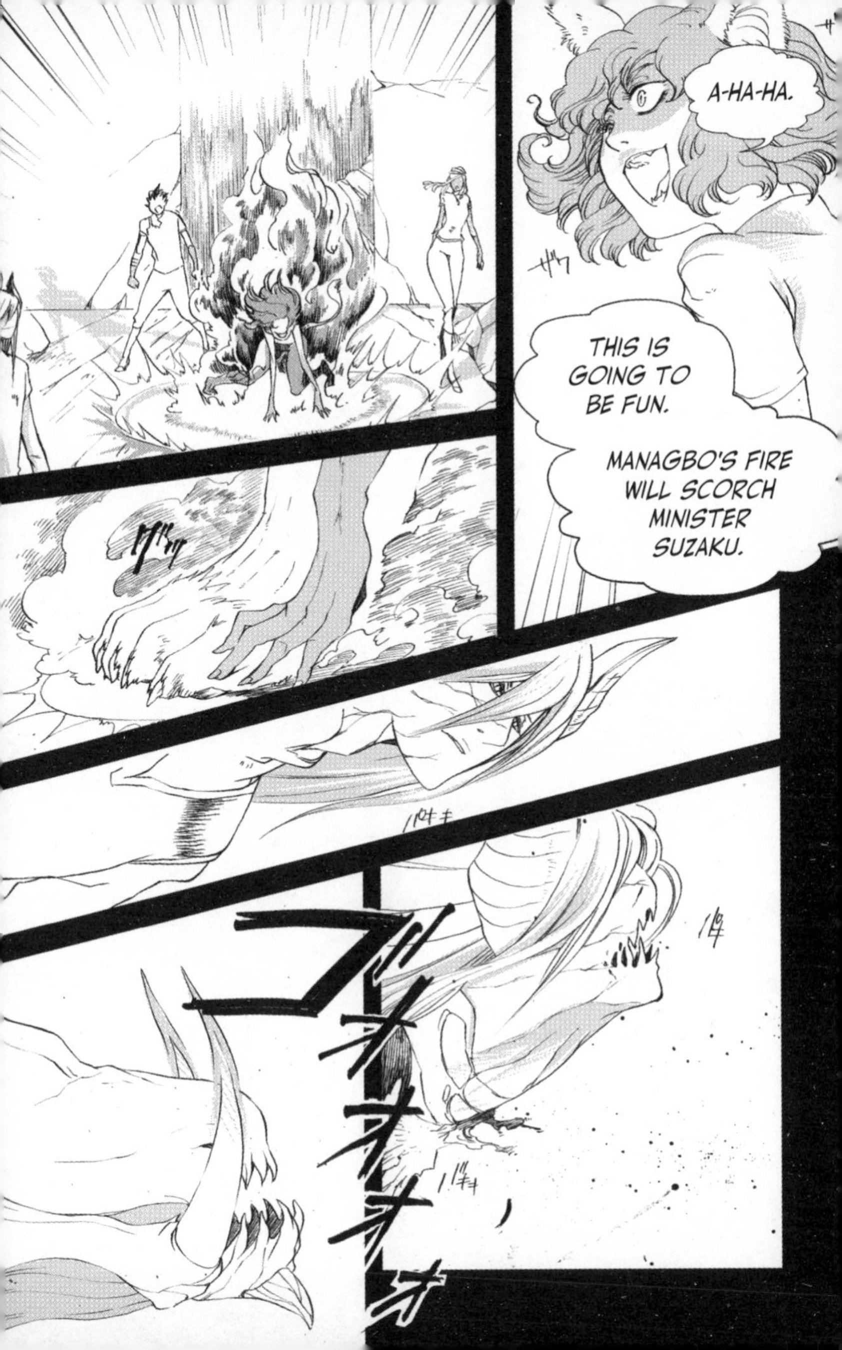
A-HA-HA.
THIS IS GOING TO BE FUN.
MANAGBO'S FIRE WILL SCORCH MINISTER SUZAKU.

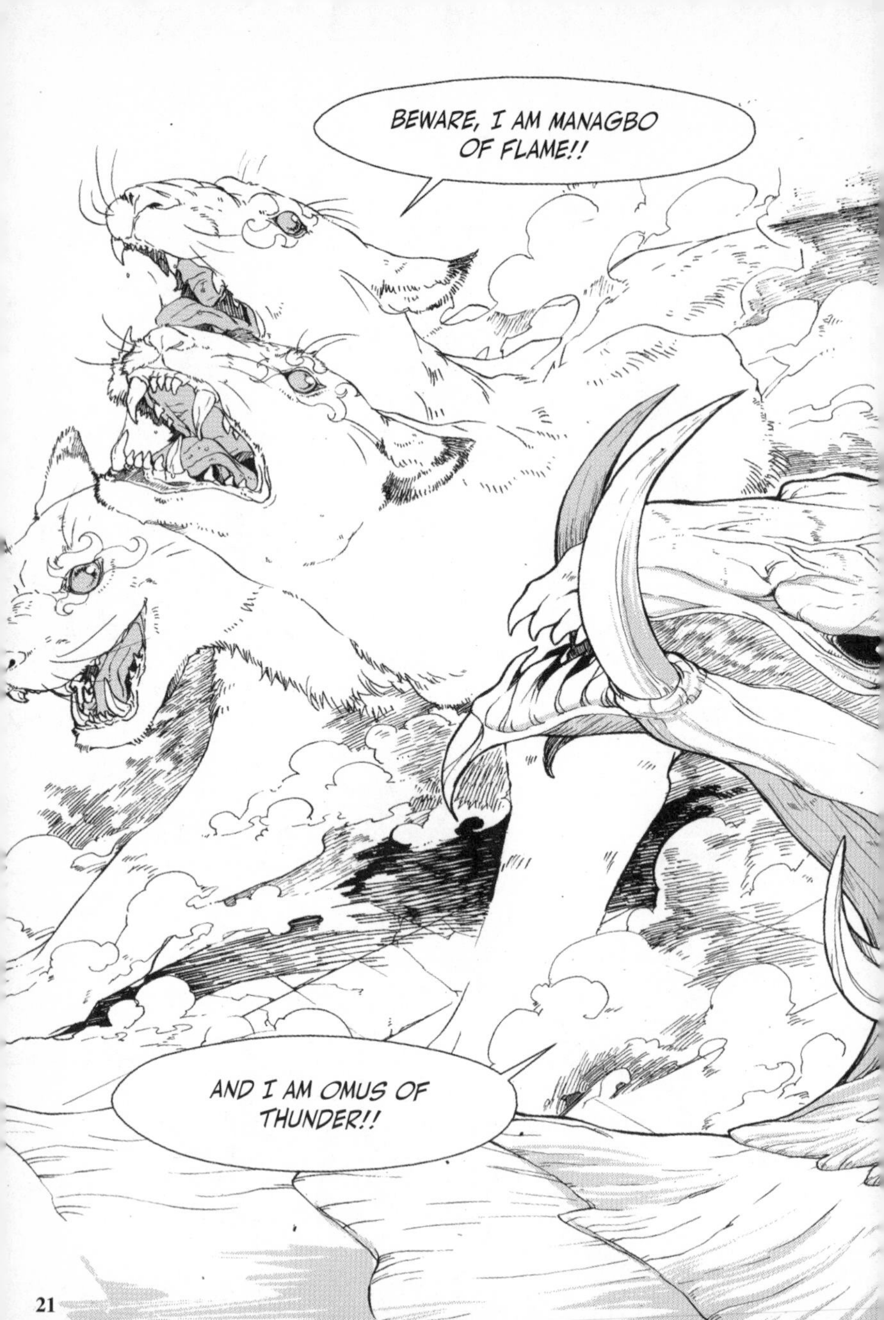
BEWARE, I AM MANAGBO OF FLAME!!
AND I AM OMUS OF THUNDER!!

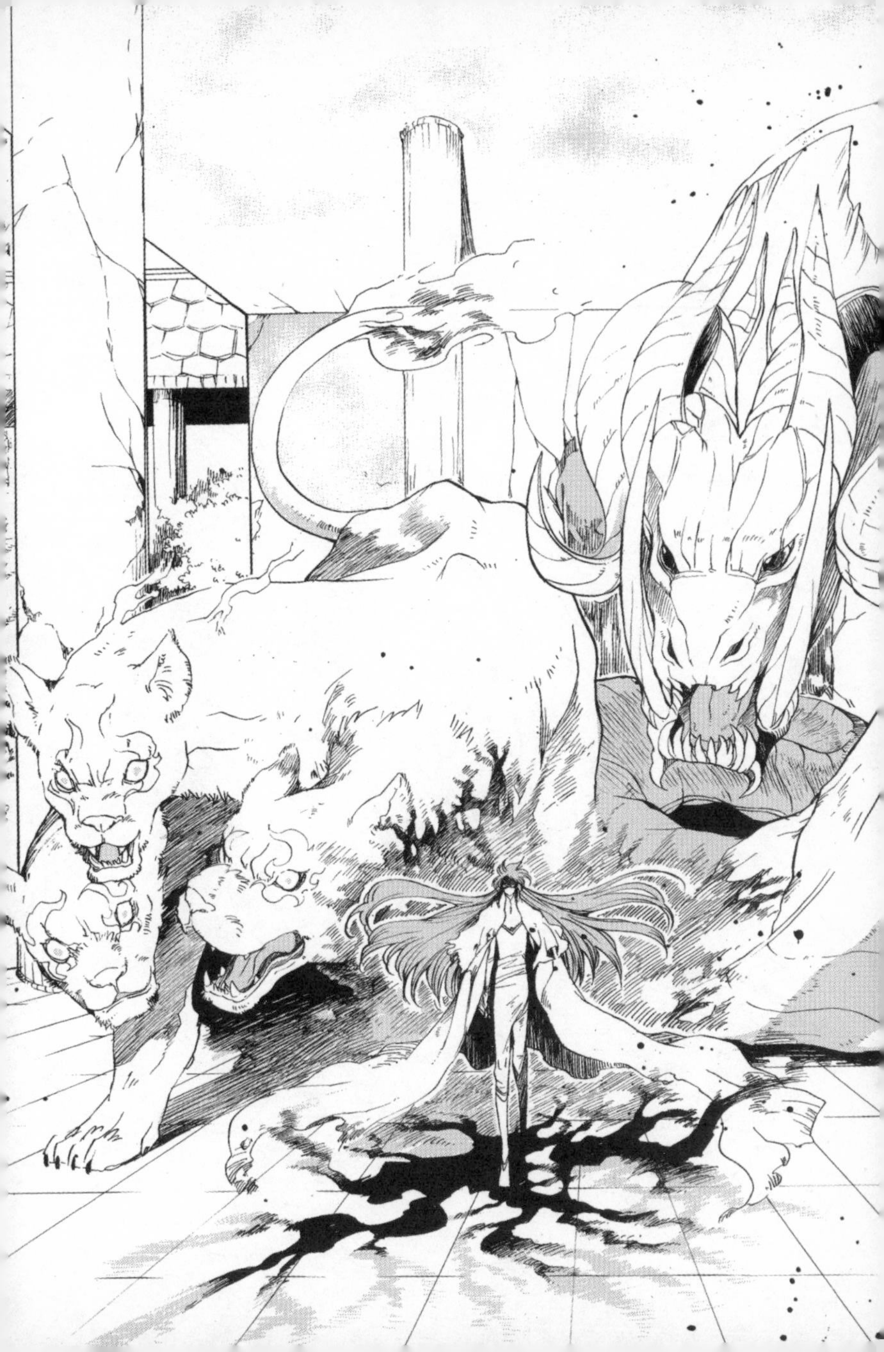

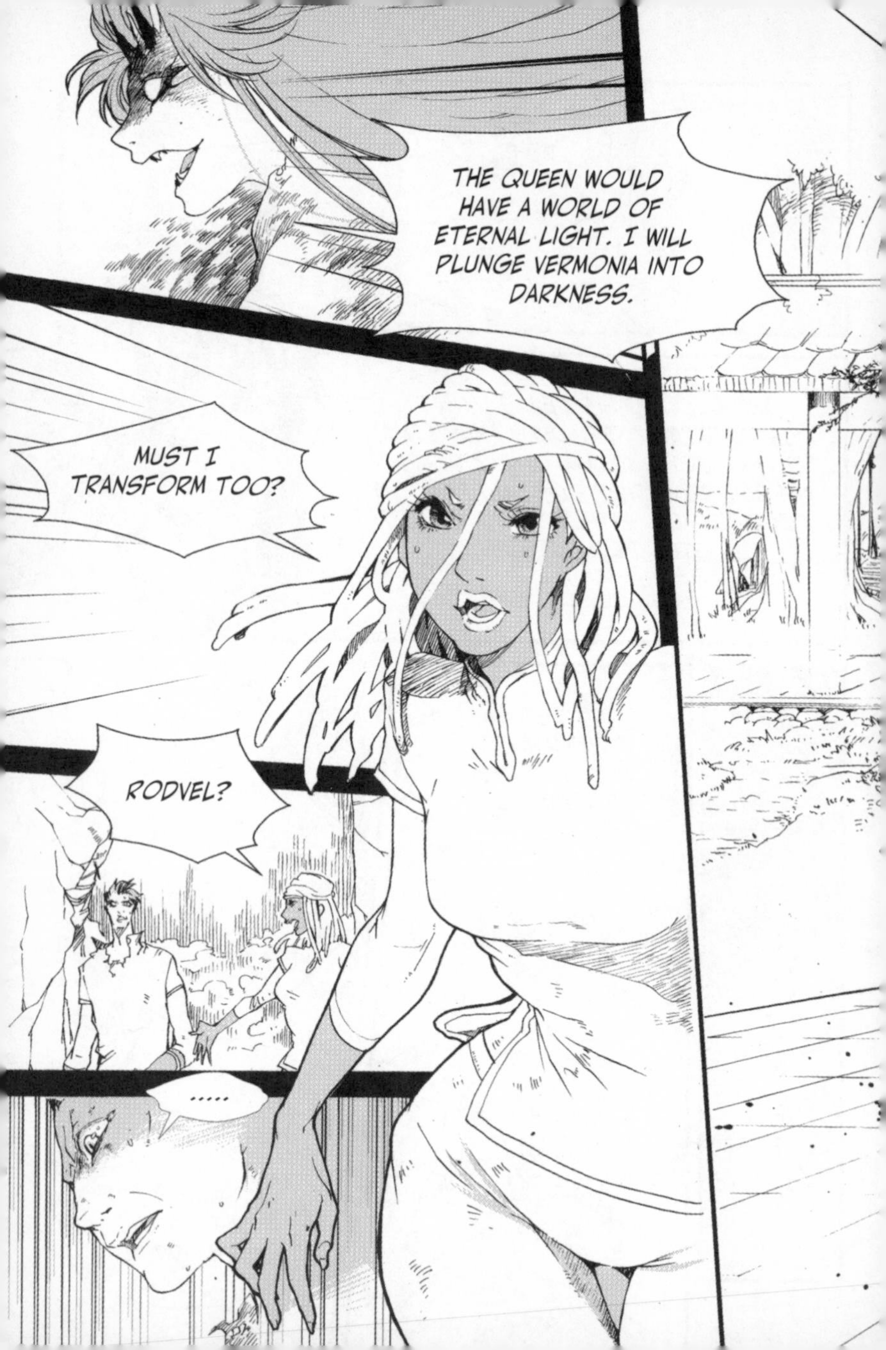
THE QUEEN WOULD HAVE A WORLD OF ETERNAL LIGHT. I WILL PLUNGE VERMONIA INTO DARKNESS.
MUST I TRANSFORM TOO?
RODVEL?
......

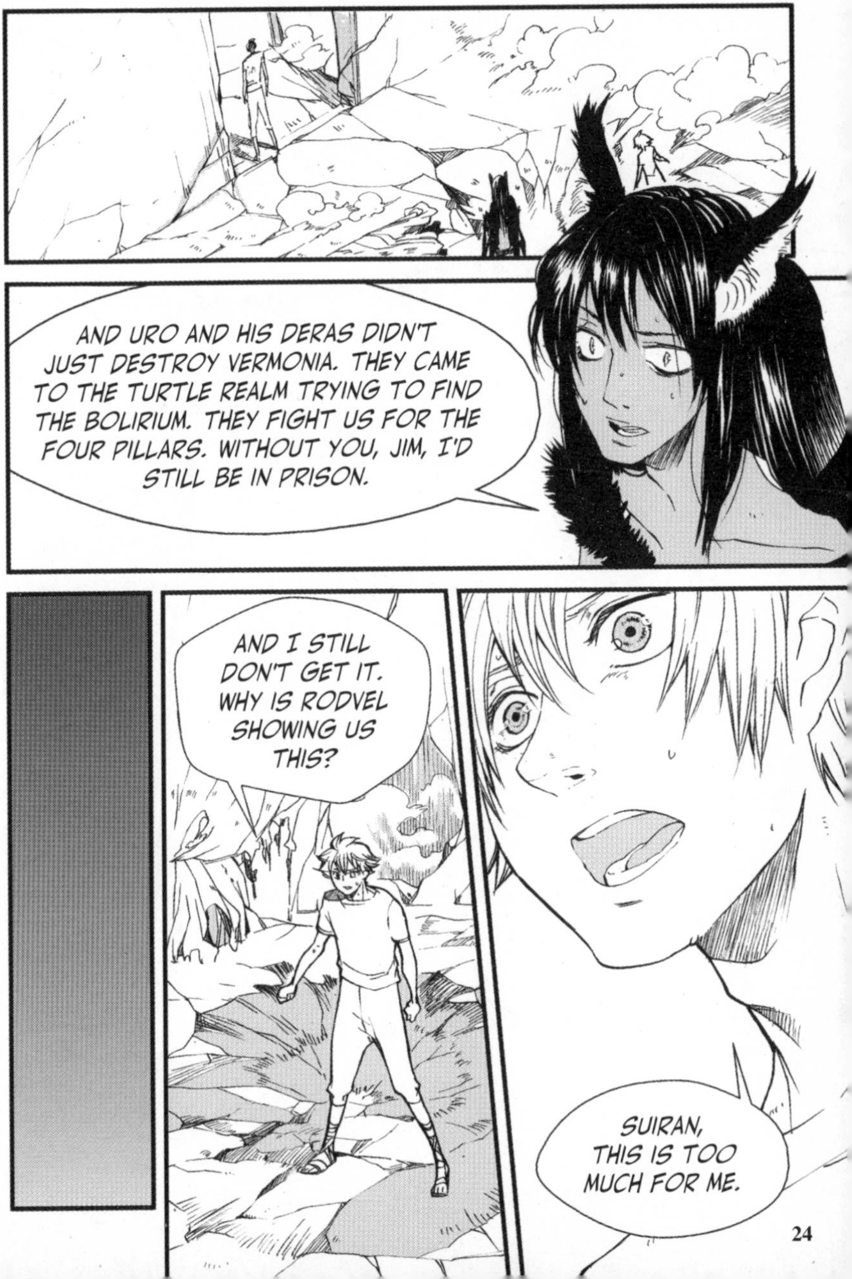
AND URO AND HIS DERAS DIDN'T JUST DESTROY VERMONIA. THEY CAME TO THE TURTLE REALM TRYING TO FIND THE BOLIRIUM. THEY FIGHT US FOR THE FOUR PILLARS. WITHOUT YOU, JIM, I'D STILL BE IN PRISON.
SUIRAN, THIS IS TOO MUCH FOR ME.
AND I STILL DON'T GET IT. WHY IS RODVEL SHOWING US THIS?

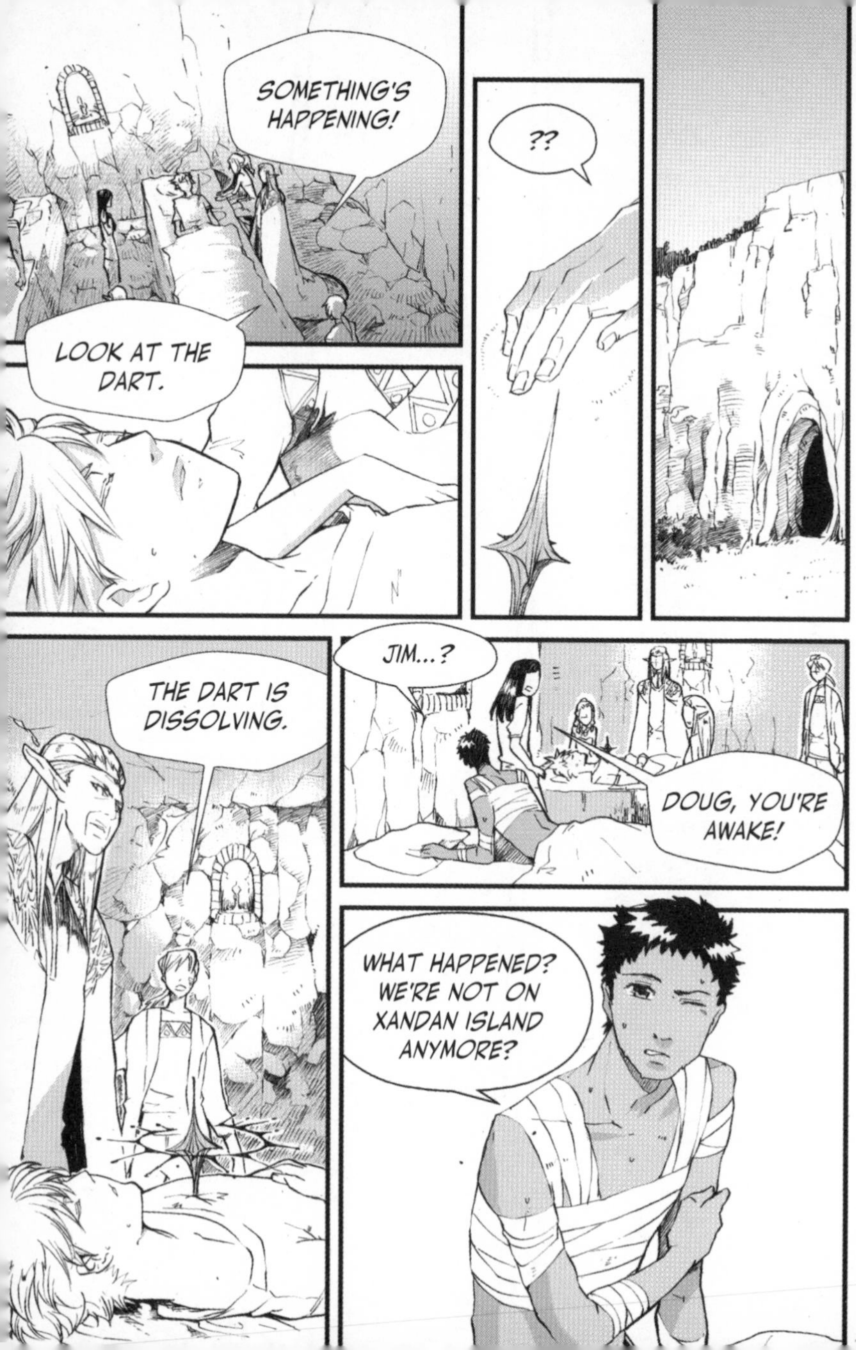
??
SOMETHING'S HAPPENING!
LOOK AT THE DART.
JIM...?
DOUG, YOU'RE AWAKE!
WHAT HAPPENED? WE'RE NOT ON XANDAN ISLAND ANYMORE?
THE DART IS DISSOLVING.

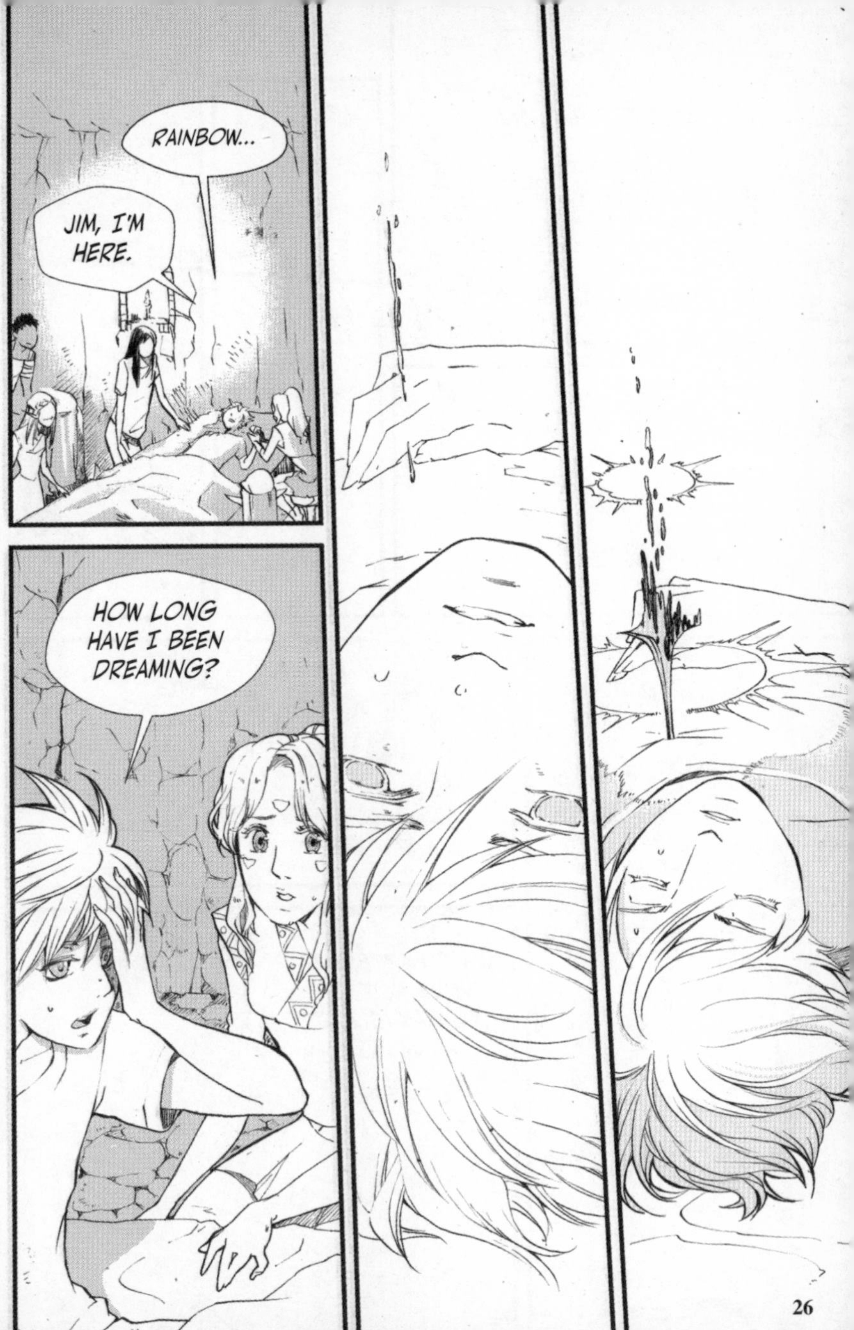
RAINBOW...
JIM, I'M HERE.
HOW LONG HAVE I BEEN DREAMING?

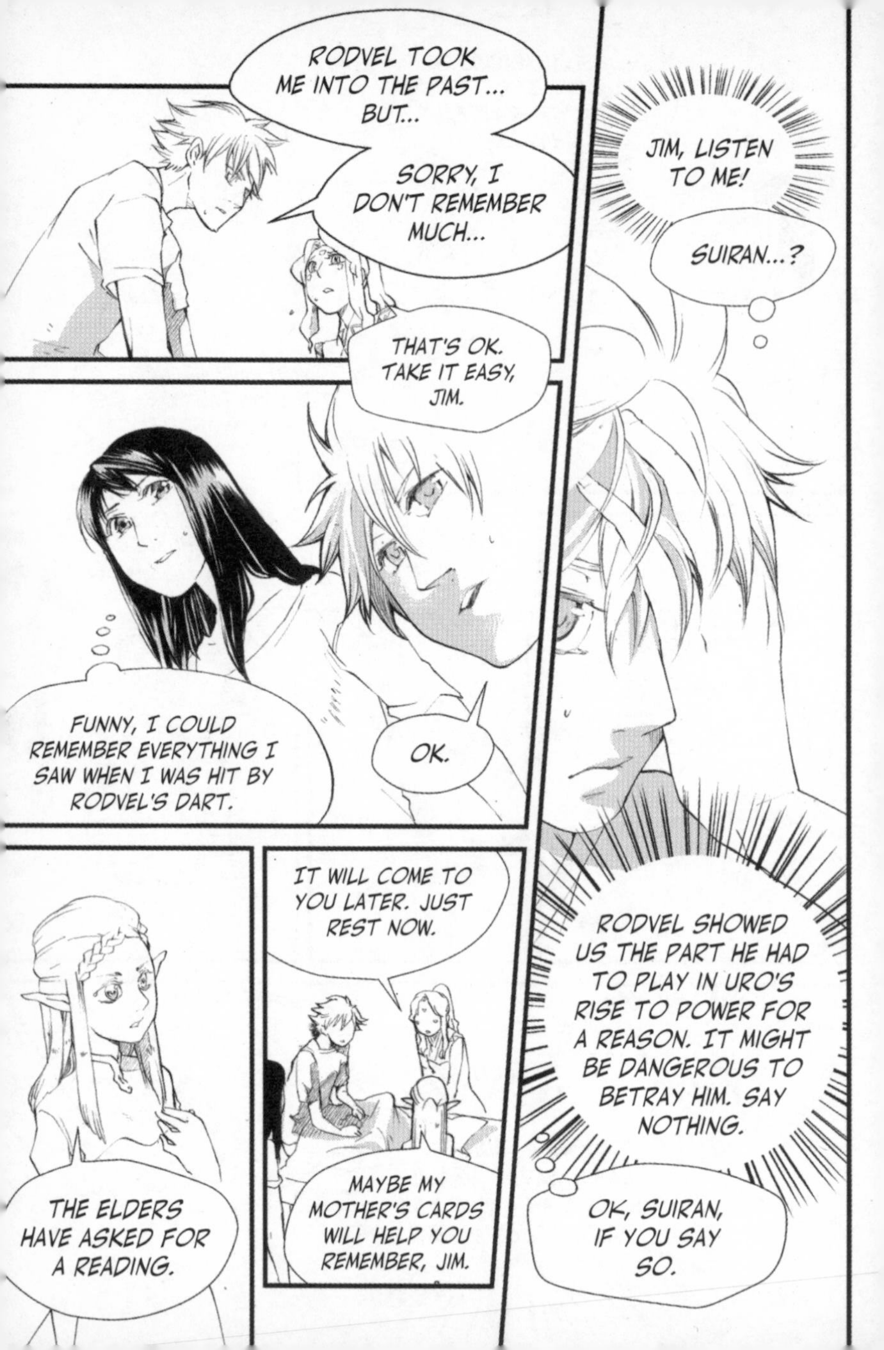

JIM, LISTEN TO ME!
SUIRAN...?
RODVEL SHOWED US THE PART HE HAD TO PLAY IN URO'S RISE TO POWER FOR A REASON. IT MIGHT BE DANGEROUS TO BETRAY HIM. SAY NOTHING.
OK, SUIRAN, IF YOU SAY SO.
RODVEL TOOK ME INTO THE PAST... BUT...
SORRY, I DON'T REMEMBER MUCH...
THAT'S OK. TAKE IT EASY, JIM.
OK.
FUNNY, I COULD REMEMBER EVERYTHING I SAW WHEN I WAS HIT BY RODVEL'S DART.
IT WILL COME TO YOU LATER. JUST REST NOW.
MAYBE MY MOTHER'S CARDS WILL HELP YOU REMEMBER, JIM.
THE ELDERS HAVE ASKED FOR A READING.

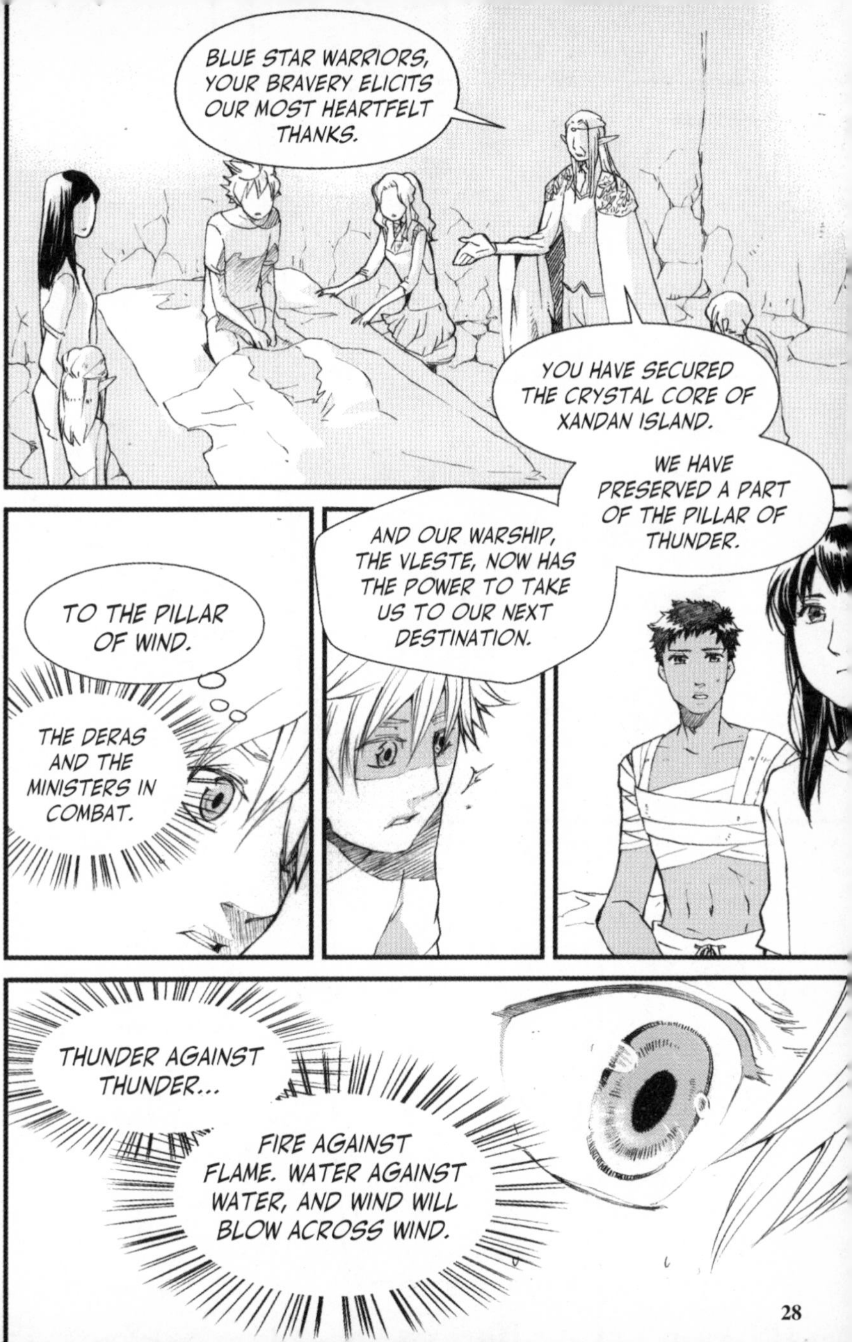
BLUE STAR WARRIORS, YOUR BRAVERY ELICITS OUR MOST HEARTFELT THANKS.
YOU HAVE SECURED THE CRYSTAL CORE OF XANDAN ISLAND.
WE HAVE PRESERVED A PART OF THE PILLAR OF THUNDER.
AND OUR WARSHIP, THE VLESTE, NOW HAS THE POWER TO TAKE US TO OUR NEXT DESTINATION.
TO THE PILLAR OF WIND.
THE DERAS AND THE MINISTERS IN COMBAT.
THUNDER AGAINST THUNDER...
FIRE AGAINST FLAME. WATER AGAINST WATER, AND WIND WILL BLOW ACROSS WIND.

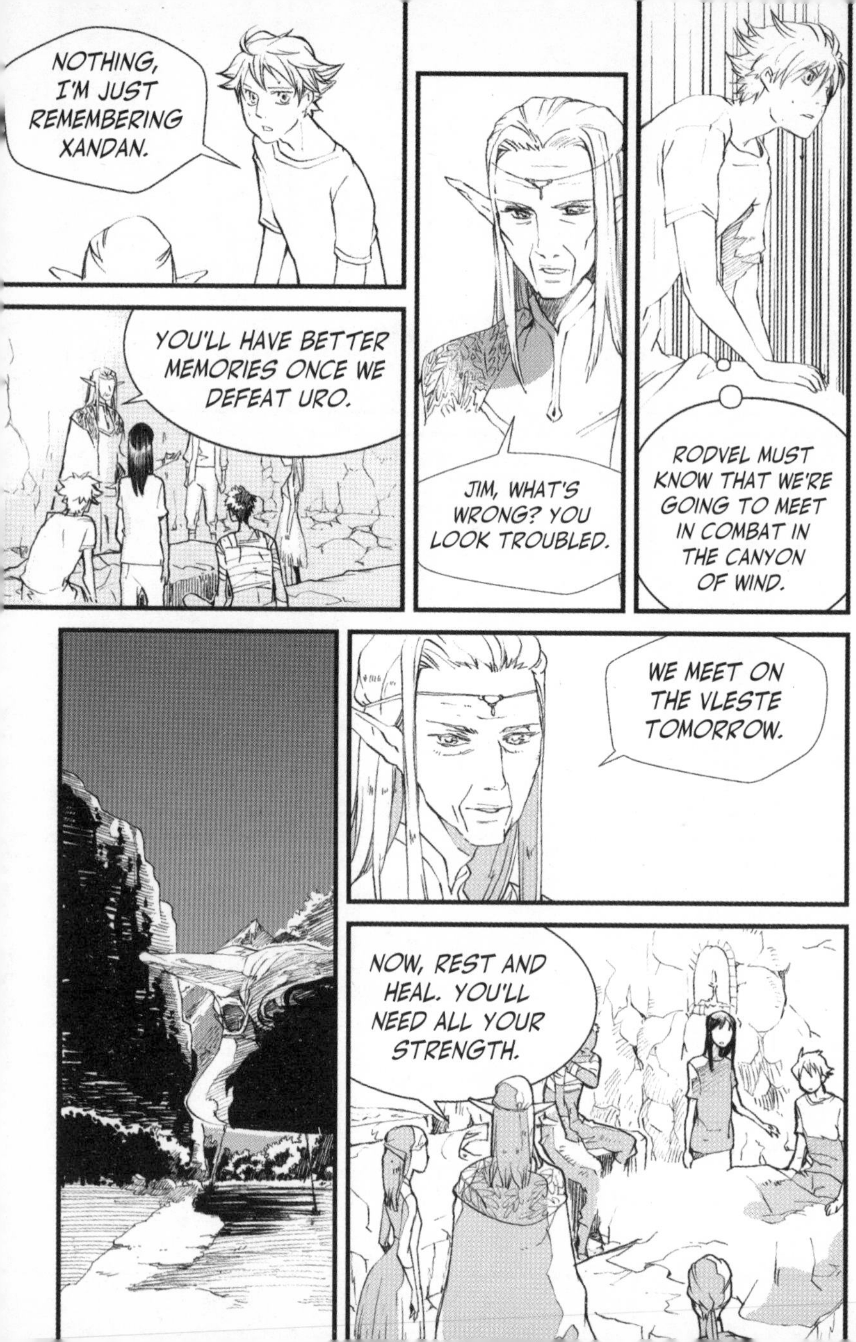
RODVEL MUST KNOW THAT WE'RE GOING TO MEET IN COMBAT IN THE CANYON OF WIND.
JIM, WHAT'S WRONG? YOU LOOK TROUBLED.
NOTHING, I'M JUST REMEMBERING XANDAN.
YOU'LL HAVE BETTER MEMORIES ONCE WE DEFEAT URO.
WE MEET ON THE VLESTE TOMORROW.
NOW, REST AND HEAL. YOU'LL NEED ALL YOUR STRENGTH.

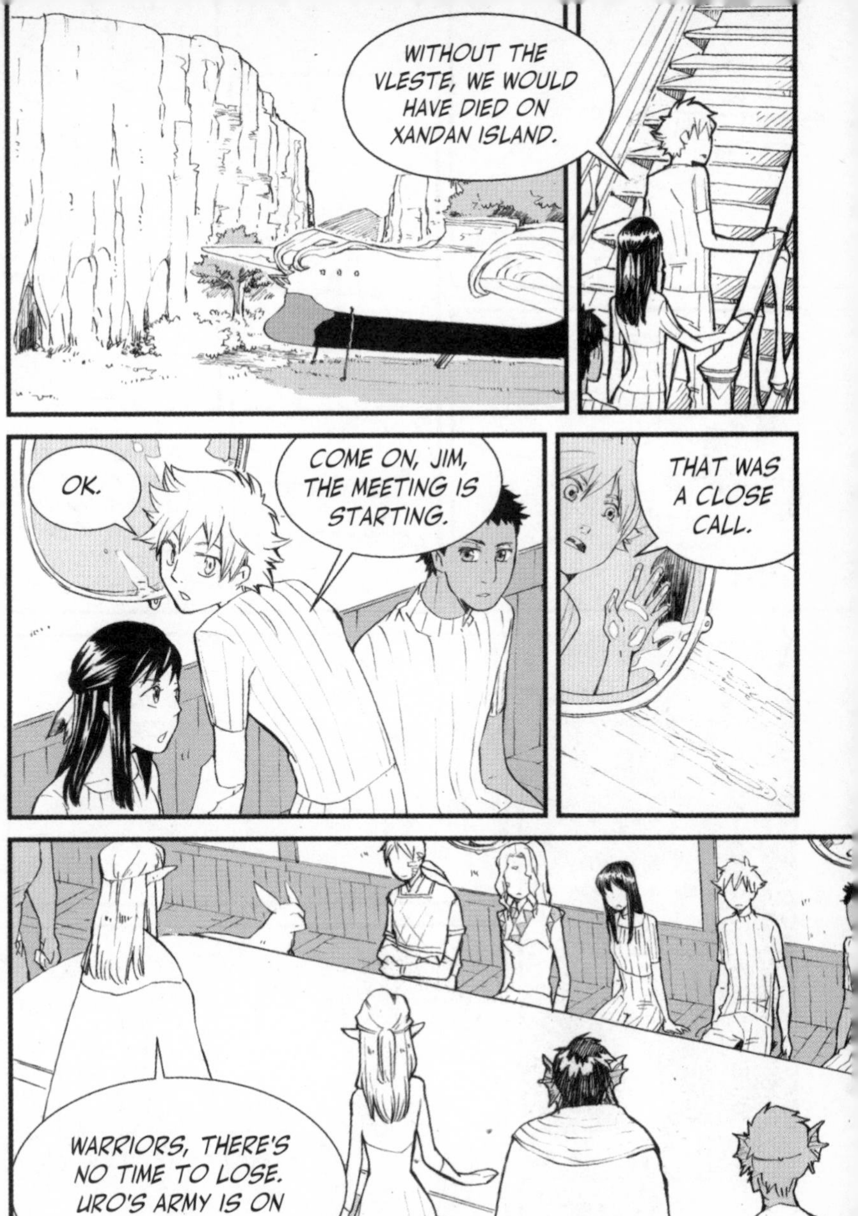
WITHOUT THE VLESTE, WE WOULD HAVE DIED ON XANDAN ISLAND.
THAT WAS A CLOSE CALL.
COME ON, JIM, THE MEETING IS STARTING.
OK.
WARRIORS, THERE'S NO TIME TO LOSE. URO'S ARMY IS ON THE MOVE.

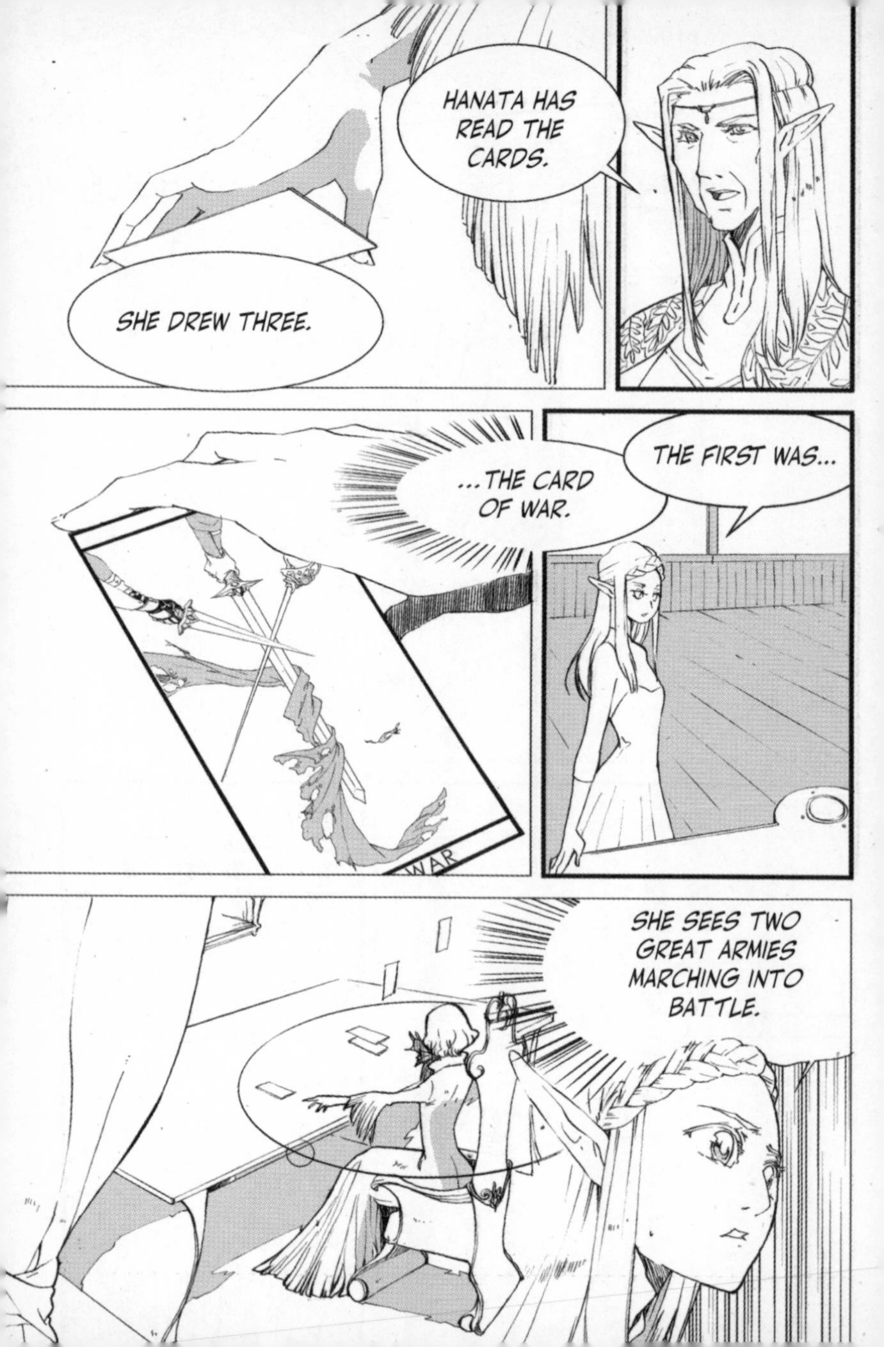
HANATA HAS READ THE CARDS.
SHE DREW THREE.
THE FIRST WAS...
...THE CARD OF WAR.
WAR
SHE SEES TWO GREAT ARMIES MARCHING INTO BATTLE.

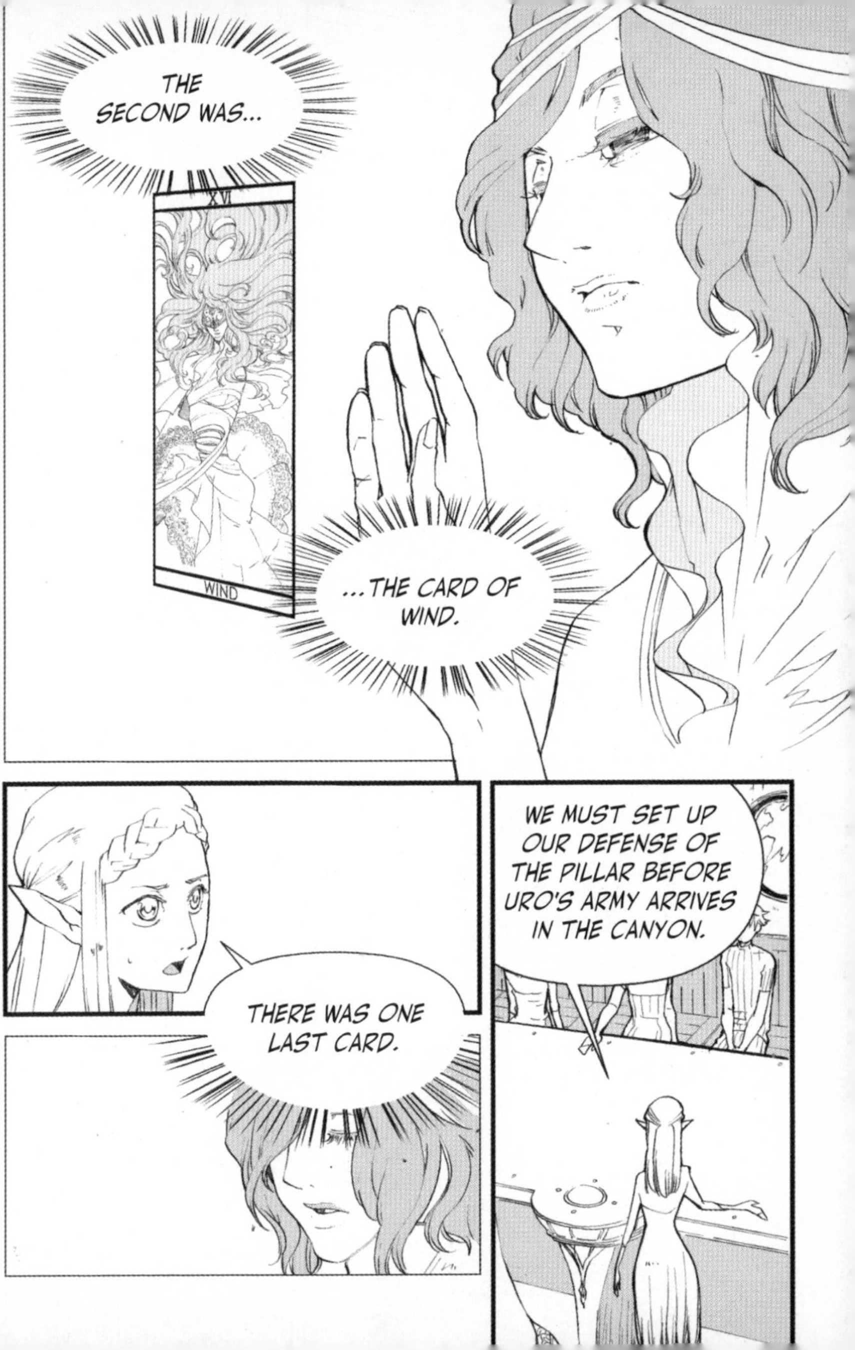
THE SECOND WAS...
XVI
WIND
...THE CARD OF WIND.
WE MUST SET UP OUR DEFENSE OF THE PILLAR BEFORE URO'S ARMY ARRIVES IN THE CANYON.
THERE WAS ONE LAST CARD.

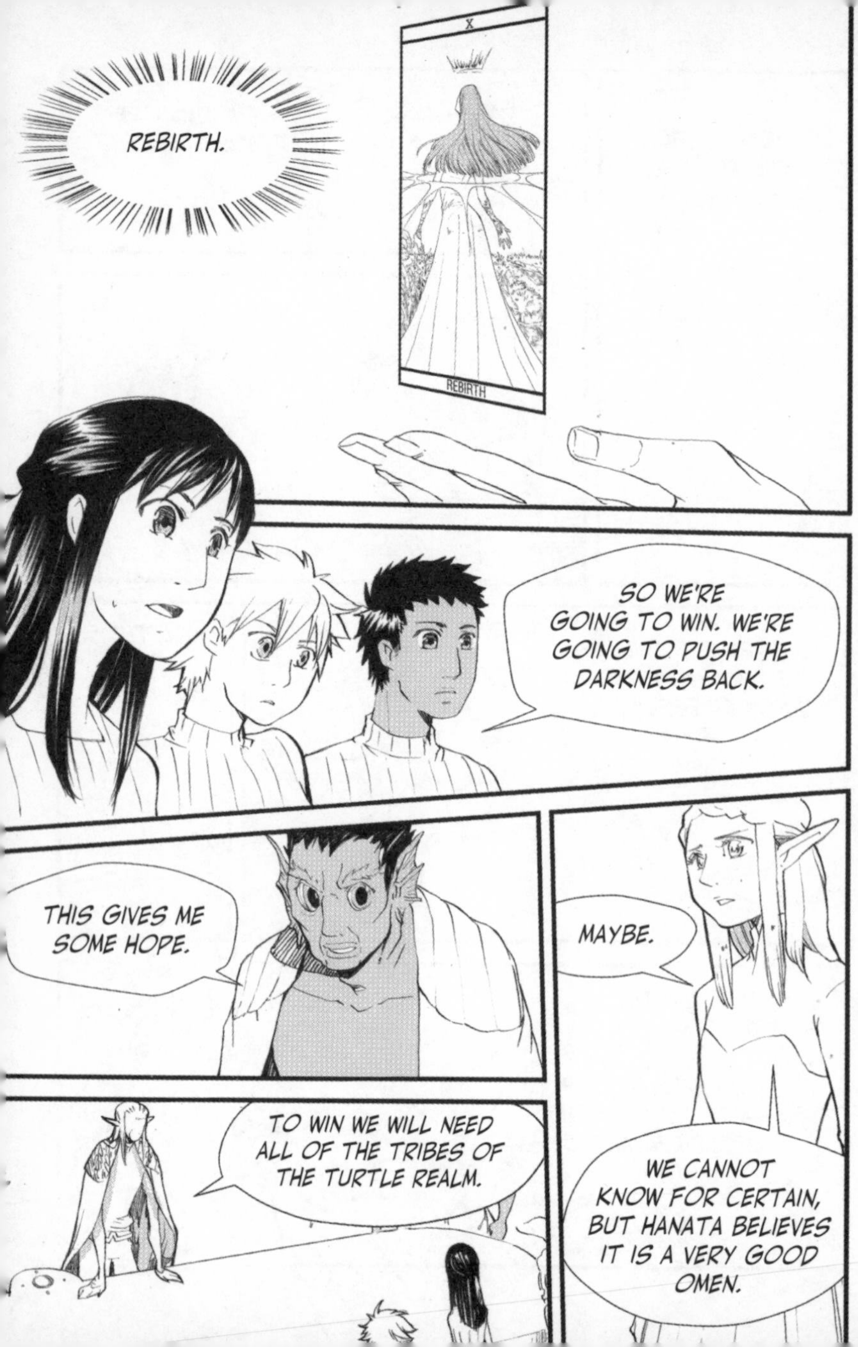
X
REBIRTH
REBIRTH.
SO WE'RE GOING TO WIN. WE'RE GOING TO PUSH THE DARKNESS BACK.
MAYBE.
WE CANNOT KNOW FOR CERTAIN, BUT HANATA BELIEVES IT IS A VERY GOOD OMEN.
THIS GIVES ME SOME HOPE.
TO WIN WE WILL NEED ALL OF THE TRIBES OF THE TURTLE REALM.

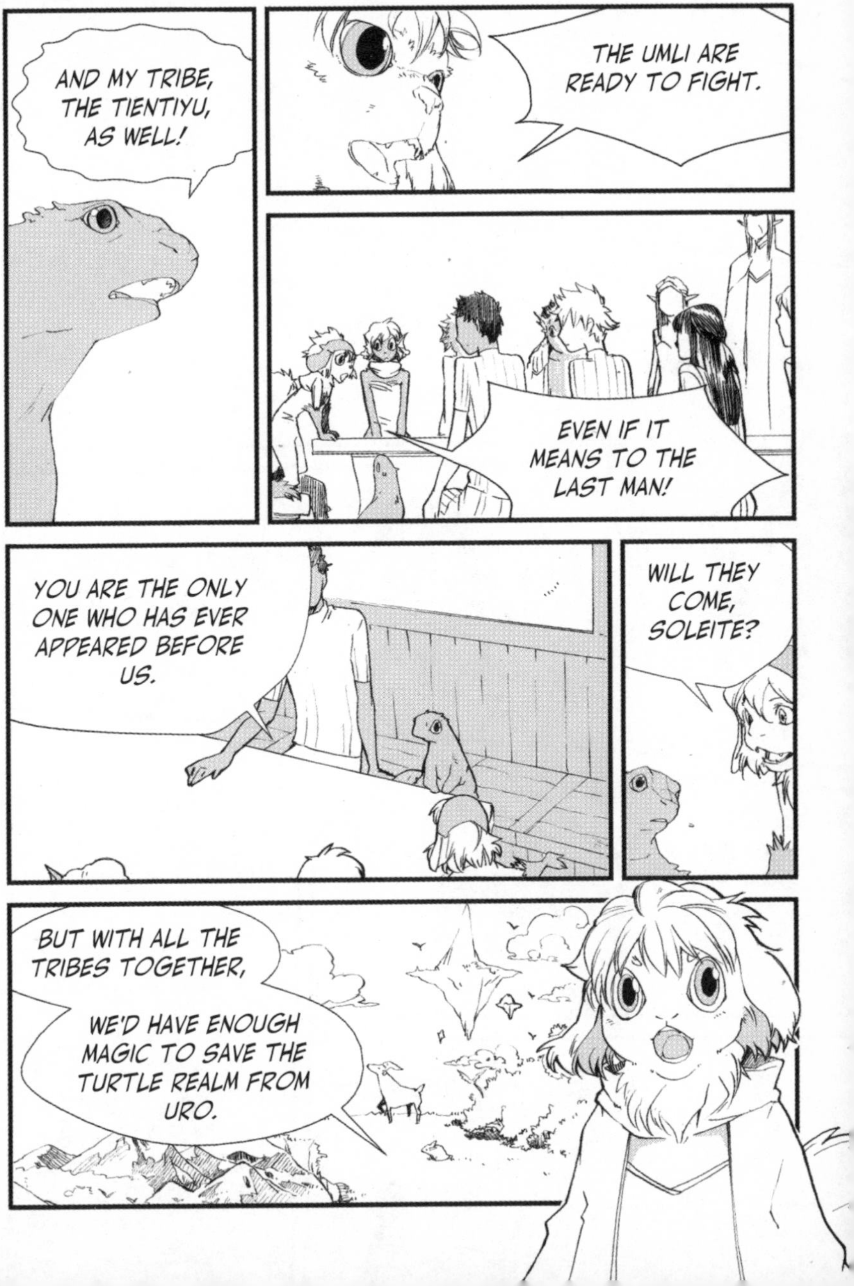
THE UMLI ARE READY TO FIGHT.
EVEN IF IT MEANS TO THE LAST MAN!
AND MY TRIBE, THE TIENTIYU, AS WELL!
WILL THEY COME, SOLEITE?
YOU ARE THE ONLY ONE WHO HAS EVER APPEARED BEFORE US.
BUT WITH ALL THE TRIBES TOGETHER,
WE'D HAVE ENOUGH MAGIC TO SAVE THE TURTLE REALM FROM URO.

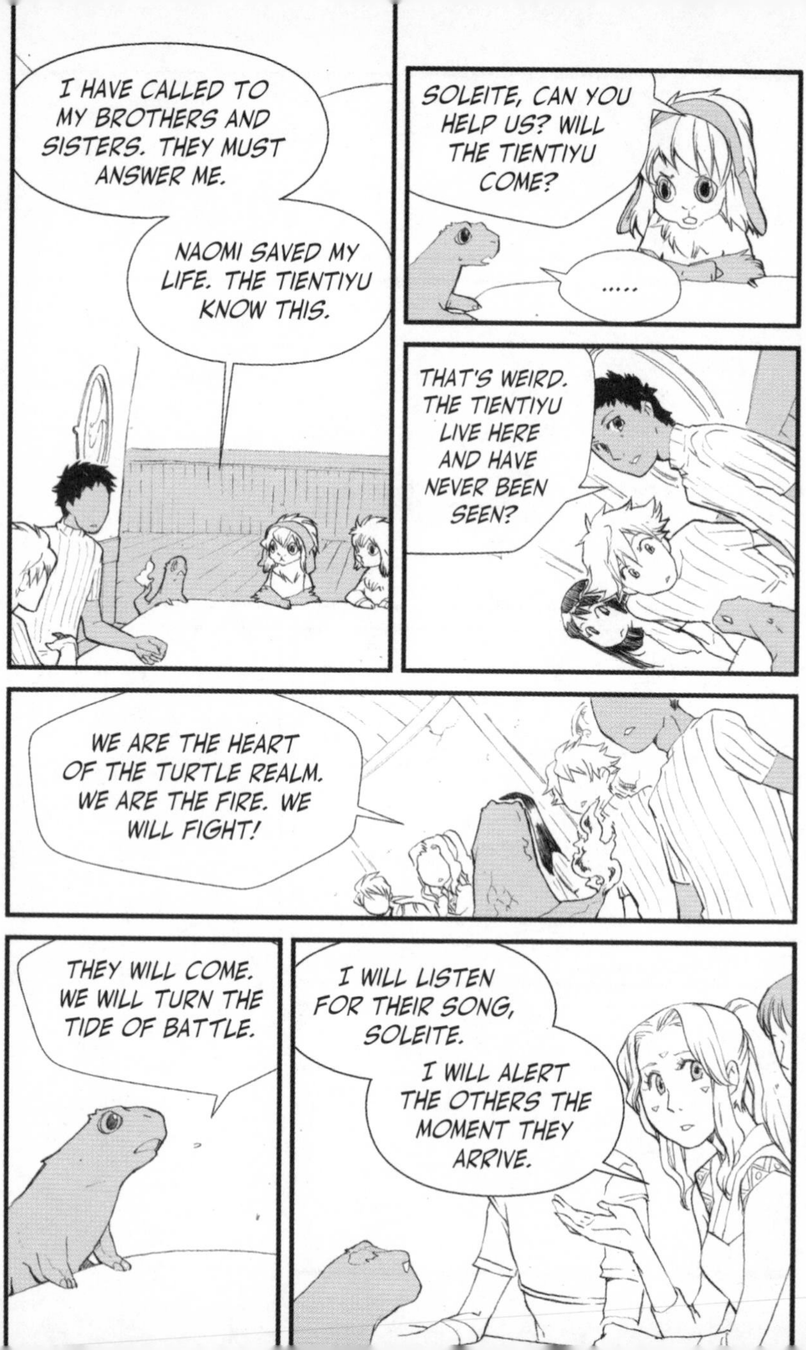
SOLEITE, CAN YOU HELP US? WILL THE TIENTIYU COME?
.....
THAT'S WEIRD. THE TIENTIYU LIVE HERE AND HAVE NEVER BEEN SEEN?
I HAVE CALLED TO MY BROTHERS AND SISTERS. THEY MUST ANSWER ME.
NAOMI SAVED MY LIFE. THE TIENTIYU KNOW THIS.
WE ARE THE HEART OF THE TURTLE REALM. WE ARE THE FIRE. WE WILL FIGHT!
I WILL LISTEN FOR THEIR SONG, SOLEITE.
I WILL ALERT THE OTHERS THE MOMENT THEY ARRIVE.
THEY WILL COME. WE WILL TURN THE TIDE OF BATTLE.

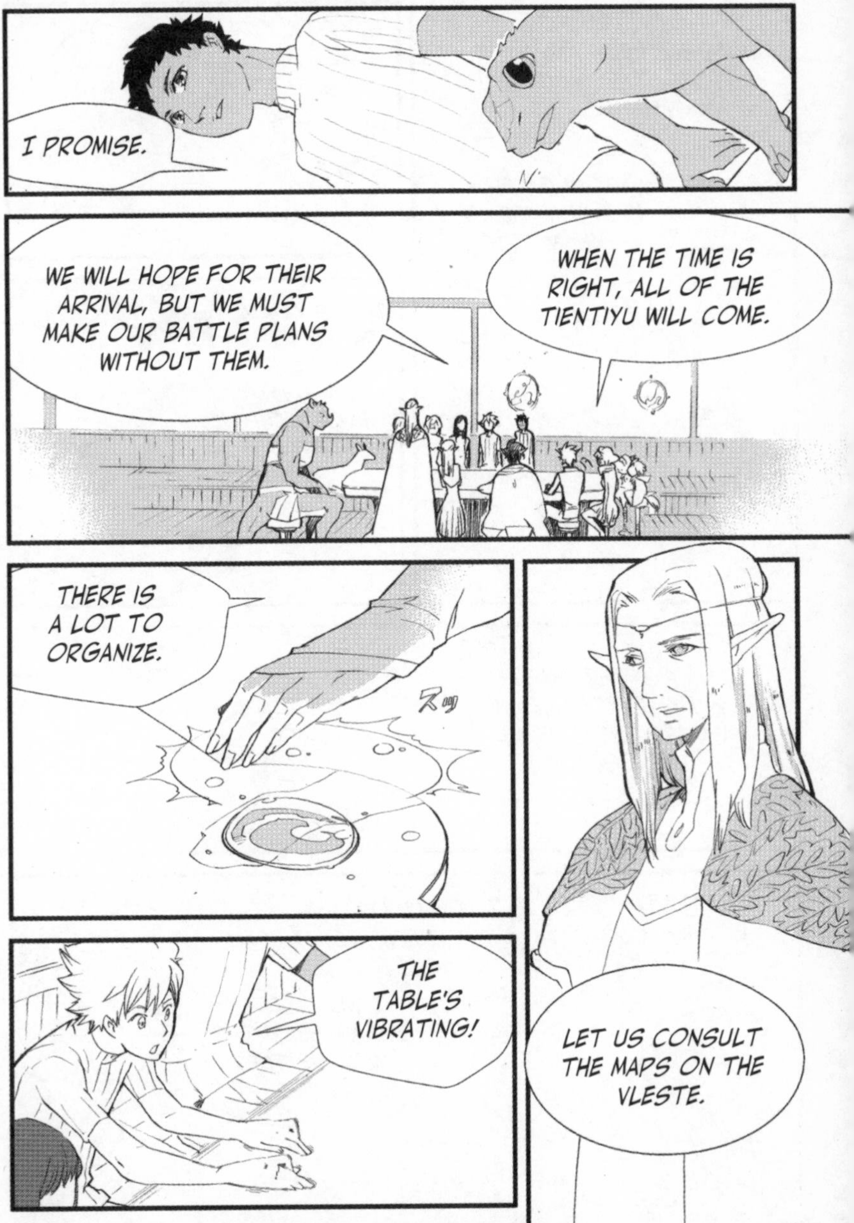
I PROMISE.
WHEN THE TIME IS RIGHT, ALL OF THE TIENTIYU WILL COME.
WE WILL HOPE FOR THEIR ARRIVAL, BUT WE MUST MAKE OUR BATTLE PLANS WITHOUT THEM.
LET US CONSULT THE MAPS ON THE VLESTE.
THERE IS A LOT TO ORGANIZE.
ズッ
THE TABLE'S VIBRATING!

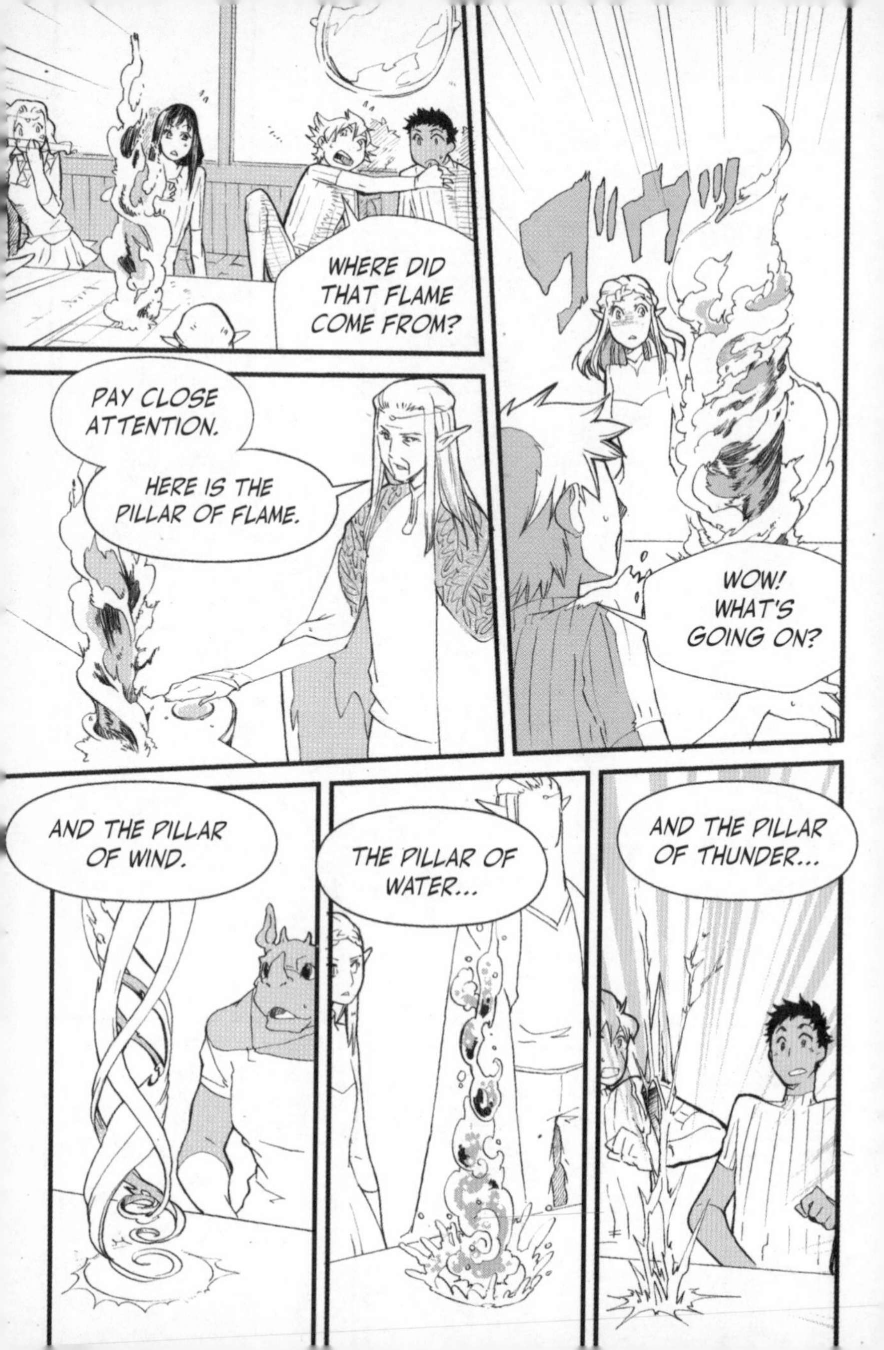
WOW! WHAT'S GOING ON?
WHERE DID THAT FLAME COME FROM?
PAY CLOSE ATTENTION.
HERE IS THE PILLAR OF FLAME.
AND THE PILLAR OF THUNDER...
THE PILLAR OF WATER...
AND THE PILLAR OF WIND.

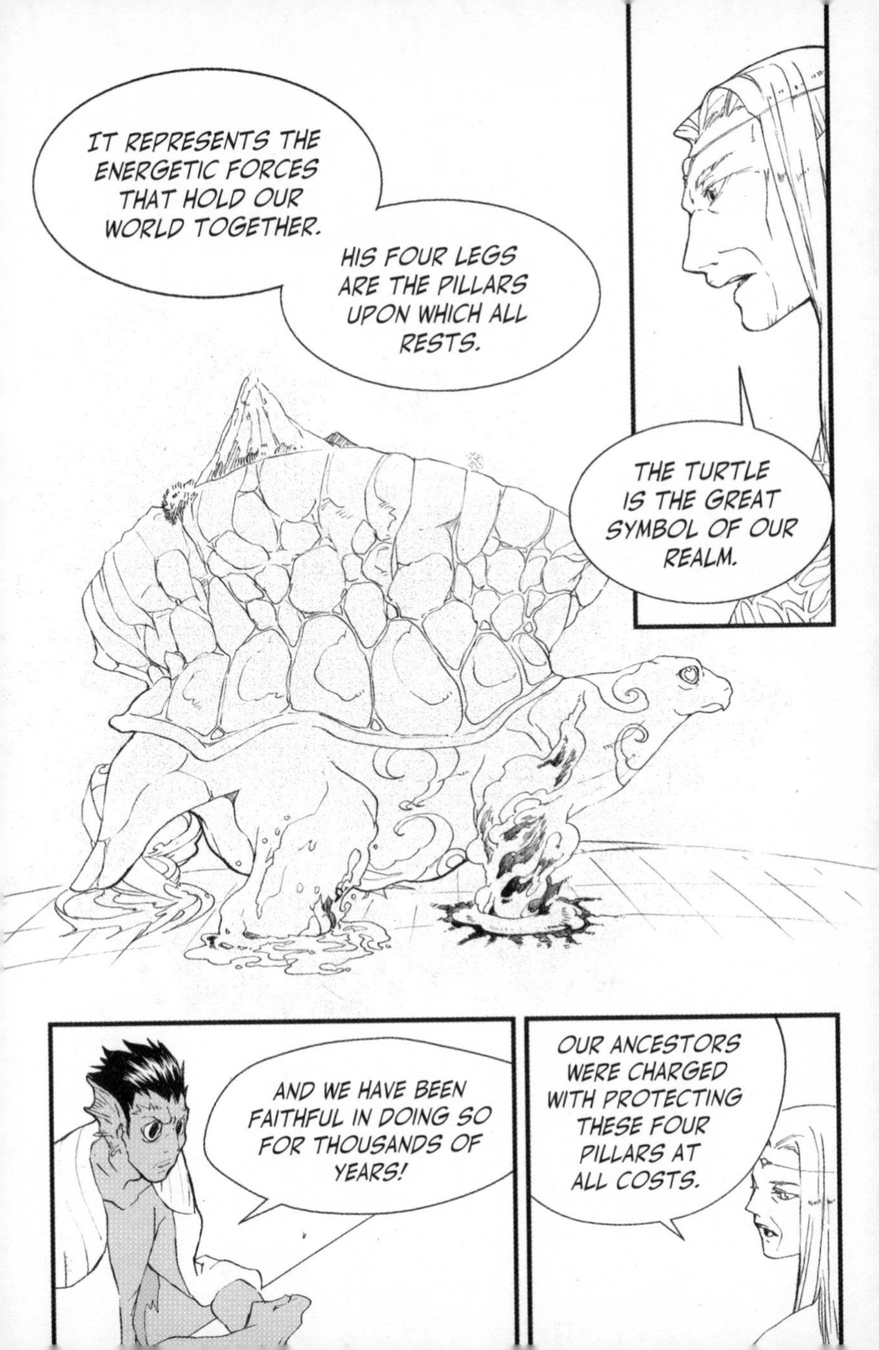
THE TURTLE IS THE GREAT SYMBOL OF OUR REALM.
IT REPRESENTS THE ENERGETIC FORCES THAT HOLD OUR WORLD TOGETHER.
HIS FOUR LEGS ARE THE PILLARS UPON WHICH ALL RESTS.
OUR ANCESTORS WERE CHARGED WITH PROTECTING THESE FOUR PILLARS AT ALL COSTS.
AND WE HAVE BEEN FAITHFUL IN DOING SO FOR THOUSANDS OF YEARS!

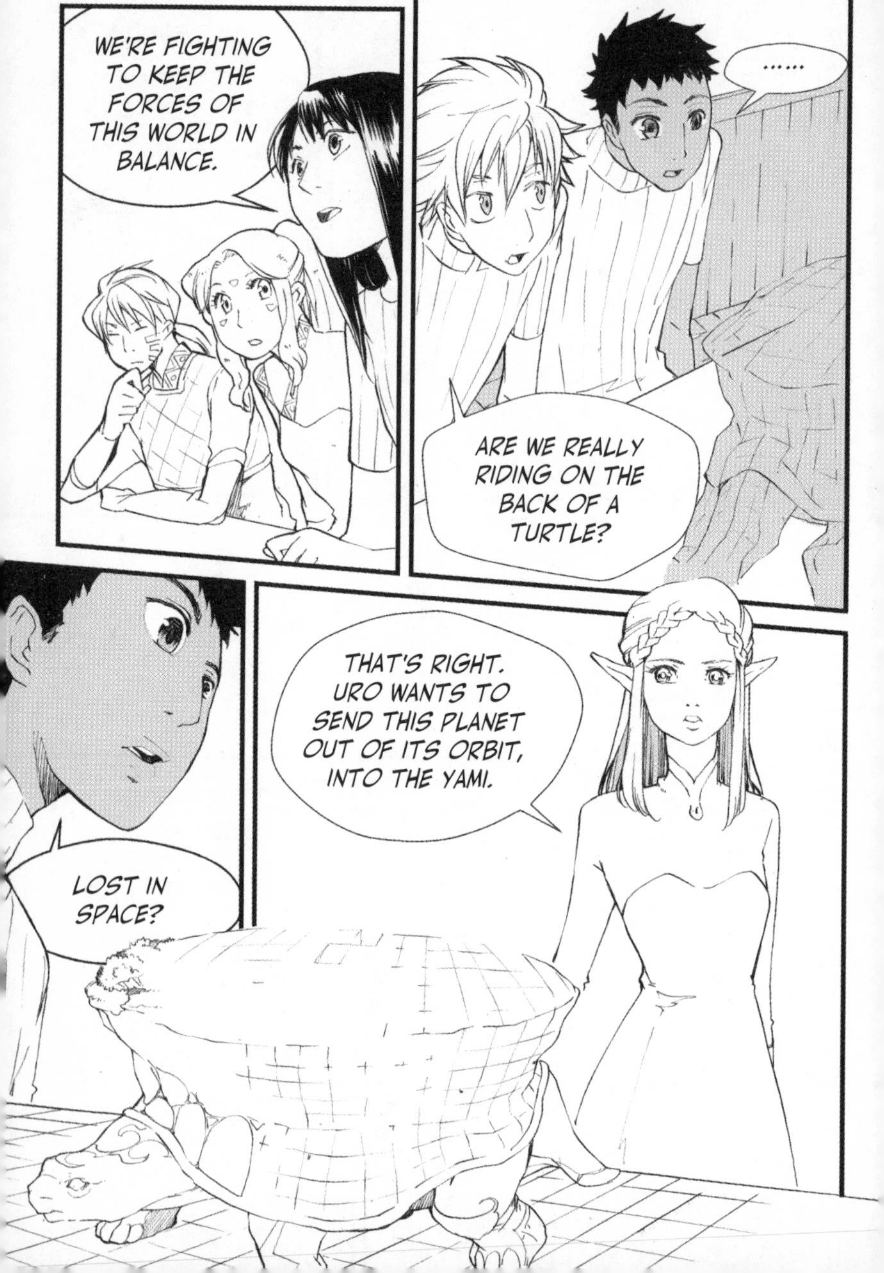
......
ARE WE REALLY RIDING ON THE BACK OF A TURTLE?
WE'RE FIGHTING TO KEEP THE FORCES OF THIS WORLD IN BALANCE.
THAT'S RIGHT. URO WANTS TO SEND THIS PLANET OUT OF ITS ORBIT, INTO THE YAMI.
LOST IN SPACE?

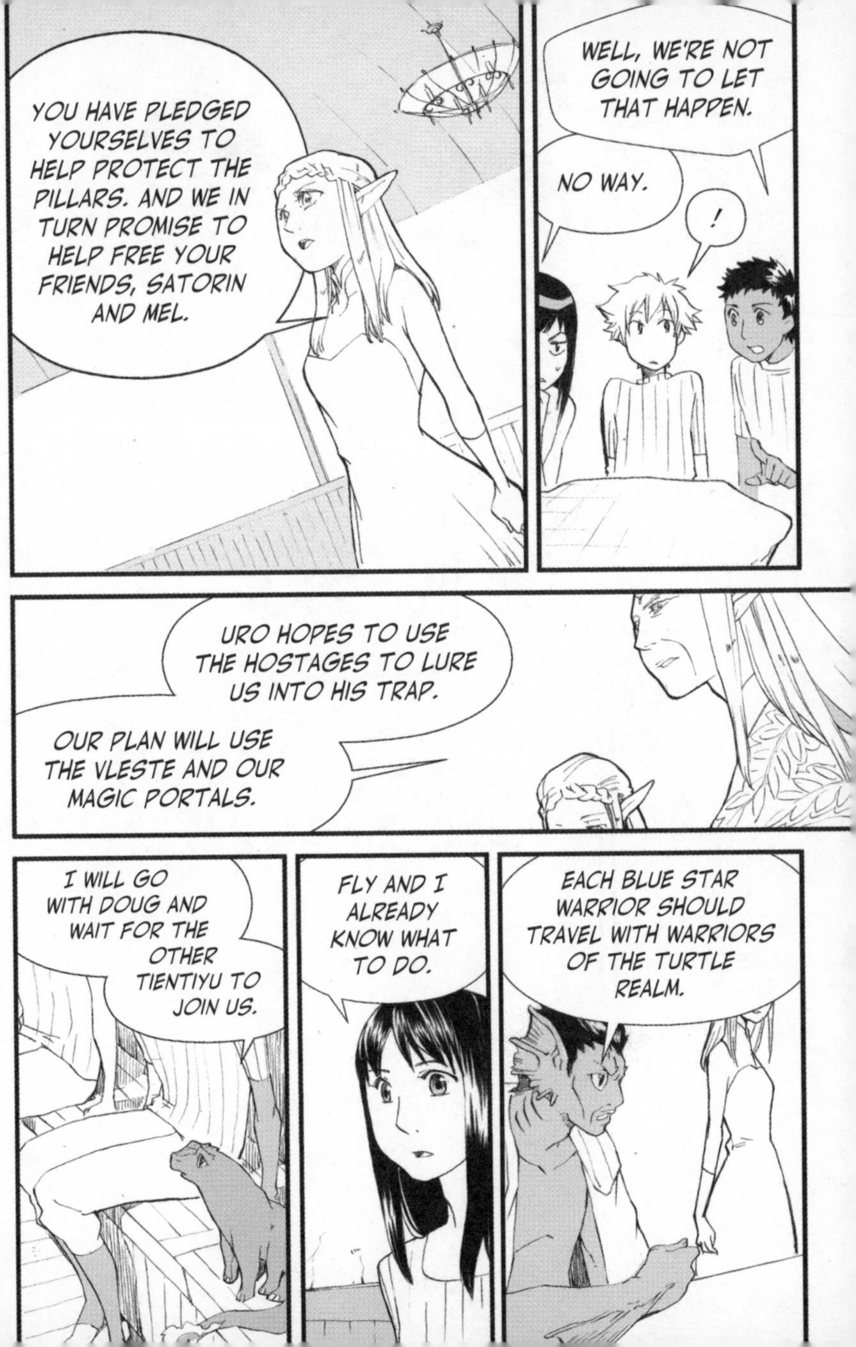
WELL, WE'RE NOT GOING TO LET THAT HAPPEN.
!
NO WAY.
YOU HAVE PLEDGED YOURSELVES TO HELP PROTECT THE PILLARS. AND WE IN TURN PROMISE TO HELP FREE YOUR FRIENDS, SATORIN AND MEL.
URO HOPES TO USE THE HOSTAGES TO LURE US INTO HIS TRAP.
OUR PLAN WILL USE THE VLESTE AND OUR MAGIC PORTALS.
EACH BLUE STAR WARRIOR SHOULD TRAVEL WITH WARRIORS OF THE TURTLE REALM.
FLY AND I ALREADY KNOW WHAT TO DO.
I WILL GO WITH DOUG AND WAIT FOR THE OTHER TIENTIYU TO JOIN US.

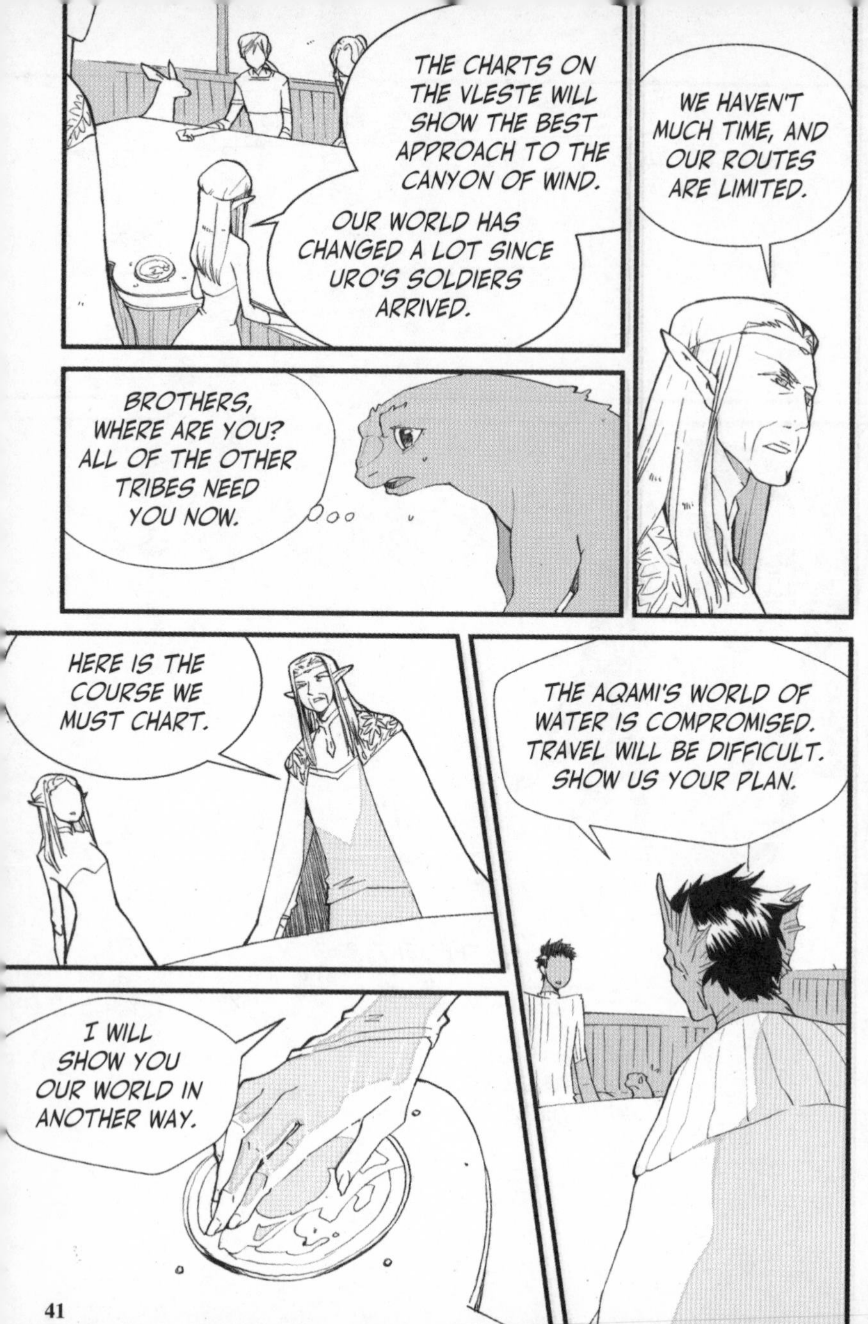
WE HAVEN'T MUCH TIME, AND OUR ROUTES ARE LIMITED.
THE CHARTS ON THE VLESTE WILL SHOW THE BEST APPROACH TO THE CANYON OF WIND.
OUR WORLD HAS CHANGED A LOT SINCE URO'S SOLDIERS ARRIVED.
BROTHERS, WHERE ARE YOU? ALL OF THE OTHER TRIBES NEED YOU NOW.
THE AQAMI'S WORLD OF WATER IS COMPROMISED. TRAVEL WILL BE DIFFICULT. SHOW US YOUR PLAN.
HERE IS THE COURSE WE MUST CHART.
I WILL SHOW YOU OUR WORLD IN ANOTHER WAY.

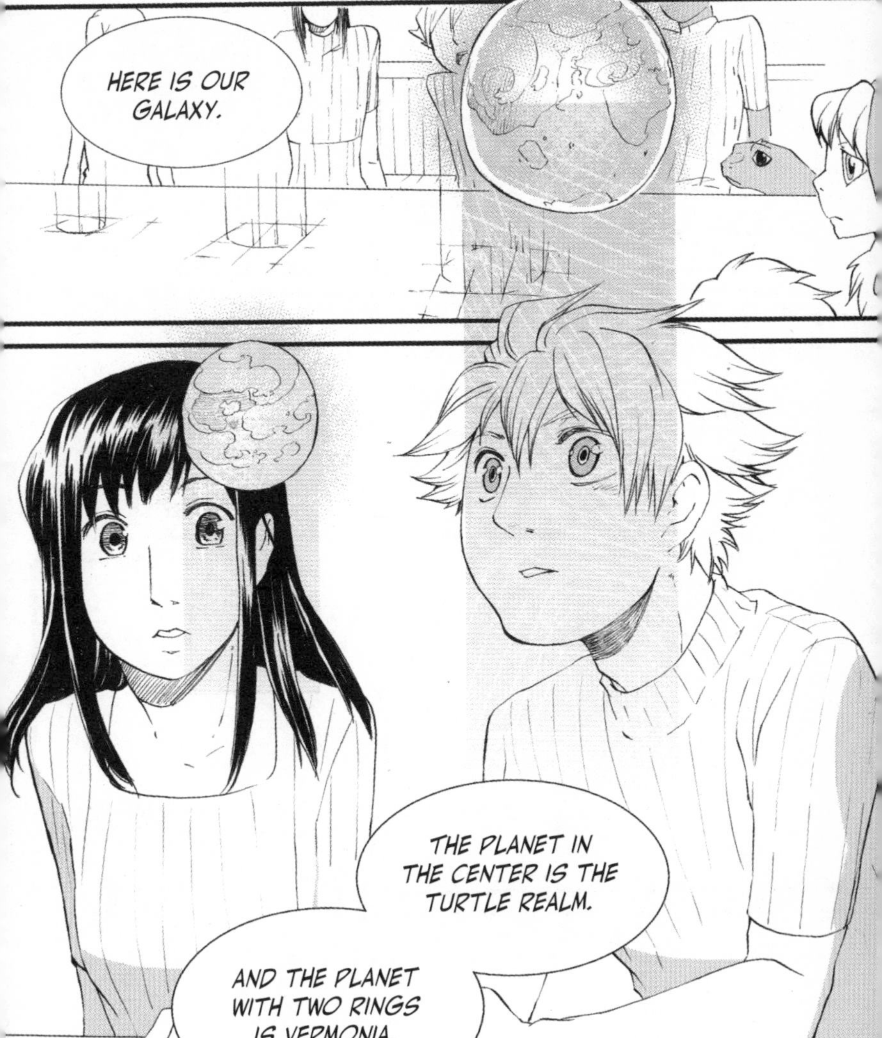
HERE IS OUR GALAXY.
THE PLANET IN THE CENTER IS THE TURTLE REALM.
AND THE PLANET WITH TWO RINGS IS VERMONIA.

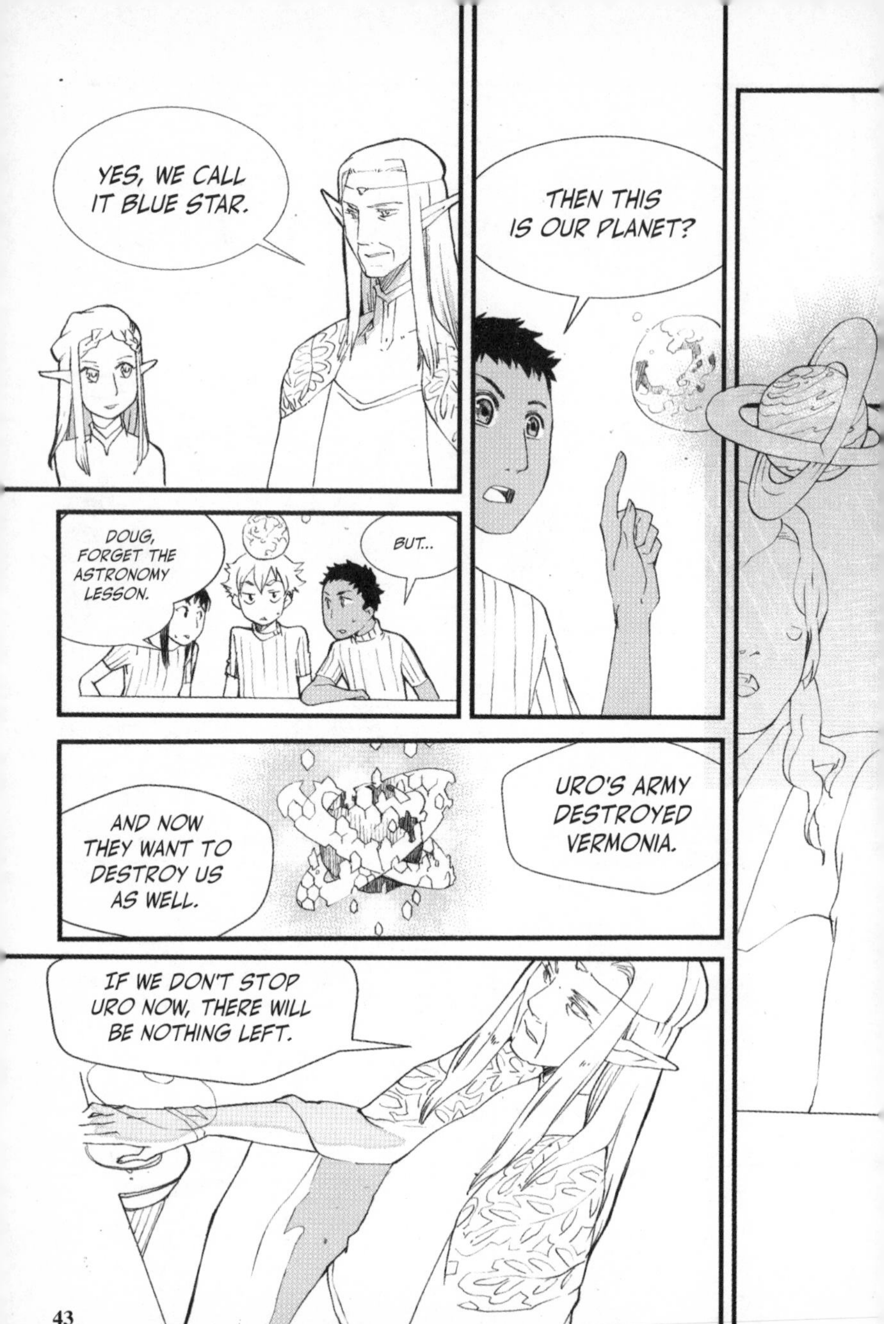
THEN THIS IS OUR PLANET?
YES, WE CALL IT BLUE STAR.
DOUG, FORGET THE ASTRONOMY LESSON.
BUT...
URO'S ARMY DESTROYED VERMONIA.
AND NOW THEY WANT TO DESTROY US AS WELL.
IF WE DON'T STOP URO NOW, THERE WILL BE NOTHING LEFT.

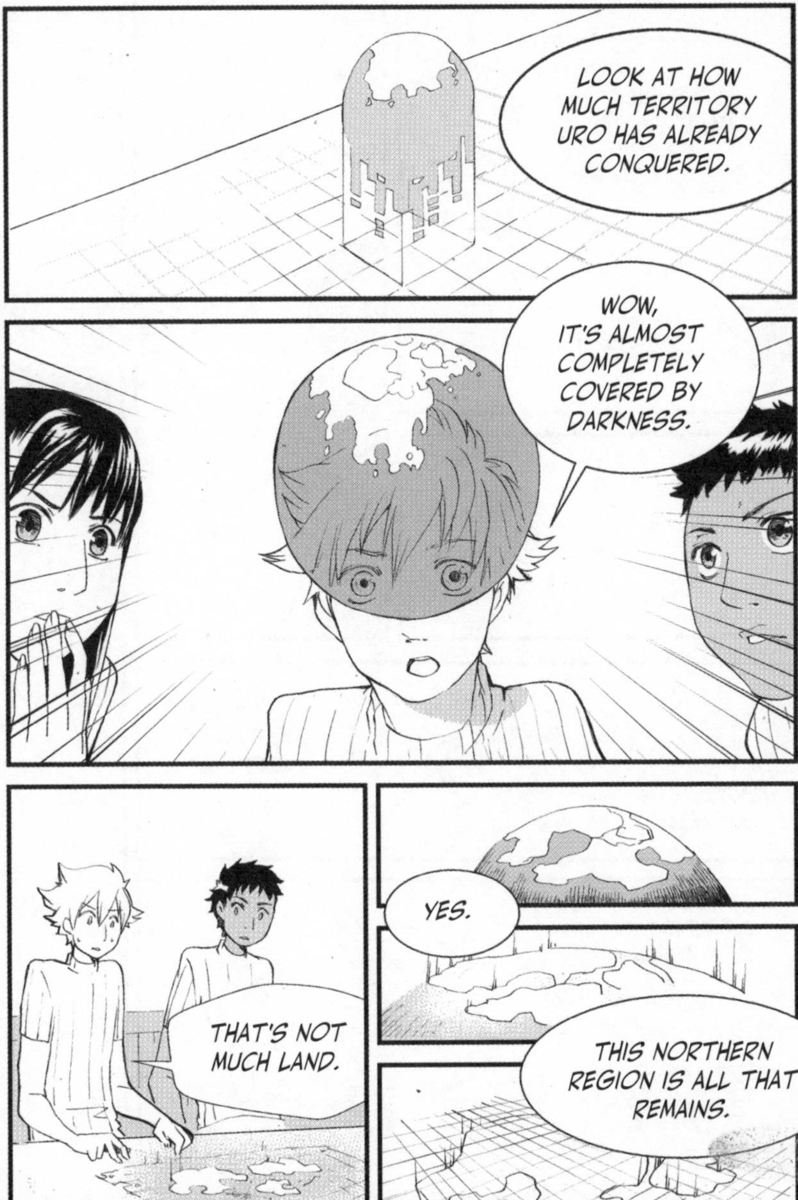
LOOK AT HOW MUCH TERRITORY URO HAS ALREADY CONQUERED.
WOW, IT'S ALMOST COMPLETELY COVERED BY DARKNESS.
YES.
THIS NORTHERN REGION IS ALL THAT REMAINS.
THAT'S NOT MUCH LAND.

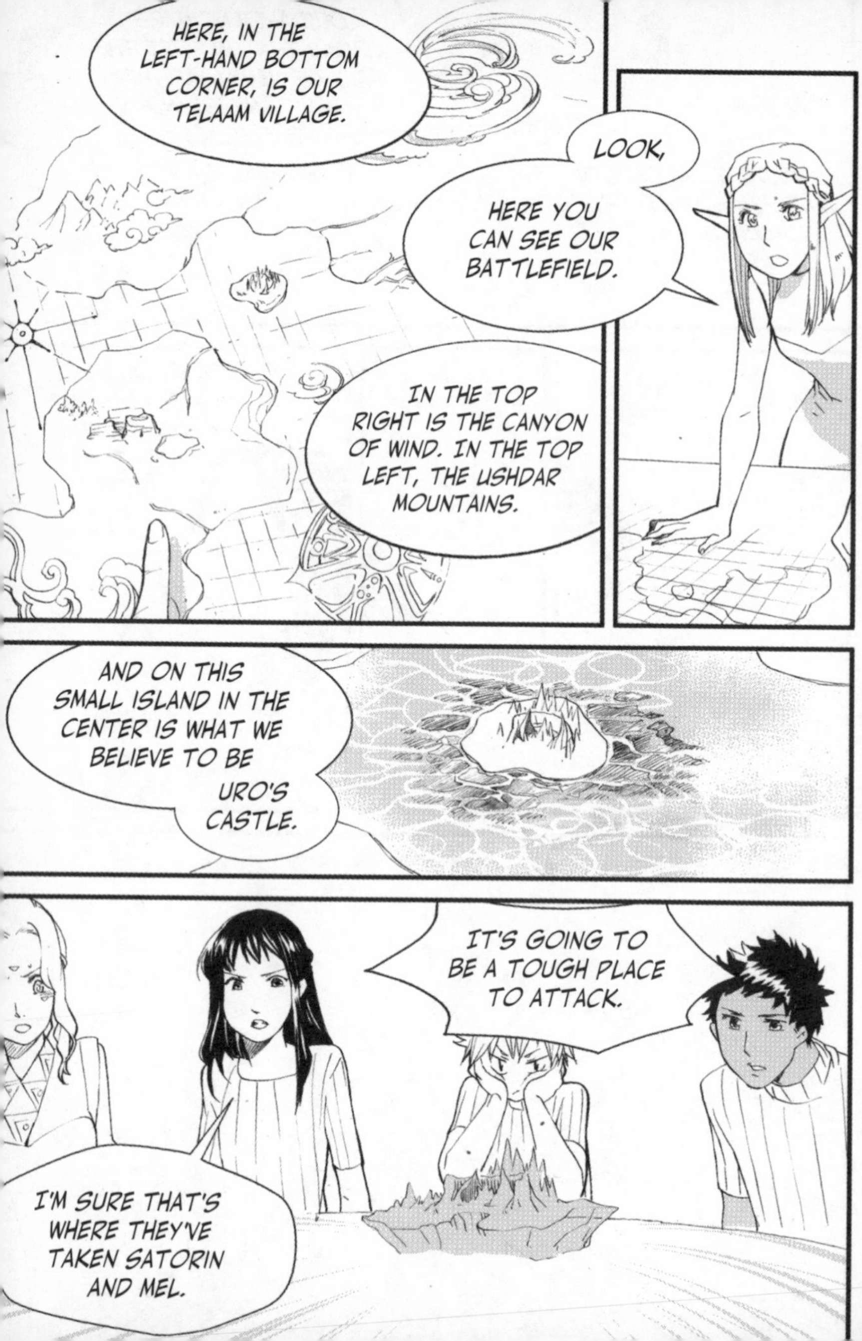
LOOK,
HERE YOU CAN SEE OUR BATTLEFIELD.
HERE, IN THE LEFT-HAND BOTTOM CORNER, IS OUR TELAAM VILLAGE.
IN THE TOP RIGHT IS THE CANYON OF WIND. IN THE TOP LEFT, THE USHDAR MOUNTAINS.
AND ON THIS SMALL ISLAND IN THE CENTER IS WHAT WE BELIEVE TO BE
URO'S CASTLE.
IT'S GOING TO BE A TOUGH PLACE TO ATTACK.
I'M SURE THAT'S WHERE THEY'VE TAKEN SATORIN AND MEL.

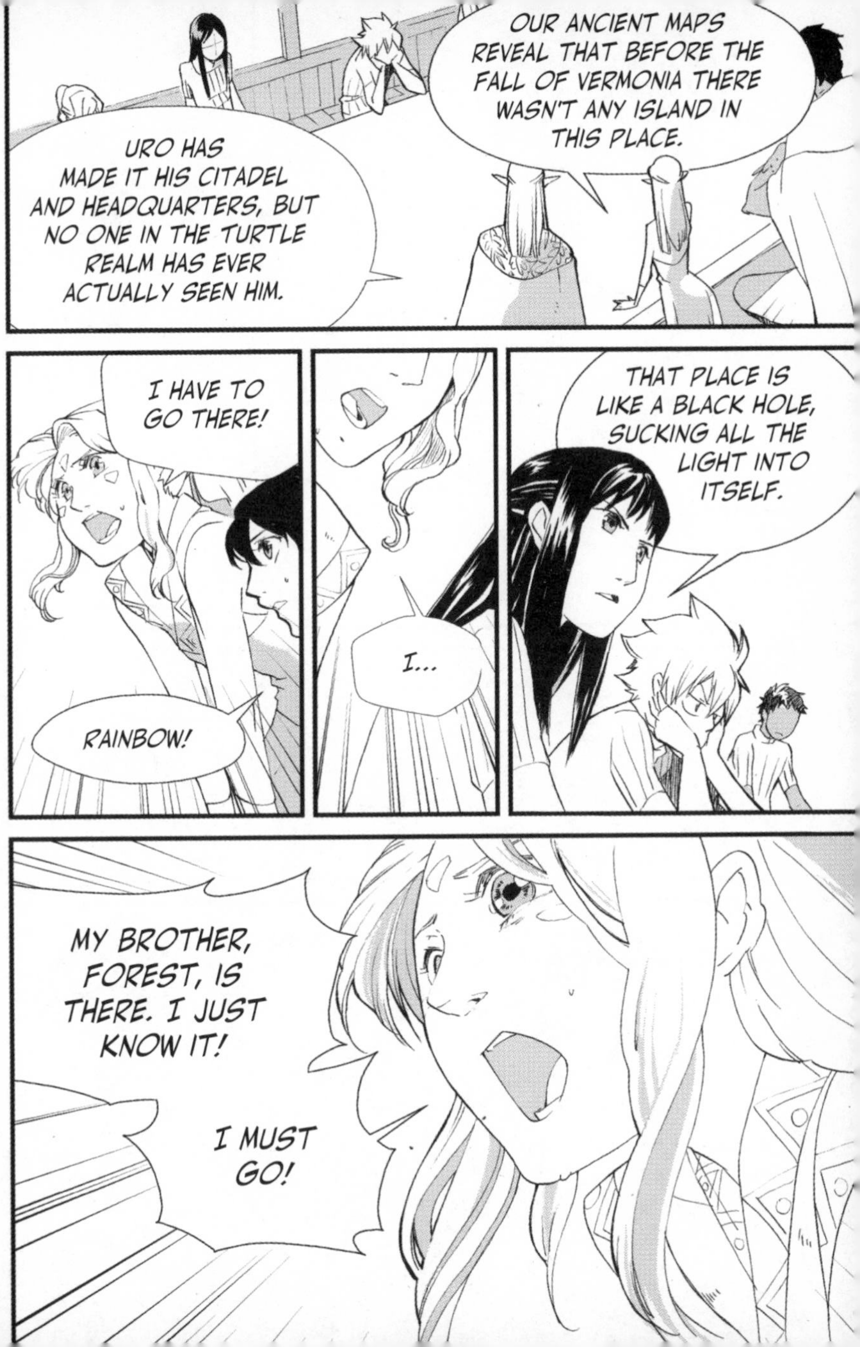
OUR ANCIENT MAPS REVEAL THAT BEFORE THE FALL OF VERMONIA THERE WASN'T ANY ISLAND IN THIS PLACE.
URO HAS MADE IT HIS CITADEL AND HEADQUARTERS, BUT NO ONE IN THE TURTLE REALM HAS EVER ACTUALLY SEEN HIM.
THAT PLACE IS LIKE A BLACK HOLE, SUCKING ALL THE LIGHT INTO ITSELF.
I...
I HAVE TO GO THERE!
RAINBOW!
MY BROTHER, FOREST, IS THERE. I JUST KNOW IT!
I MUST GO!

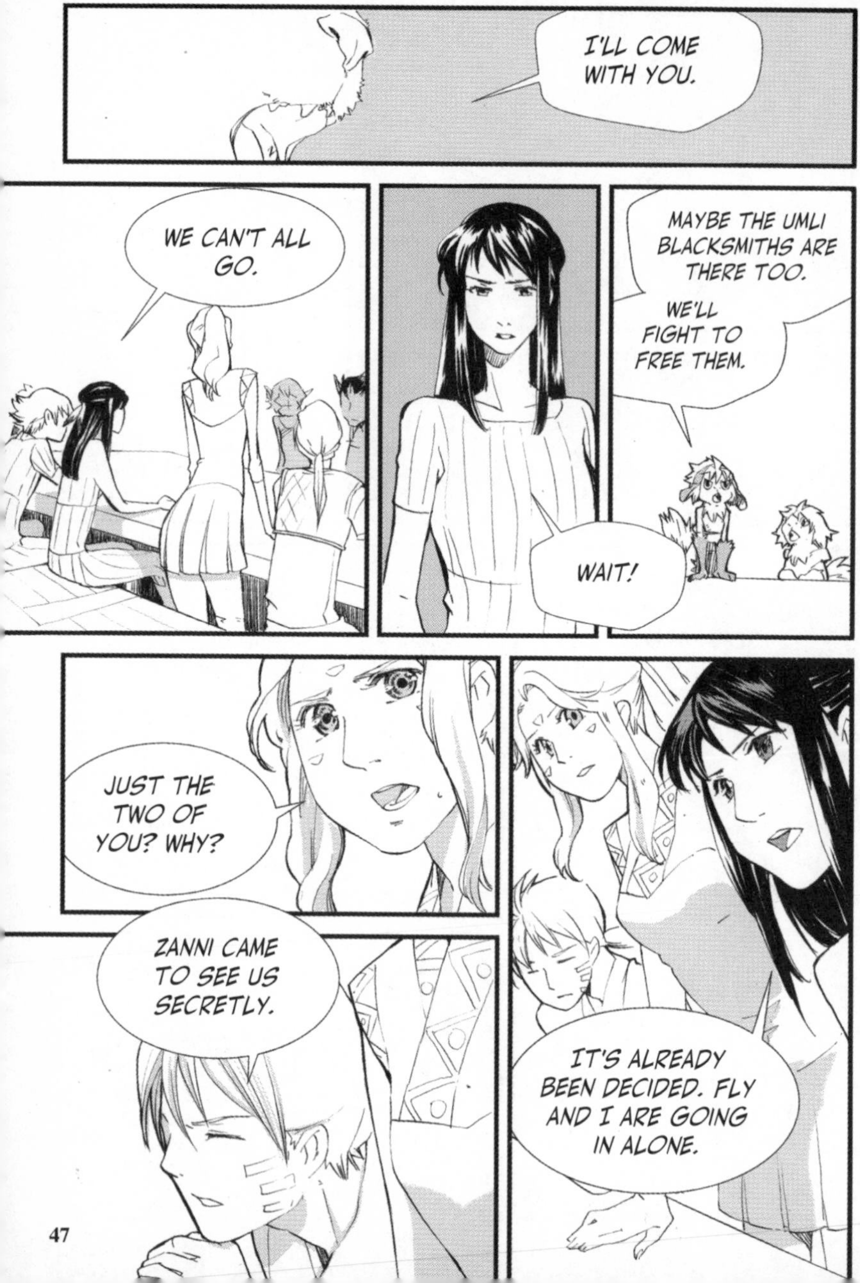
I'LL COME WITH YOU.
MAYBE THE UMLI BLACKSMITHS ARE THERE TOO.
WE'LL FIGHT TO FREE THEM.
WAIT!
WE CAN'T ALL GO.
IT'S ALREADY BEEN DECIDED. FLY AND I ARE GOING IN ALONE.
JUST THE TWO OF YOU? WHY?
ZANNI CAME TO SEE US SECRETLY.

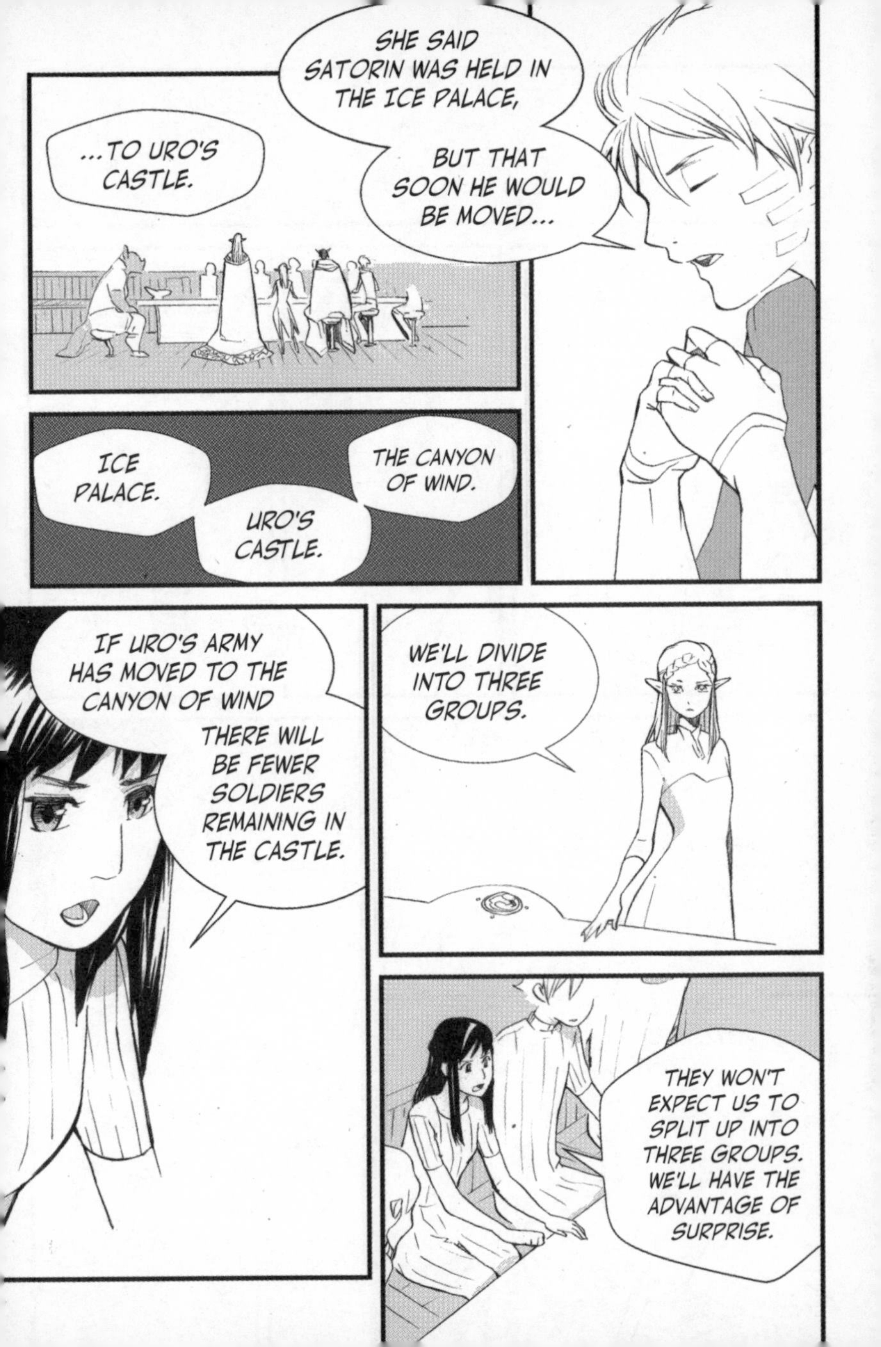
SHE SAID SATORIN WAS HELD IN THE ICE PALACE,
BUT THAT SOON HE WOULD BE MOVED...
...TO URO'S CASTLE.
THE CANYON OF WIND.
ICE PALACE.
URO'S CASTLE.
WE'LL DIVIDE INTO THREE GROUPS.
THEY WON'T EXPECT US TO SPLIT UP INTO THREE GROUPS. WE'LL HAVE THE ADVANTAGE OF SURPRISE.
IF URO'S ARMY HAS MOVED TO THE CANYON OF WIND
THERE WILL BE FEWER SOLDIERS REMAINING IN THE CASTLE.

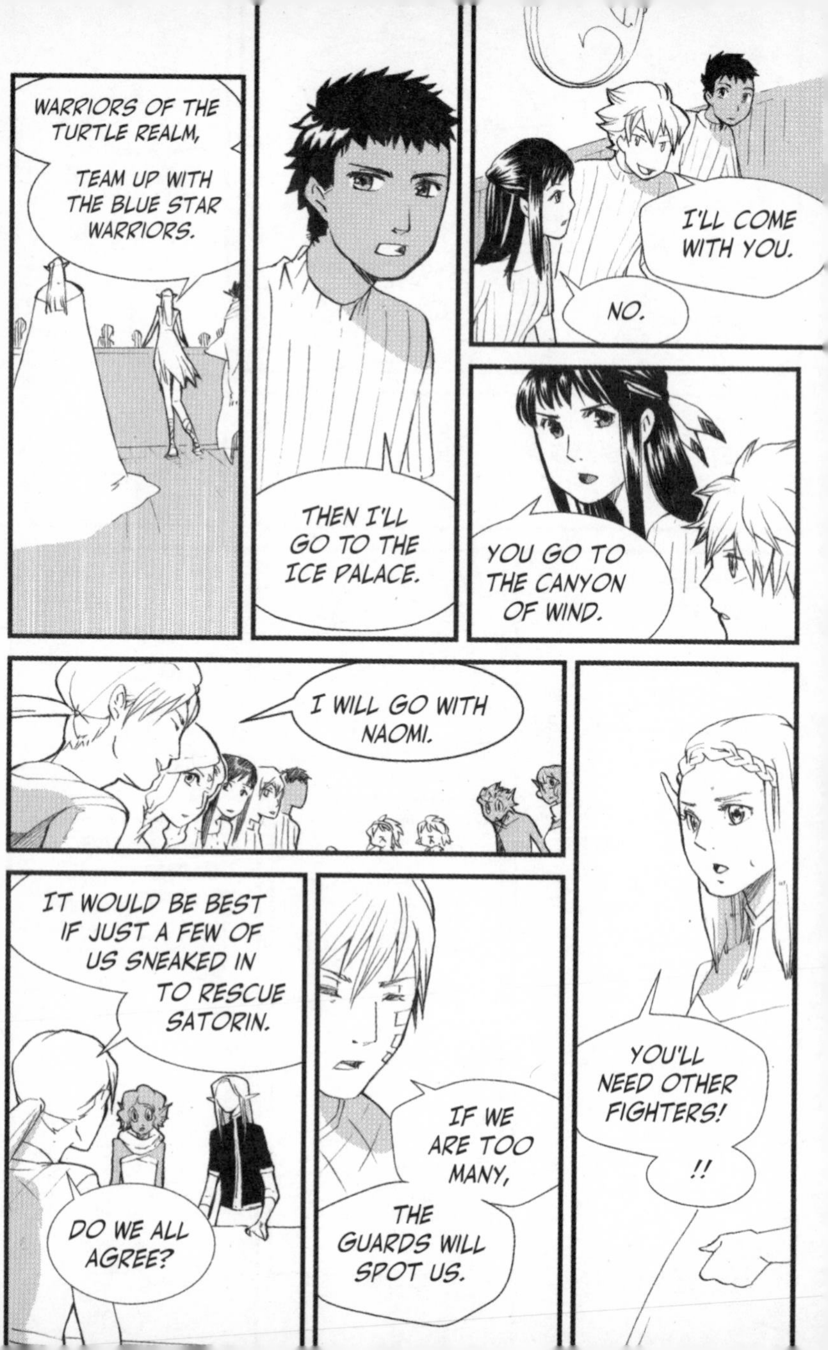
I'LL COME WITH YOU.
NO.
YOU GO TO THE CANYON OF WIND.
THEN I'LL GO TO THE ICE PALACE.
WARRIORS OF THE TURTLE REALM,
TEAM UP WITH THE BLUE STAR WARRIORS.
YOU'LL NEED OTHER FIGHTERS!
!!
I WILL GO WITH NAOMI.
IF WE ARE TOO MANY,
THE GUARDS WILL SPOT US.
IT WOULD BE BEST IF JUST A FEW OF US SNEAKED IN
TO RESCUE SATORIN.
DO WE ALL AGREE?

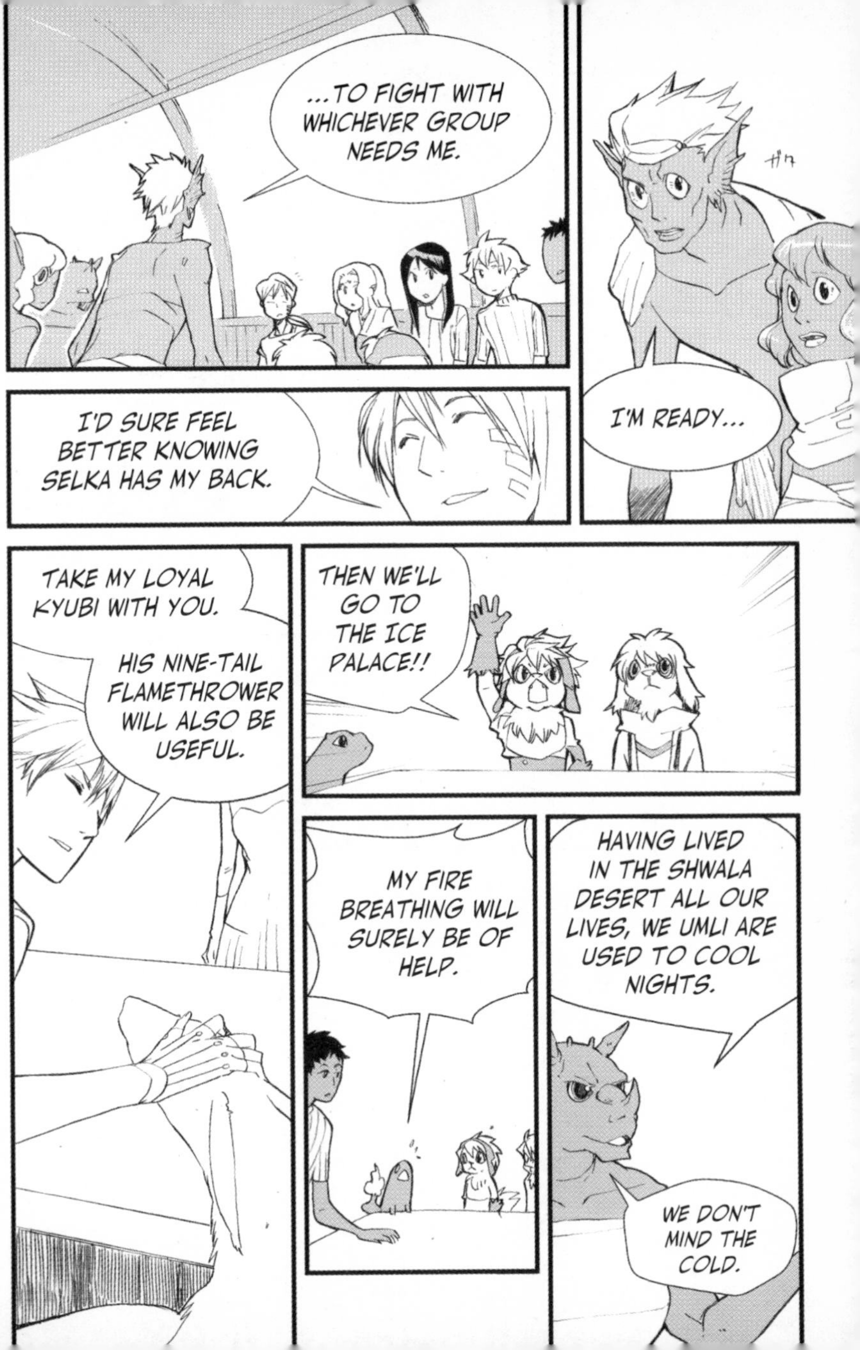
ザッ
I'M READY...
...TO FIGHT WITH WHICHEVER GROUP NEEDS ME.
I'D SURE FEEL BETTER KNOWING SELKA HAS MY BACK.
THEN WE'LL GO TO THE ICE PALACE!!
HAVING LIVED IN THE SHWALA DESERT ALL OUR LIVES, WE UMLI ARE USED TO COOL NIGHTS.
WE DON'T MIND THE COLD.
MY FIRE BREATHING WILL SURELY BE OF HELP.
TAKE MY LOYAL KYUBI WITH YOU.
HIS NINE-TAIL FLAMETHROWER WILL ALSO BE USEFUL.

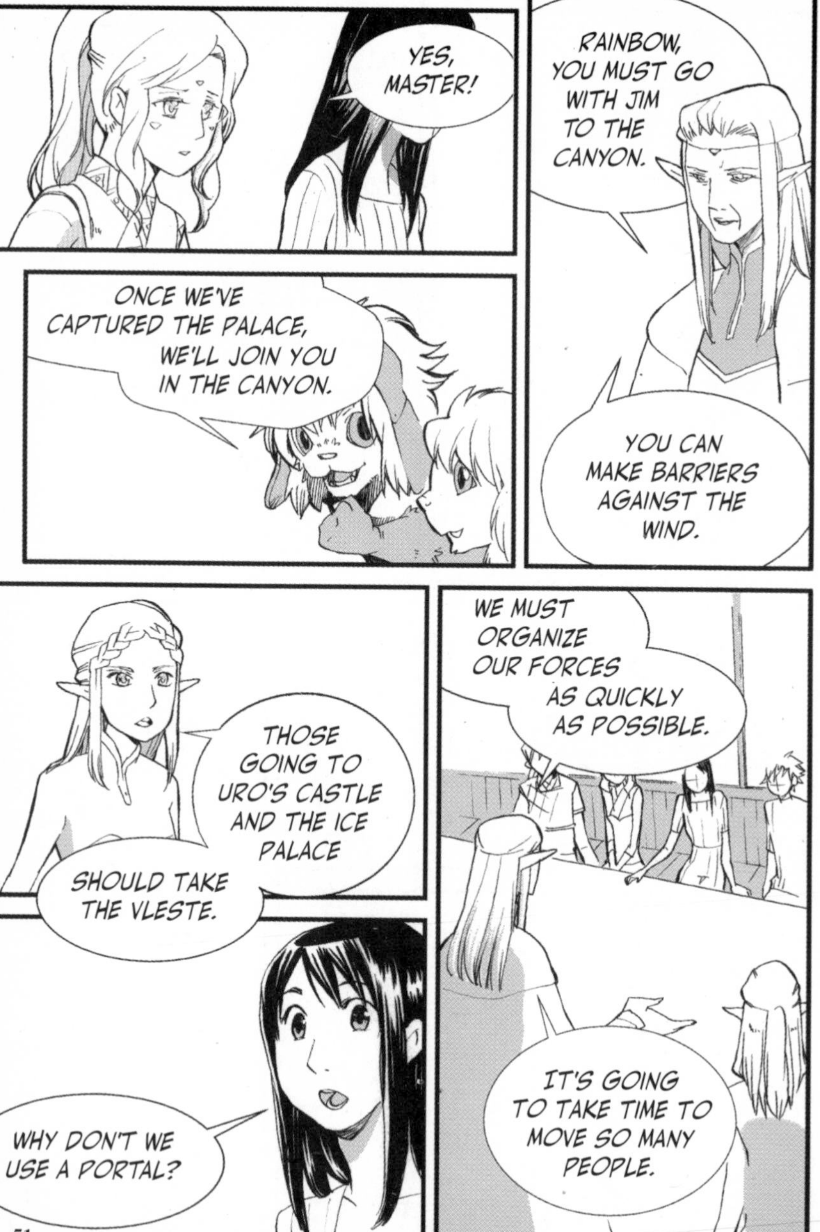
RAINBOW, YOU MUST GO WITH JIM TO THE CANYON.
YOU CAN MAKE BARRIERS AGAINST THE WIND.
YES, MASTER!
ONCE WE'VE CAPTURED THE PALACE, WE'LL JOIN YOU IN THE CANYON.
WE MUST ORGANIZE OUR FORCES AS QUICKLY AS POSSIBLE.
IT'S GOING TO TAKE TIME TO MOVE SO MANY PEOPLE.
THOSE GOING TO URO'S CASTLE AND THE ICE PALACE
SHOULD TAKE THE VLESTE.
WHY DON'T WE USE A PORTAL?

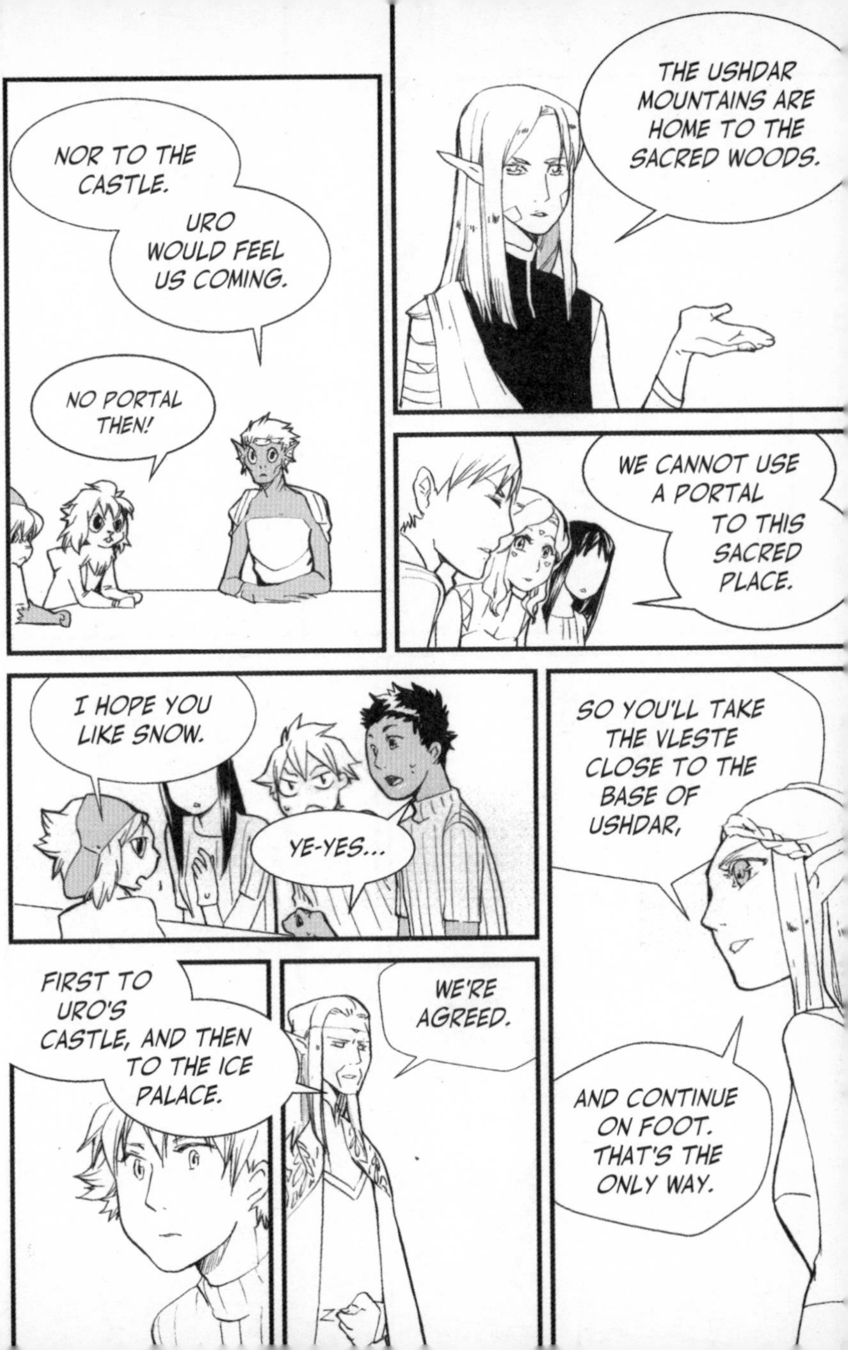
THE USHDAR MOUNTAINS ARE HOME TO THE SACRED WOODS.
WE CANNOT USE A PORTAL TO THIS SACRED PLACE.
NOR TO THE CASTLE.
URO WOULD FEEL US COMING.
NO PORTAL THEN!
SO YOU'LL TAKE THE VLESTE CLOSE TO THE BASE OF USHDAR,
AND CONTINUE ON FOOT. THAT'S THE ONLY WAY.
I HOPE YOU LIKE SNOW.
YE-YES...
WE'RE AGREED.
FIRST TO URO'S CASTLE, AND THEN TO THE ICE PALACE.

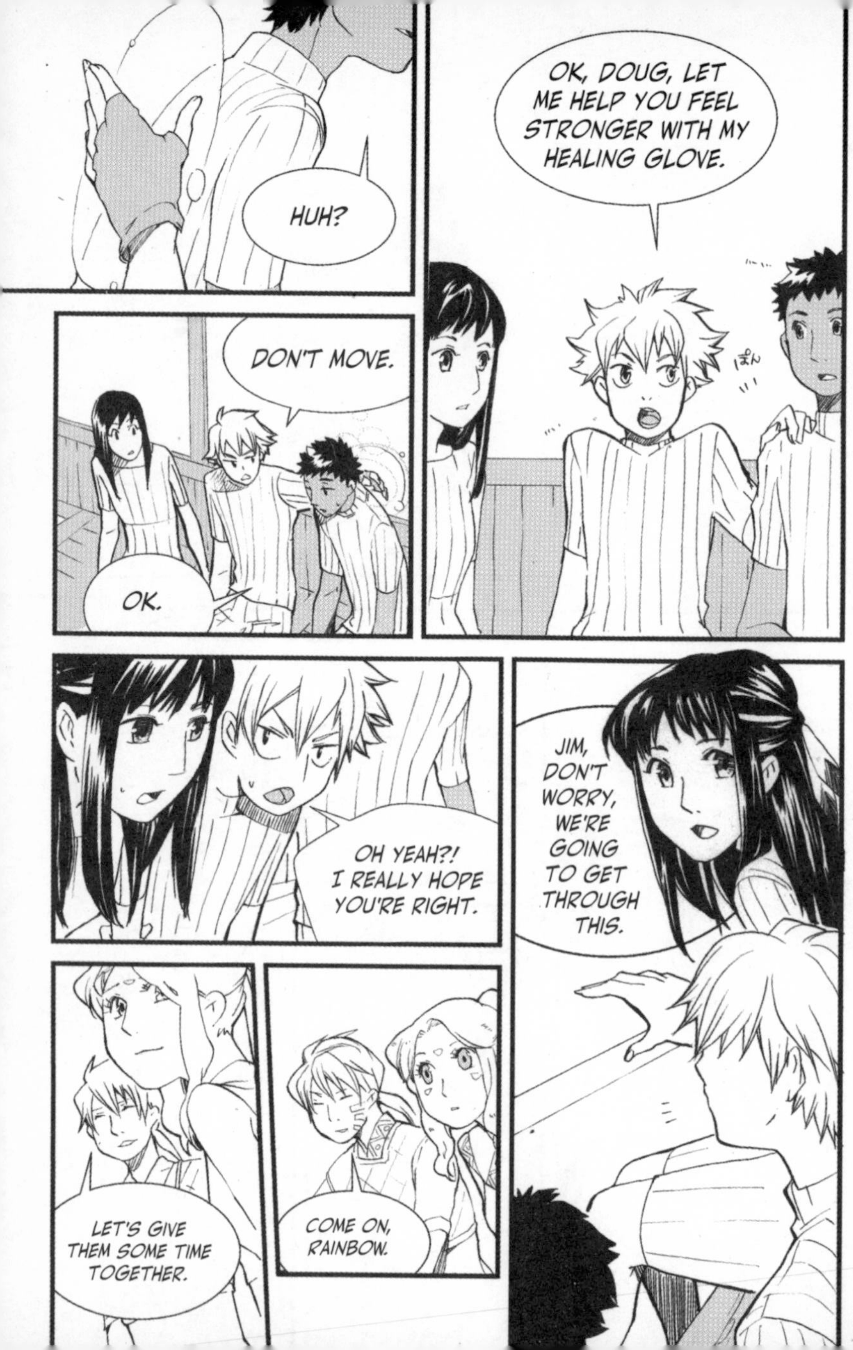
OK, DOUG, LET ME HELP YOU FEEL STRONGER WITH MY HEALING GLOVE.
ぱん
HUH?
DON'T MOVE.
OK.
JIM, DON'T WORRY, WE'RE GOING TO GET THROUGH THIS.
OH YEAH?! I REALLY HOPE YOU'RE RIGHT.
COME ON, RAINBOW.
LET'S GIVE THEM SOME TIME TOGETHER.

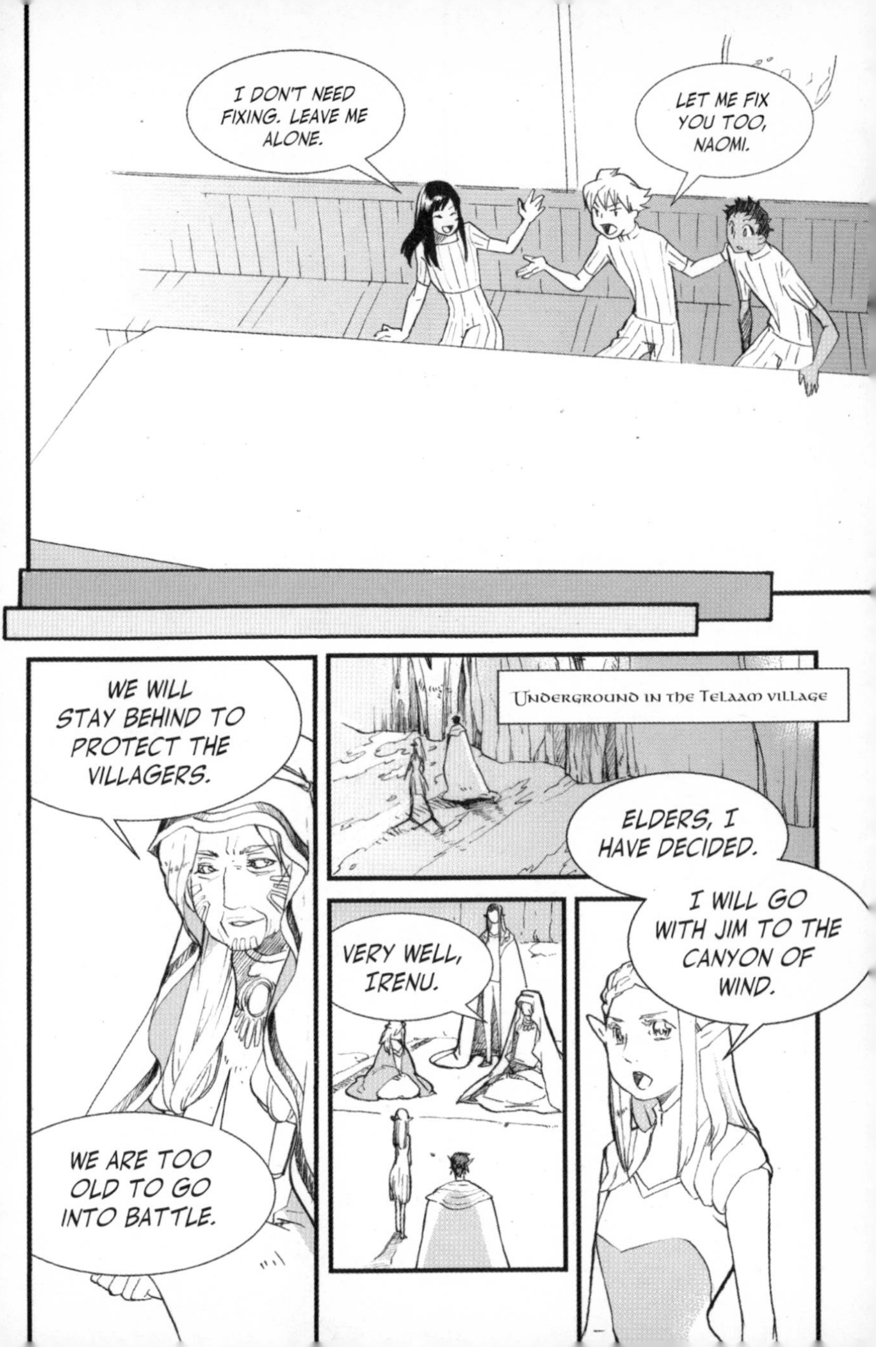
LET ME FIX YOU TOO, NAOMI.
I DON'T NEED FIXING. LEAVE ME ALONE.
Underground in the Telaam village
ELDERS, I HAVE DECIDED.
I WILL GO WITH JIM TO THE CANYON OF WIND.
VERY WELL, IRENU.
WE WILL STAY BEHIND TO PROTECT THE VILLAGERS.
WE ARE TOO OLD TO GO INTO BATTLE.

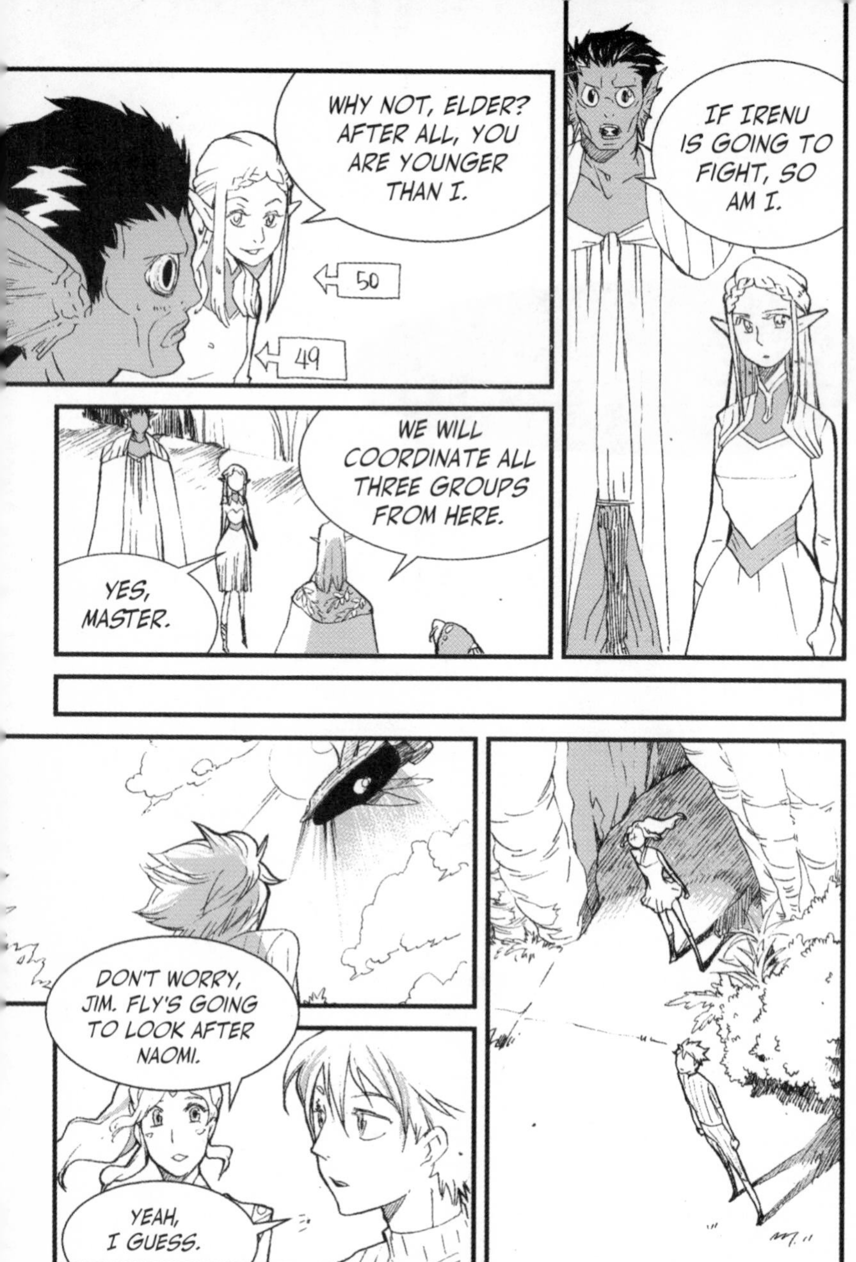
IF IRENU IS GOING TO FIGHT, SO AM I.
WHY NOT, ELDER? AFTER ALL, YOU ARE YOUNGER THAN I.
50
49
WE WILL COORDINATE ALL THREE GROUPS FROM HERE.
YES, MASTER.
DON'T WORRY, JIM. FLY'S GOING TO LOOK AFTER NAOMI.
YEAH, I GUESS.

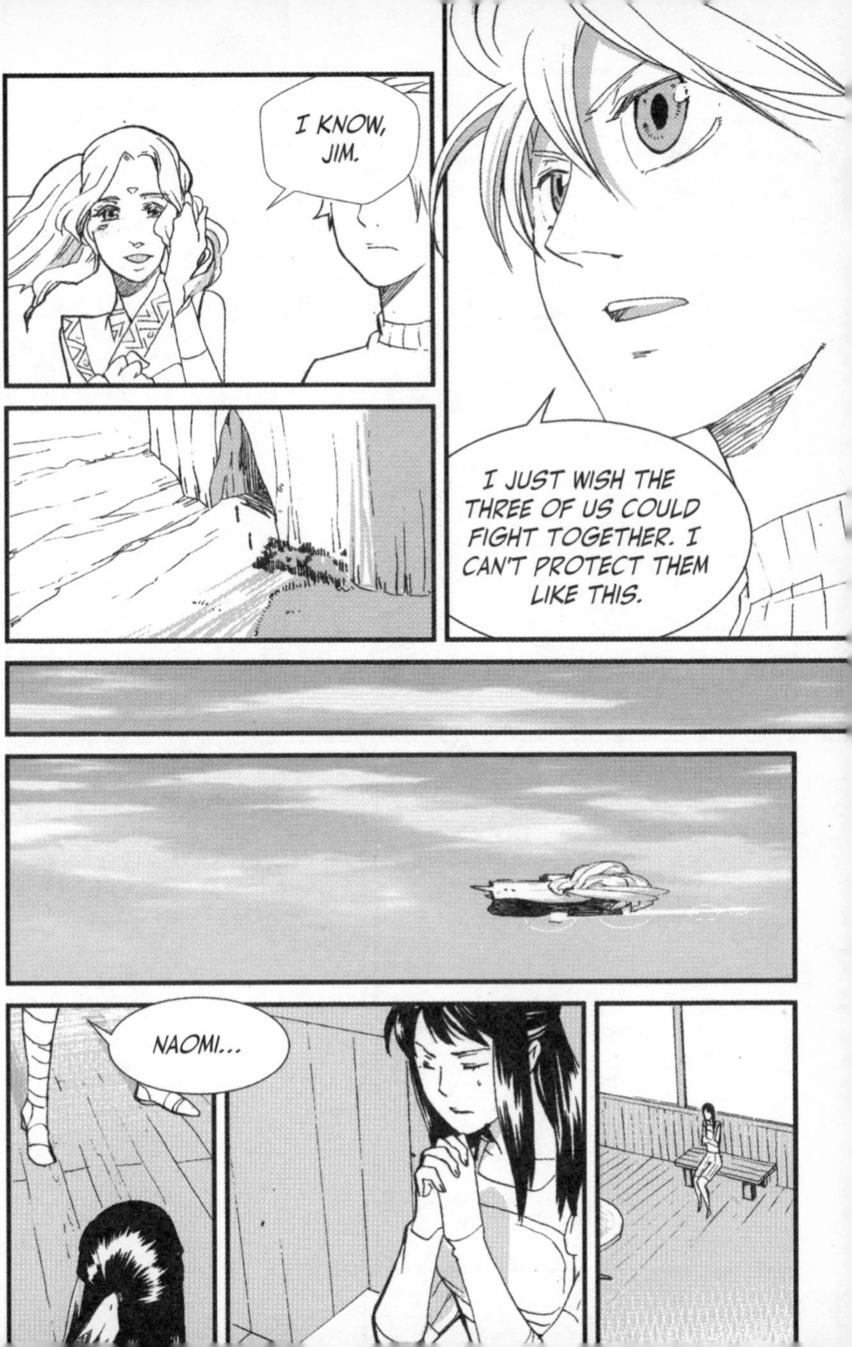
I JUST WISH THE THREE OF US COULD FIGHT TOGETHER. I CAN'T PROTECT THEM LIKE THIS.
I KNOW, JIM.
NAOMI...

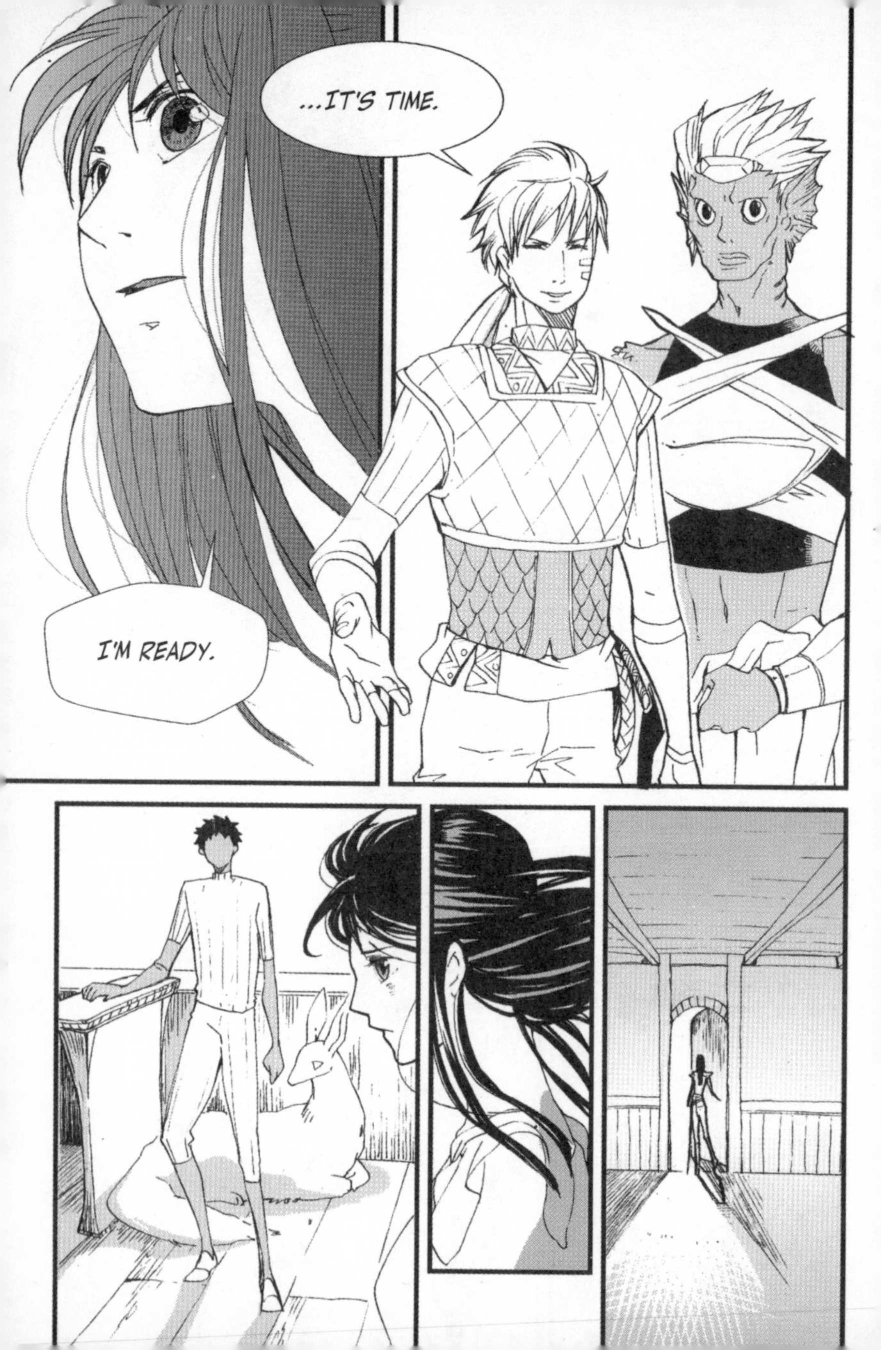
...IT'S TIME.
I'M READY.

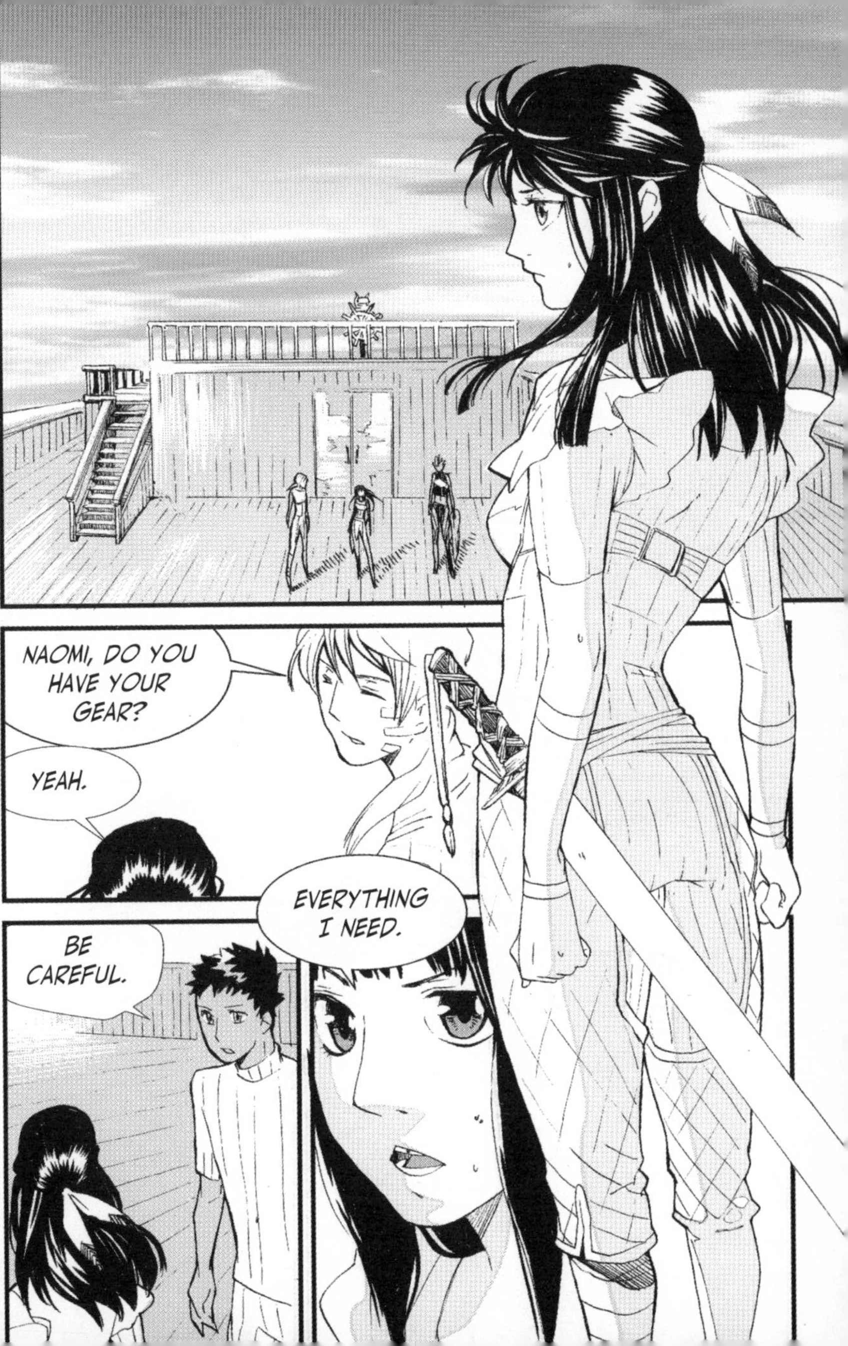
NAOMI, DO YOU HAVE YOUR GEAR?
YEAH.
EVERYTHING I NEED.
BE CAREFUL.

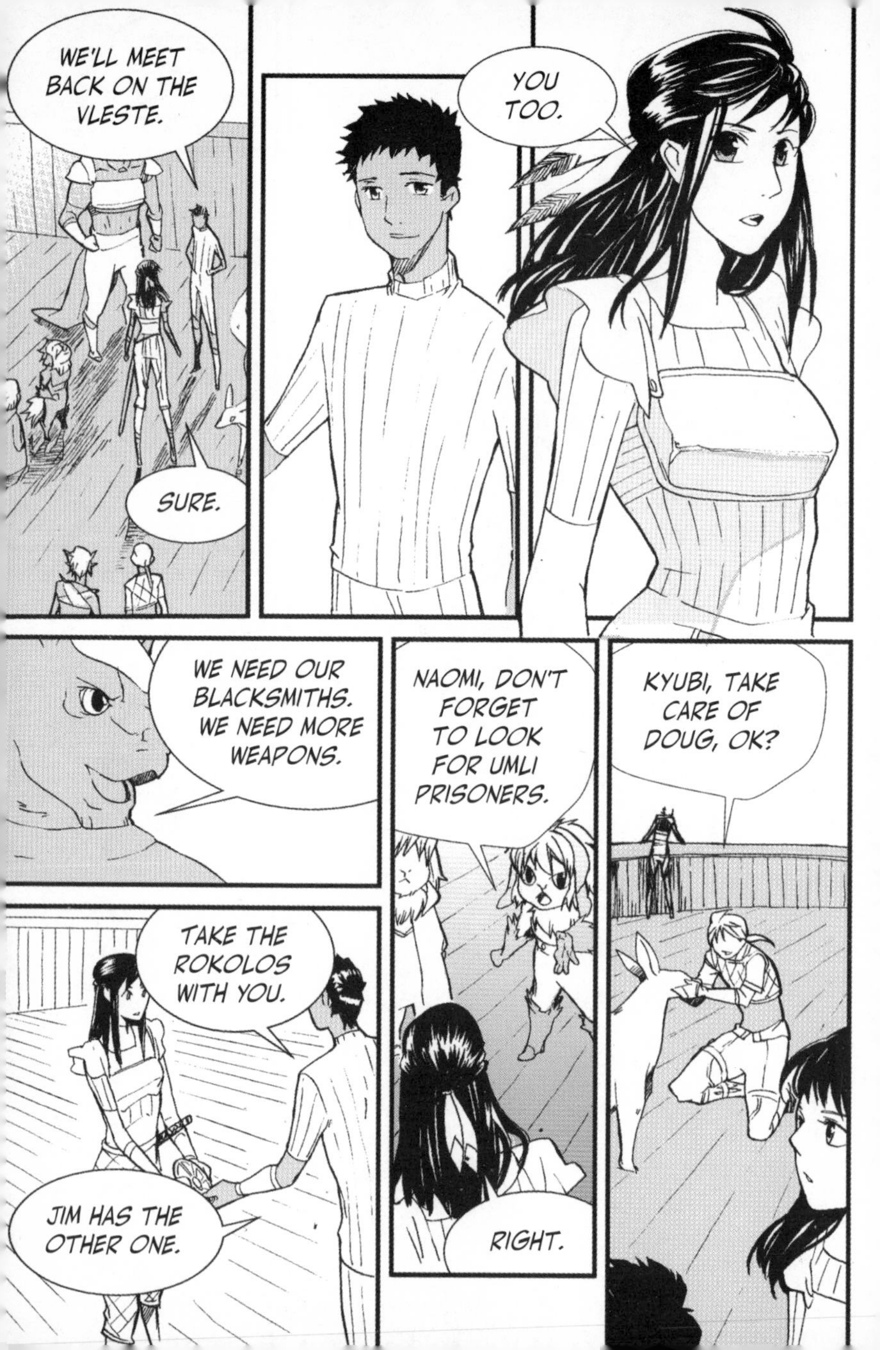
YOU TOO.
WE'LL MEET BACK ON THE VLESTE.
SURE.
KYUBI, TAKE CARE OF DOUG, OK?
NAOMI, DON'T FORGET TO LOOK FOR UMLI PRISONERS.
RIGHT.
WE NEED OUR BLACKSMITHS. WE NEED MORE WEAPONS.
TAKE THE ROKOLOS WITH YOU.
JIM HAS THE OTHER ONE.

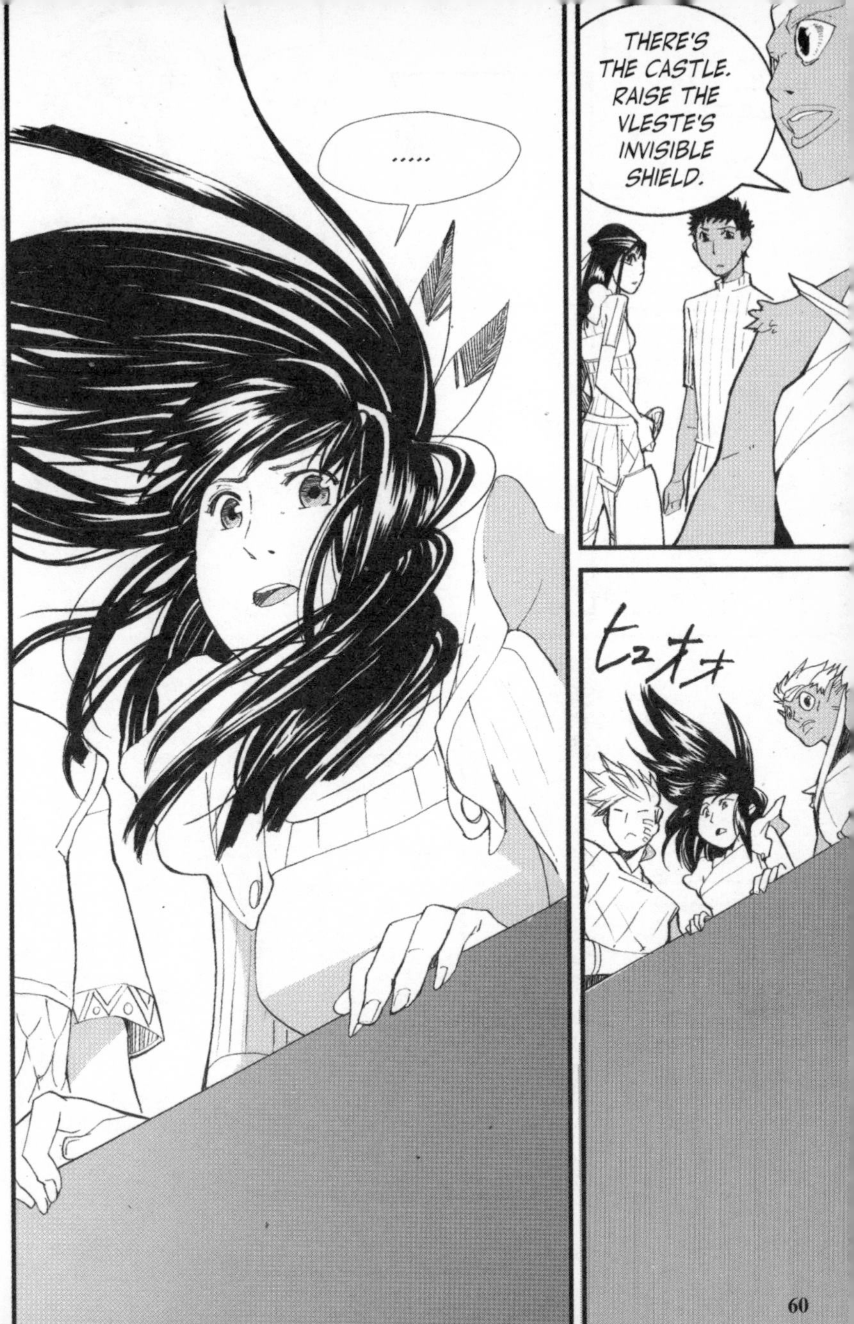
THERE'S THE CASTLE. RAISE THE VLESTE'S INVISIBLE SHIELD.
ヒュオオ
......

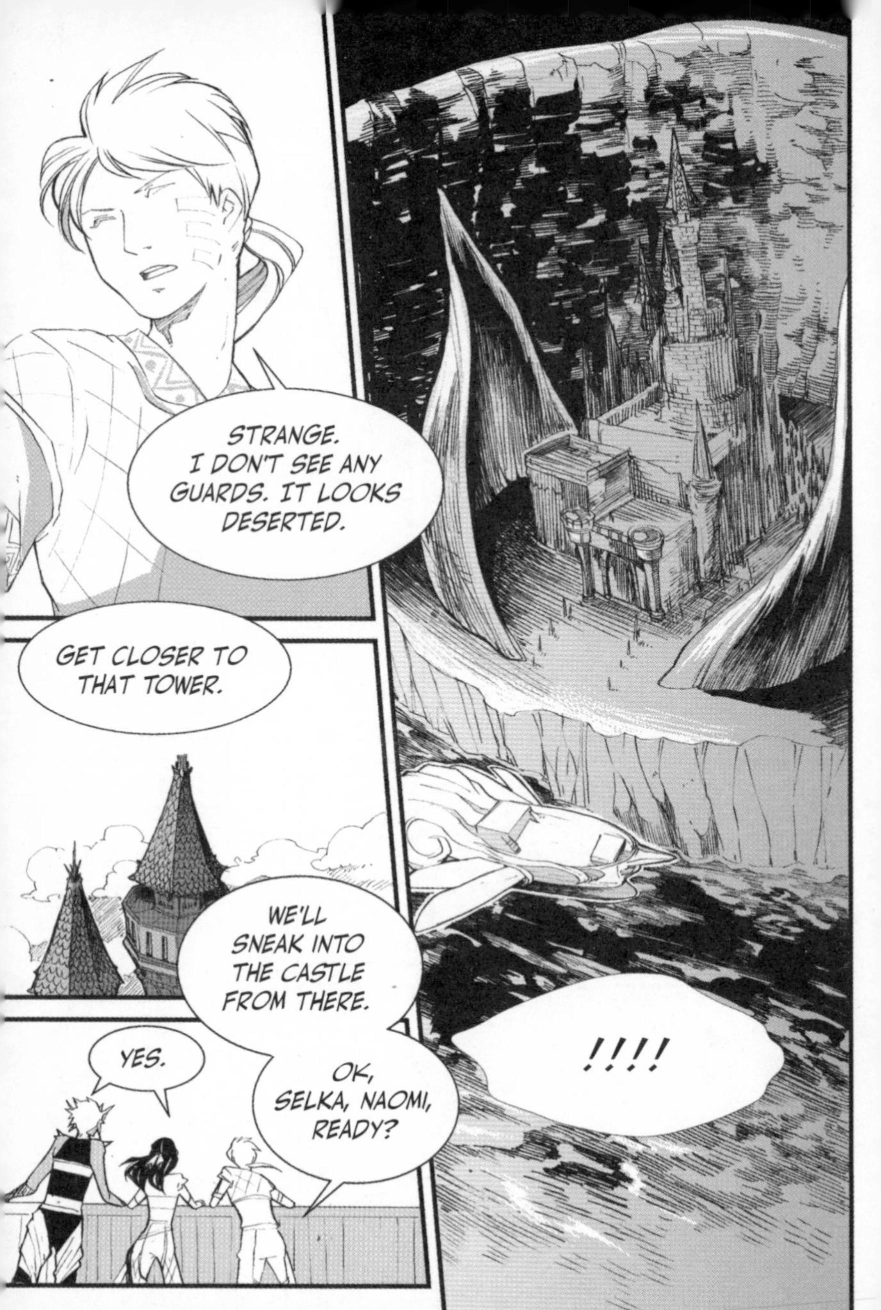
!!!!
STRANGE. I DON'T SEE ANY GUARDS. IT LOOKS DESERTED.
GET CLOSER TO THAT TOWER.
WE'LL SNEAK INTO THE CASTLE FROM THERE.
OK, SELKA, NAOMI, READY?
YES.

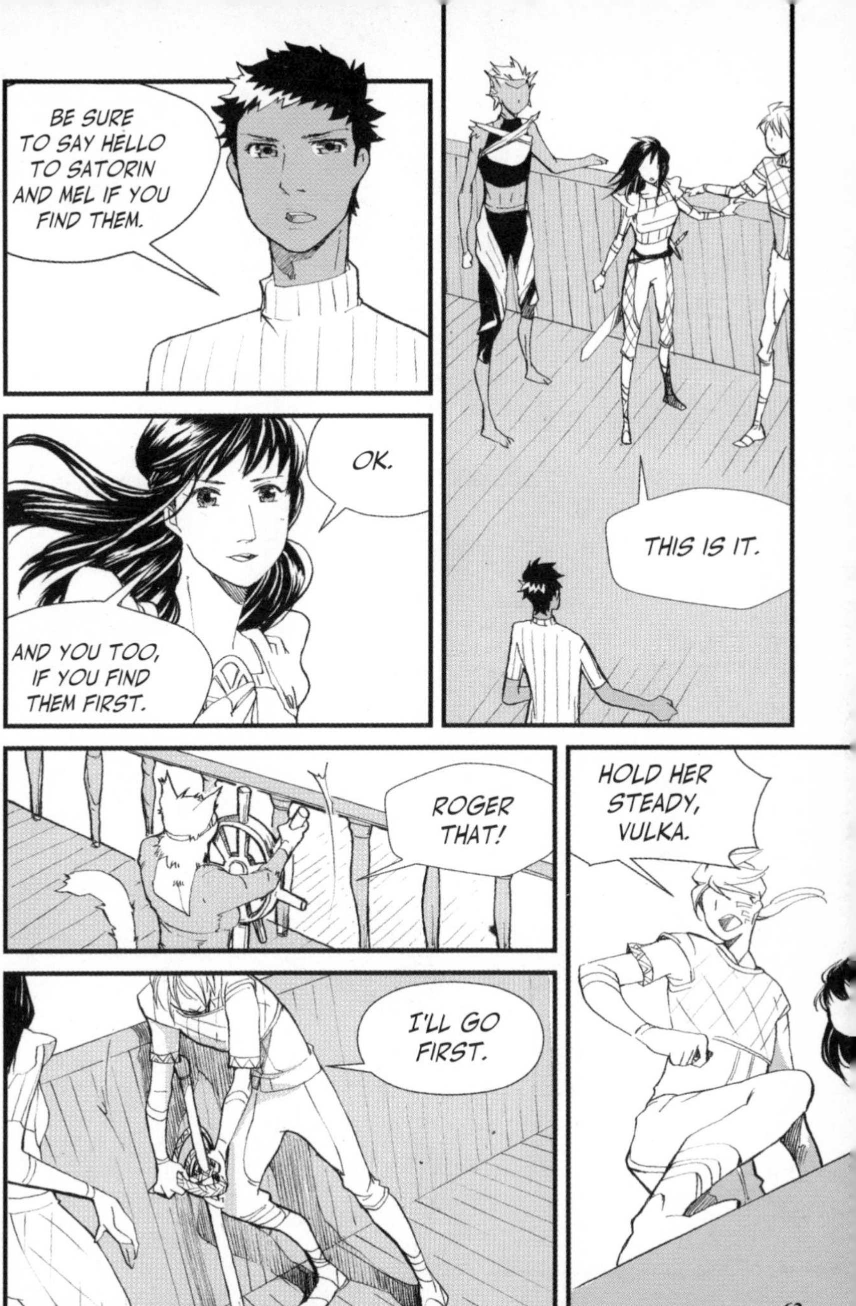
THIS IS IT.
BE SURE TO SAY HELLO TO SATORIN AND MEL IF YOU FIND THEM.
OK.
AND YOU TOO, IF YOU FIND THEM FIRST.
HOLD HER STEADY, VULKA.
ROGER THAT!
I'LL GO FIRST.

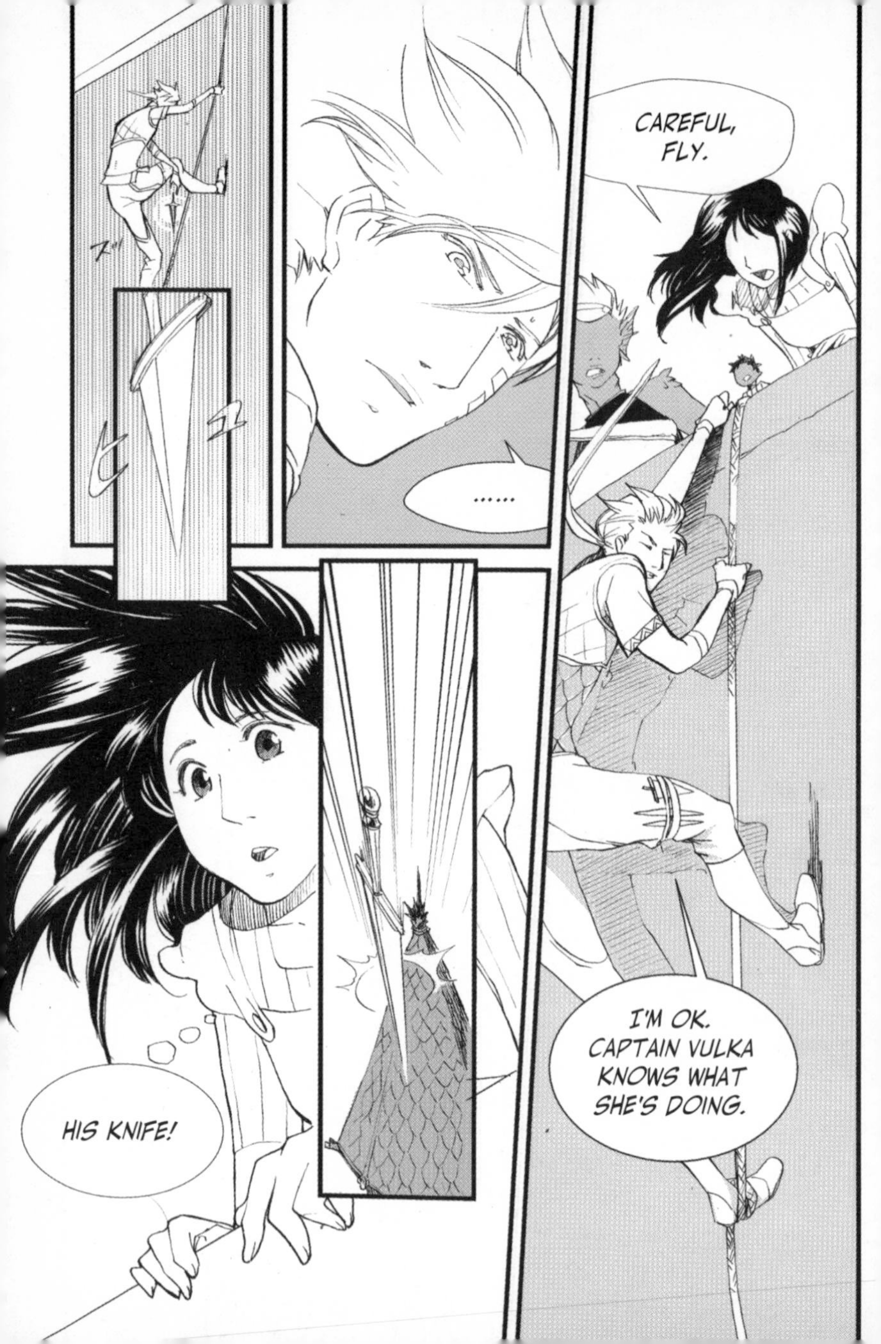
CAREFUL, FLY.
I'M OK. CAPTAIN VULKA KNOWS WHAT SHE'S DOING.
……
HIS KNIFE!

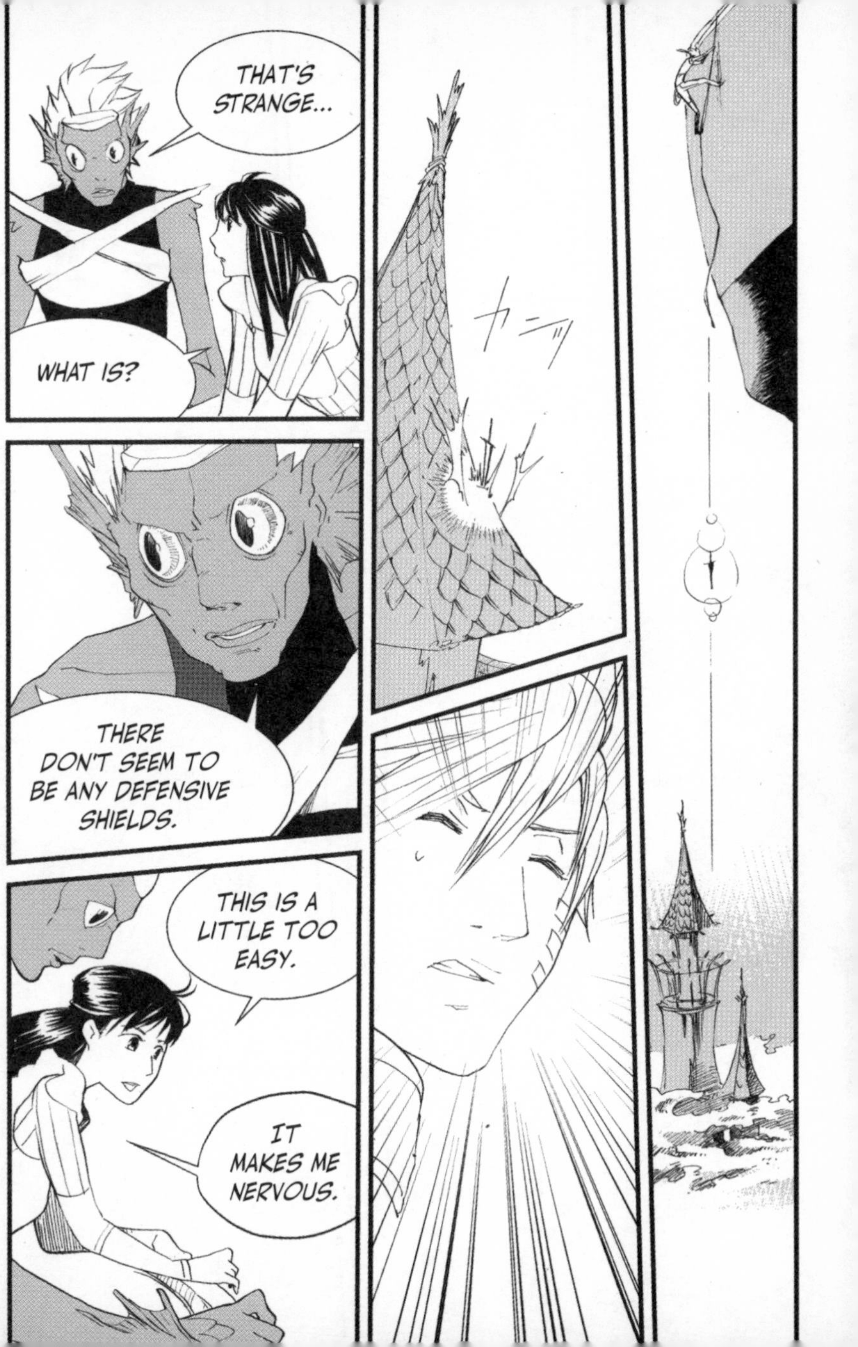
カニッ
THAT'S STRANGE...
WHAT IS?
THERE DON'T SEEM TO BE ANY DEFENSIVE SHIELDS.
THIS IS A LITTLE TOO EASY.
IT MAKES ME NERVOUS.

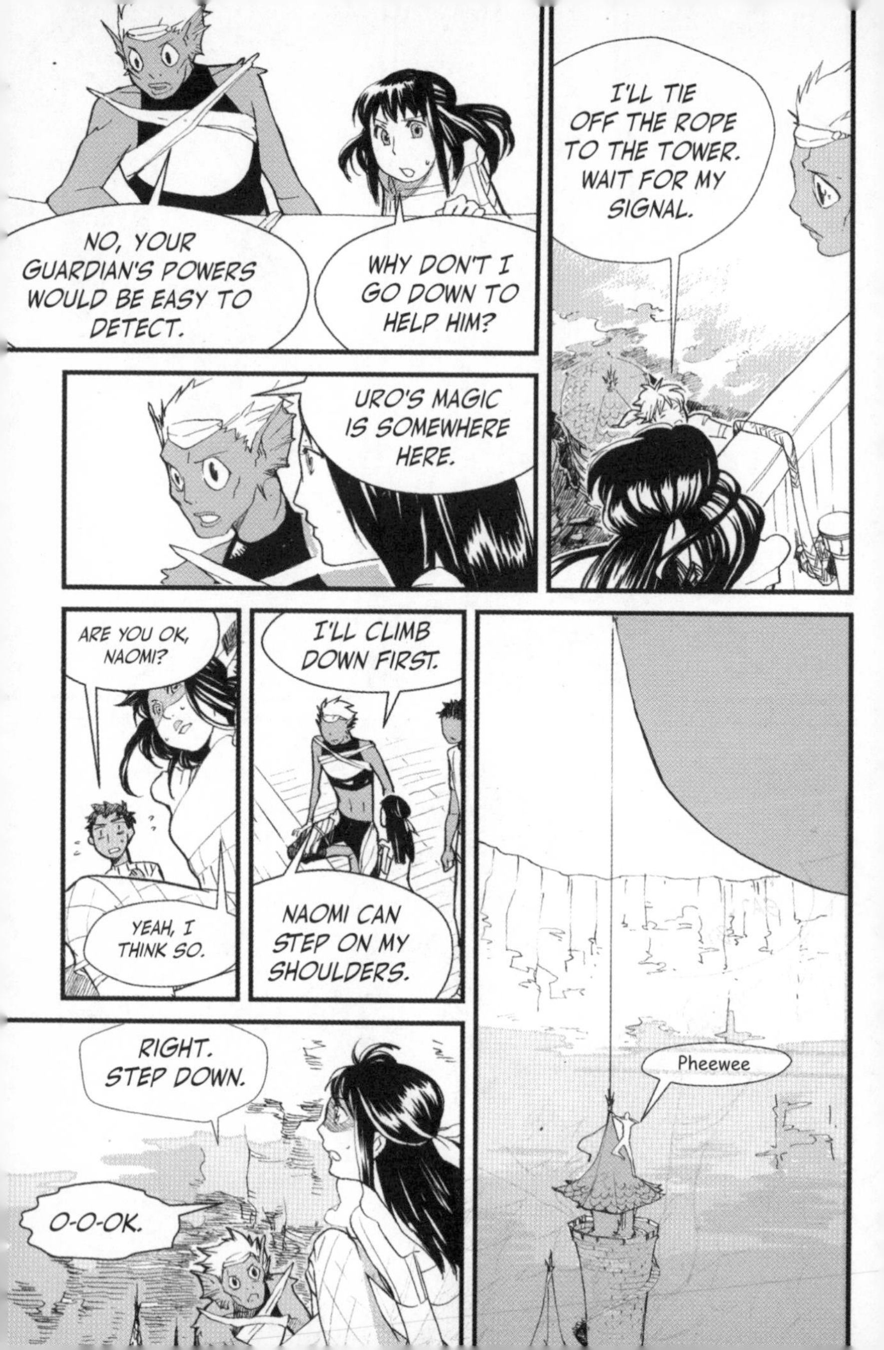
I'LL TIE OFF THE ROPE TO THE TOWER. WAIT FOR MY SIGNAL.
WHY DON'T I GO DOWN TO HELP HIM?
NO, YOUR GUARDIAN'S POWERS WOULD BE EASY TO DETECT.
URO'S MAGIC IS SOMEWHERE HERE.
Pheewee
I'LL CLIMB DOWN FIRST.
NAOMI CAN STEP ON MY SHOULDERS.
ARE YOU OK, NAOMI?
YEAH, I THINK SO.
RIGHT. STEP DOWN.
O-O-OK.

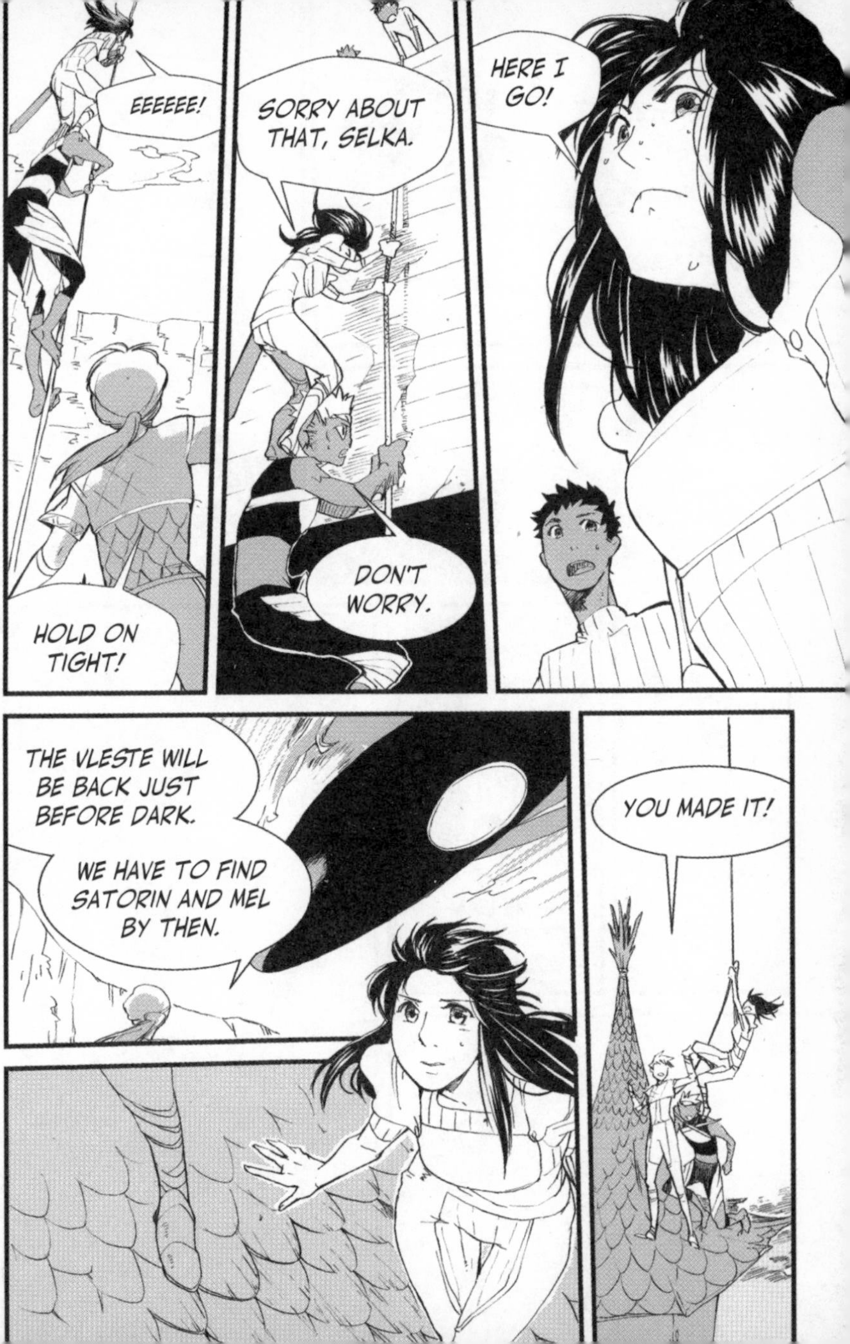
HERE I GO!
SORRY ABOUT THAT, SELKA.
DON'T WORRY.
EEEEEE!
HOLD ON TIGHT!
YOU MADE IT!
THE VLESTE WILL BE BACK JUST BEFORE DARK.
WE HAVE TO FIND SATORIN AND MEL BY THEN.

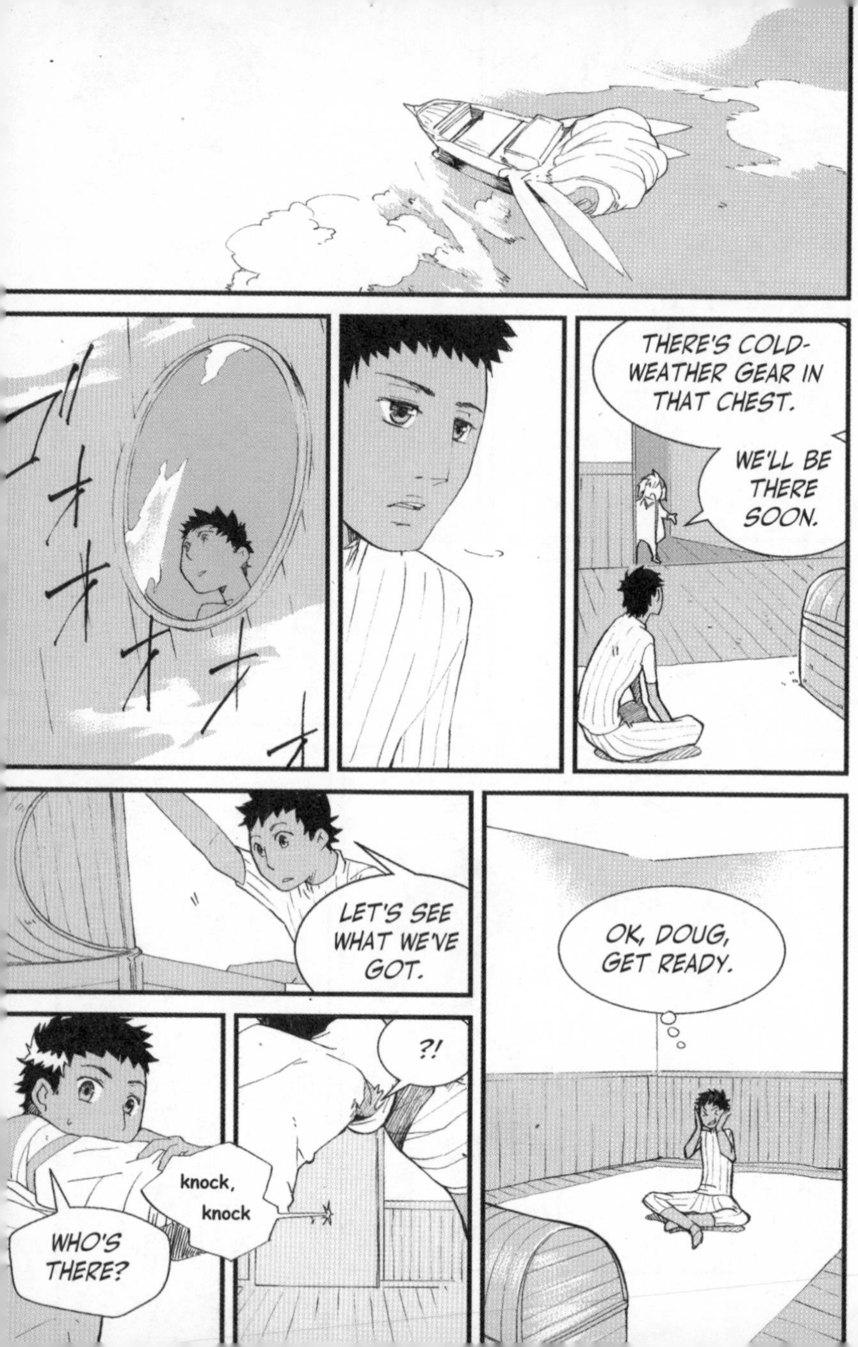
THERE'S COLD-WEATHER GEAR IN THAT CHEST.
WE'LL BE THERE SOON.
ゴオオオオオ
OK, DOUG, GET READY.
LET'S SEE WHAT WE'VE GOT.
?!
knock, knock
WHO'S THERE?

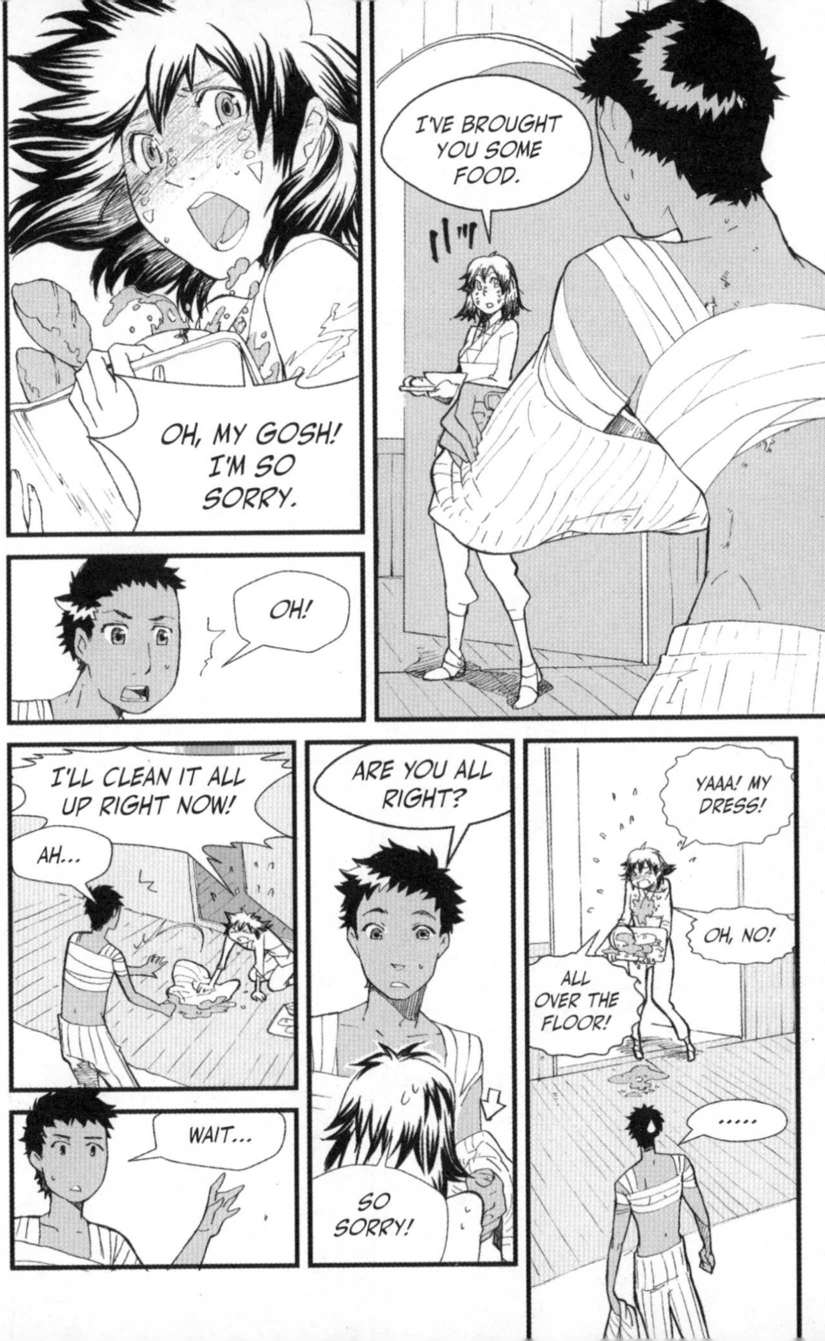
I'VE BROUGHT YOU SOME FOOD.
OH, MY GOSH! I'M SO SORRY.
OH!
YAAA! MY DRESS!
OH, NO!
ALL OVER THE FLOOR!
......
ARE YOU ALL RIGHT?
SO SORRY!
I'LL CLEAN IT ALL UP RIGHT NOW!
AH...
WAIT...

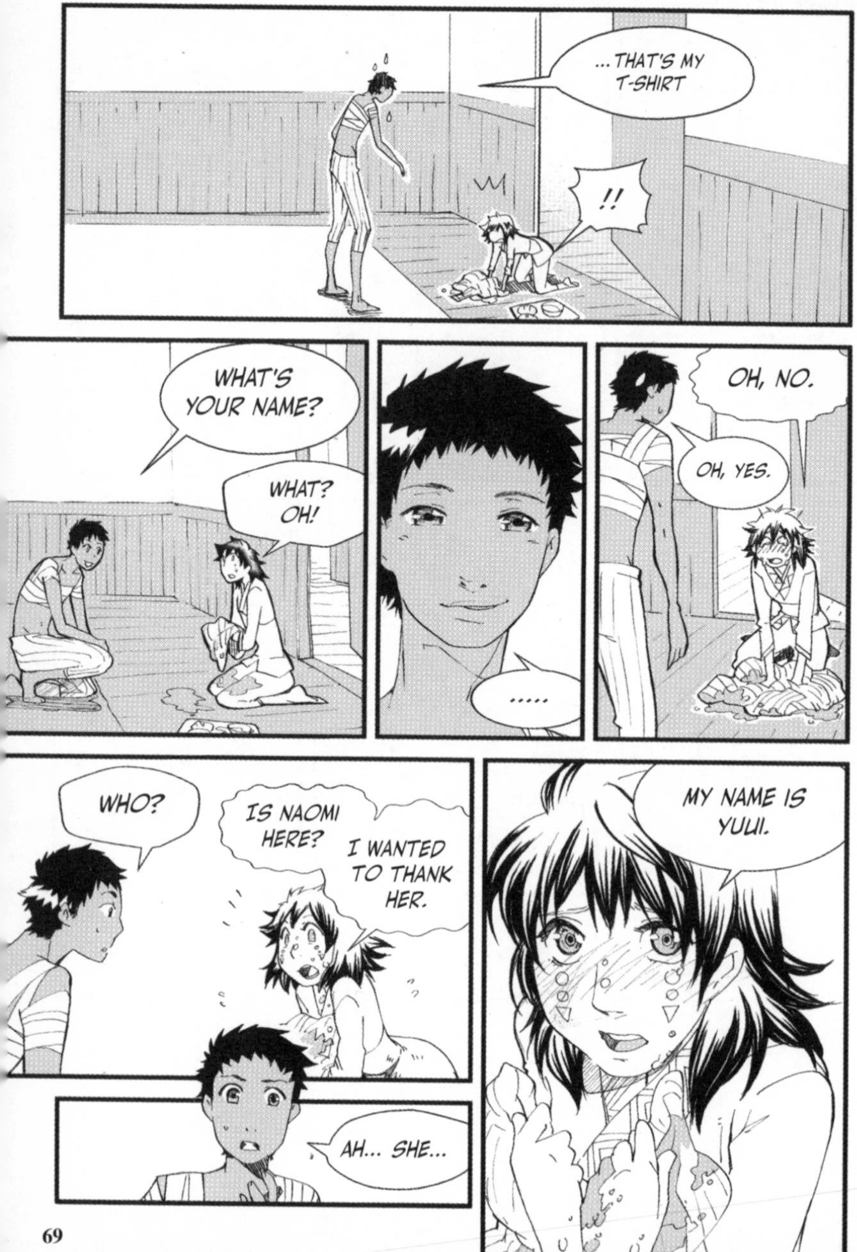
...THAT'S MY T-SHIRT
!!
OH, NO.
OH, YES.
.....
WHAT'S YOUR NAME?
WHAT? OH!
MY NAME IS YUUI.
IS NAOMI HERE?
I WANTED TO THANK HER.
WHO?
AH... SHE...

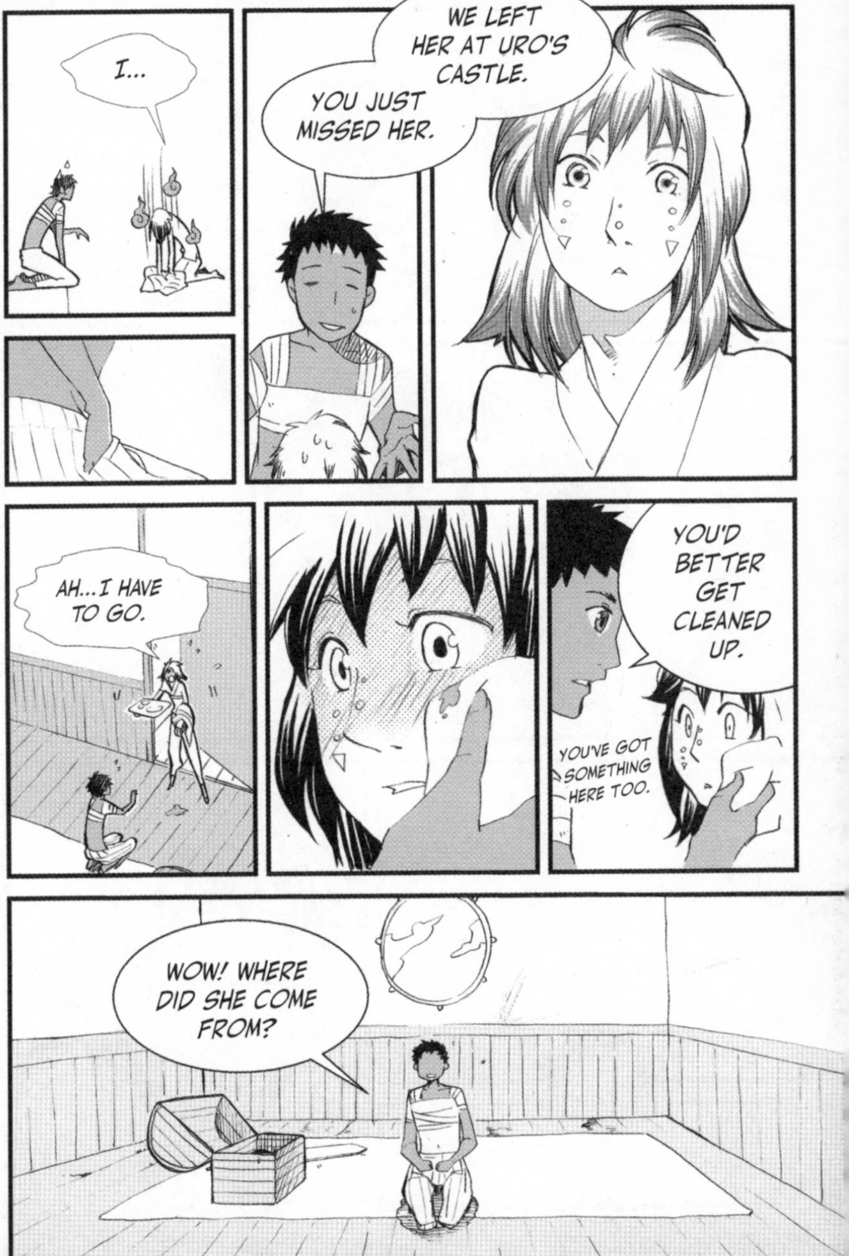
WE LEFT HER AT URO'S CASTLE.
YOU JUST MISSED HER.
I...
YOU'D BETTER GET CLEANED UP.
YOU'VE GOT SOMETHING HERE TOO.
AH...I HAVE TO GO.
WOW! WHERE DID SHE COME FROM?

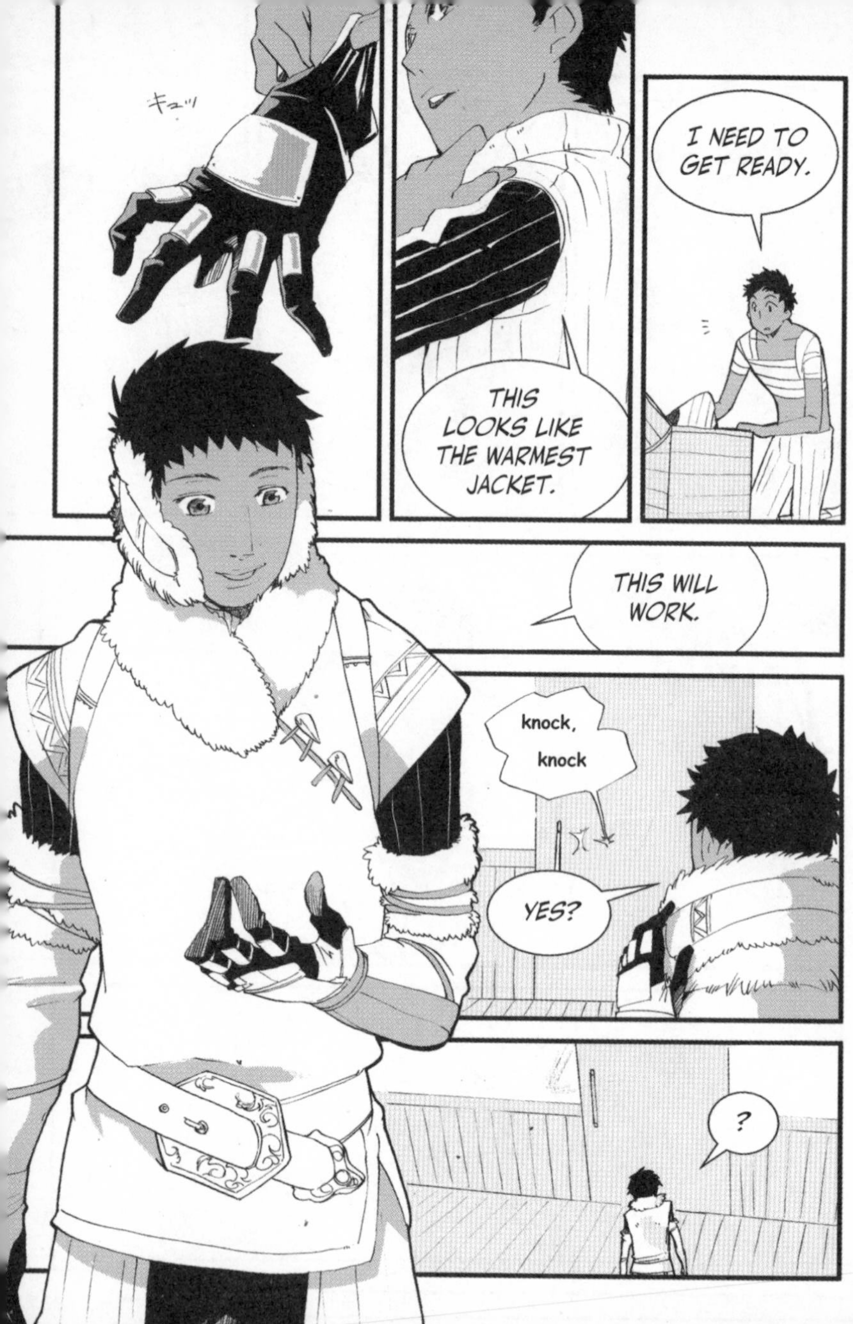

I NEED TO GET READY.
THIS LOOKS LIKE THE WARMEST JACKET.
キュッ
THIS WILL WORK.
knock, knock
YES?
?

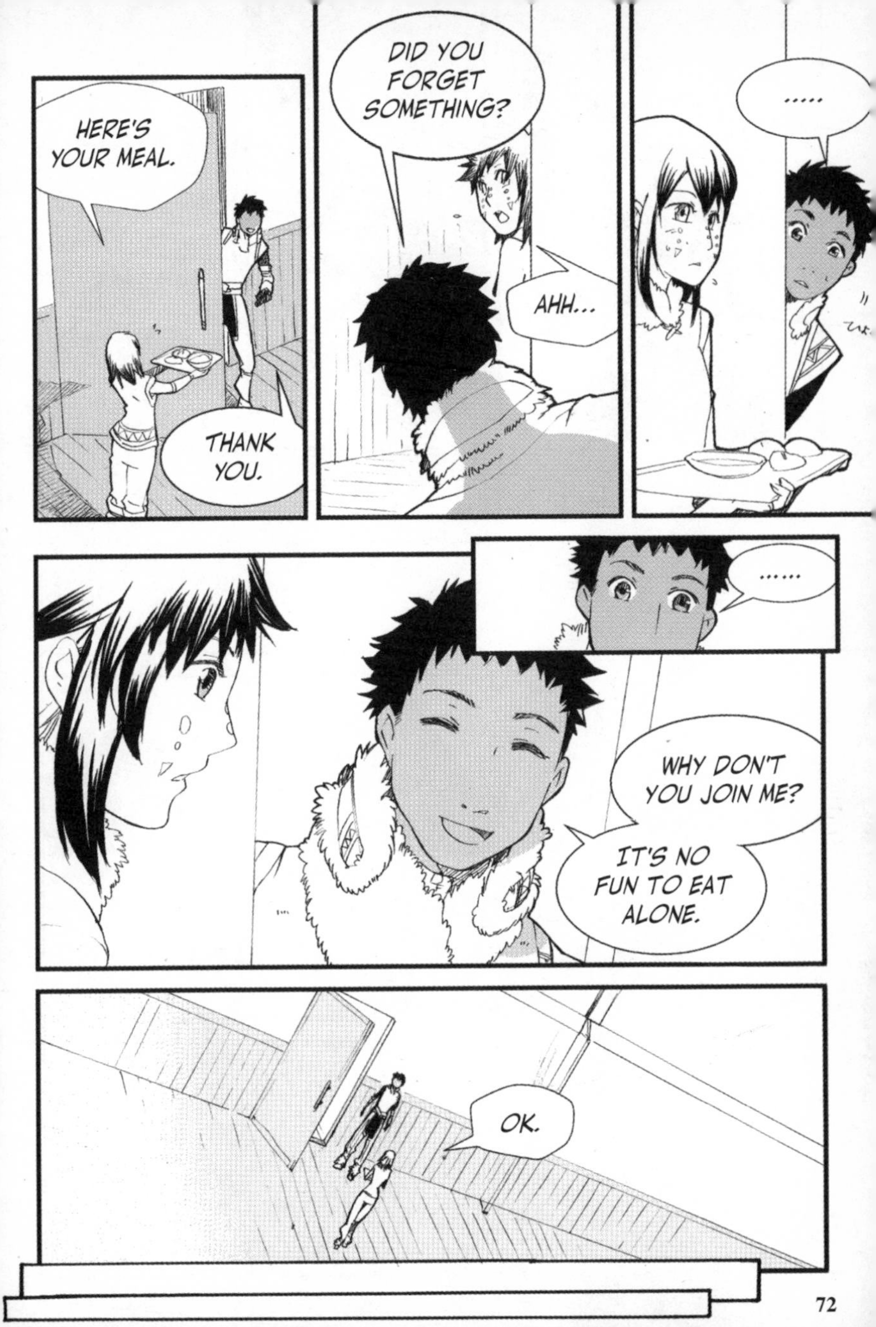
......
DID YOU FORGET SOMETHING?
AHH...
HERE'S YOUR MEAL.
THANK YOU.
......
WHY DON'T YOU JOIN ME?
IT'S NO FUN TO EAT ALONE.
OK.

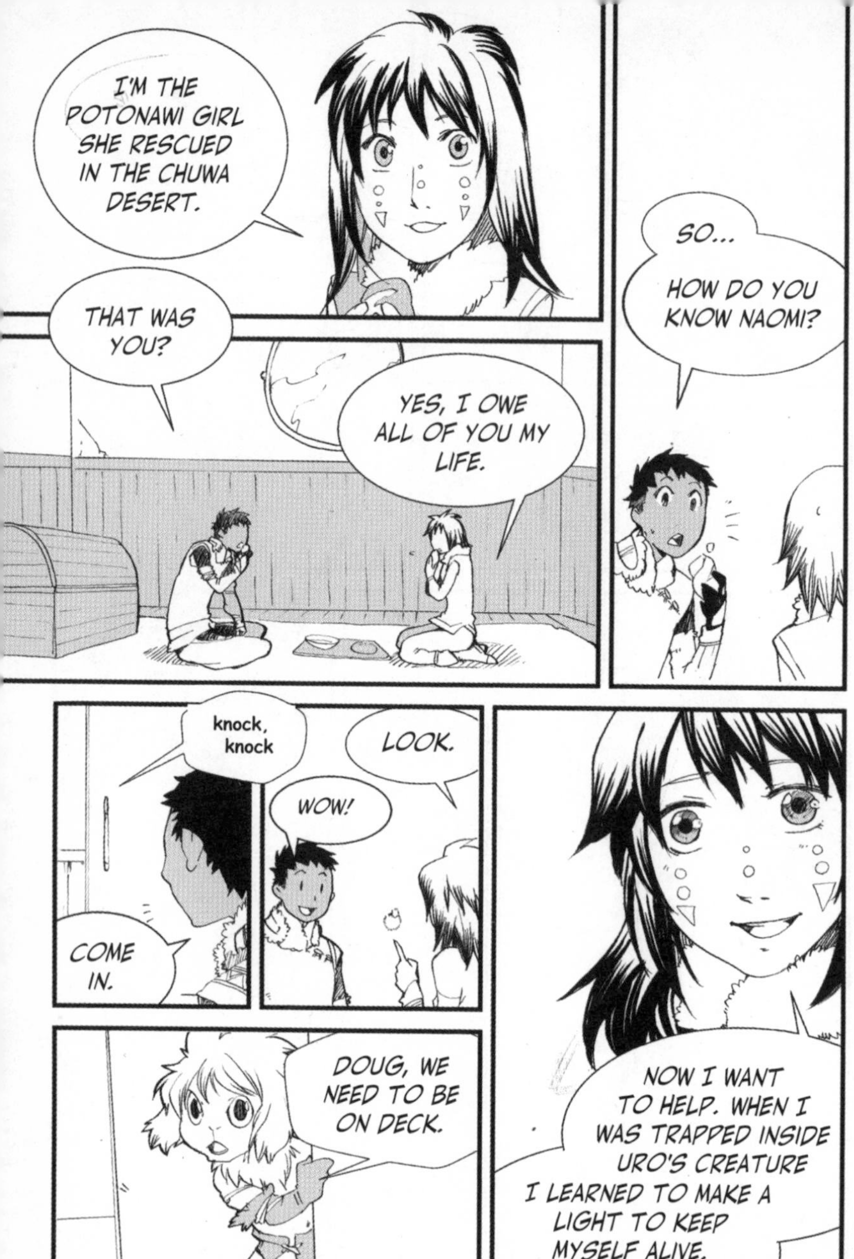
SO...
HOW DO YOU KNOW NAOMI?
I'M THE POTONAWI GIRL SHE RESCUED IN THE CHUWA DESERT.
THAT WAS YOU?
YES, I OWE ALL OF YOU MY LIFE.
NOW I WANT TO HELP. WHEN I WAS TRAPPED INSIDE URO'S CREATURE I LEARNED TO MAKE A LIGHT TO KEEP MYSELF ALIVE.
LOOK.
WOW!
knock, knock
COME IN.
DOUG, WE NEED TO BE ON DECK.

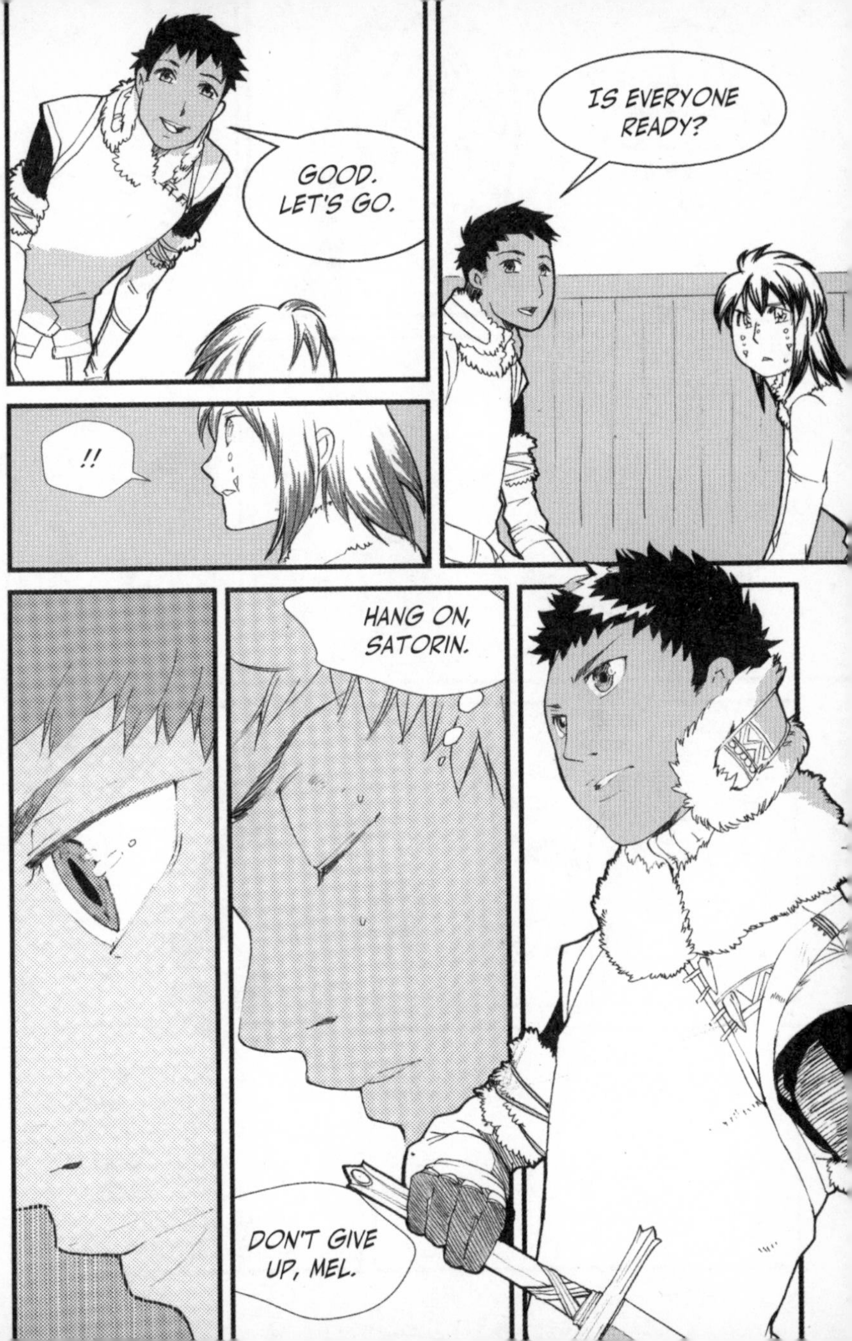
IS EVERYONE READY?
GOOD. LET'S GO.
!!
HANG ON, SATORIN.
DON'T GIVE UP, MEL.

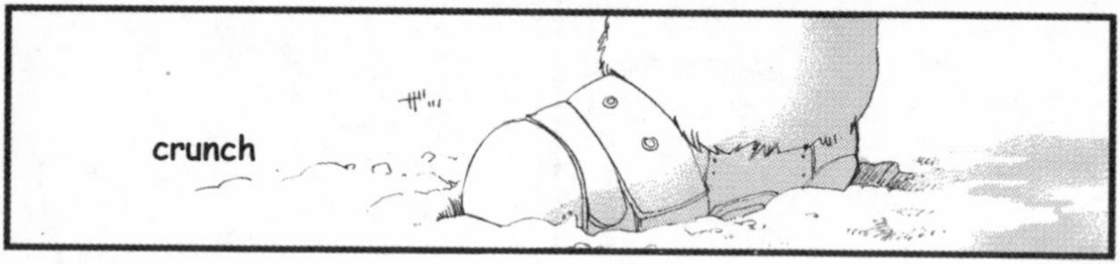
crunch

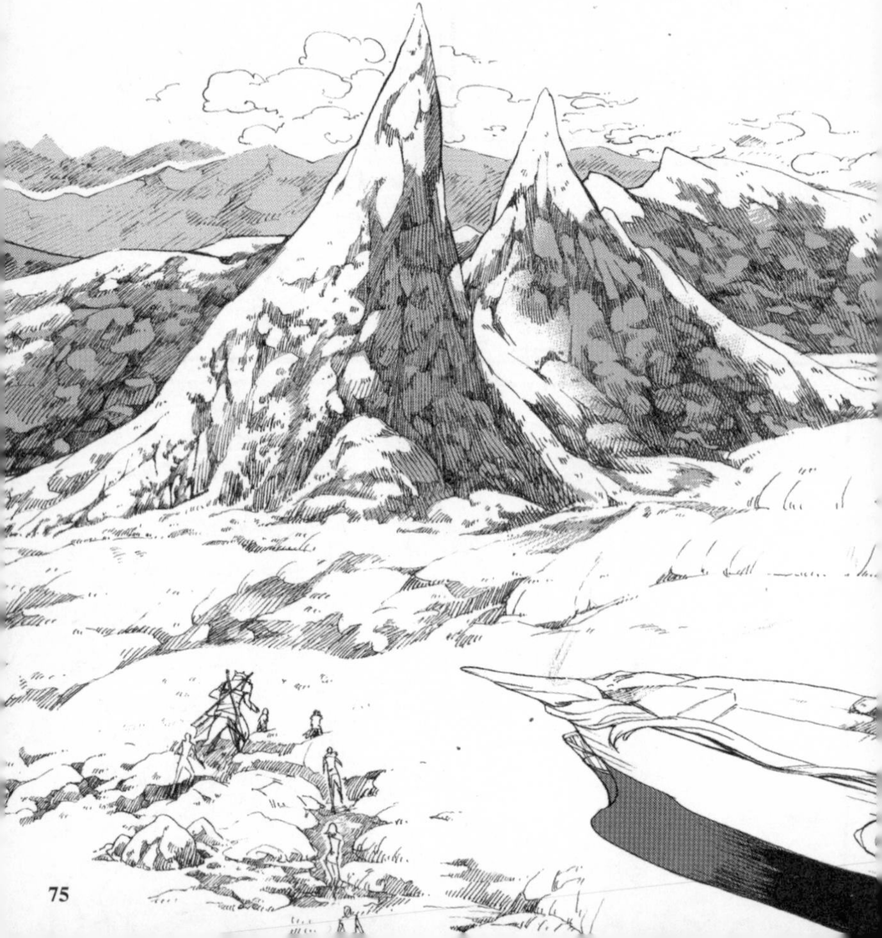

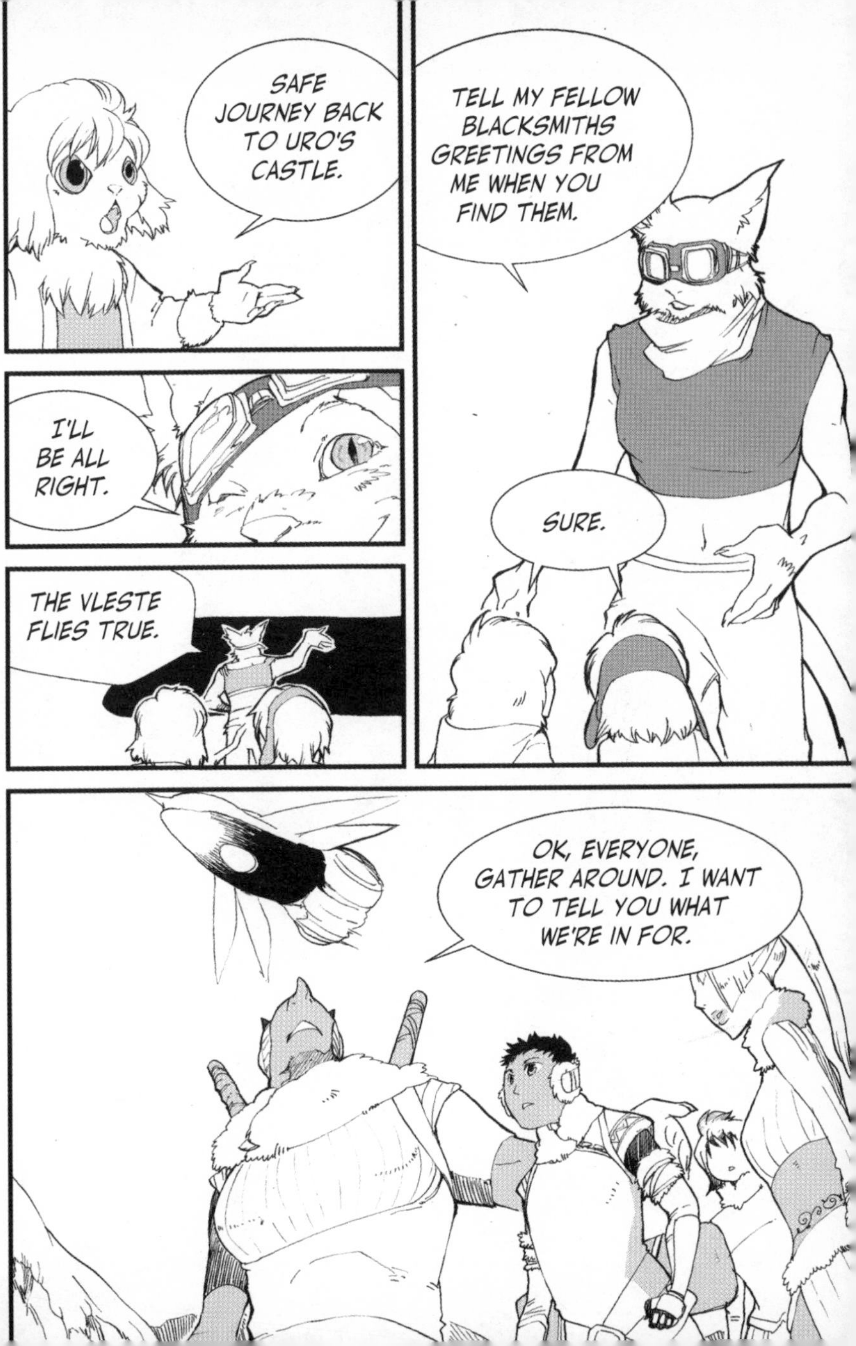
TELL MY FELLOW BLACKSMITHS GREETINGS FROM ME WHEN YOU FIND THEM.
SURE.
SAFE JOURNEY BACK TO URO'S CASTLE.
I'LL BE ALL RIGHT.
THE VLESTE FLIES TRUE.
OK, EVERYONE, GATHER AROUND. I WANT TO TELL YOU WHAT WE'RE IN FOR.

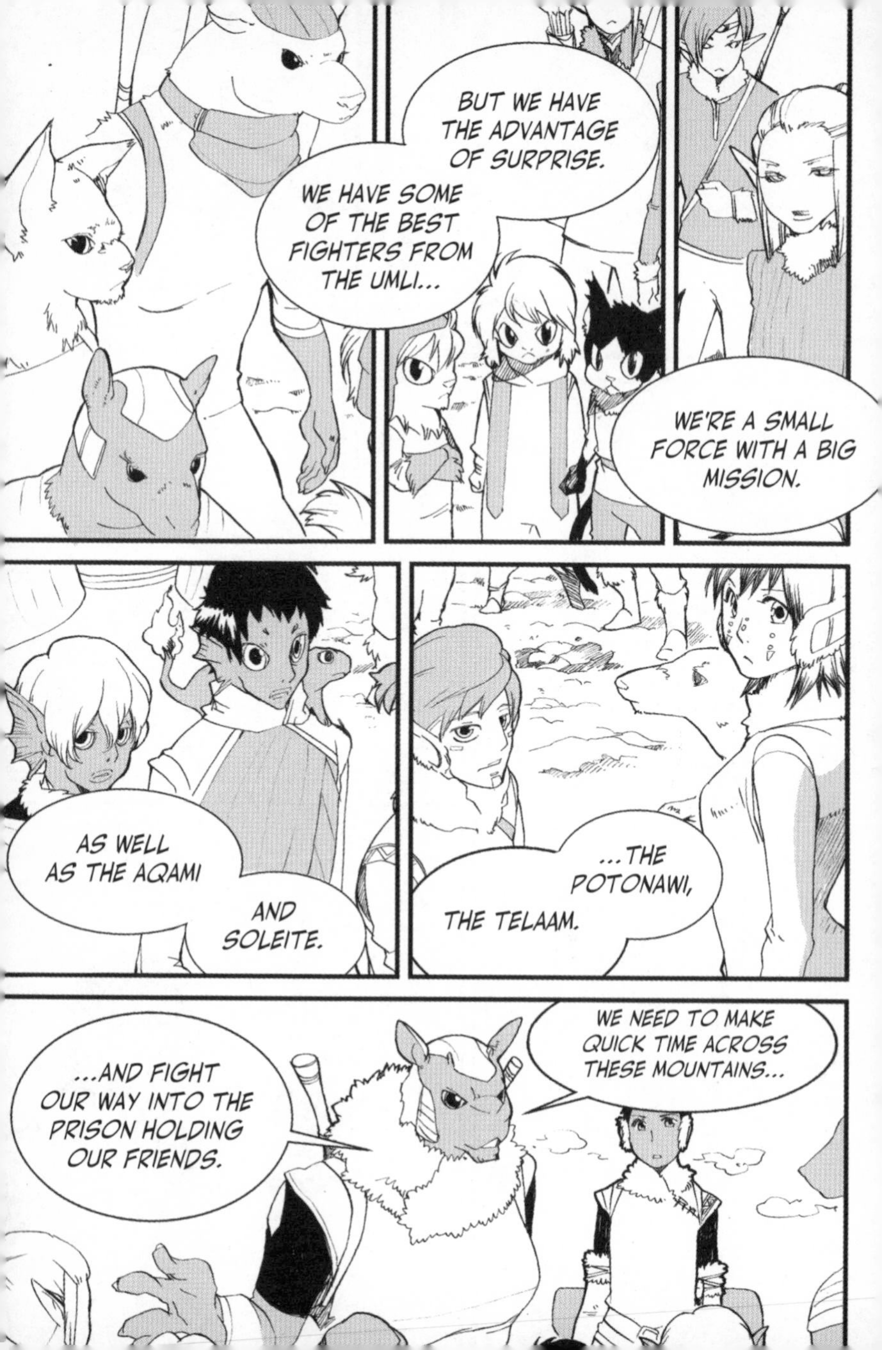
WE'RE A SMALL FORCE WITH A BIG MISSION.
BUT WE HAVE THE ADVANTAGE OF SURPRISE.
WE HAVE SOME OF THE BEST FIGHTERS FROM THE UMLI...
...THE POTONAWI,
THE TELAAM.
AS WELL AS THE AQAMI
AND SOLEITE.
WE NEED TO MAKE QUICK TIME ACROSS THESE MOUNTAINS...
...AND FIGHT OUR WAY INTO THE PRISON HOLDING OUR FRIENDS.

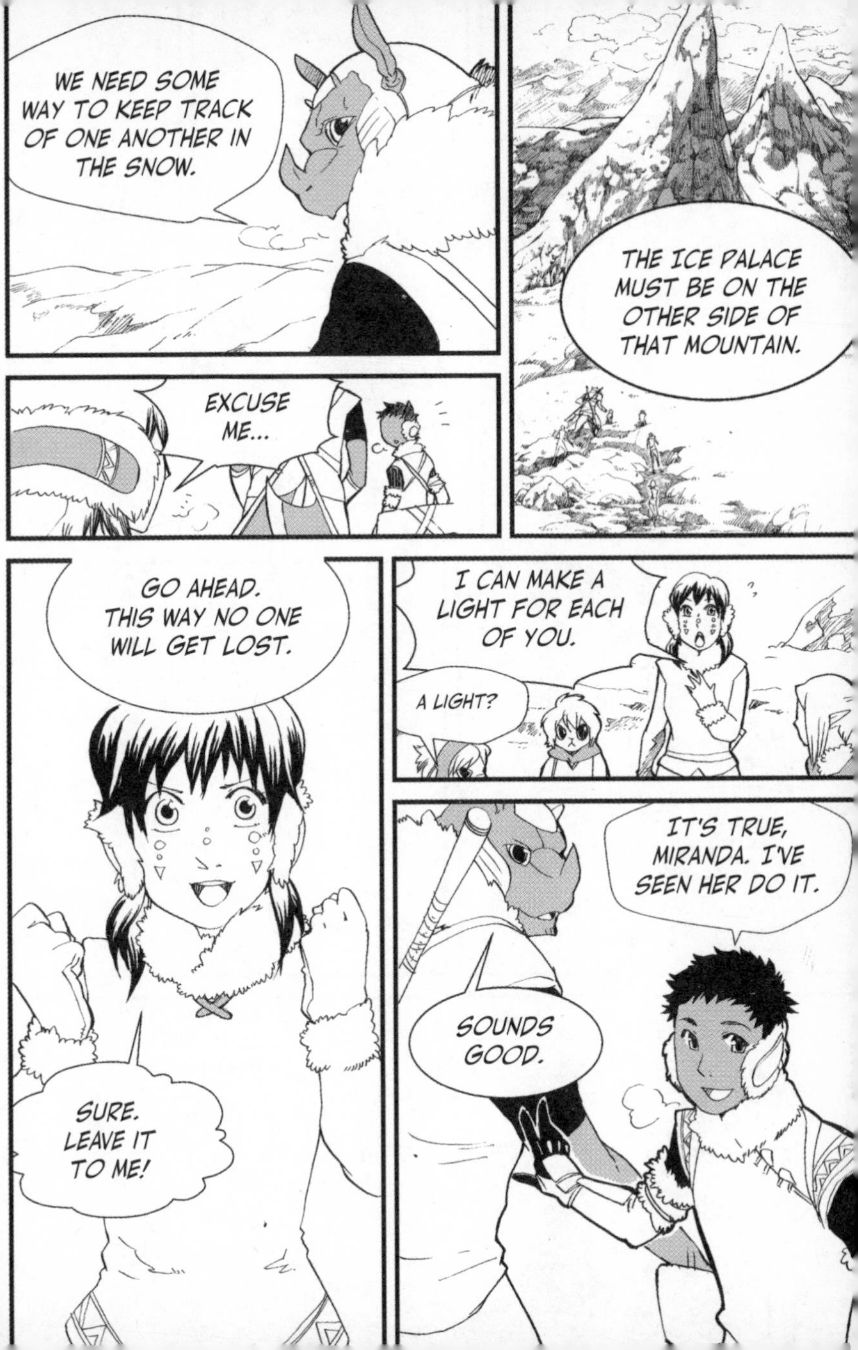
WE NEED SOME WAY TO KEEP TRACK OF ONE ANOTHER IN THE SNOW.
EXCUSE ME...
THE ICE PALACE MUST BE ON THE OTHER SIDE OF THAT MOUNTAIN.
GO AHEAD. THIS WAY NO ONE WILL GET LOST.
SURE. LEAVE IT TO ME!
I CAN MAKE A LIGHT FOR EACH OF YOU.
A LIGHT?
IT'S TRUE, MIRANDA. I'VE SEEN HER DO IT.
SOUNDS GOOD.

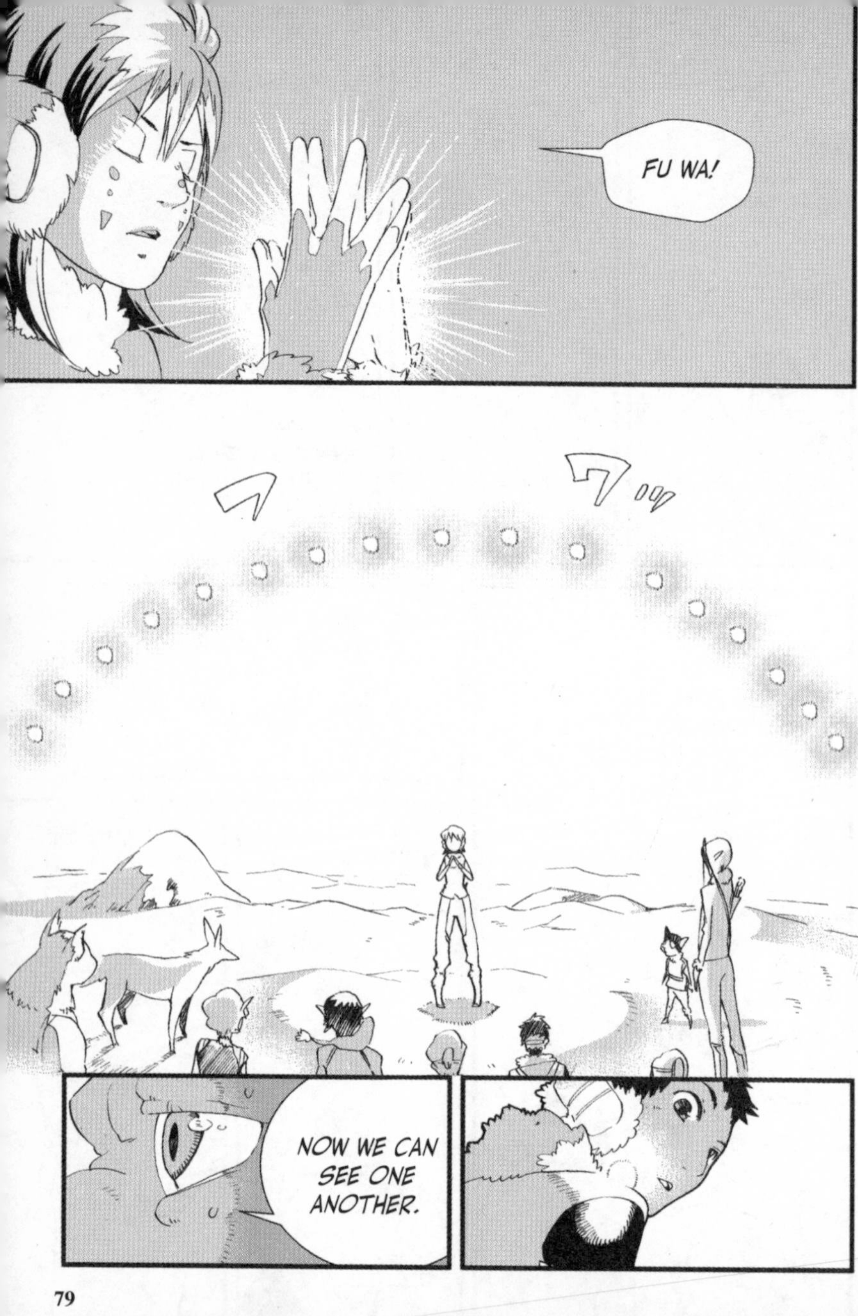
FU WA!
フワッ
NOW WE CAN SEE ONE ANOTHER.

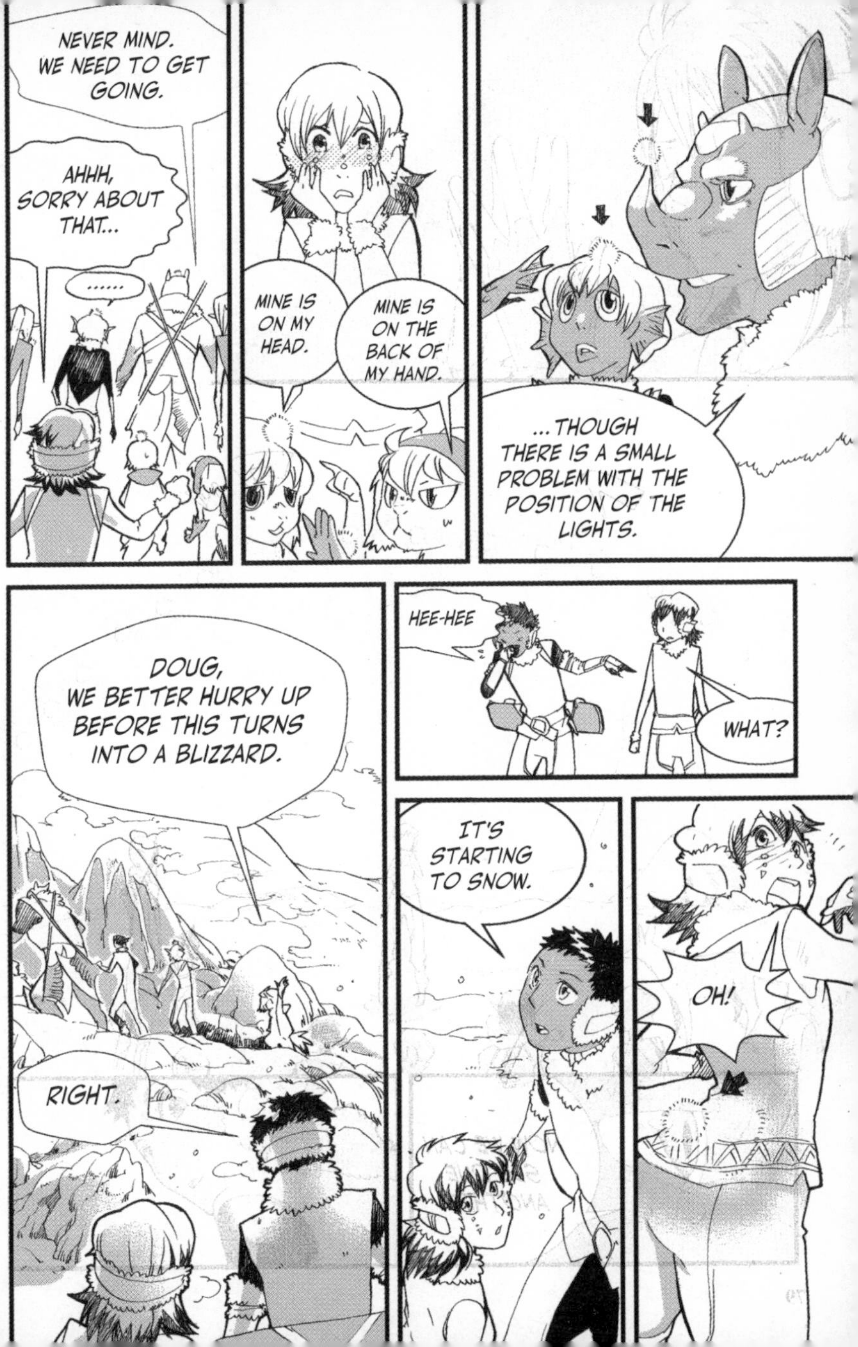
...THOUGH THERE IS A SMALL PROBLEM WITH THE POSITION OF THE LIGHTS.
MINE IS ON THE BACK OF MY HAND.
MINE IS ON MY HEAD.
NEVER MIND. WE NEED TO GET GOING.
AHHH, SORRY ABOUT THAT...
....
HEE-HEE
WHAT?
OH!
IT'S STARTING TO SNOW.
DOUG, WE BETTER HURRY UP BEFORE THIS TURNS INTO A BLIZZARD.
RIGHT.

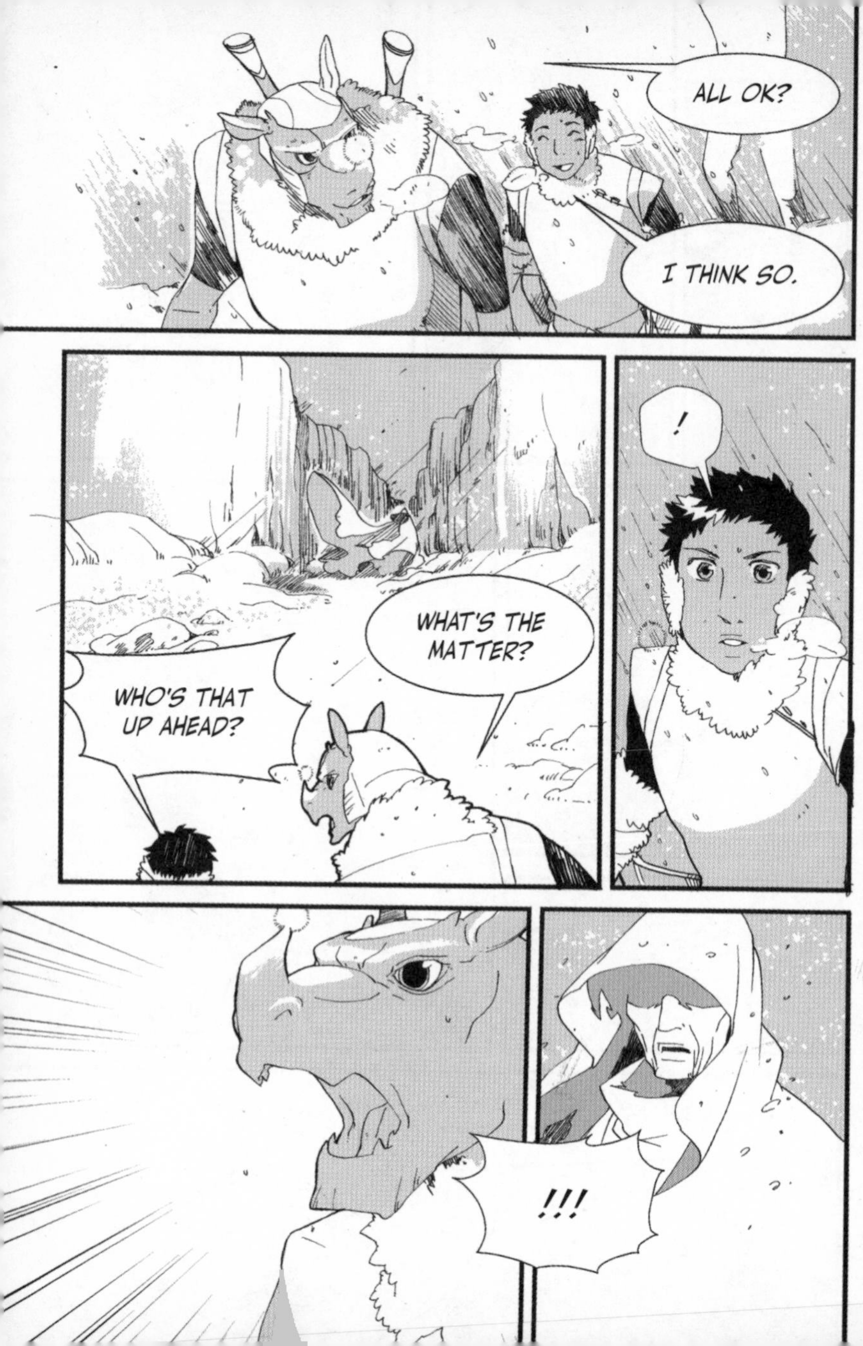
ALL OK?
I THINK SO.
!
WHAT'S THE MATTER?
WHO'S THAT UP AHEAD?
!!!

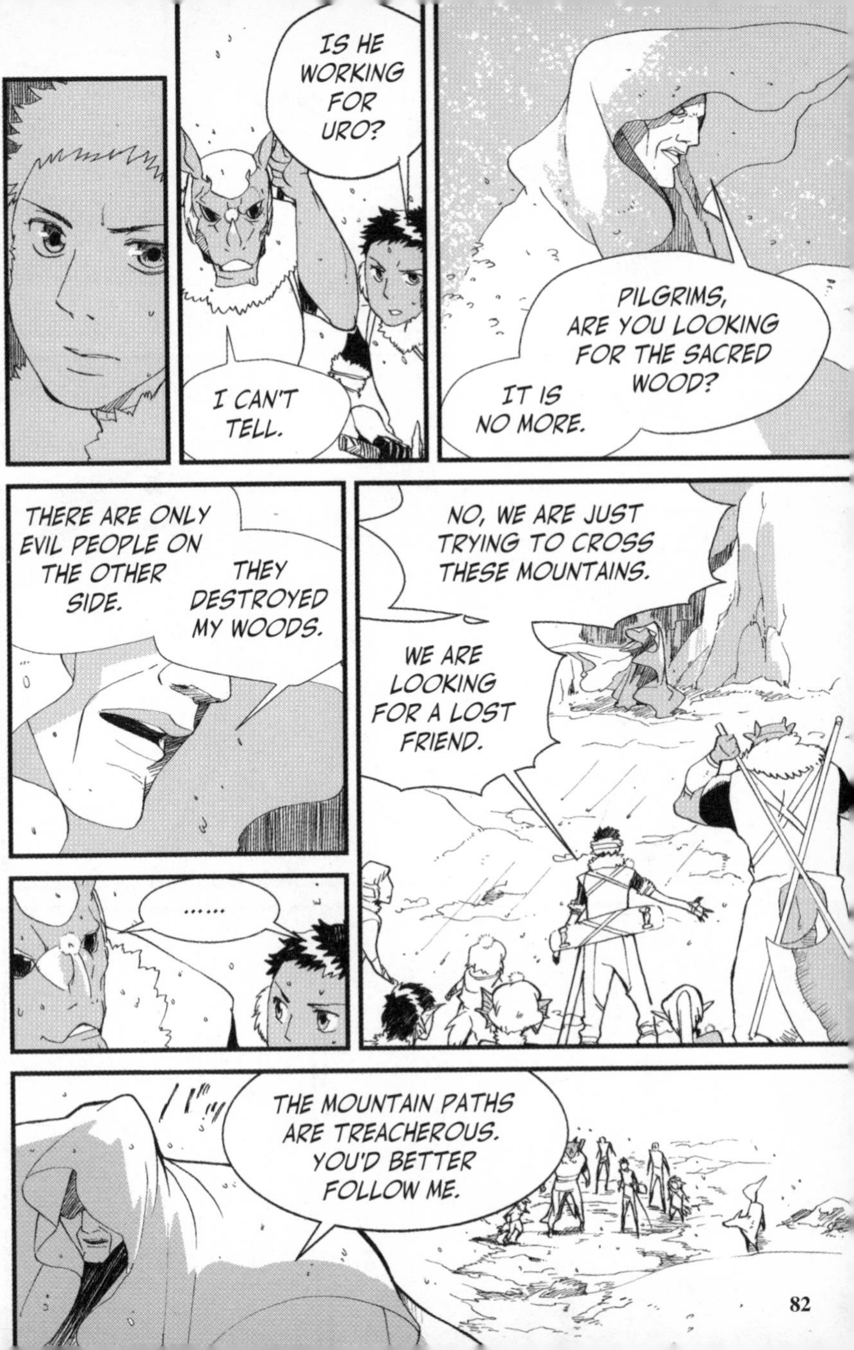
PILGRIMS, ARE YOU LOOKING FOR THE SACRED WOOD?
IT IS NO MORE.
IS HE WORKING FOR URO?
I CAN'T TELL.
NO, WE ARE JUST TRYING TO CROSS THESE MOUNTAINS.
WE ARE LOOKING FOR A LOST FRIEND.
THERE ARE ONLY EVIL PEOPLE ON THE OTHER SIDE.
THEY DESTROYED MY WOODS.
……
THE MOUNTAIN PATHS ARE TREACHEROUS. YOU'D BETTER FOLLOW ME.

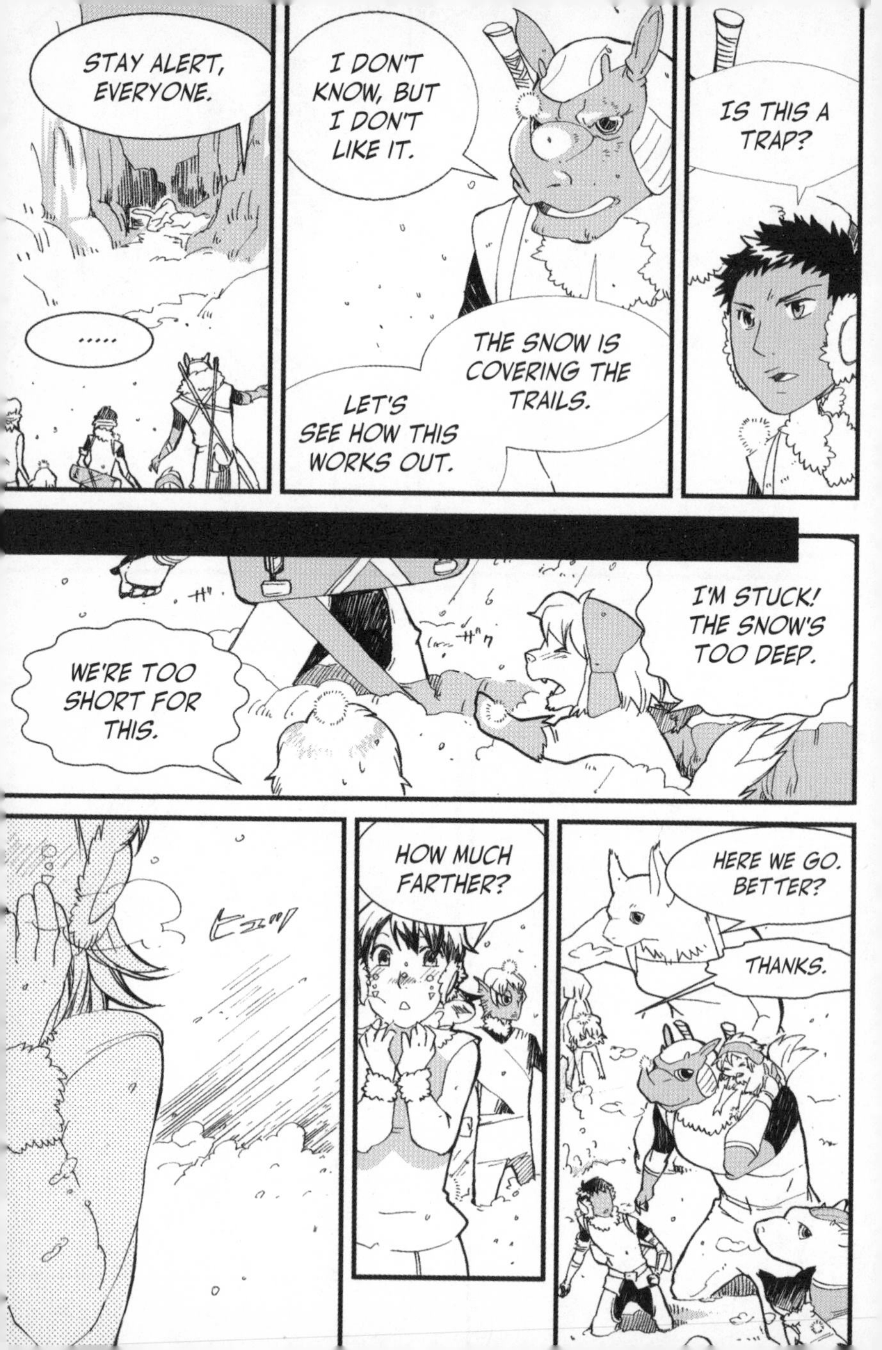
IS THIS A TRAP?
I DON'T KNOW, BUT I DON'T LIKE IT.
THE SNOW IS COVERING THE TRAILS.
LET'S SEE HOW THIS WORKS OUT.
STAY ALERT, EVERYONE.
......
I'M STUCK! THE SNOW'S TOO DEEP.
WE'RE TOO SHORT FOR THIS.
HERE WE GO. BETTER?
THANKS.
HOW MUCH FARTHER?

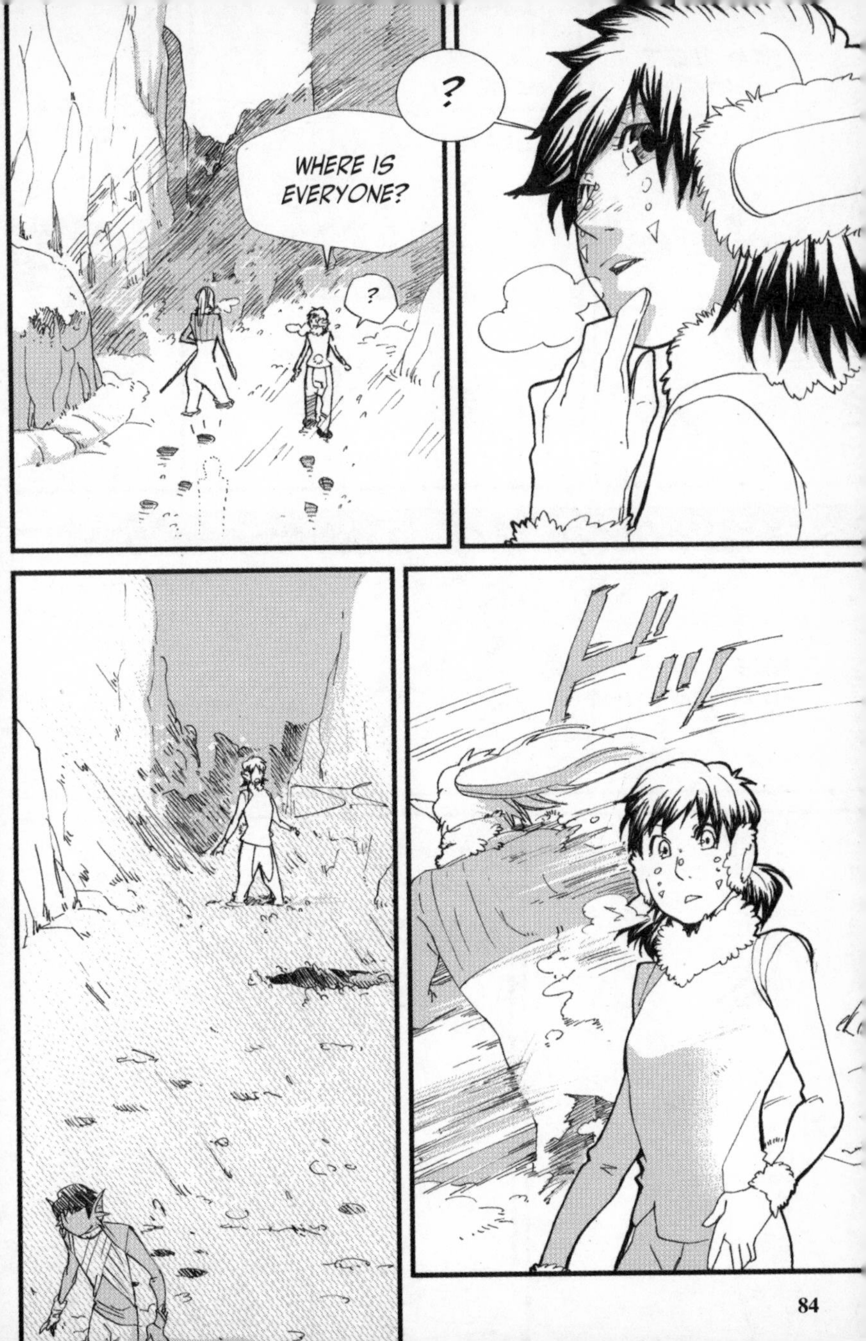
?
WHERE IS EVERYONE?
?

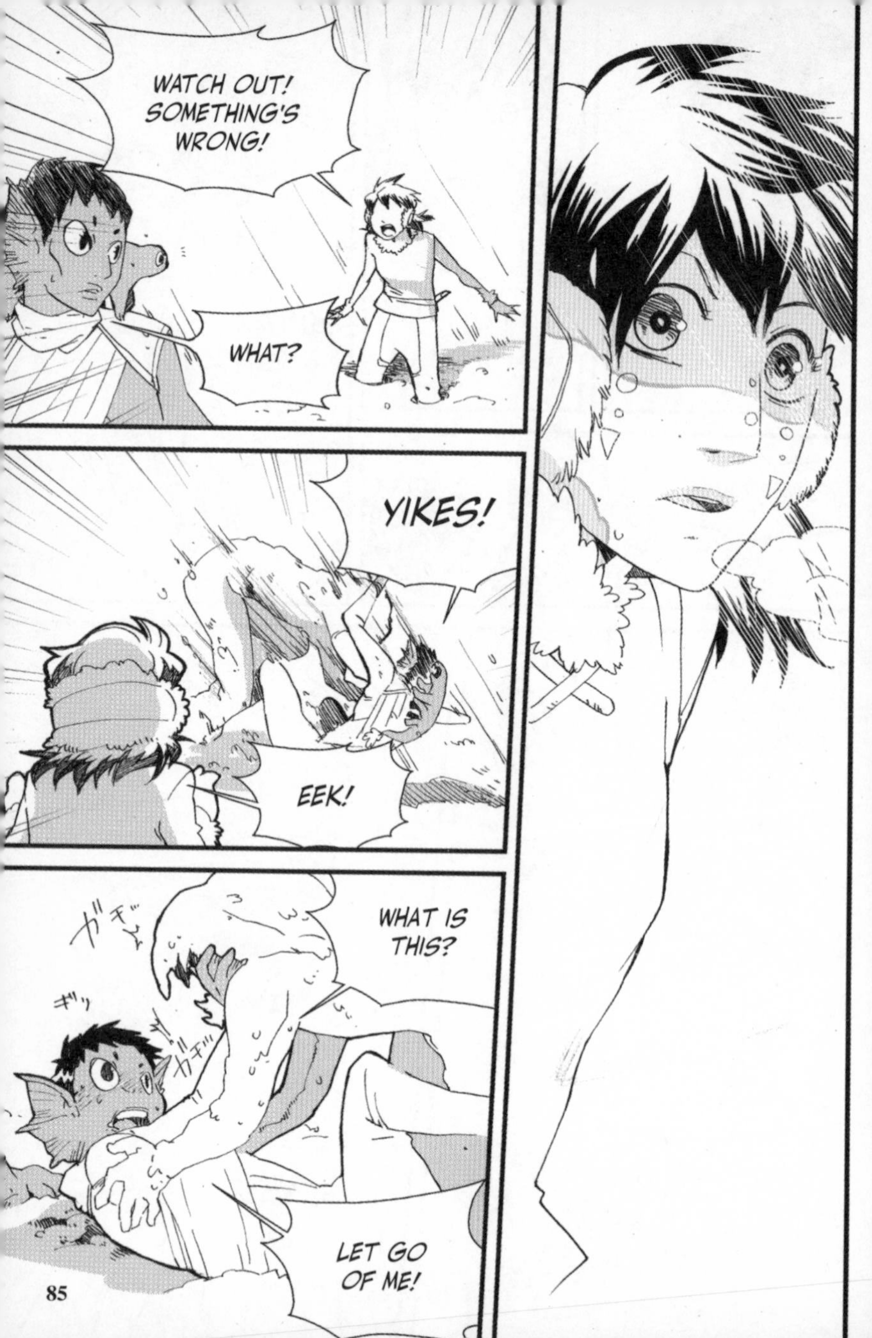
WATCH OUT! SOMETHING'S WRONG!
WHAT?
YIKES!
EEK!
WHAT IS THIS?
LET GO OF ME!

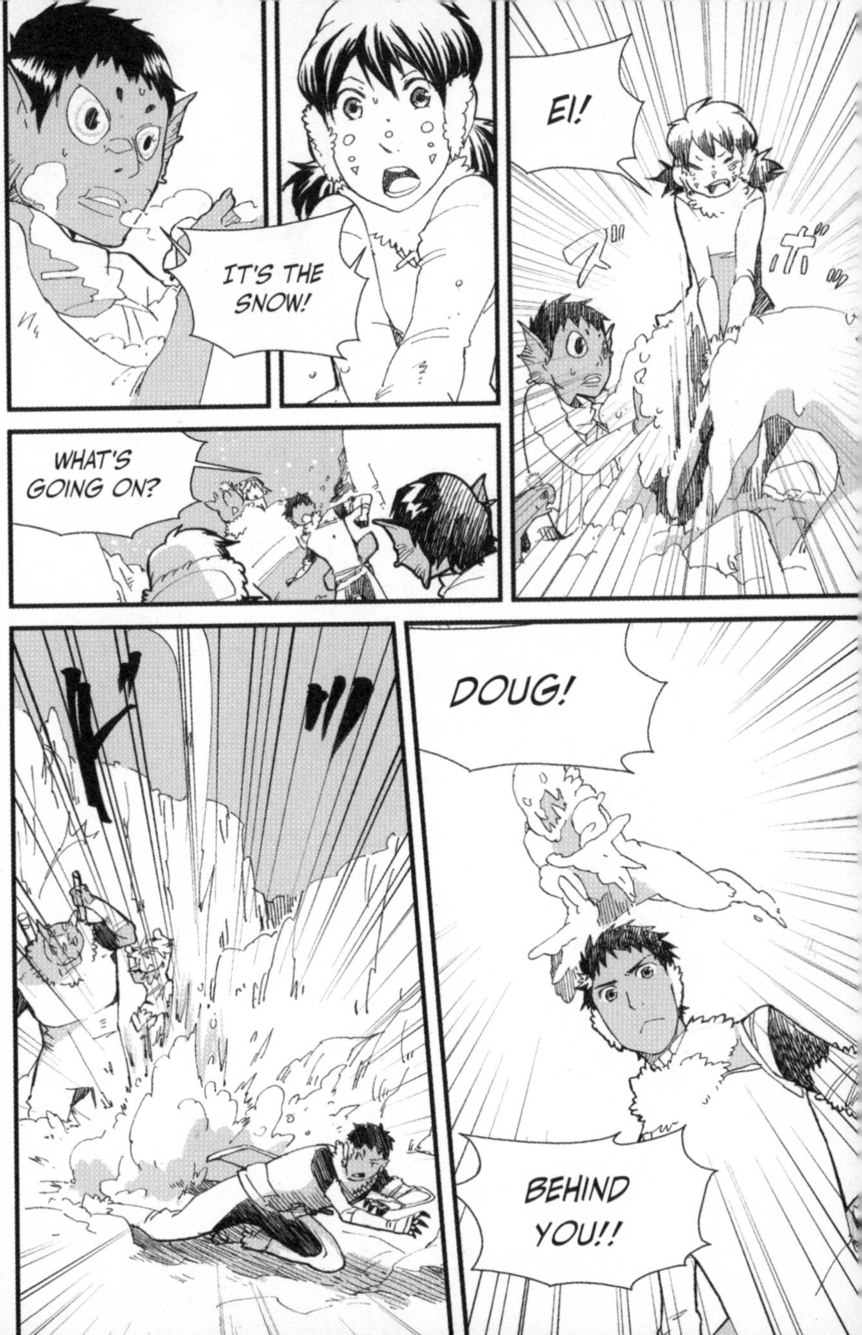
EI!
IT'S THE SNOW!
WHAT'S GOING ON?
DOUG!
BEHIND YOU!!

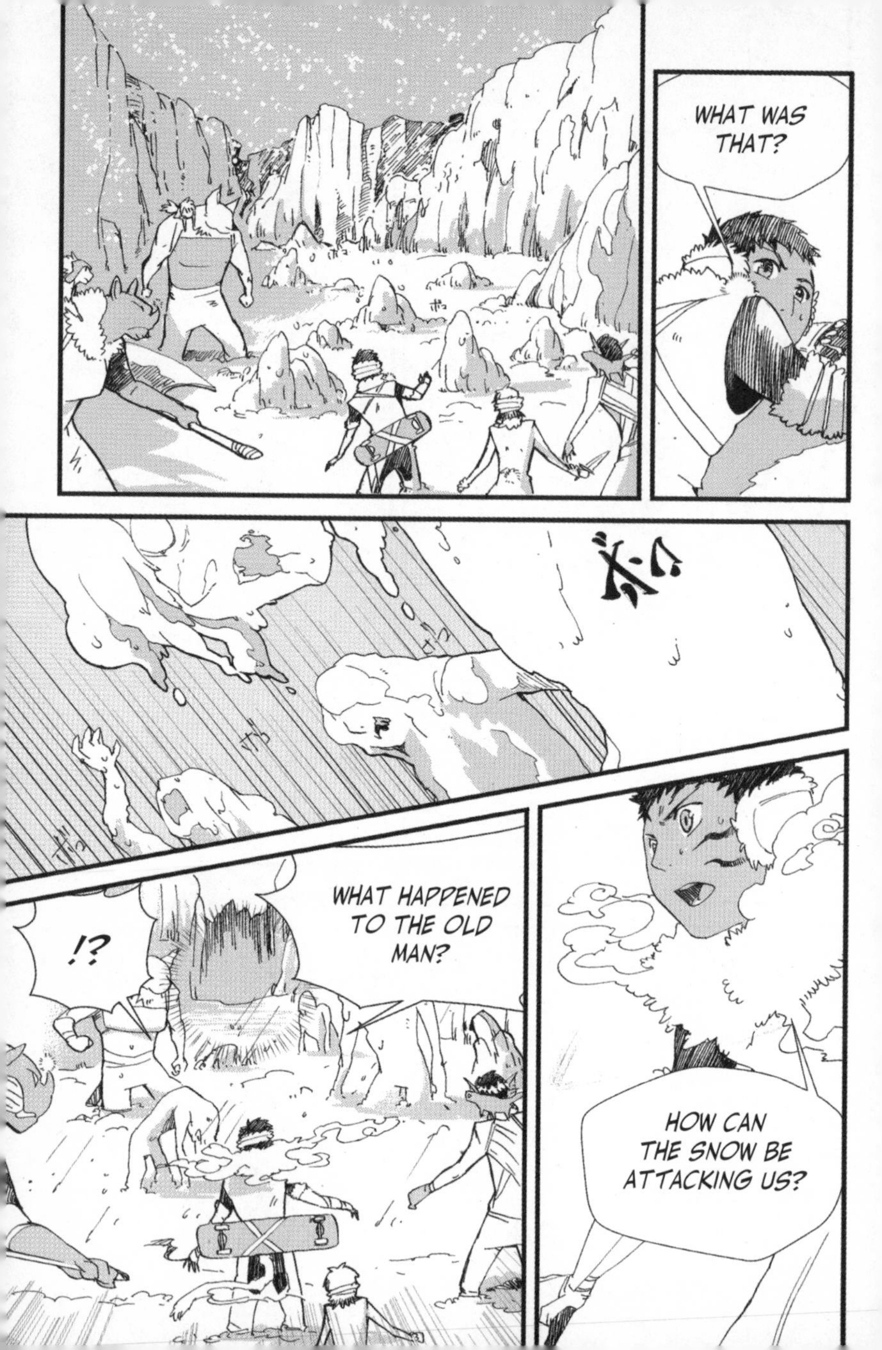
WHAT WAS THAT?
HOW CAN THE SNOW BE ATTACKING US?
WHAT HAPPENED TO THE OLD MAN?
!?

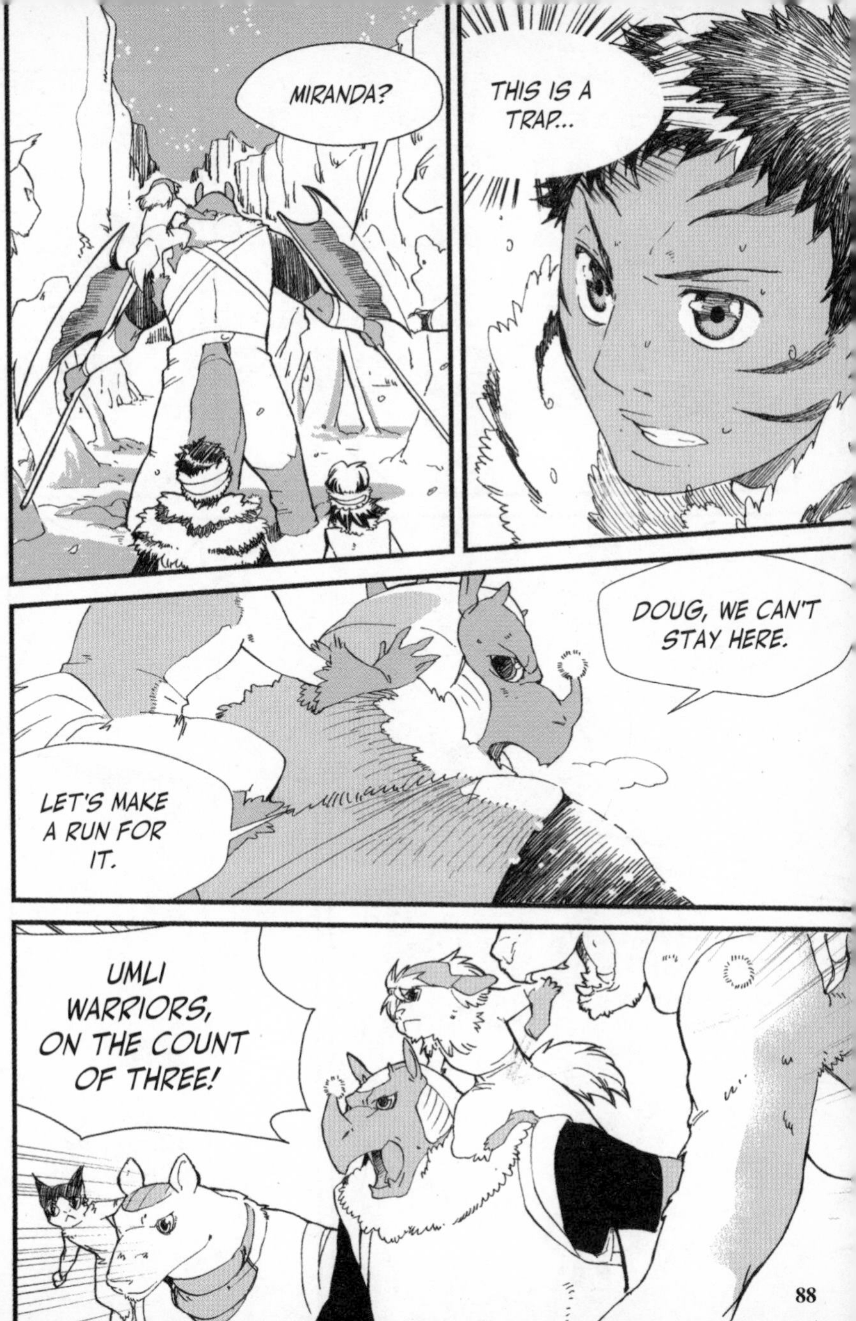
THIS IS A TRAP...
MIRANDA?
DOUG, WE CAN'T STAY HERE.
LET'S MAKE A RUN FOR IT.
UMLI WARRIORS, ON THE COUNT OF THREE!

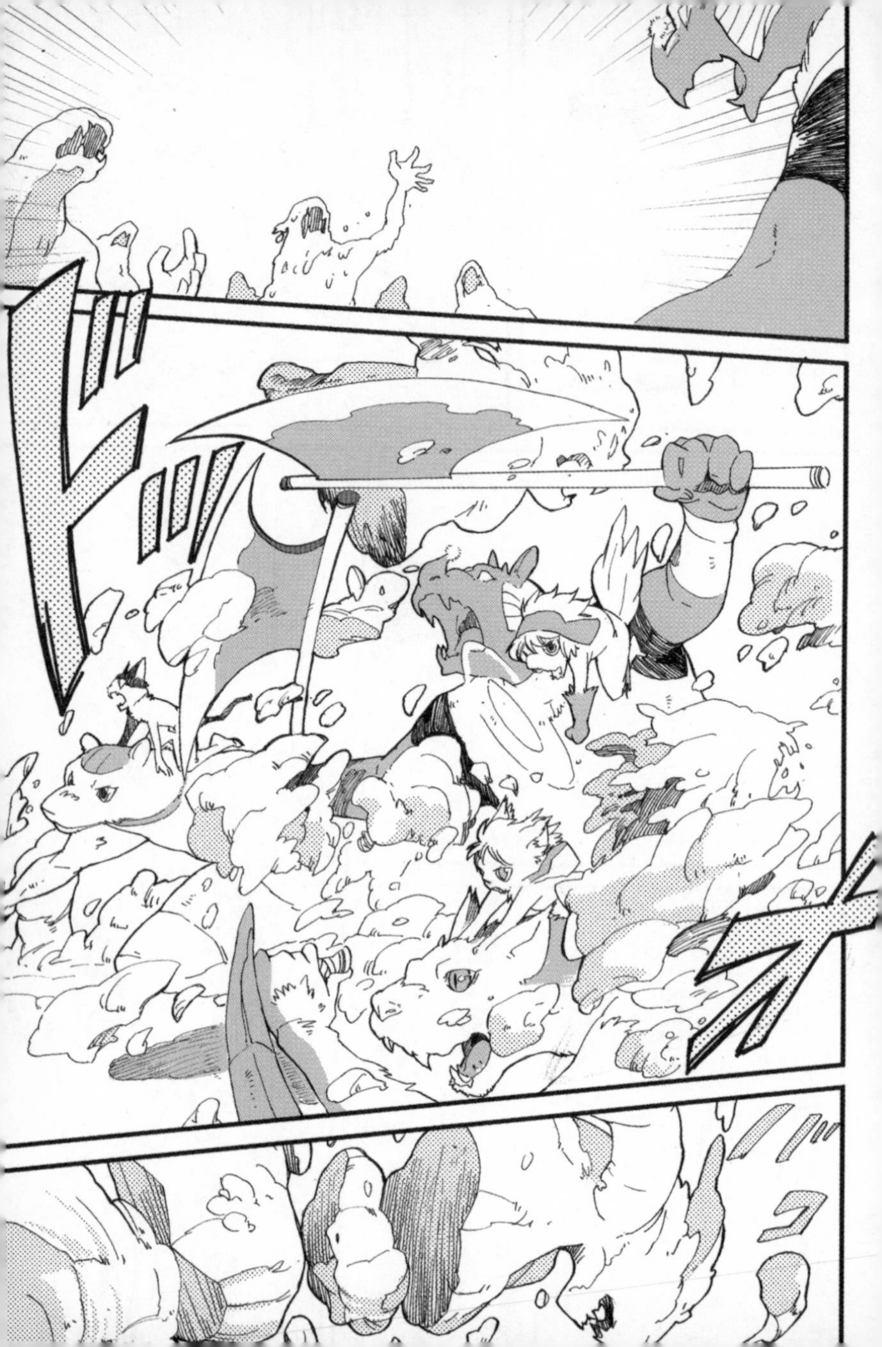

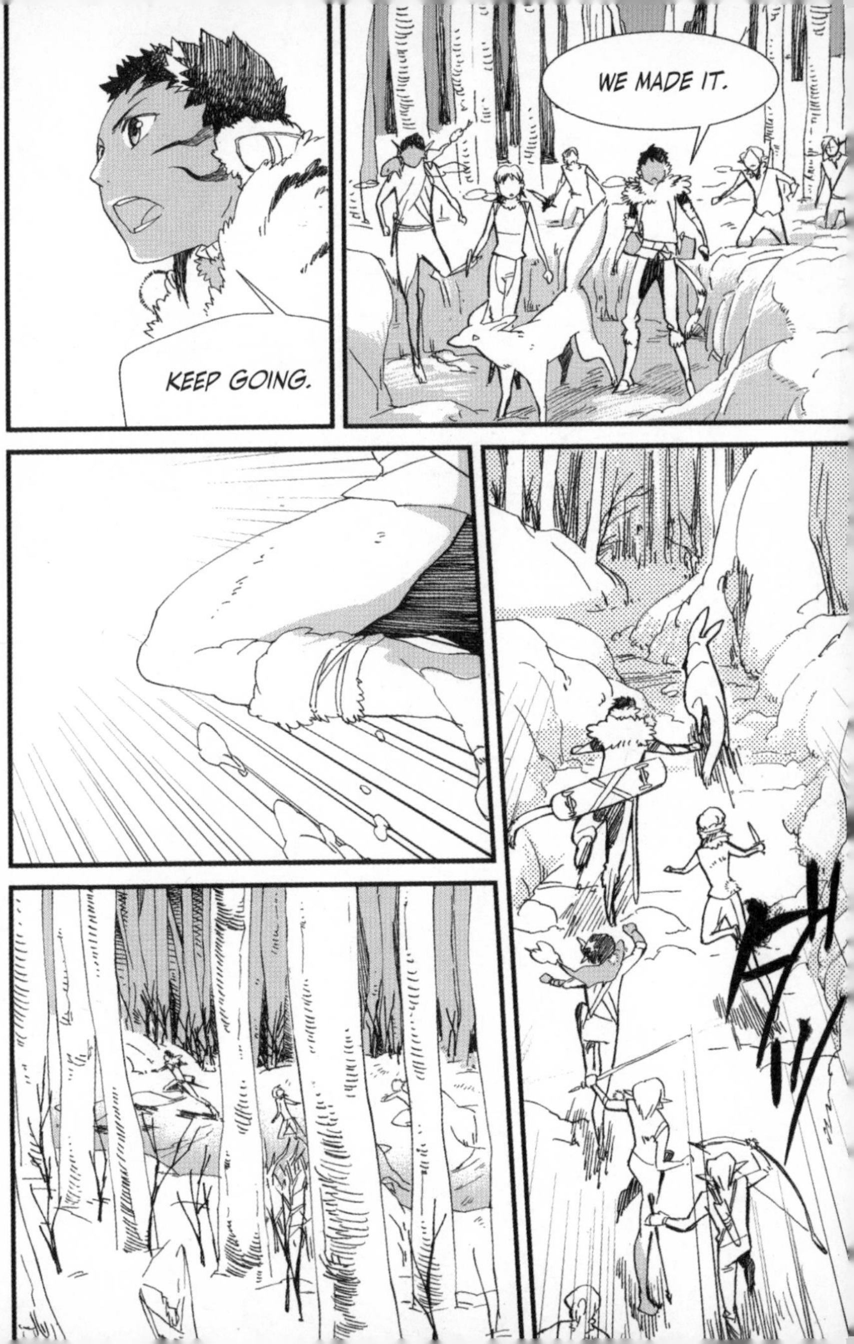
WE MADE IT.
KEEP GOING.

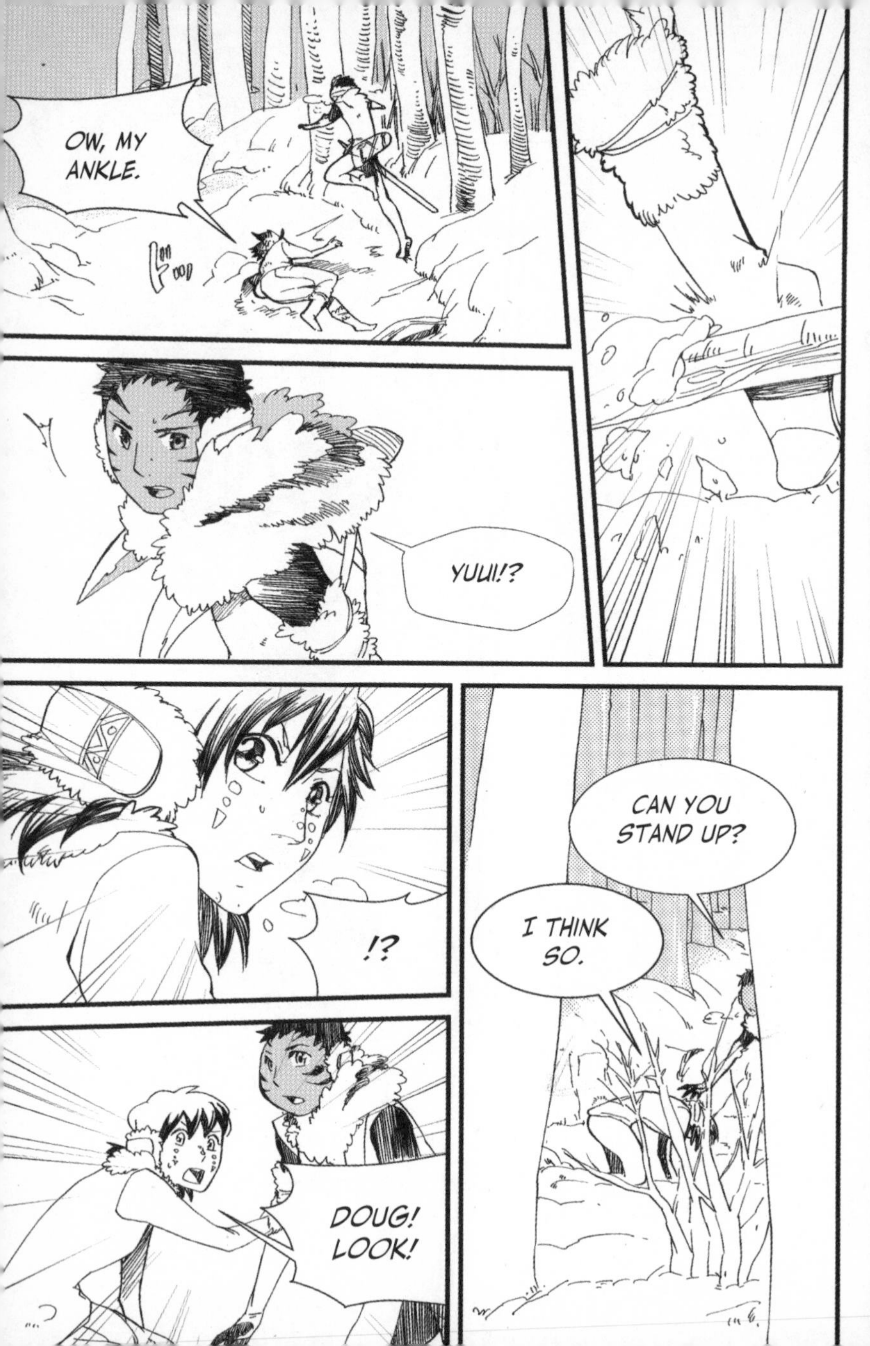
OW, MY ANKLE.
YUUI!?
CAN YOU STAND UP?
I THINK SO.
!?
DOUG! LOOK!

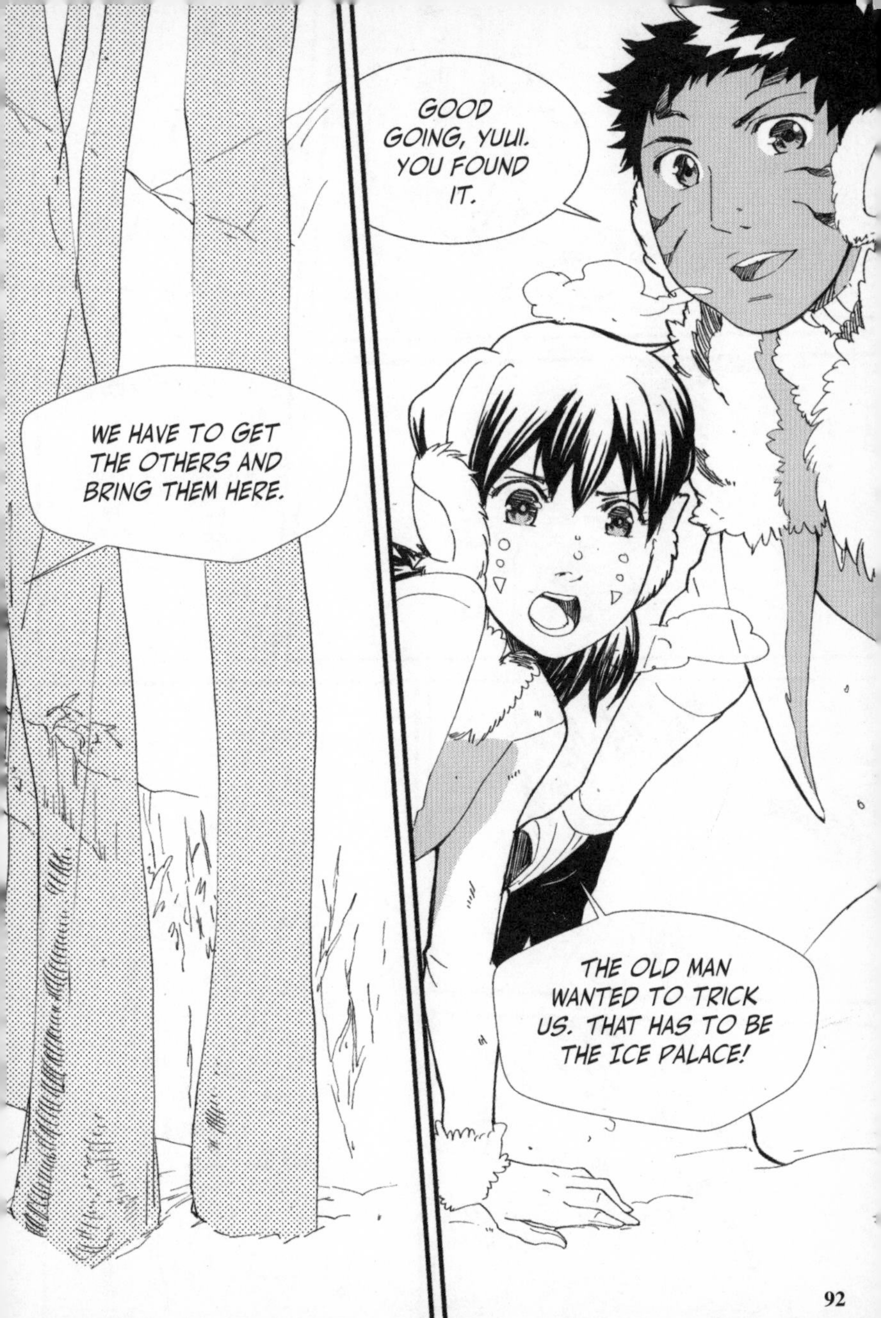
GOOD GOING, YUUI. YOU FOUND IT.
THE OLD MAN WANTED TO TRICK US. THAT HAS TO BE THE ICE PALACE!
WE HAVE TO GET THE OTHERS AND BRING THEM HERE.

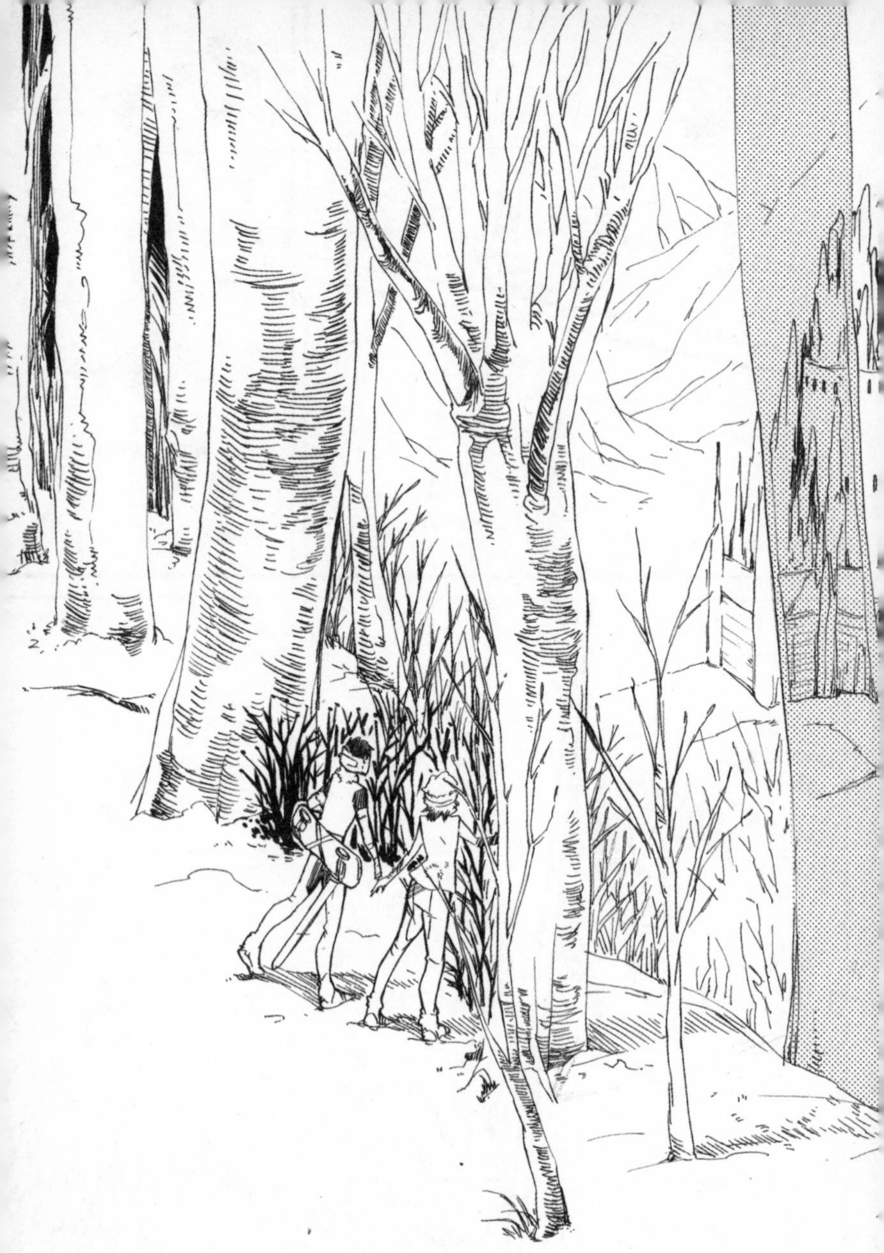

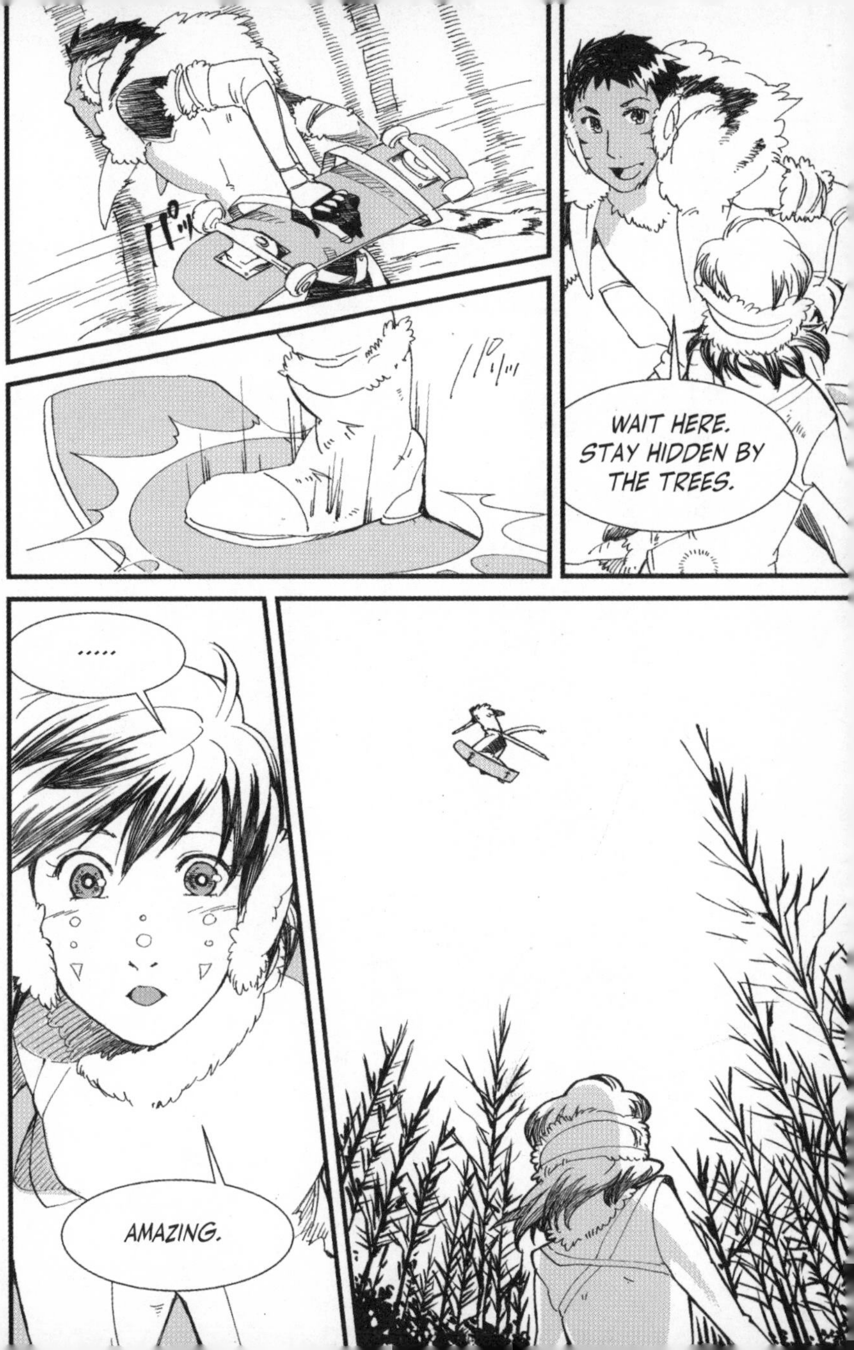
WAIT HERE. STAY HIDDEN BY THE TREES.
.....
AMAZING.

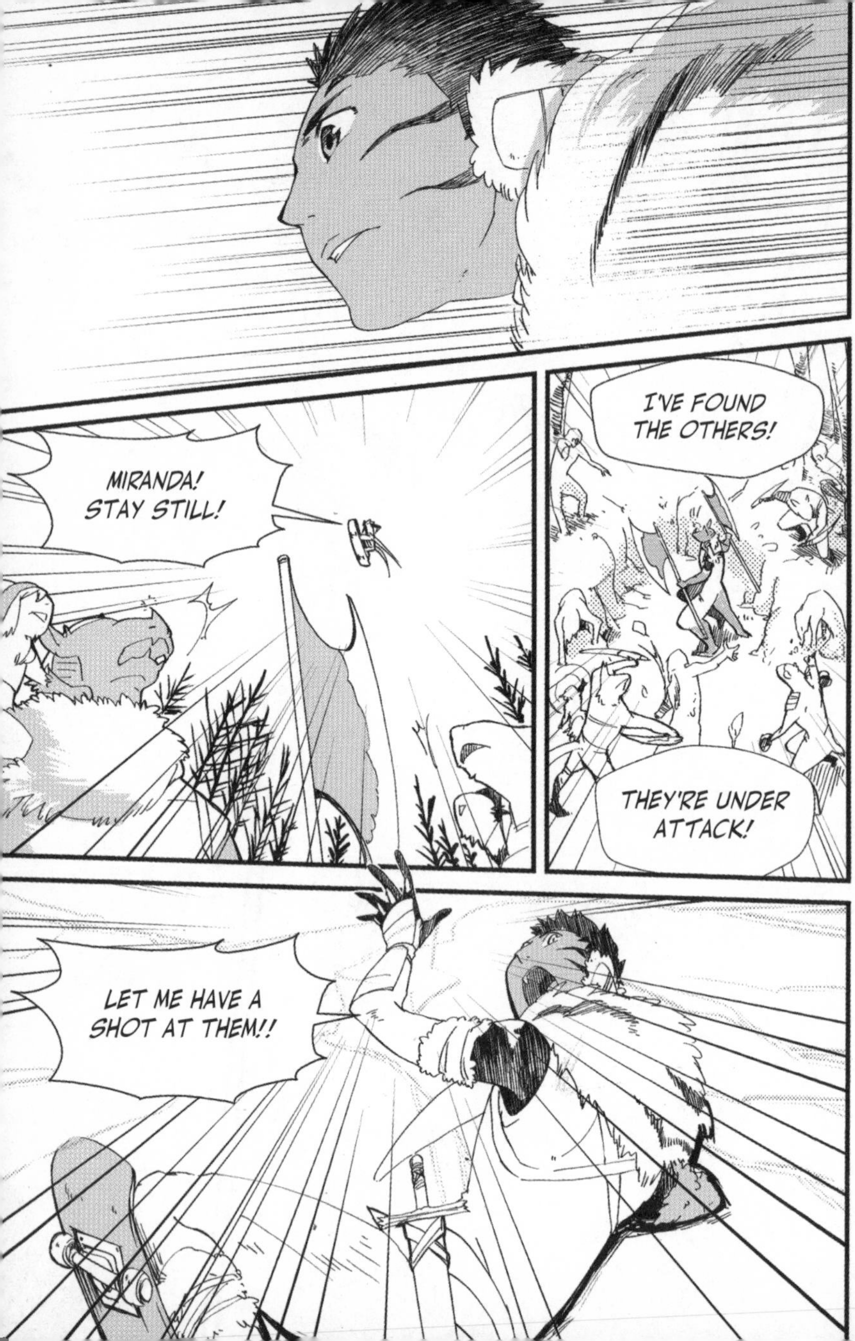
I'VE FOUND THE OTHERS!
THEY'RE UNDER ATTACK!
MIRANDA! STAY STILL!
LET ME HAVE A SHOT AT THEM!!

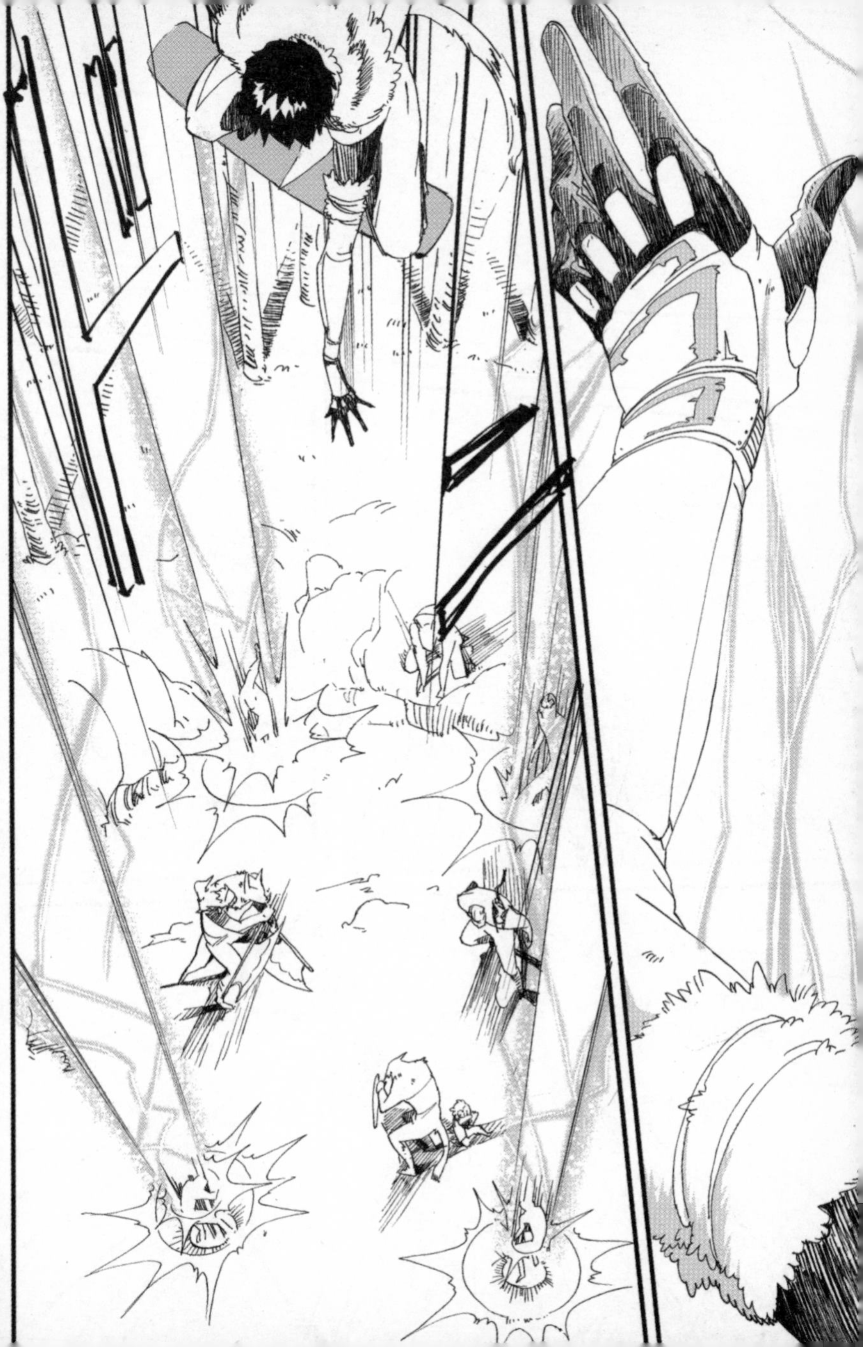

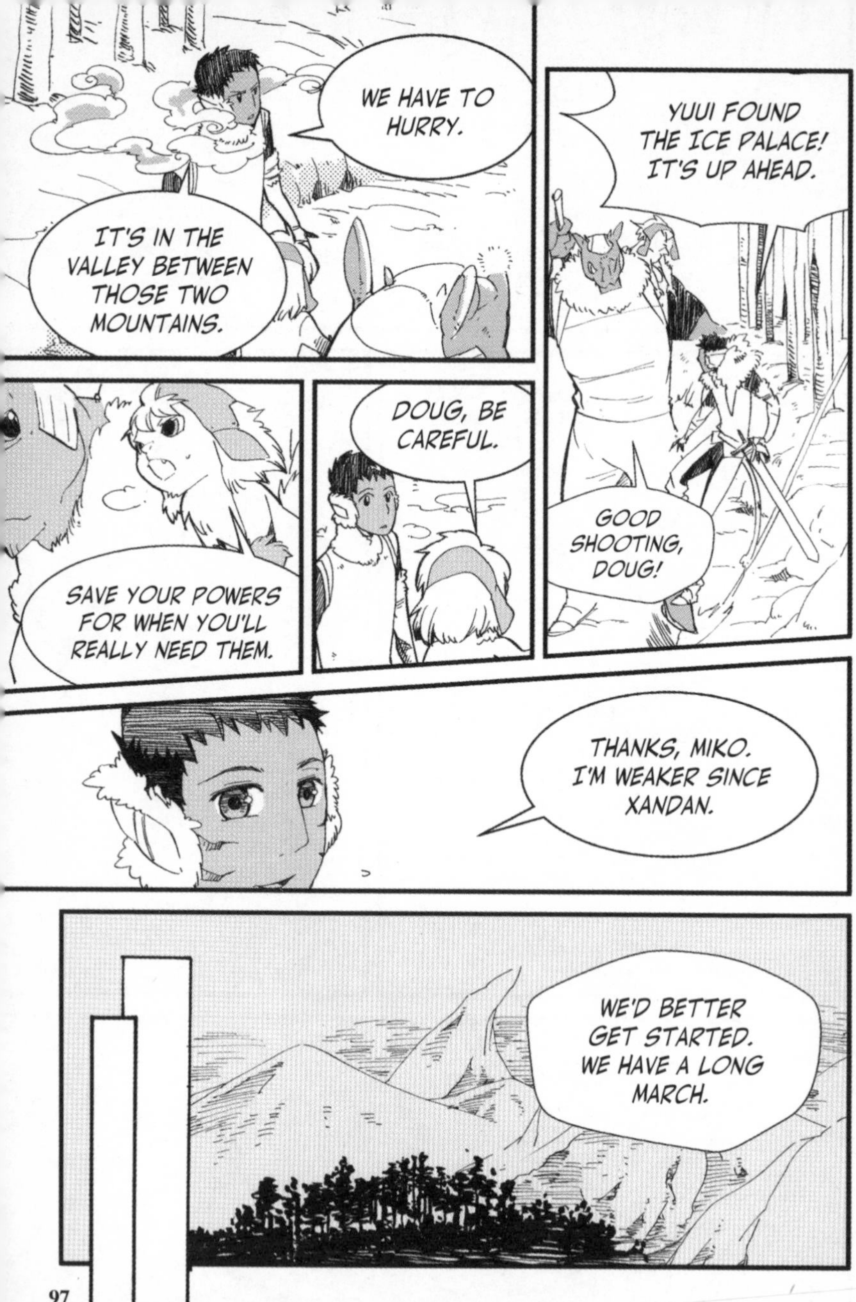
YUUI FOUND THE ICE PALACE! IT'S UP AHEAD.
GOOD SHOOTING, DOUG!
WE HAVE TO HURRY.
IT'S IN THE VALLEY BETWEEN THOSE TWO MOUNTAINS.
DOUG, BE CAREFUL.
SAVE YOUR POWERS FOR WHEN YOU'LL REALLY NEED THEM.
THANKS, MIKO. I'M WEAKER SINCE XANDAN.
WE'D BETTER GET STARTED. WE HAVE A LONG MARCH.

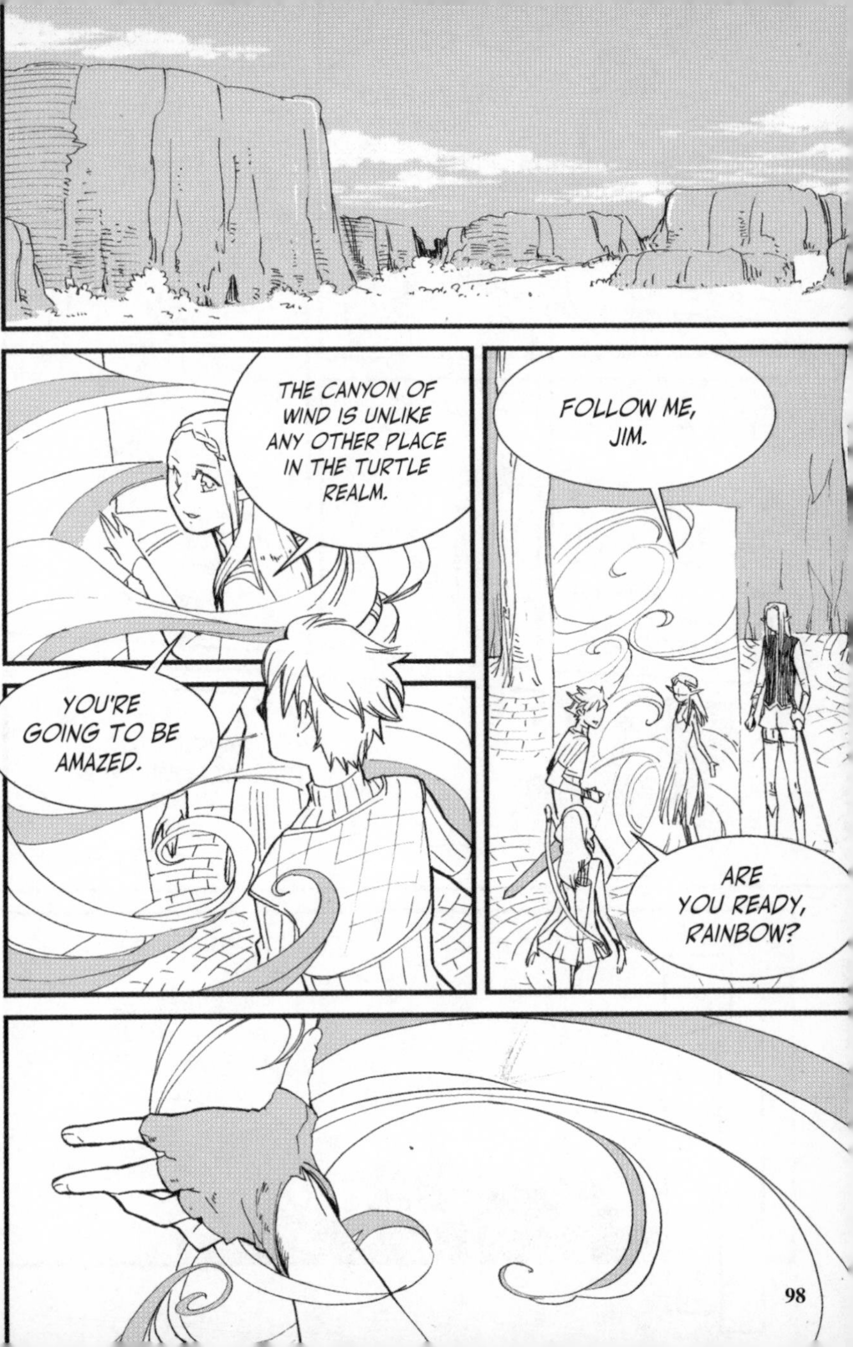
FOLLOW ME, JIM.
ARE YOU READY, RAINBOW?
THE CANYON OF WIND IS UNLIKE ANY OTHER PLACE IN THE TURTLE REALM.
YOU'RE GOING TO BE AMAZED.

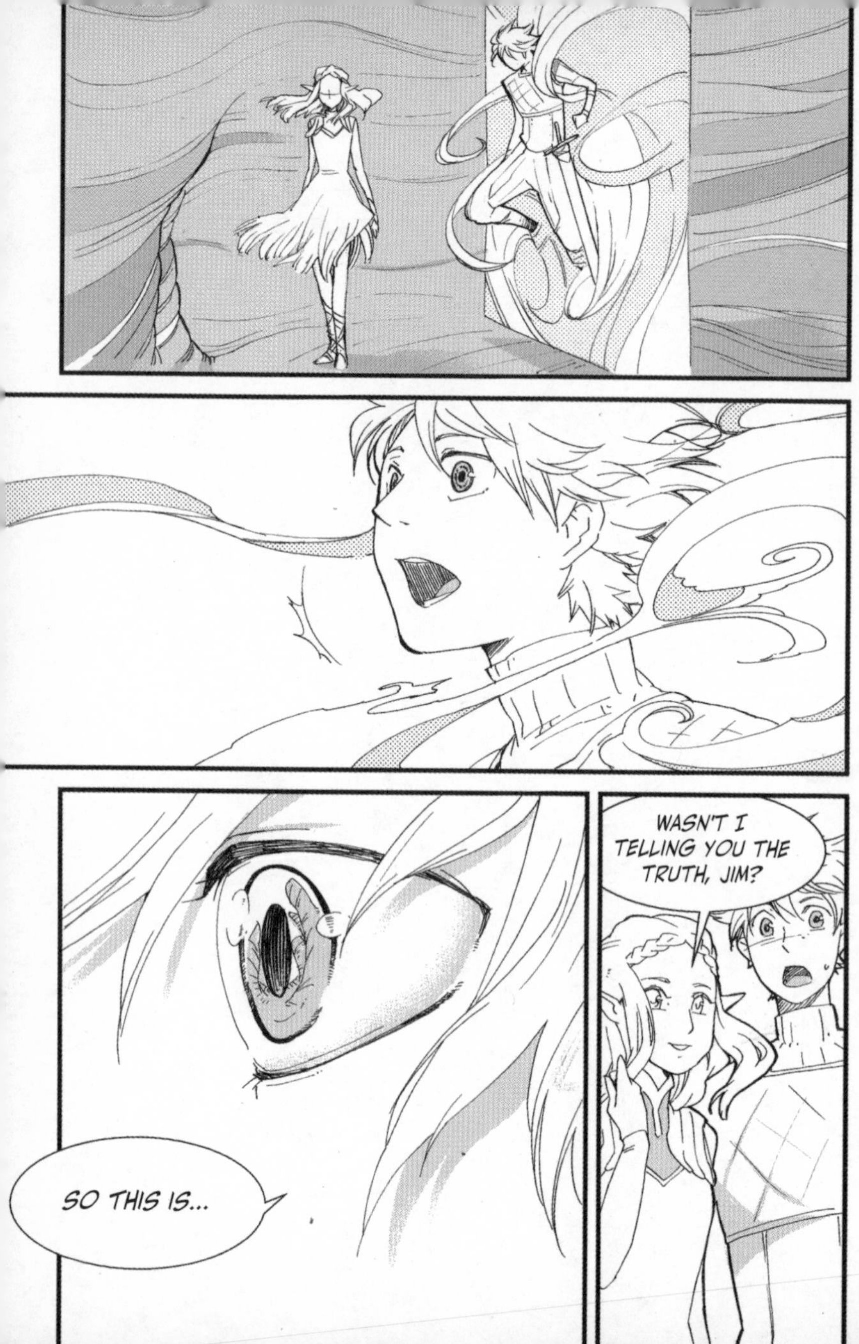
WASN'T I TELLING YOU THE TRUTH, JIM?
SO THIS IS...

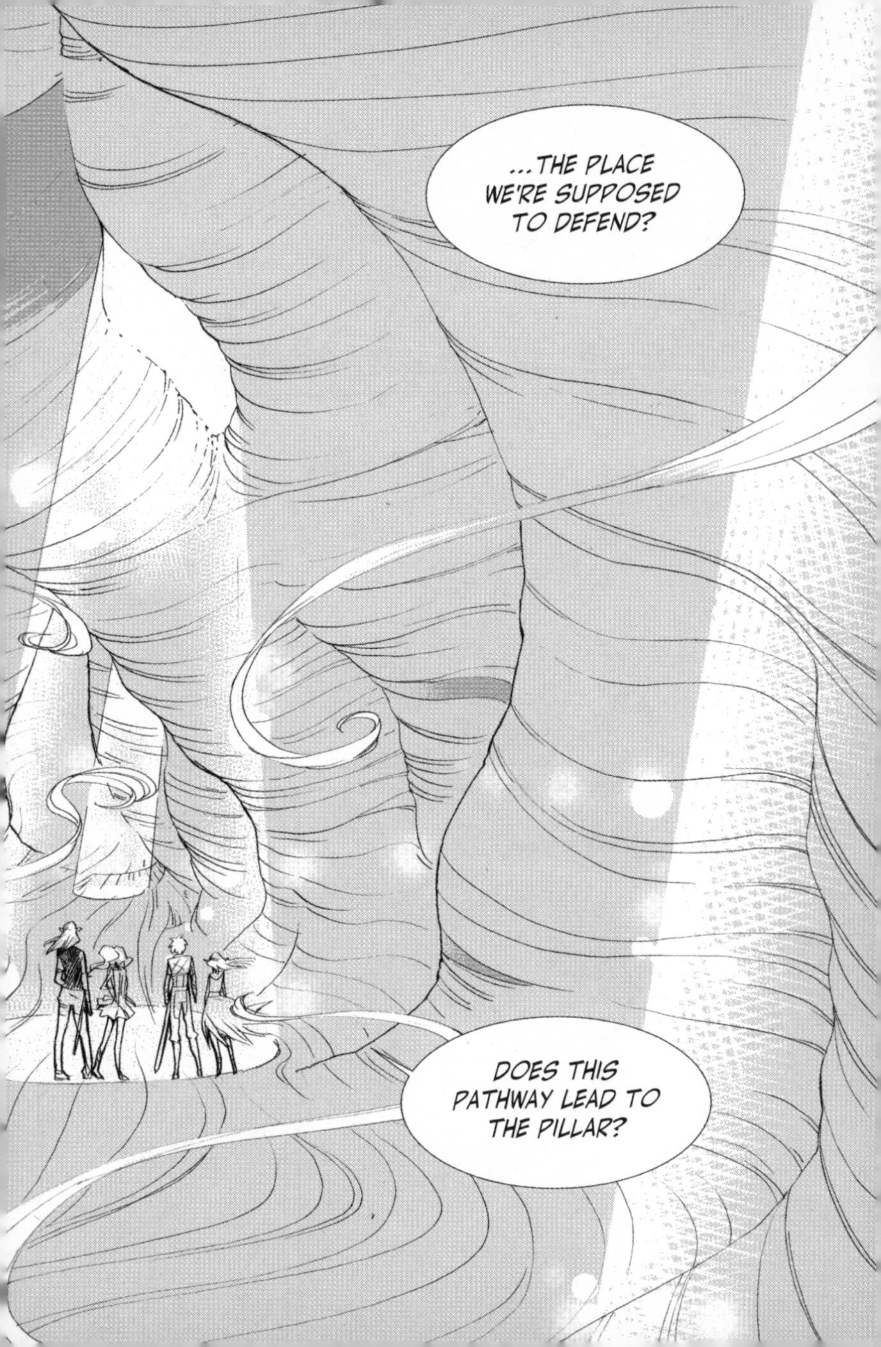
...THE PLACE WE'RE SUPPOSED TO DEFEND?
DOES THIS PATHWAY LEAD TO THE PILLAR?

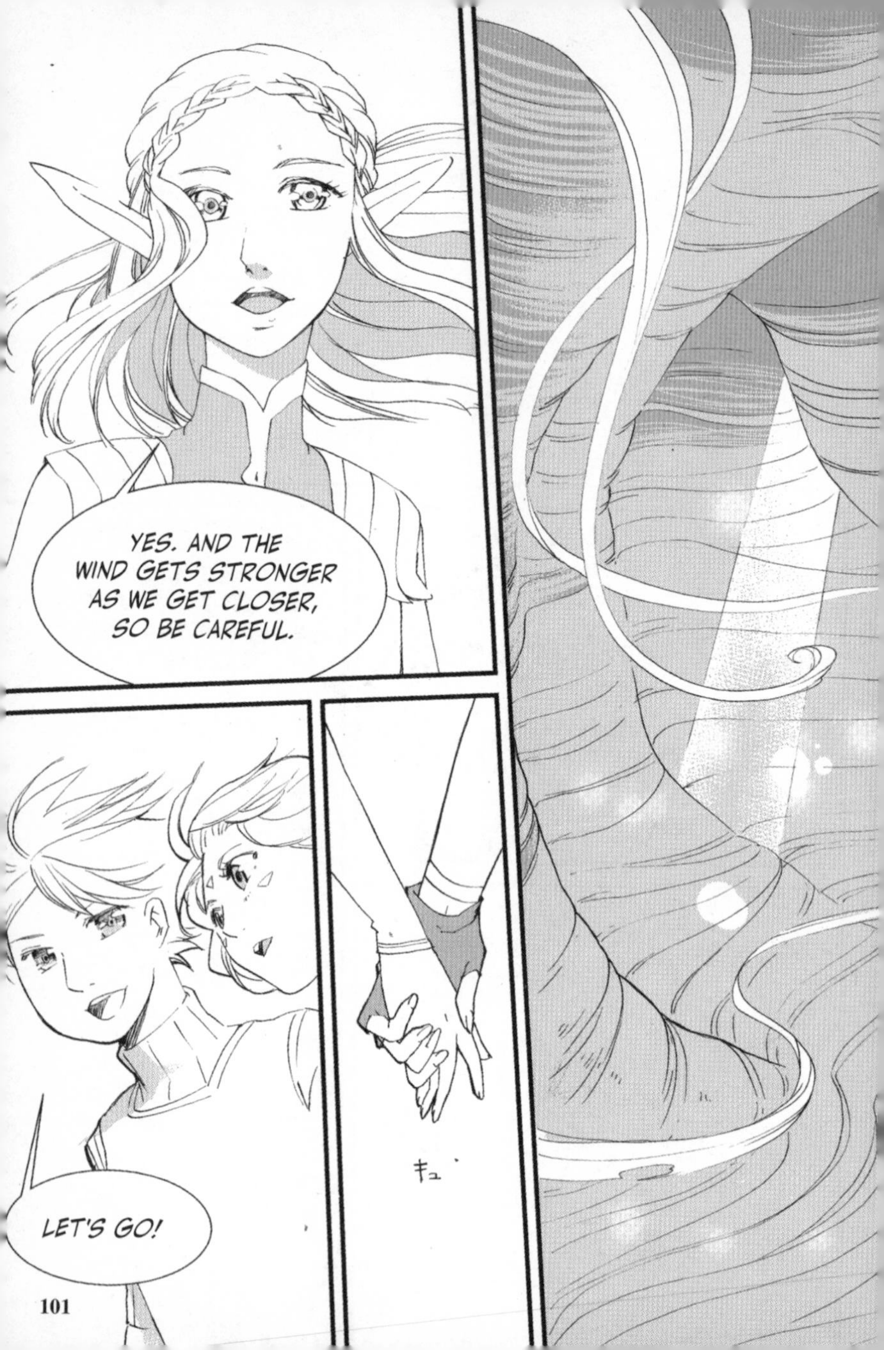
YES. AND THE WIND GETS STRONGER AS WE GET CLOSER, SO BE CAREFUL.
キュ
LET'S GO!

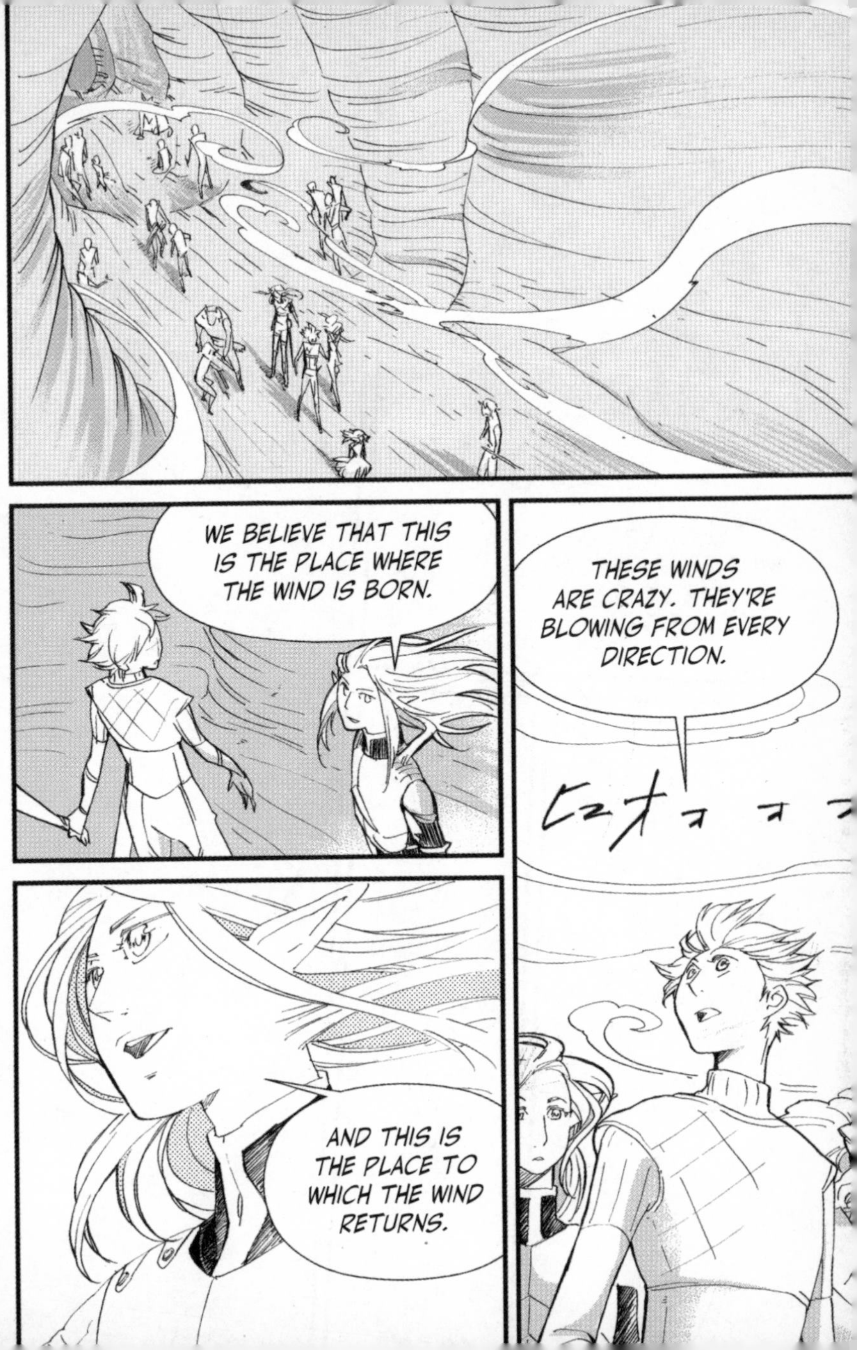
THESE WINDS ARE CRAZY. THEY'RE BLOWING FROM EVERY DIRECTION.
WE BELIEVE THAT THIS IS THE PLACE WHERE THE WIND IS BORN.
AND THIS IS THE PLACE TO WHICH THE WIND RETURNS.

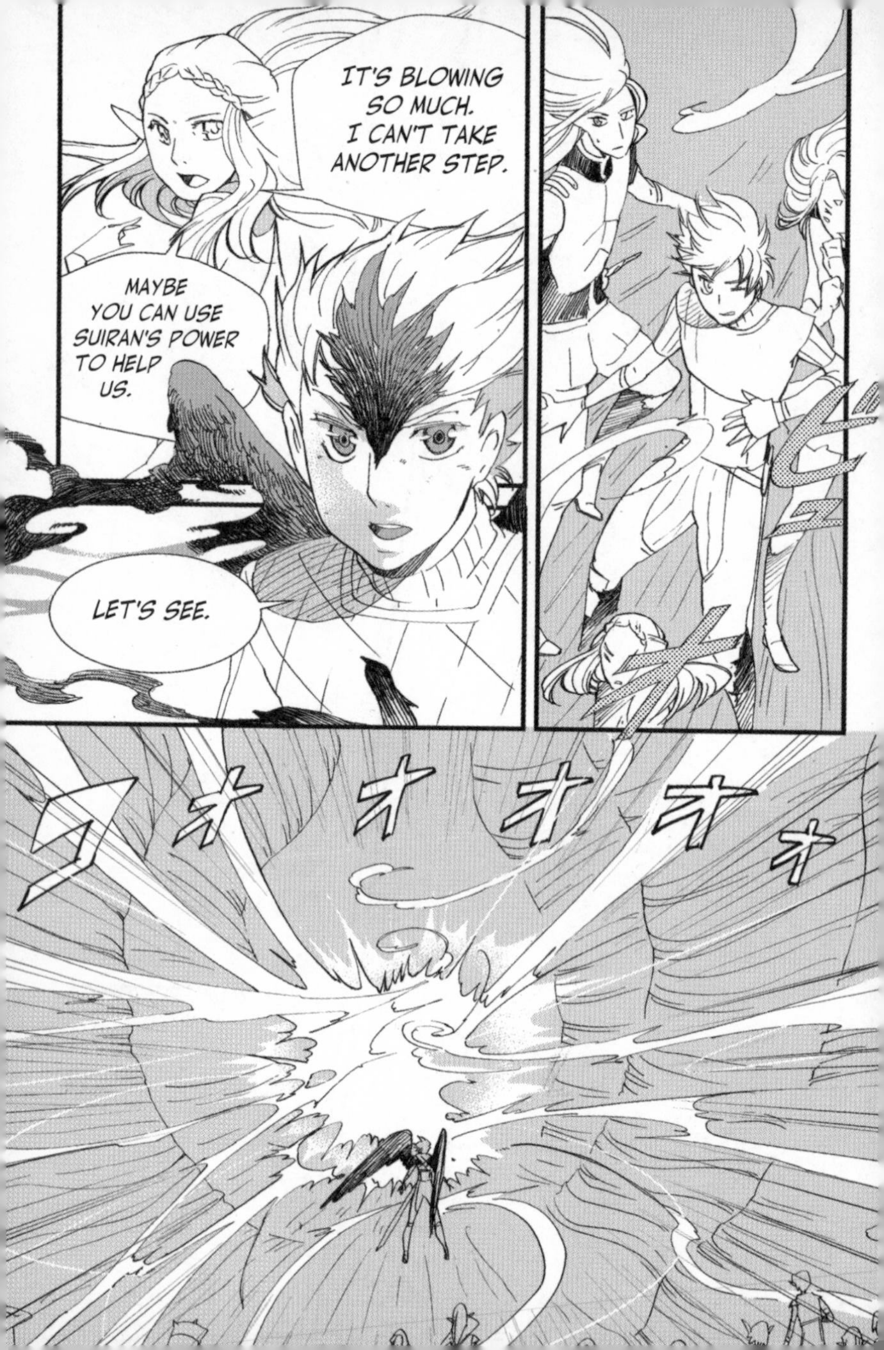
IT'S BLOWING SO MUCH. I CAN'T TAKE ANOTHER STEP.
MAYBE YOU CAN USE SUIRAN'S POWER TO HELP US.
LET'S SEE.
ウォオオオォ

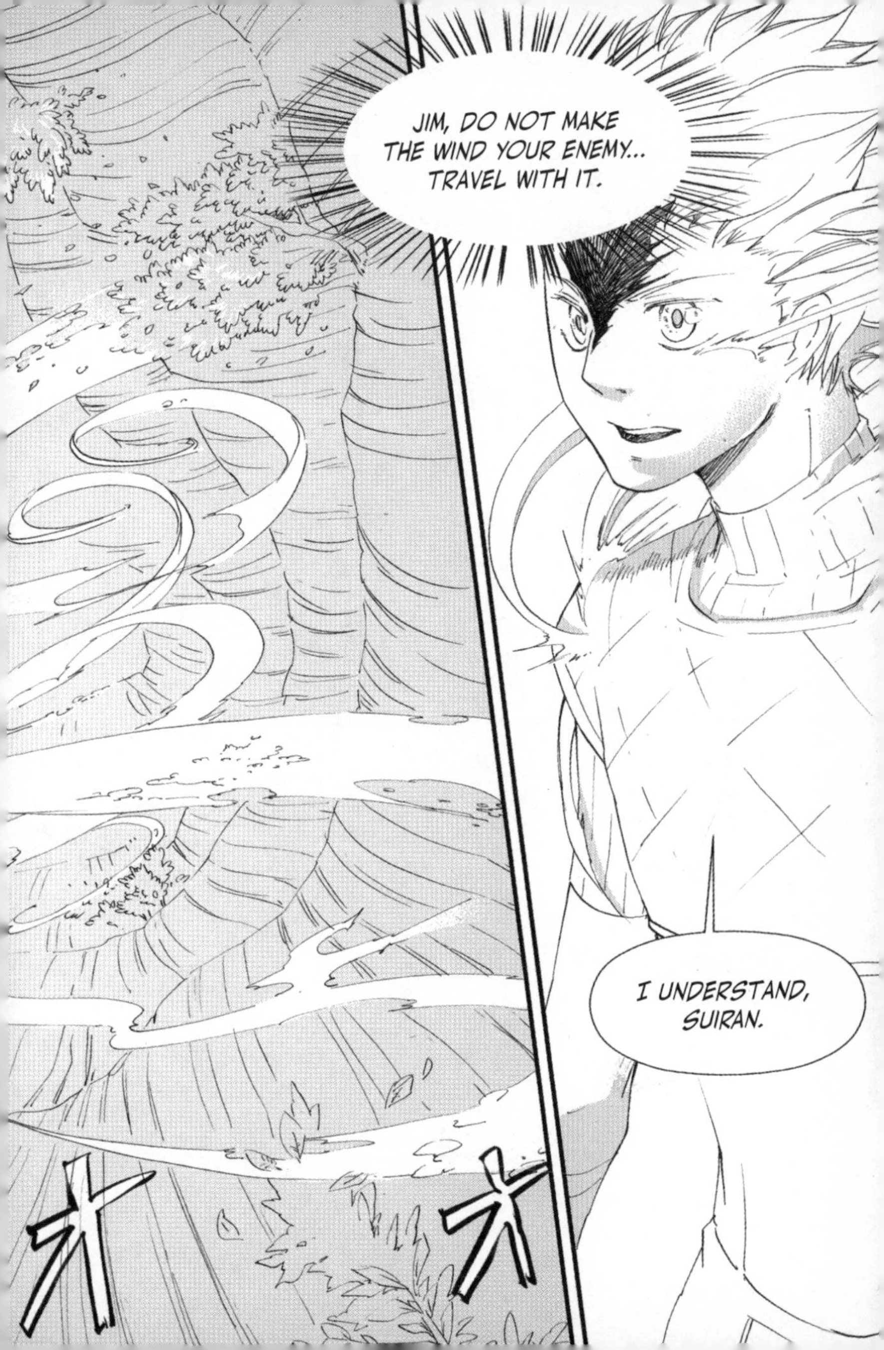
JIM, DO NOT MAKE THE WIND YOUR ENEMY... TRAVEL WITH IT.
I UNDERSTAND, SUIRAN.

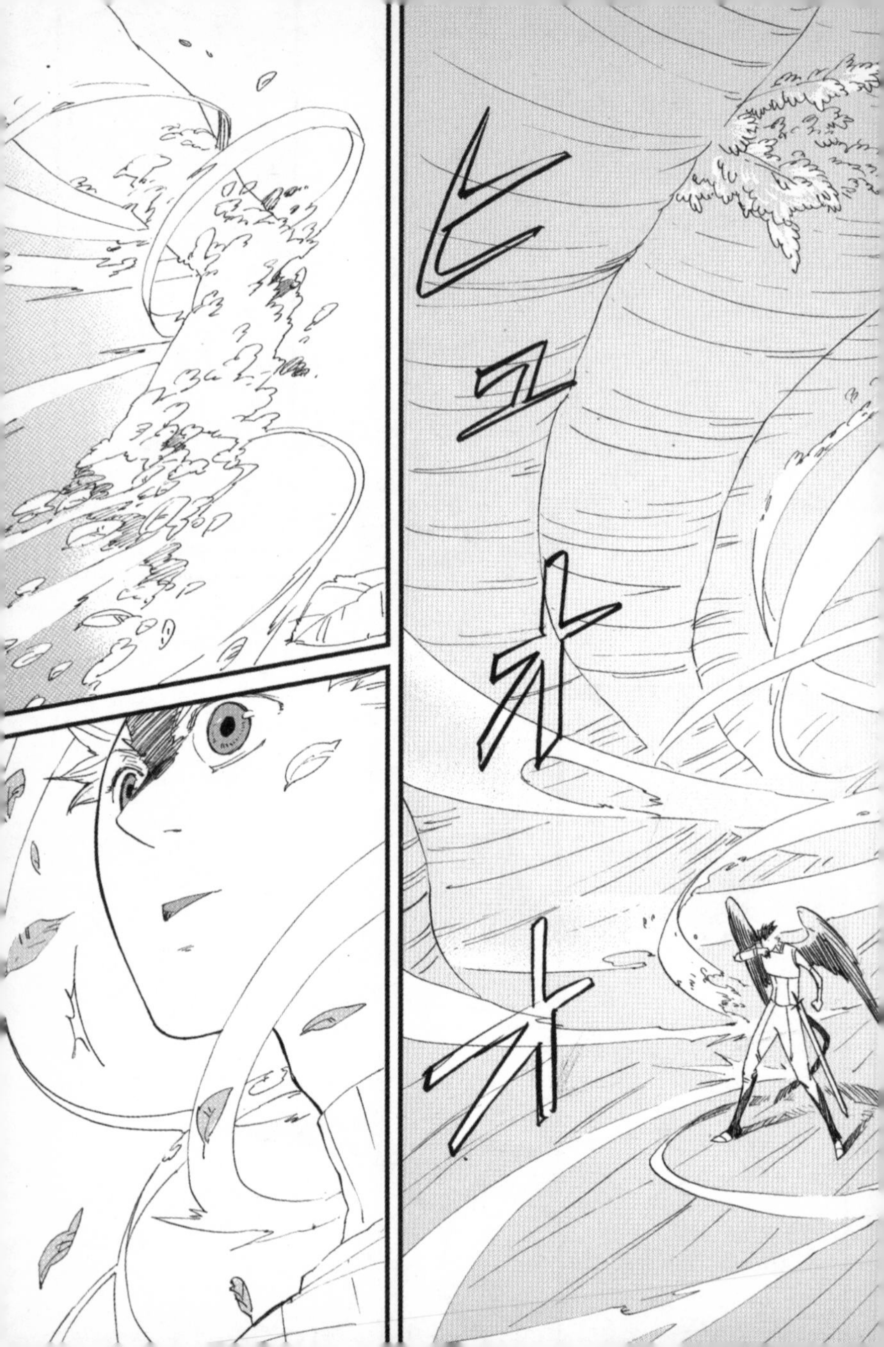
ヒュオオ

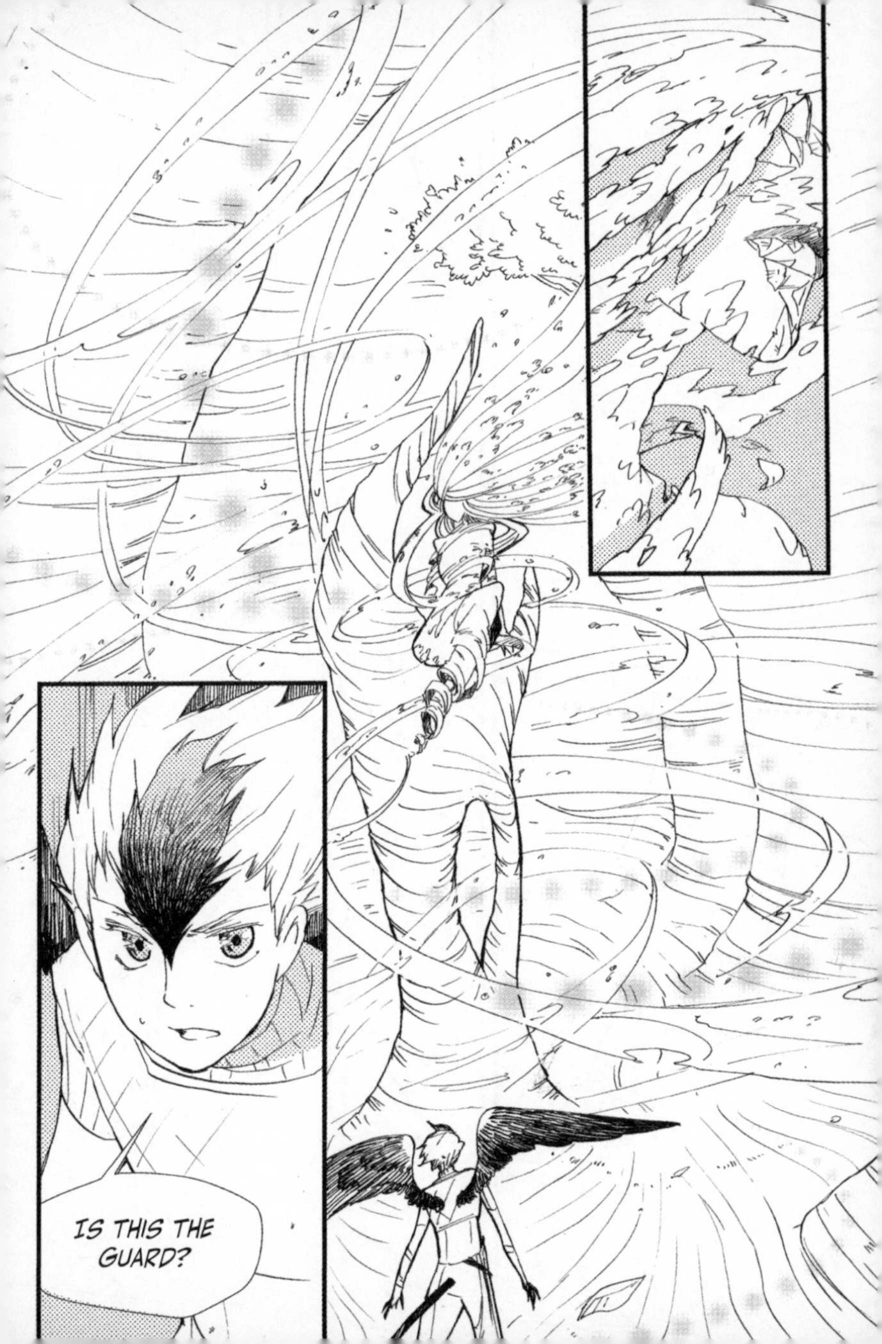
IS THIS THE GUARD?

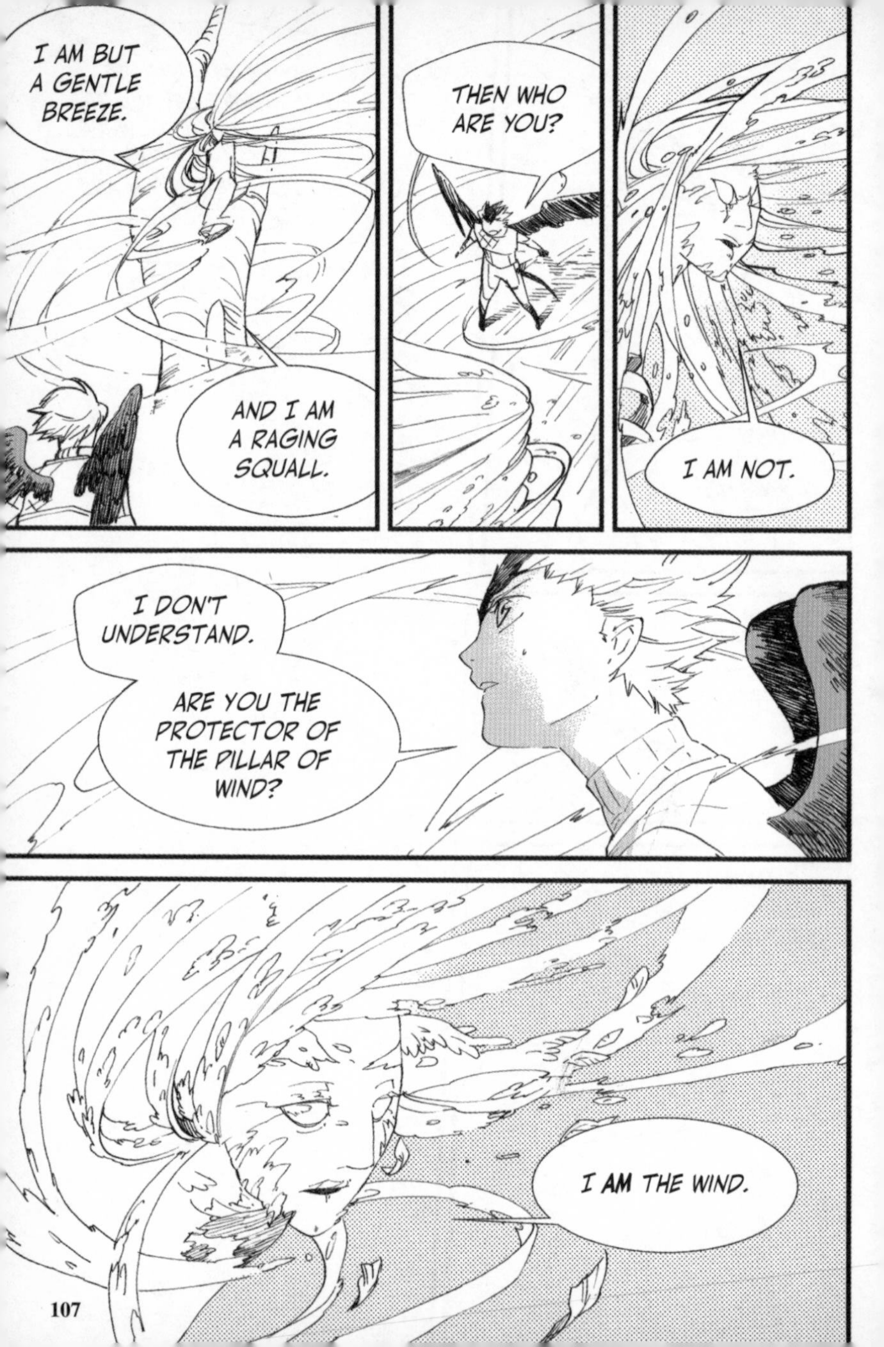
I AM NOT.
THEN WHO ARE YOU?
I AM BUT A GENTLE BREEZE.
AND I AM A RAGING SQUALL.
I DON'T UNDERSTAND.
ARE YOU THE PROTECTOR OF THE PILLAR OF WIND?
I AM THE WIND.

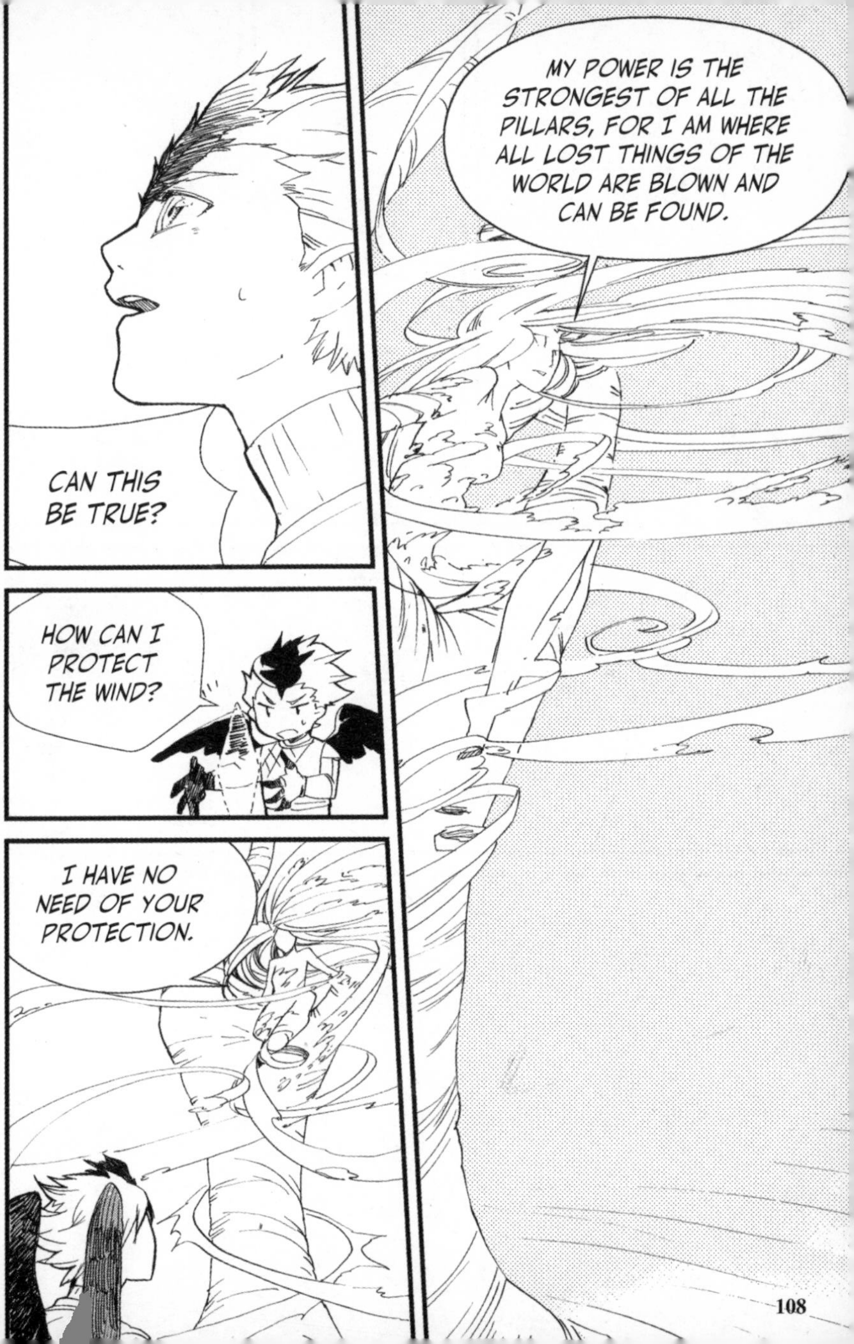
MY POWER IS THE STRONGEST OF ALL THE PILLARS, FOR I AM WHERE ALL LOST THINGS OF THE WORLD ARE BLOWN AND CAN BE FOUND.
CAN THIS BE TRUE?
HOW CAN I PROTECT THE WIND?
I HAVE NO NEED OF YOUR PROTECTION.

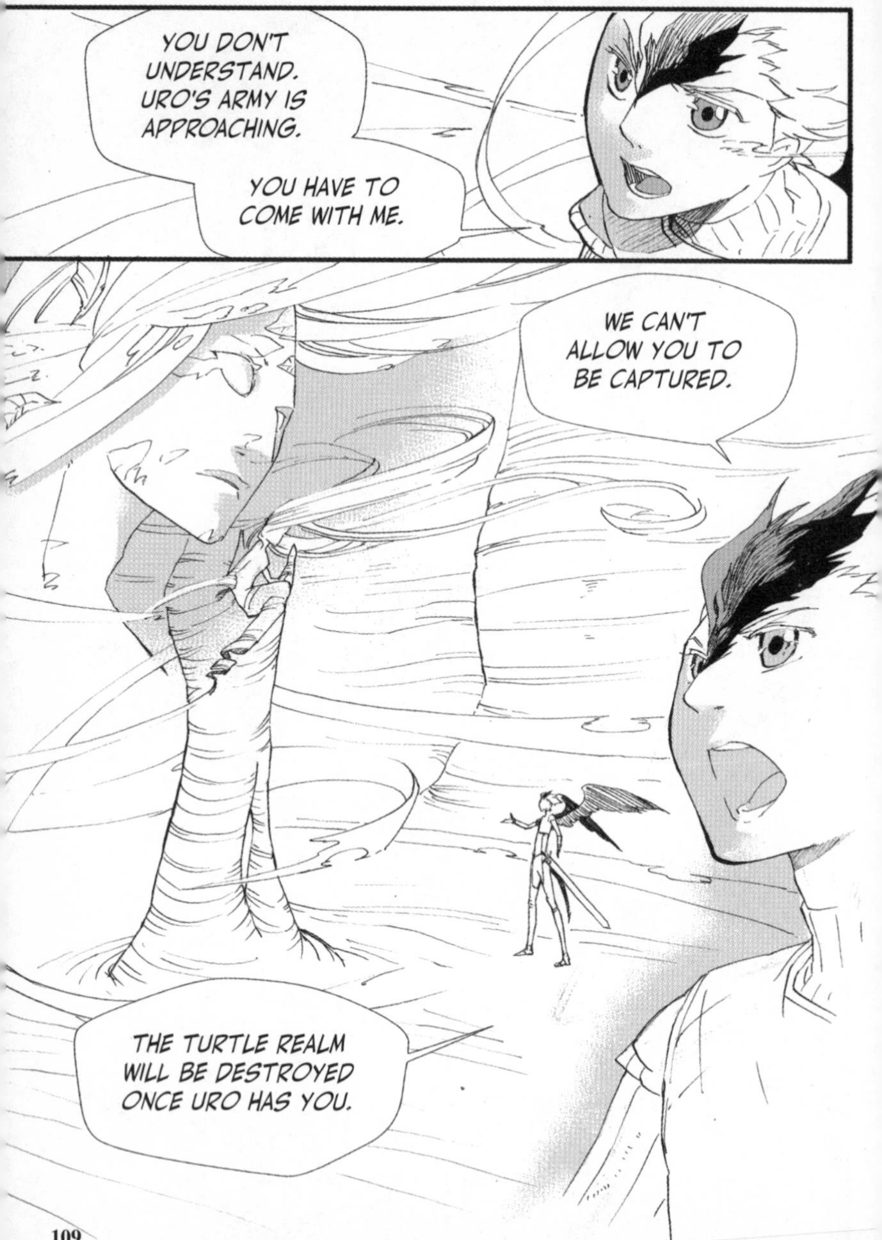
YOU DON'T UNDERSTAND. URO'S ARMY IS APPROACHING.
YOU HAVE TO COME WITH ME.
WE CAN'T ALLOW YOU TO BE CAPTURED.
THE TURTLE REALM WILL BE DESTROYED ONCE URO HAS YOU.

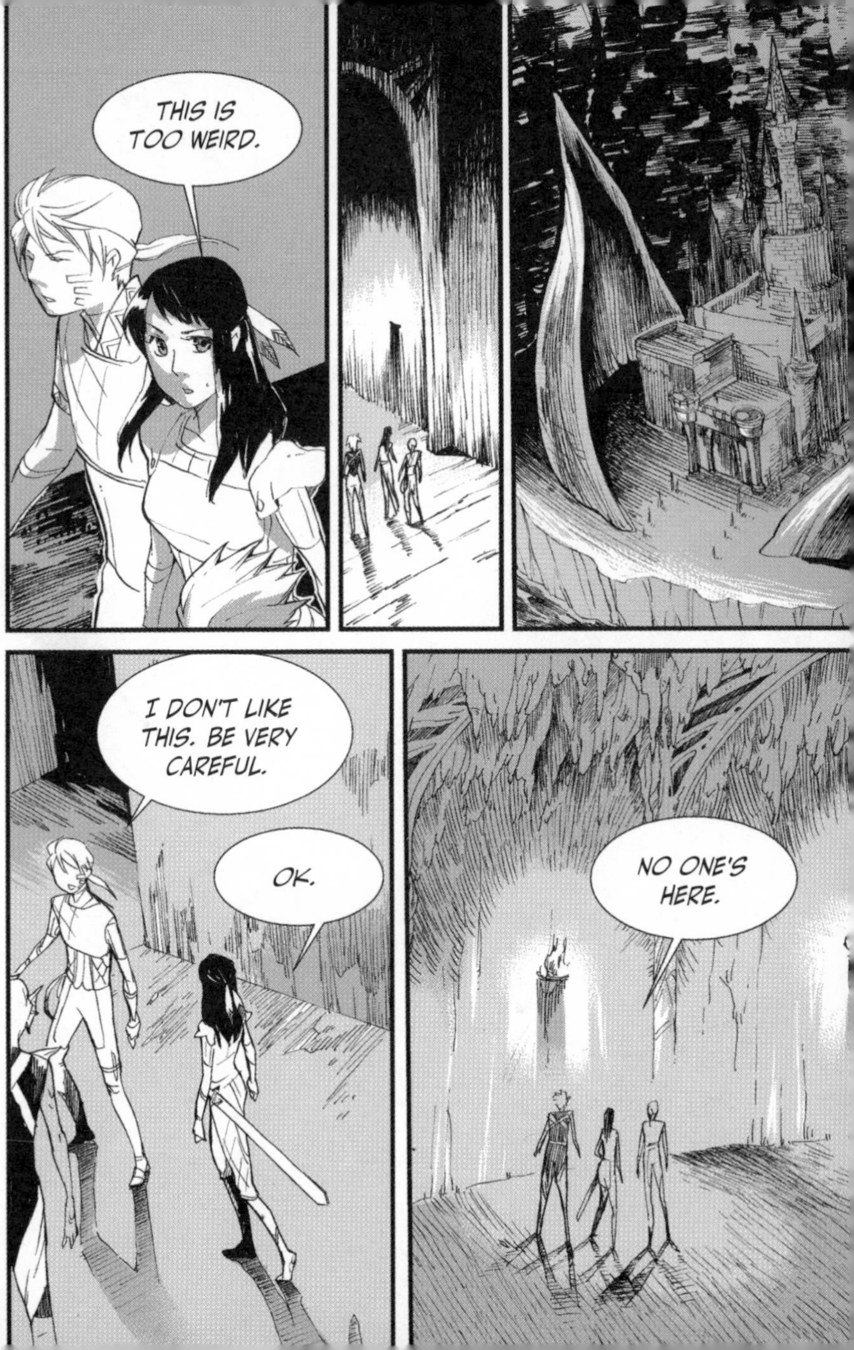
THIS IS TOO WEIRD.
NO ONE'S HERE.
I DON'T LIKE THIS. BE VERY CAREFUL.
OK.

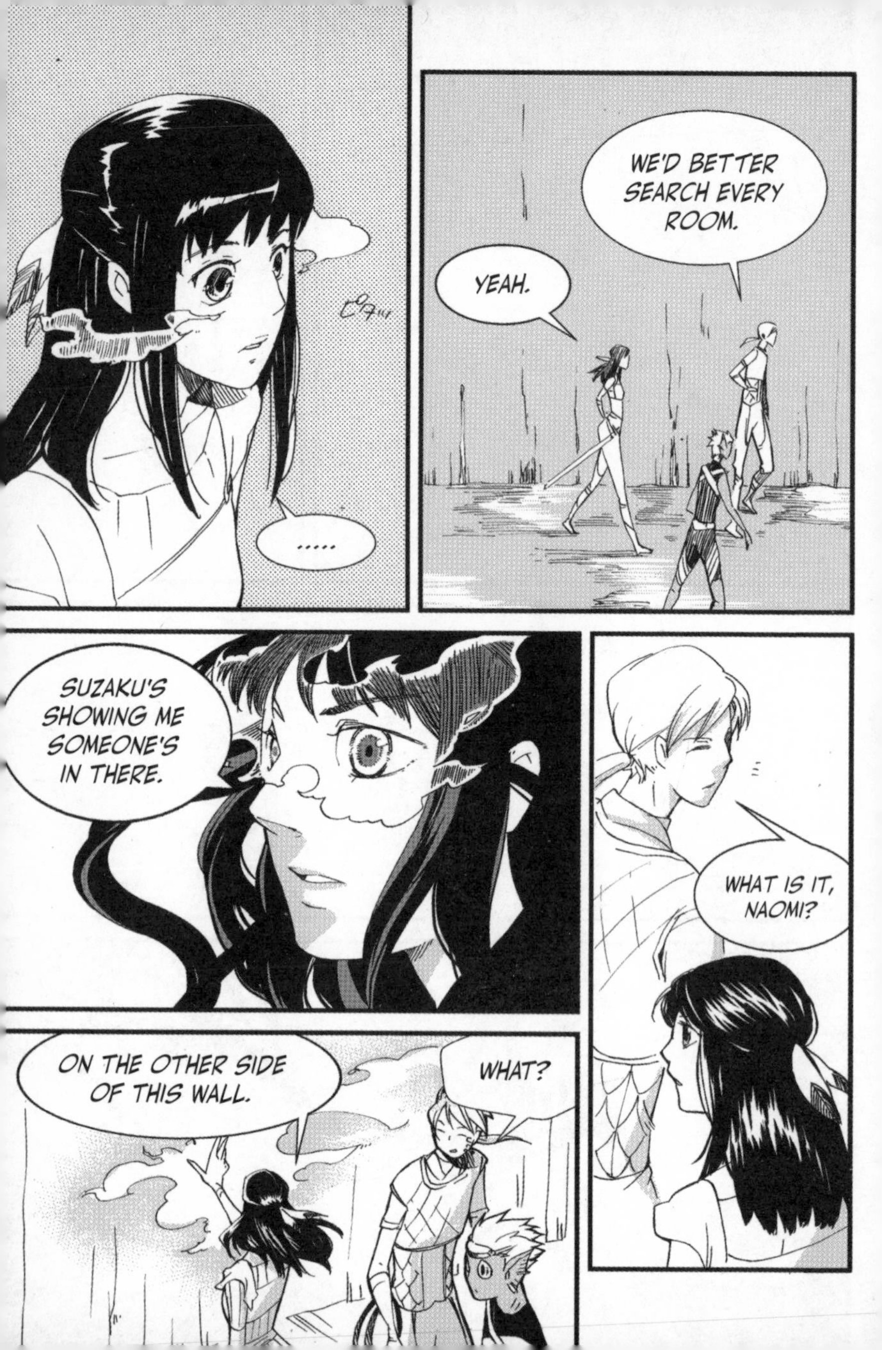
WE'D BETTER SEARCH EVERY ROOM.
YEAH.
......
WHAT IS IT, NAOMI?
SUZAKU'S SHOWING ME SOMEONE'S IN THERE.
WHAT?
ON THE OTHER SIDE OF THIS WALL.

THERE'S A GROUP OF PEOPLE HUDDLED TOGETHER.

MOVE BACK.

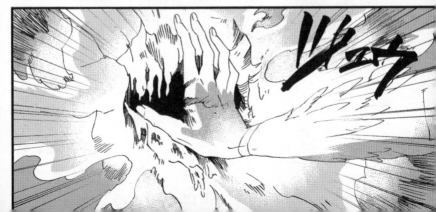

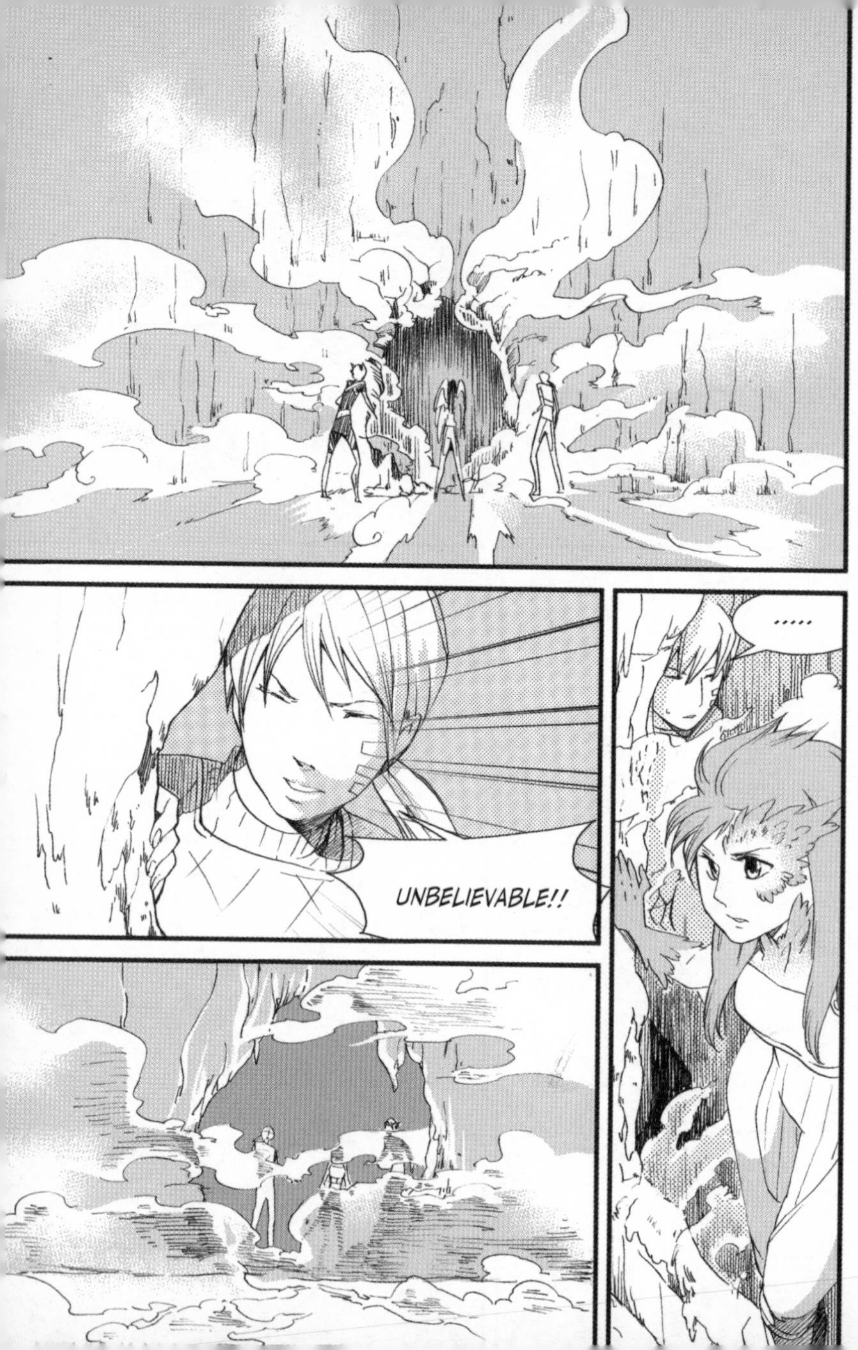
......
UNBELIEVABLE!!

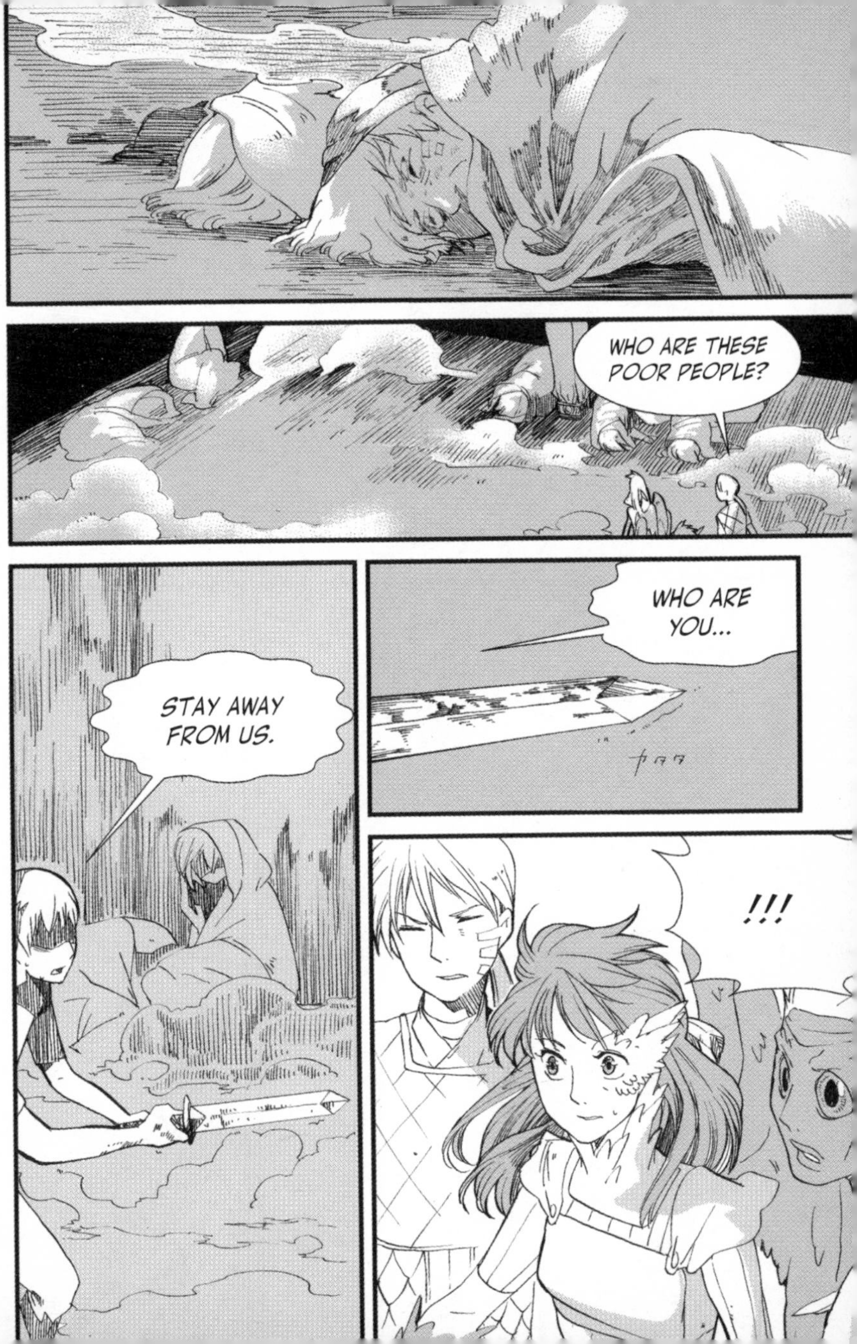
WHO ARE THESE POOR PEOPLE?
WHO ARE YOU...
!!!
STAY AWAY FROM US.

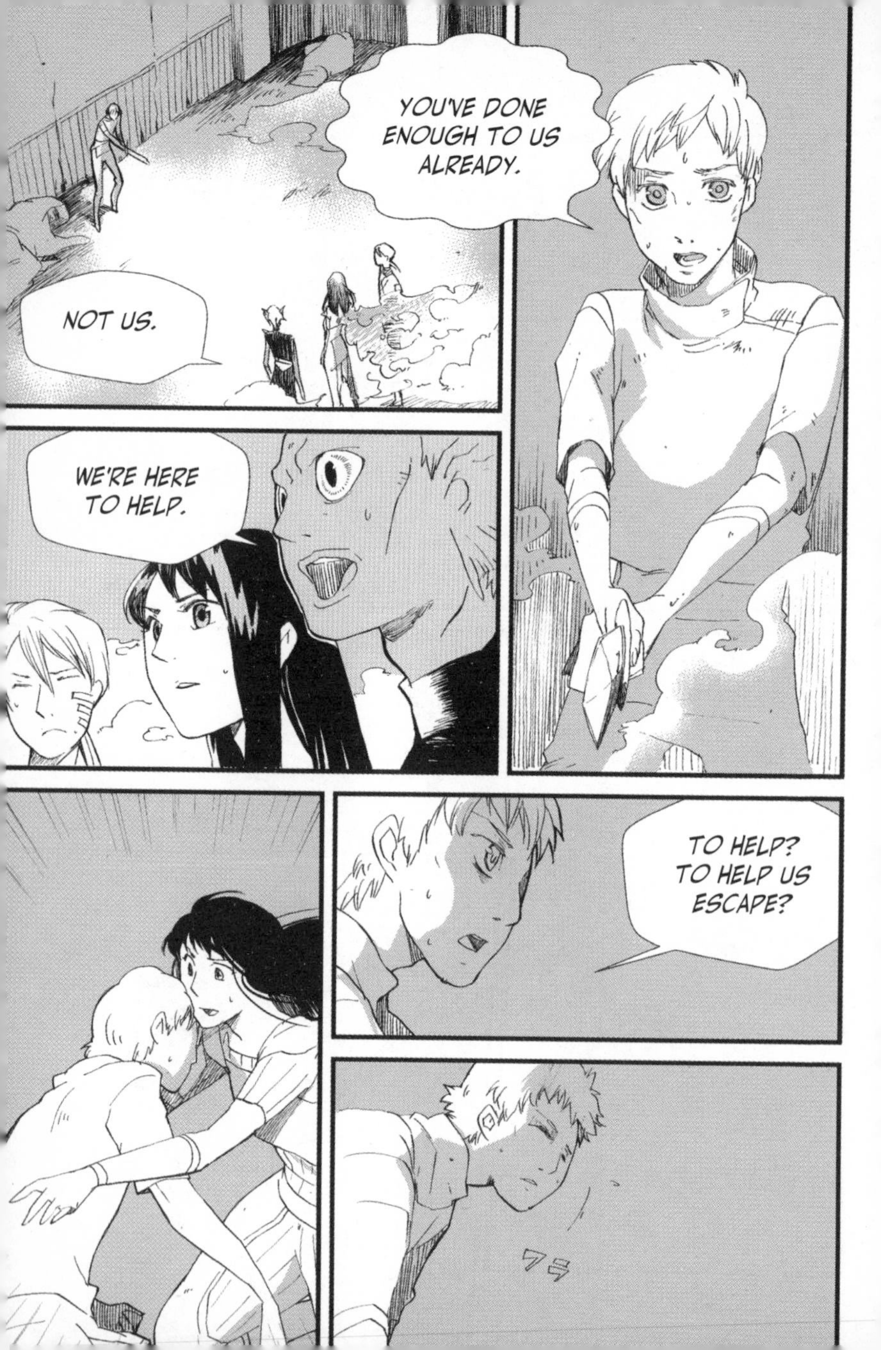
YOU'VE DONE ENOUGH TO US ALREADY.
NOT US.
WE'RE HERE TO HELP.
TO HELP? TO HELP US ESCAPE?
フラ

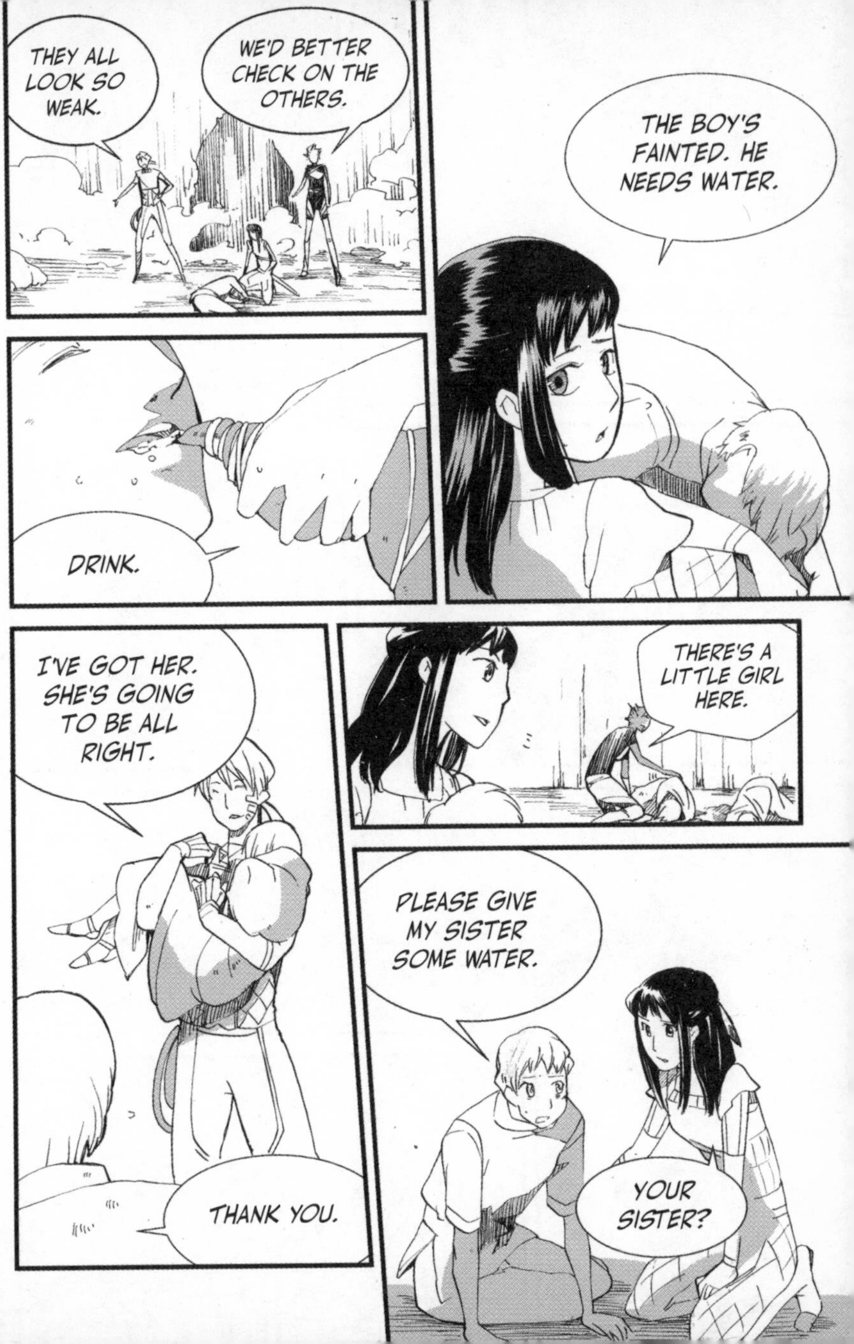
THE BOY'S FAINTED. HE NEEDS WATER.
WE'D BETTER CHECK ON THE OTHERS.
THEY ALL LOOK SO WEAK.
DRINK.
THERE'S A LITTLE GIRL HERE.
PLEASE GIVE MY SISTER SOME WATER.
YOUR SISTER?
I'VE GOT HER. SHE'S GOING TO BE ALL RIGHT.
THANK YOU.

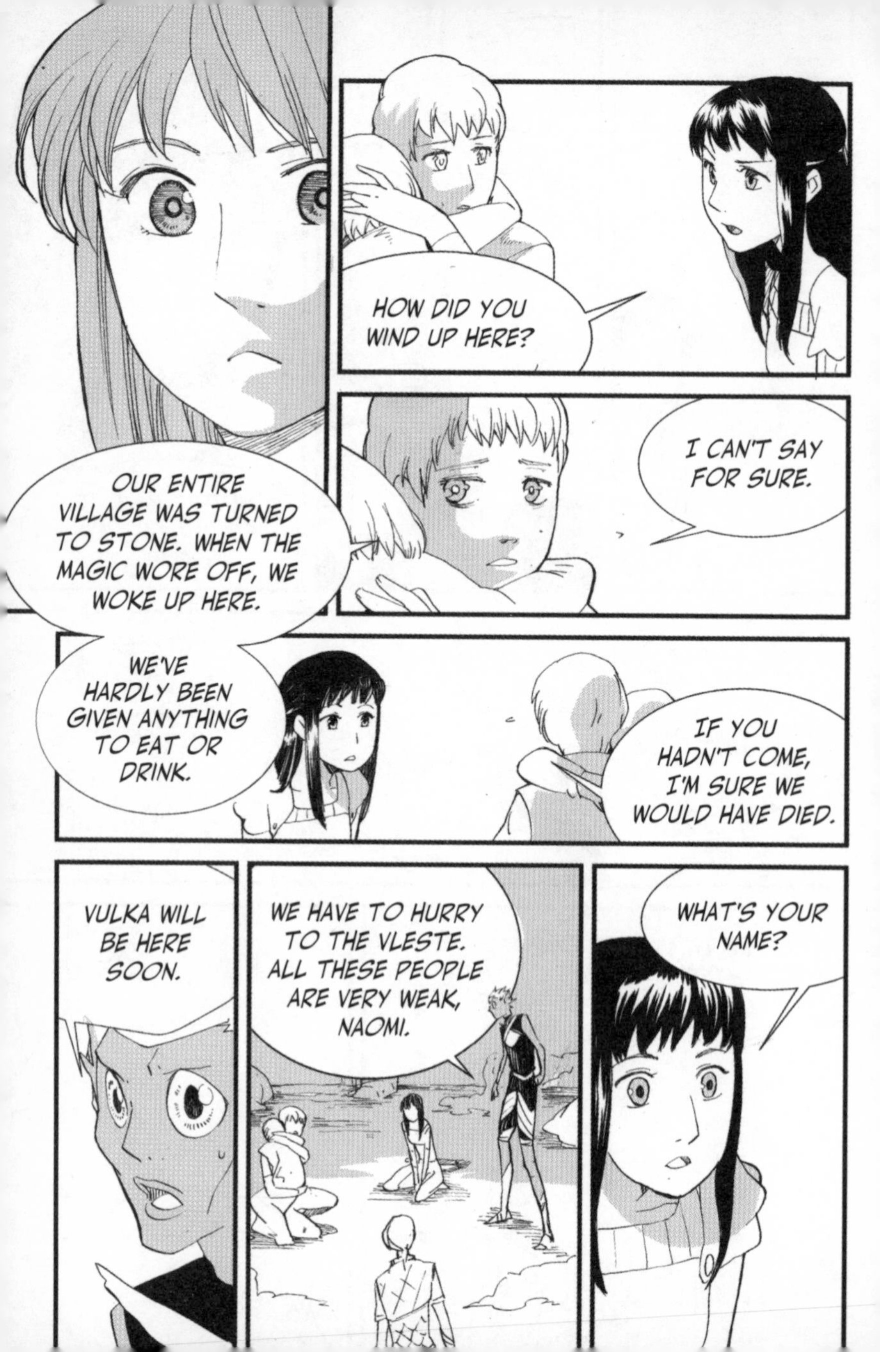
HOW DID YOU WIND UP HERE?
I CAN'T SAY FOR SURE.
OUR ENTIRE VILLAGE WAS TURNED TO STONE. WHEN THE MAGIC WORE OFF, WE WOKE UP HERE.
WE'VE HARDLY BEEN GIVEN ANYTHING TO EAT OR DRINK.
IF YOU HADN'T COME, I'M SURE WE WOULD HAVE DIED.
WHAT'S YOUR NAME?
WE HAVE TO HURRY TO THE VLESTE. ALL THESE PEOPLE ARE VERY WEAK, NAOMI.
VULKA WILL BE HERE SOON.

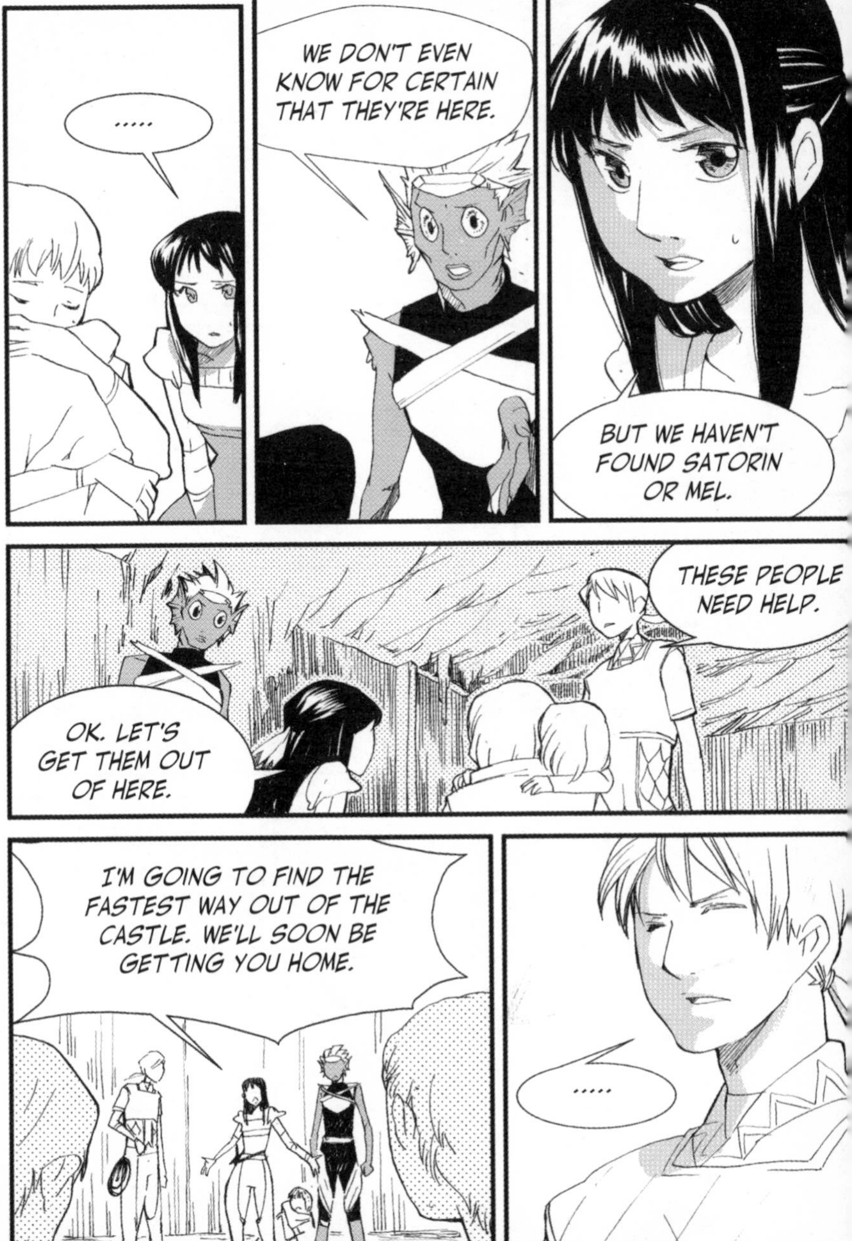
BUT WE HAVEN'T FOUND SATORIN OR MEL.
WE DON'T EVEN KNOW FOR CERTAIN THAT THEY'RE HERE.
.....
THESE PEOPLE NEED HELP.
OK. LET'S GET THEM OUT OF HERE.
.....
I'M GOING TO FIND THE FASTEST WAY OUT OF THE CASTLE. WE'LL SOON BE GETTING YOU HOME.

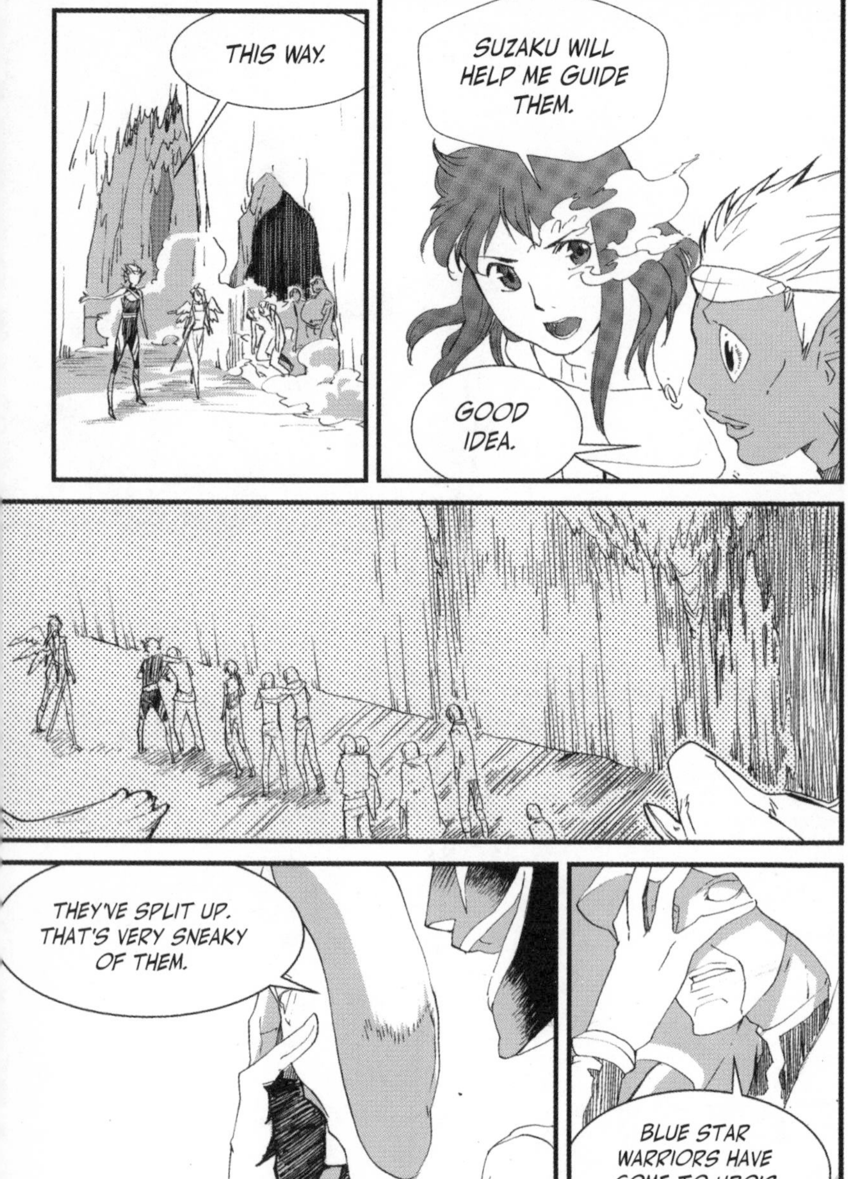
SUZAKU WILL HELP ME GUIDE THEM.
GOOD IDEA.
THIS WAY.
BLUE STAR WARRIORS HAVE COME TO URO'S CASTLE.
THEY'VE SPLIT UP. THAT'S VERY SNEAKY OF THEM.

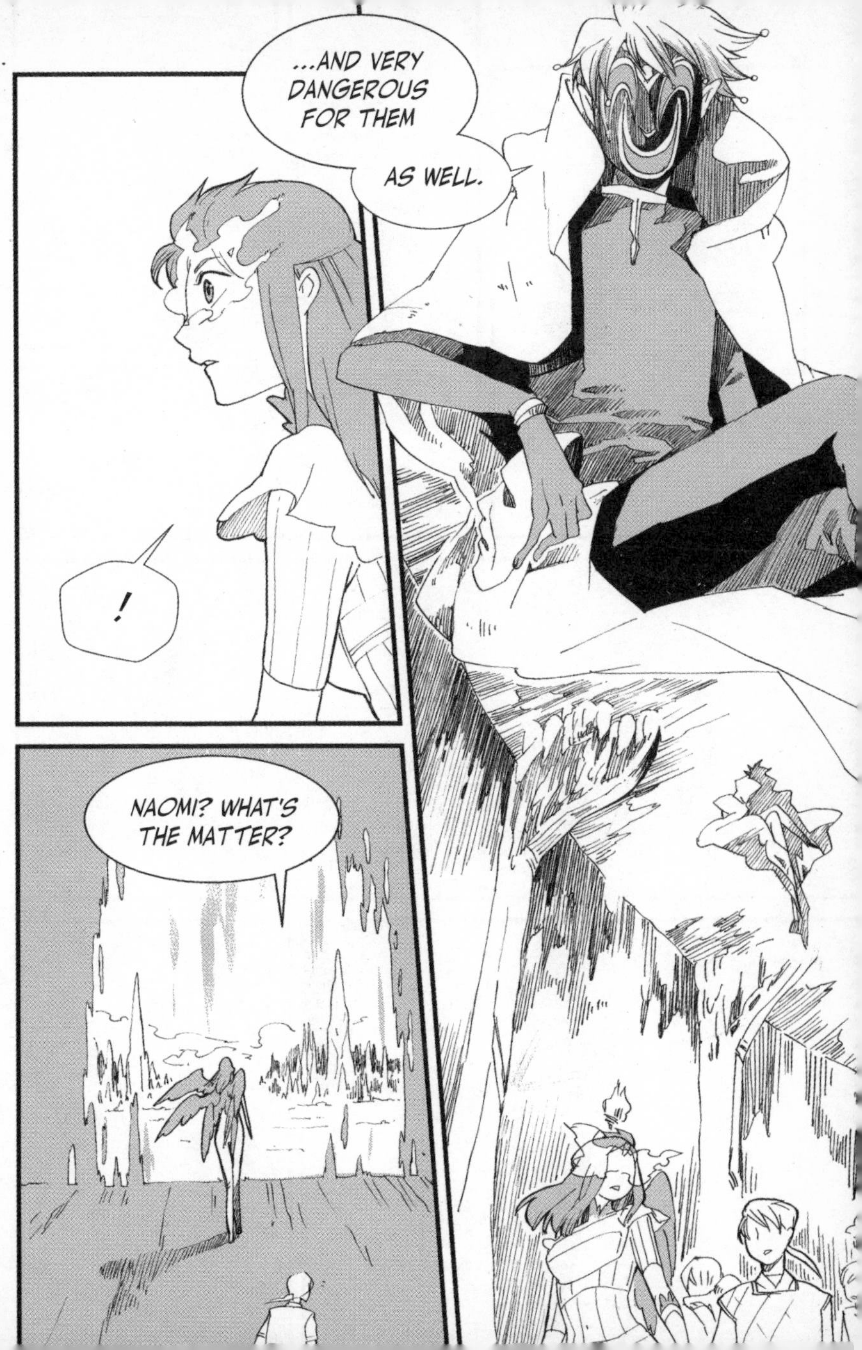
...AND VERY DANGEROUS FOR THEM
AS WELL.
!
NAOMI? WHAT'S THE MATTER?

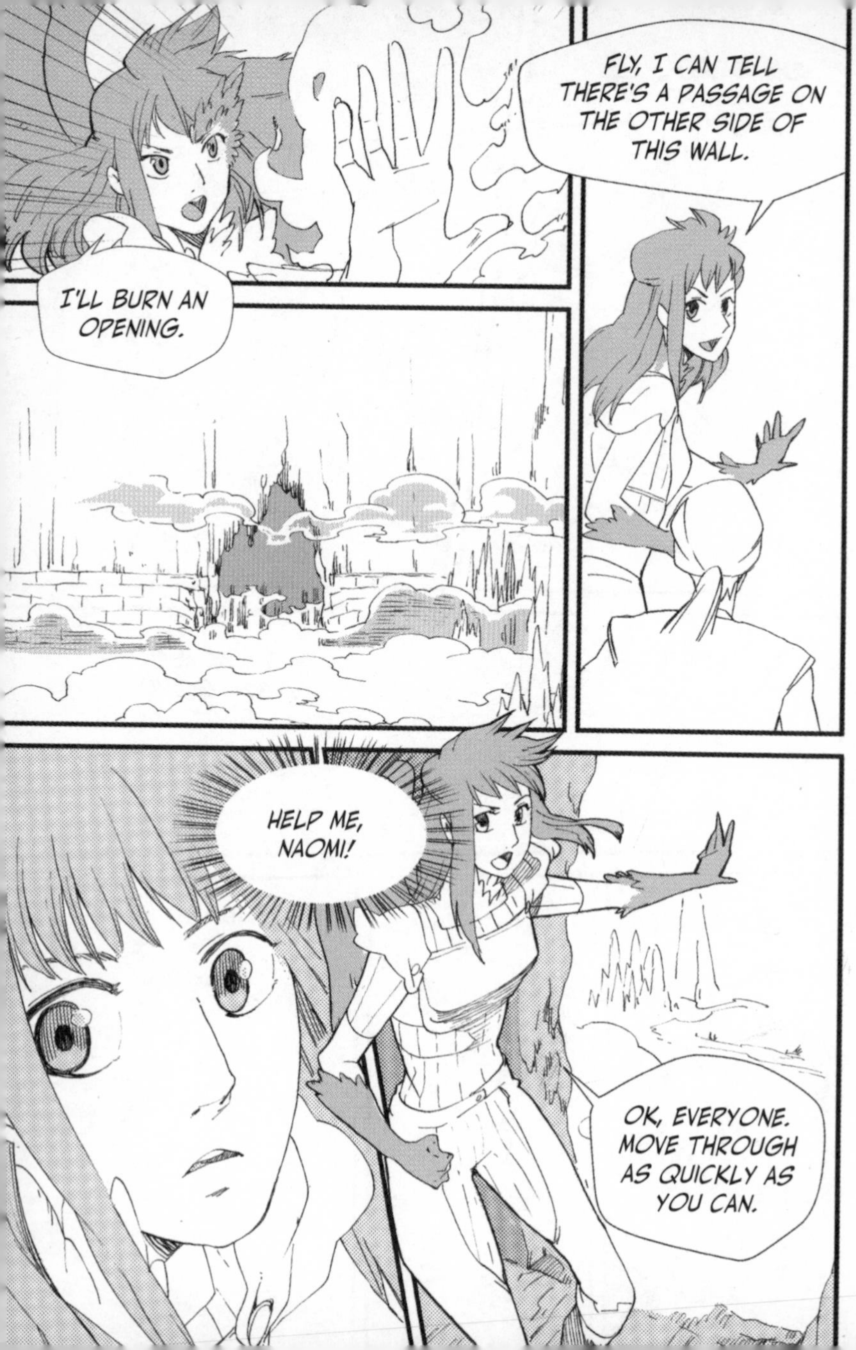
FLY, I CAN TELL THERE'S A PASSAGE ON THE OTHER SIDE OF THIS WALL.
I'LL BURN AN OPENING.
HELP ME, NAOMI!
OK, EVERYONE. MOVE THROUGH AS QUICKLY AS YOU CAN.

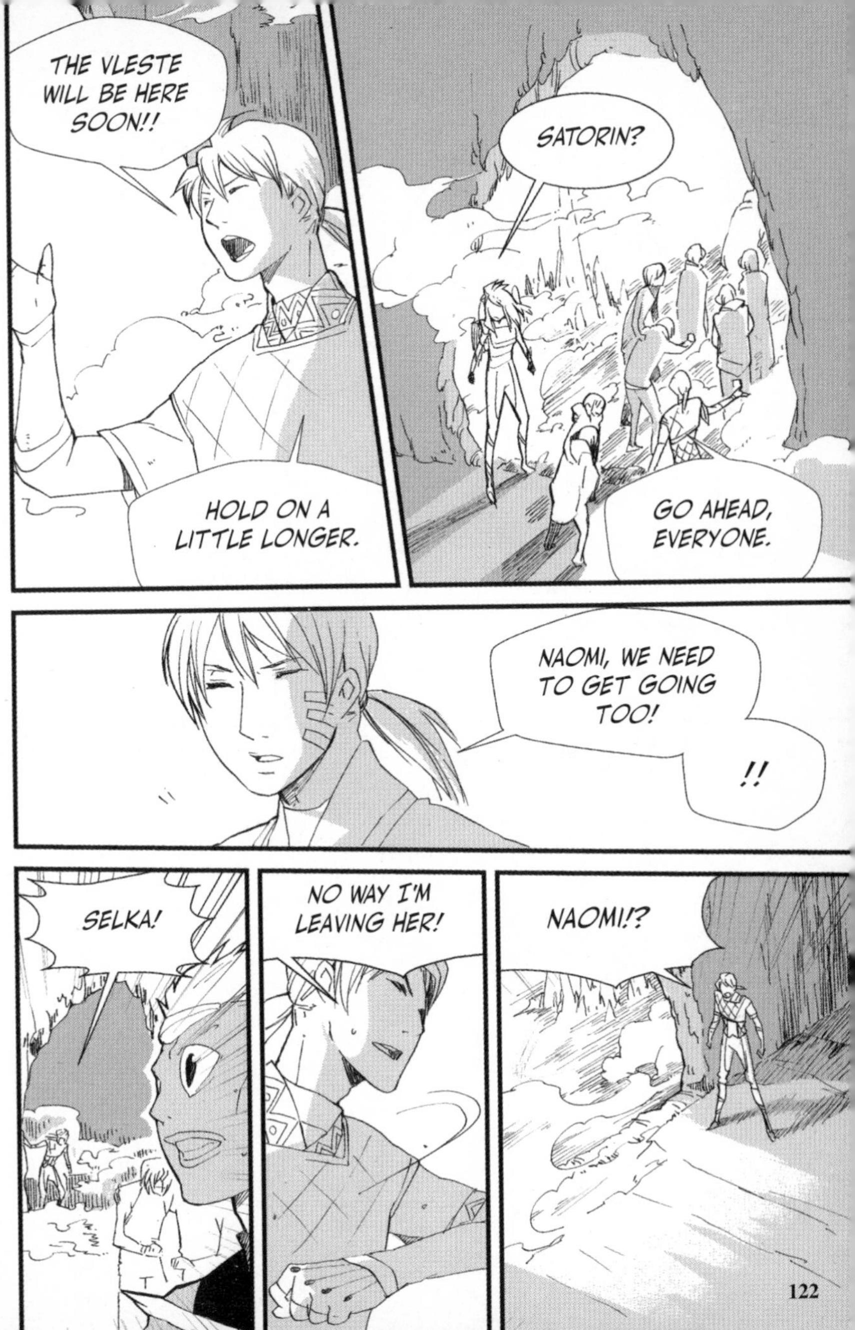
SATORIN?
GO AHEAD, EVERYONE.
THE VLESTE WILL BE HERE SOON!!
HOLD ON A LITTLE LONGER.
NAOMI, WE NEED TO GET GOING TOO!
!!
NAOMI!?
NO WAY I'M LEAVING HER!
SELKA!

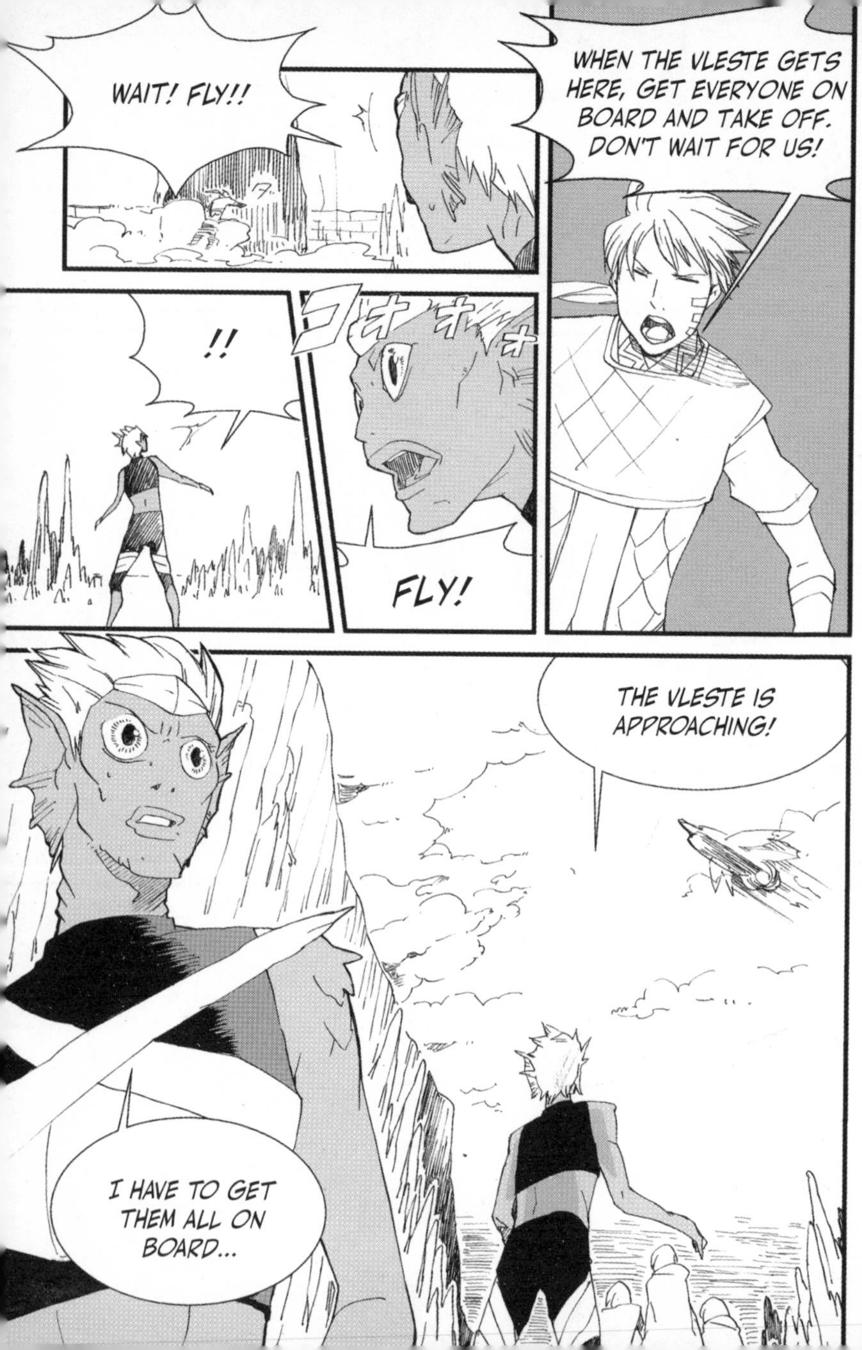
WHEN THE VLESTE GETS HERE, GET EVERYONE ON BOARD AND TAKE OFF. DON'T WAIT FOR US!
WAIT! FLY!!
FLY!
!!
THE VLESTE IS APPROACHING!
I HAVE TO GET THEM ALL ON BOARD...

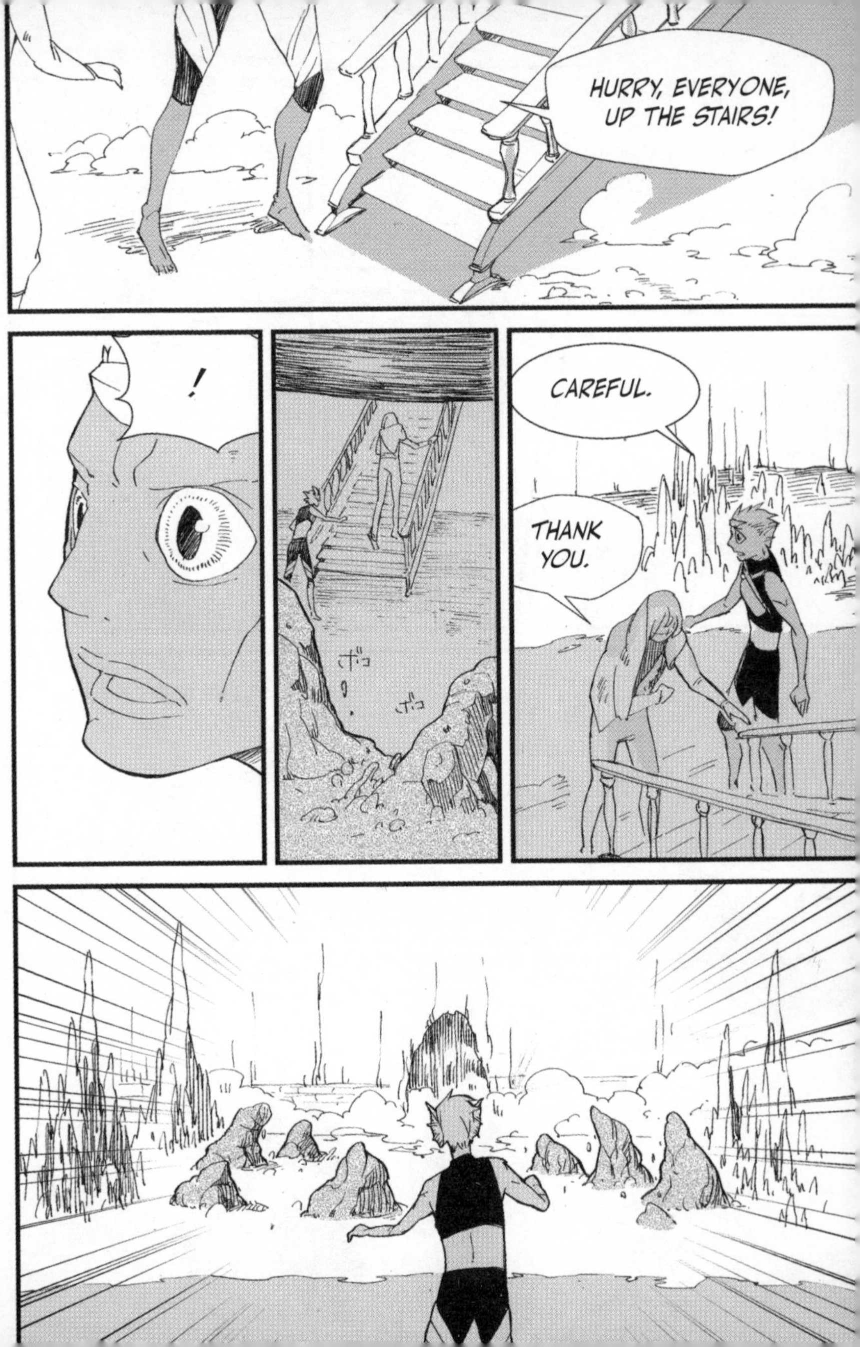
HURRY, EVERYONE, UP THE STAIRS!
CAREFUL.
THANK YOU.
!

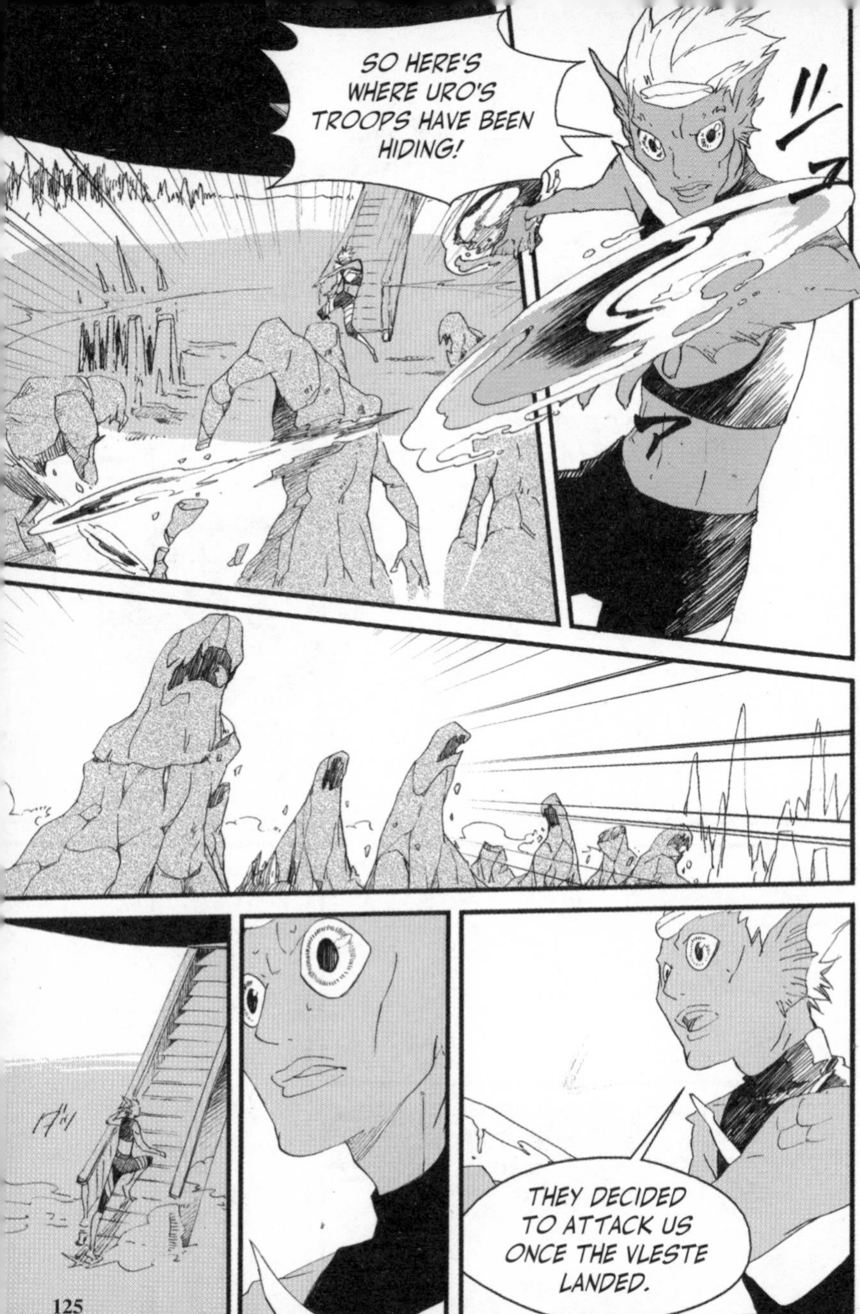
SO HERE'S WHERE URO'S TROOPS HAVE BEEN HIDING!
THEY DECIDED TO ATTACK US ONCE THE VLESTE LANDED.

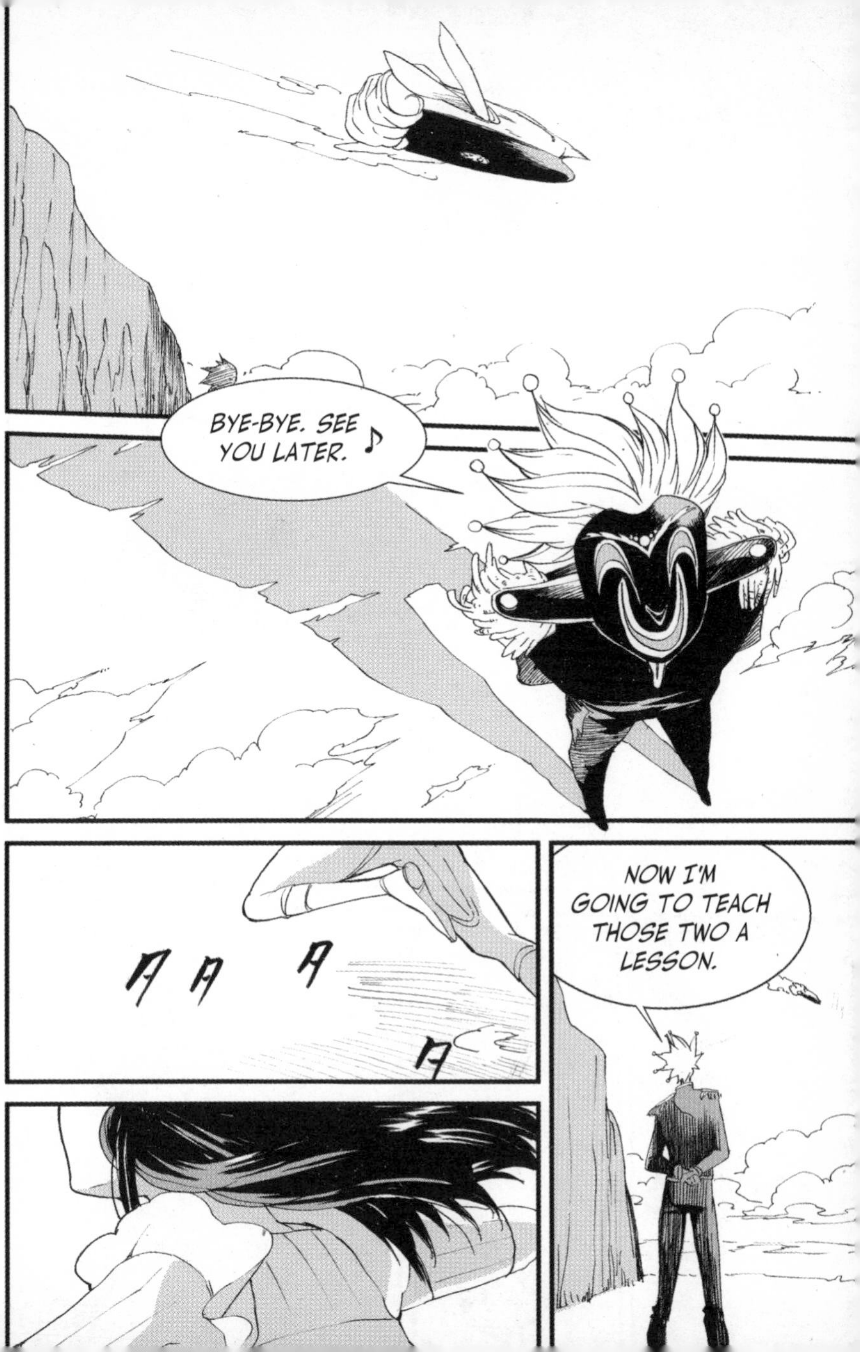

BYE-BYE. SEE YOU LATER. ♪
NOW I'M GOING TO TEACH THOSE TWO A LESSON.
A A A
A

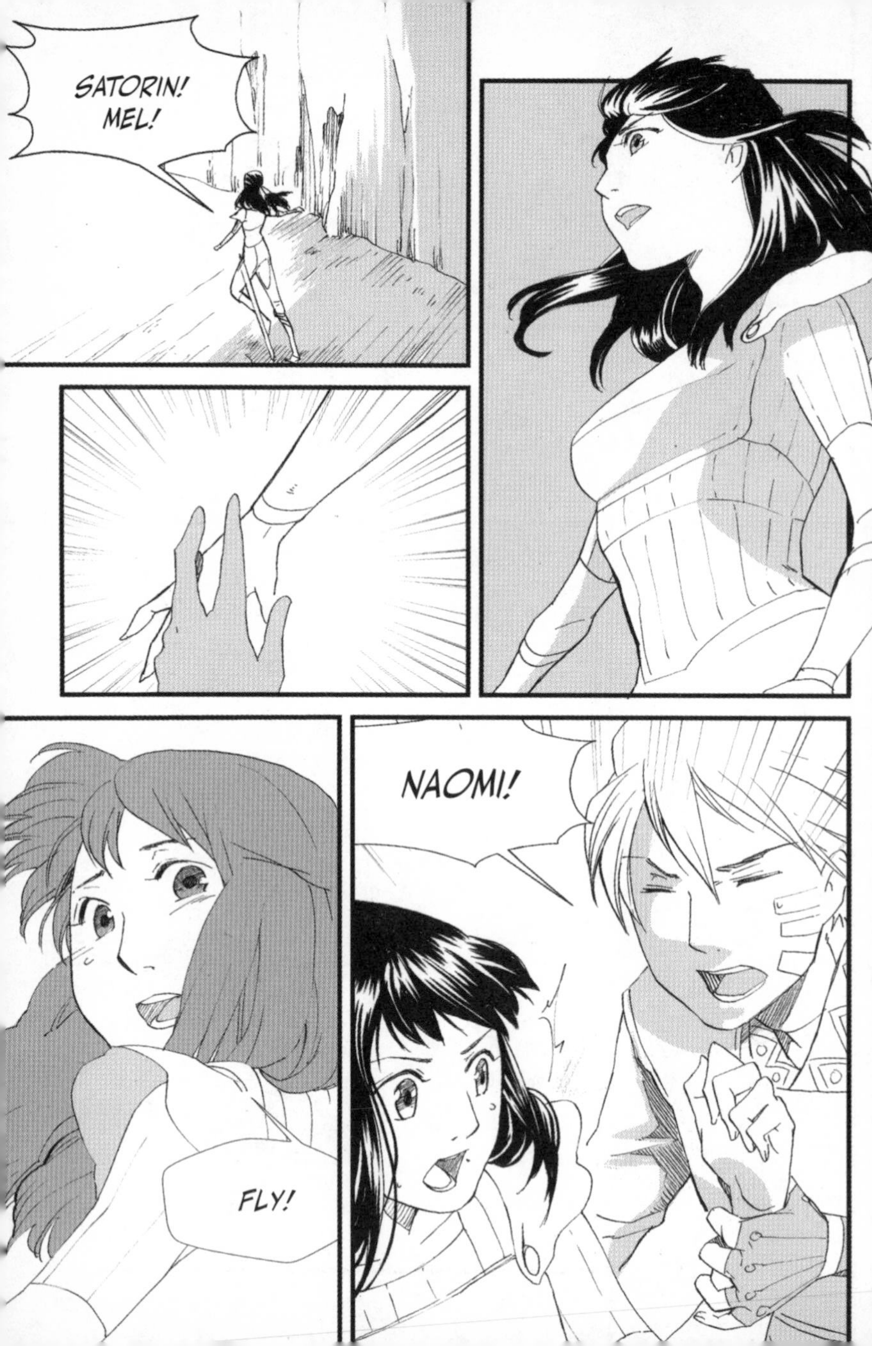
SATORIN! MEL!
NAOMI!
FLY!

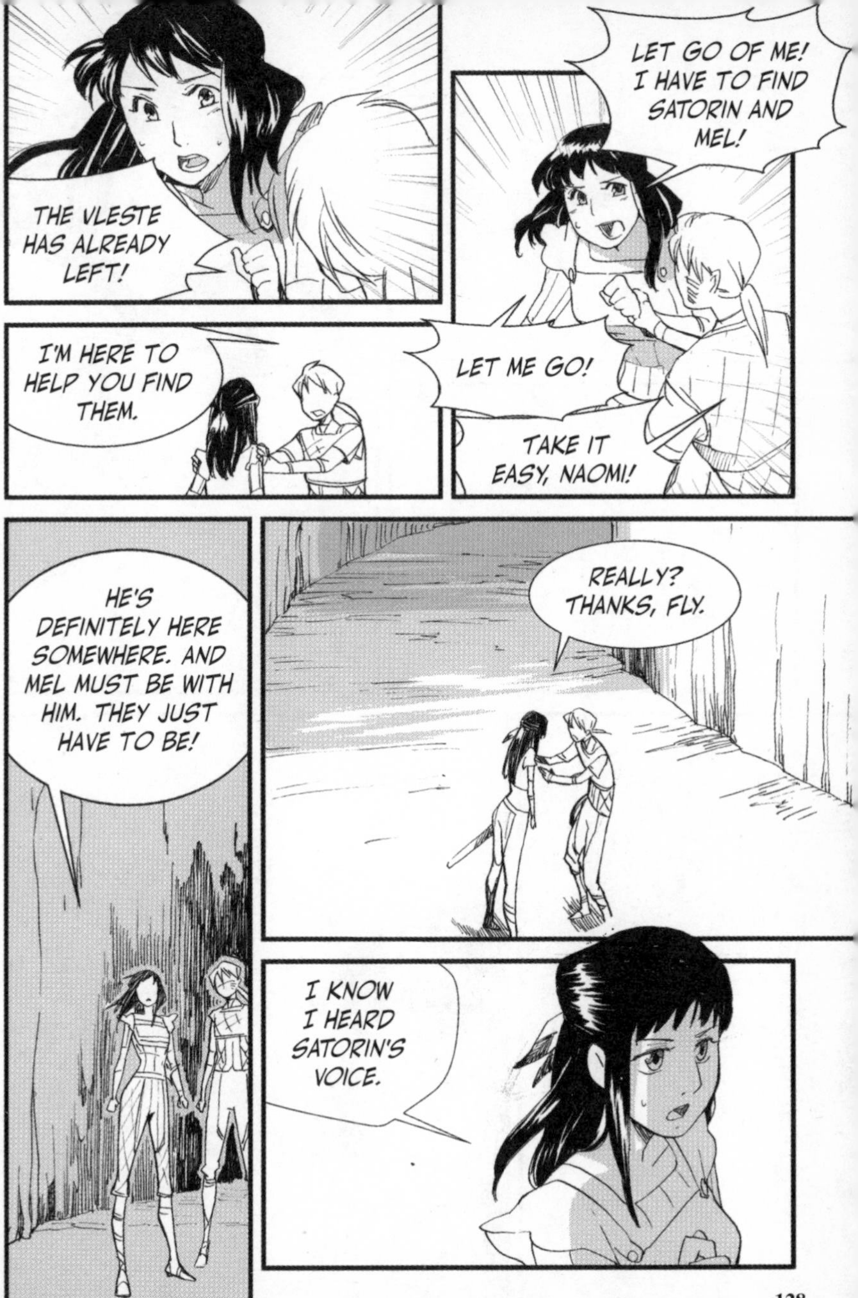
LET GO OF ME! I HAVE TO FIND SATORIN AND MEL!
LET ME GO!
TAKE IT EASY, NAOMI!
THE VLESTE HAS ALREADY LEFT!
I'M HERE TO HELP YOU FIND THEM.
REALLY? THANKS, FLY.
I KNOW I HEARD SATORIN'S VOICE.
HE'S DEFINITELY HERE SOMEWHERE. AND MEL MUST BE WITH HIM. THEY JUST HAVE TO BE!

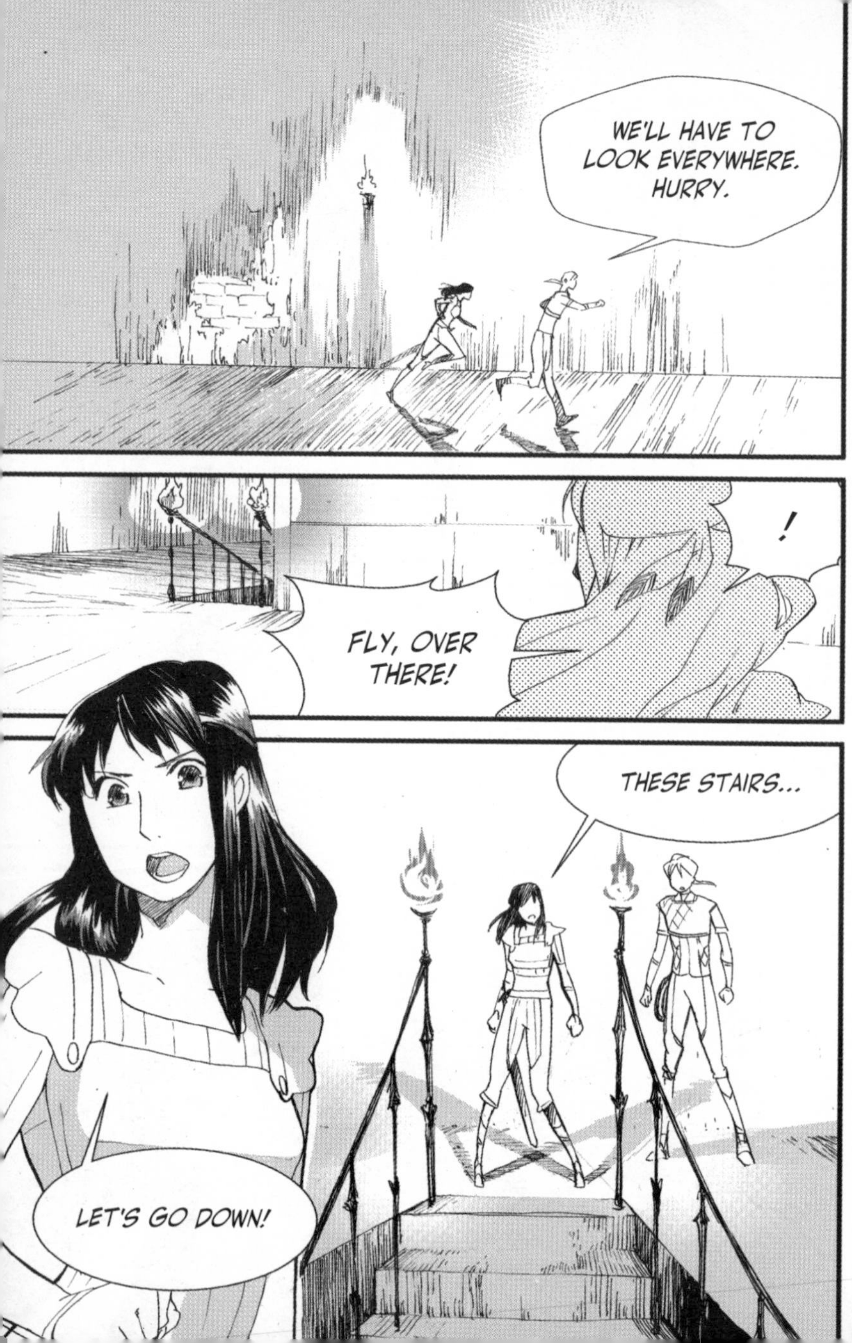
WE'LL HAVE TO LOOK EVERYWHERE. HURRY.
!
FLY, OVER THERE!
THESE STAIRS...
LET'S GO DOWN!

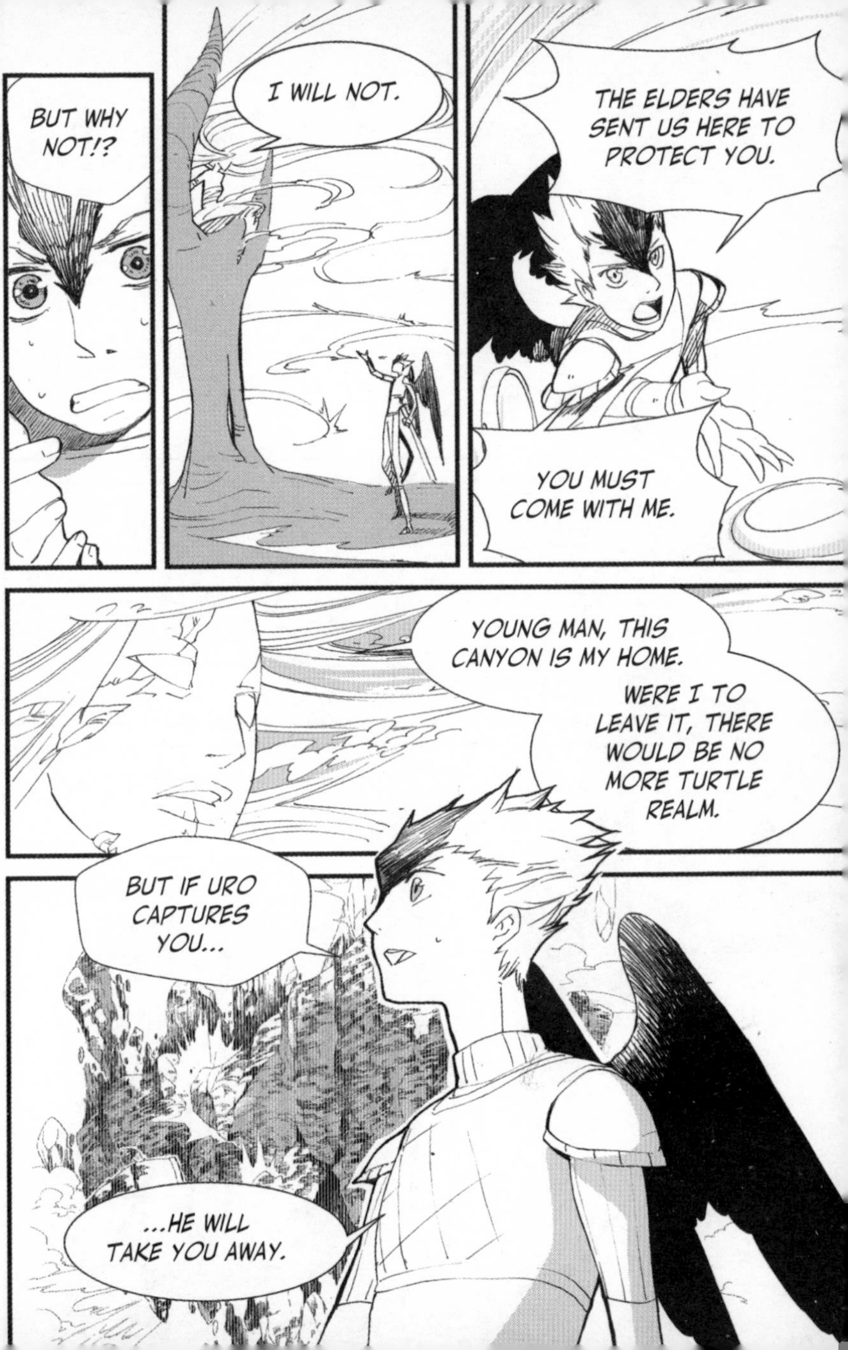
THE ELDERS HAVE SENT US HERE TO PROTECT YOU.
YOU MUST COME WITH ME.
I WILL NOT.
BUT WHY NOT!?
YOUNG MAN, THIS CANYON IS MY HOME.
WERE I TO LEAVE IT, THERE WOULD BE NO MORE TURTLE REALM.
BUT IF URO CAPTURES YOU...
...HE WILL TAKE YOU AWAY.

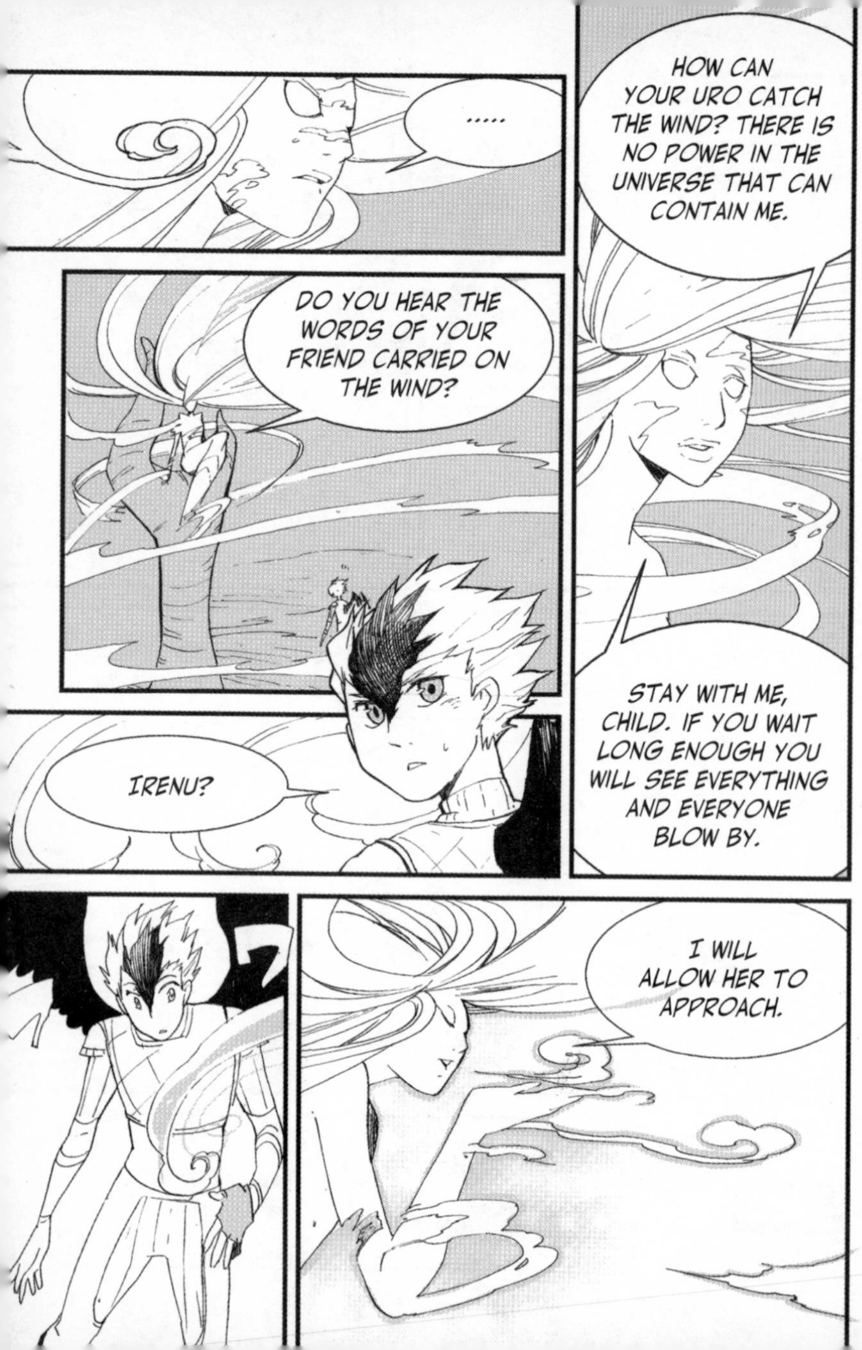
HOW CAN YOUR URO CATCH THE WIND? THERE IS NO POWER IN THE UNIVERSE THAT CAN CONTAIN ME.
STAY WITH ME, CHILD. IF YOU WAIT LONG ENOUGH YOU WILL SEE EVERYTHING AND EVERYONE BLOW BY.
......
DO YOU HEAR THE WORDS OF YOUR FRIEND CARRIED ON THE WIND?
IRENU?
I WILL ALLOW HER TO APPROACH.

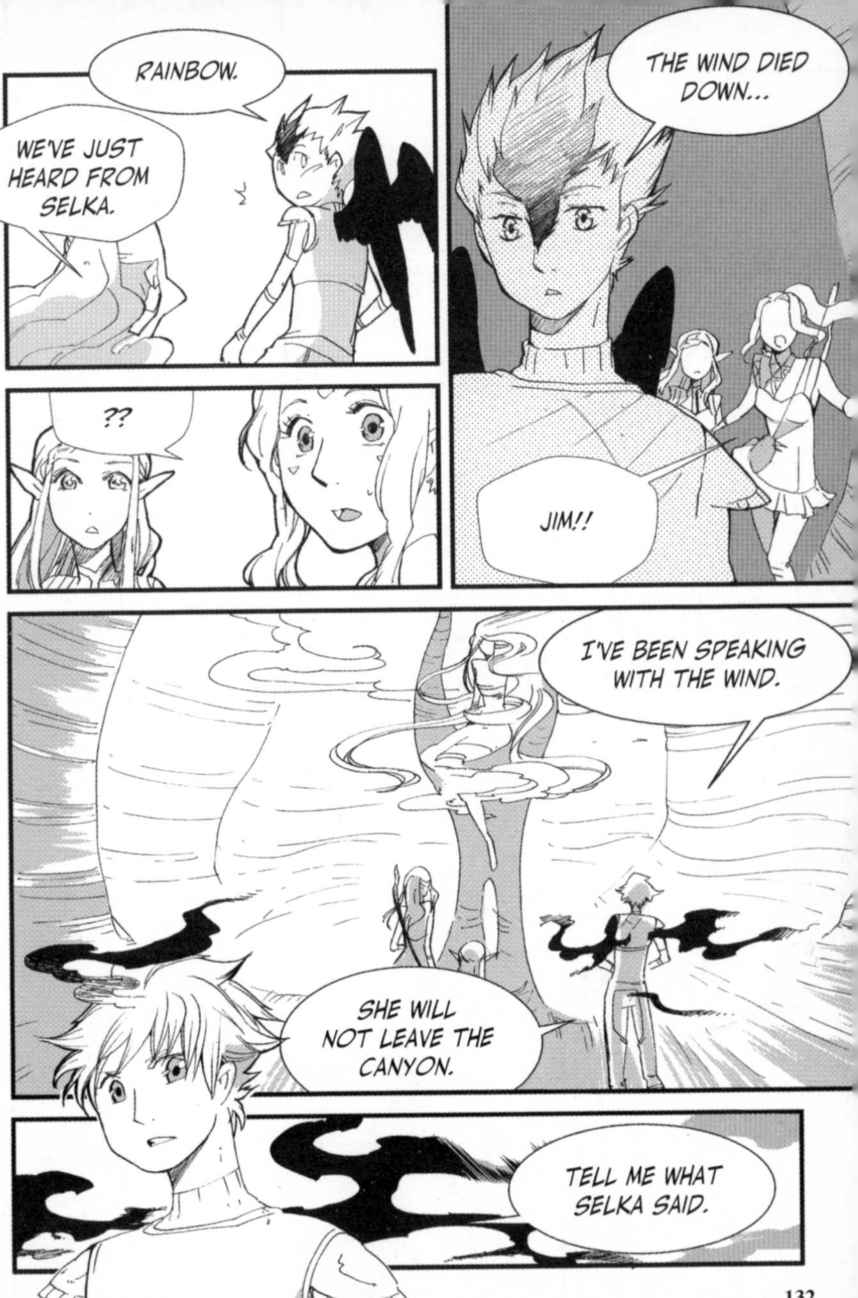
RAINBOW.
WE'VE JUST HEARD FROM SELKA.
??
THE WIND DIED DOWN...
JIM!!
I'VE BEEN SPEAKING WITH THE WIND.
SHE WILL NOT LEAVE THE CANYON.
TELL ME WHAT SELKA SAID.

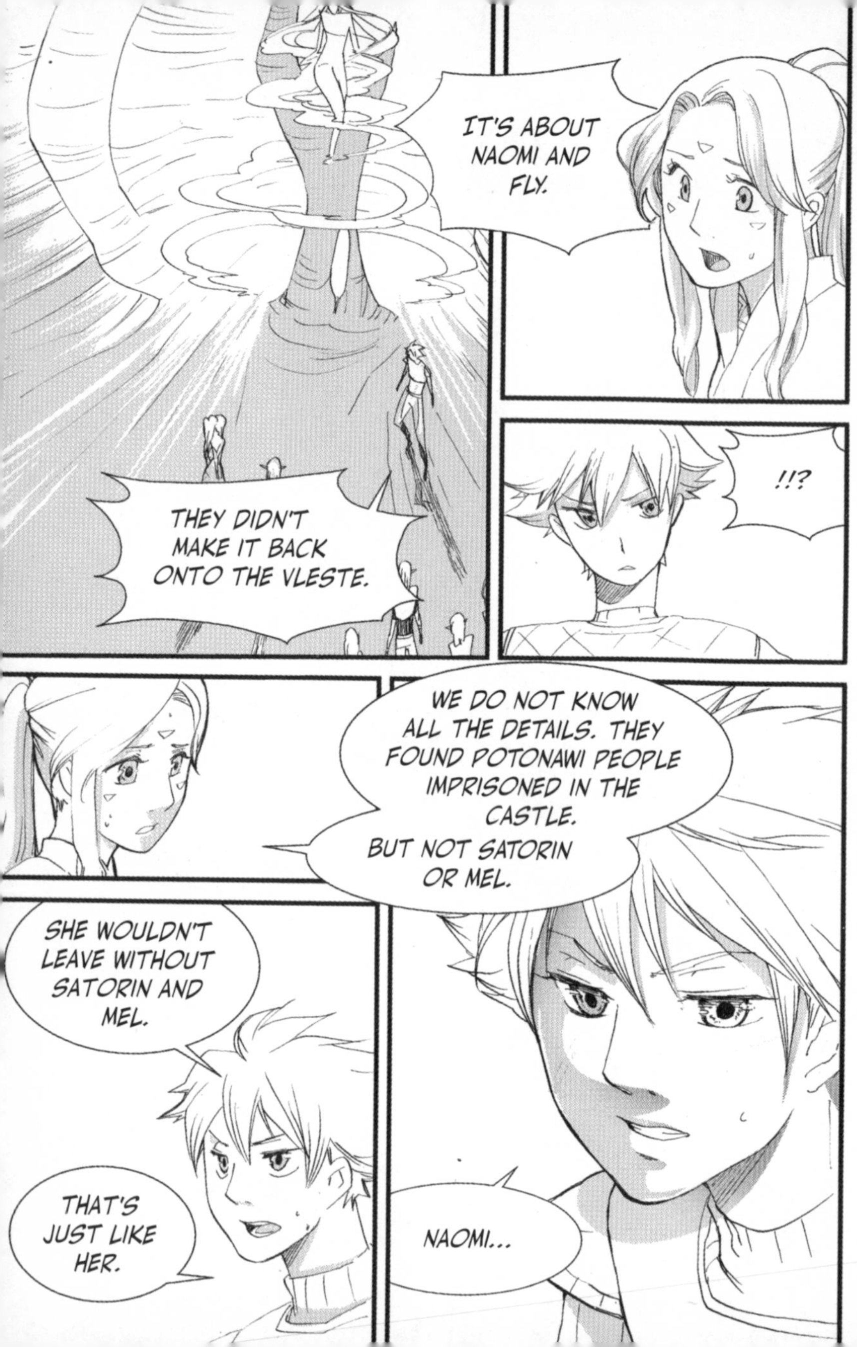
IT'S ABOUT NAOMI AND FLY.
!!?
THEY DIDN'T MAKE IT BACK ONTO THE VLESTE.
WE DO NOT KNOW ALL THE DETAILS. THEY FOUND POTONAWI PEOPLE IMPRISONED IN THE CASTLE.
BUT NOT SATORIN OR MEL.
NAOMI...
SHE WOULDN'T LEAVE WITHOUT SATORIN AND MEL.
THAT'S JUST LIKE HER.

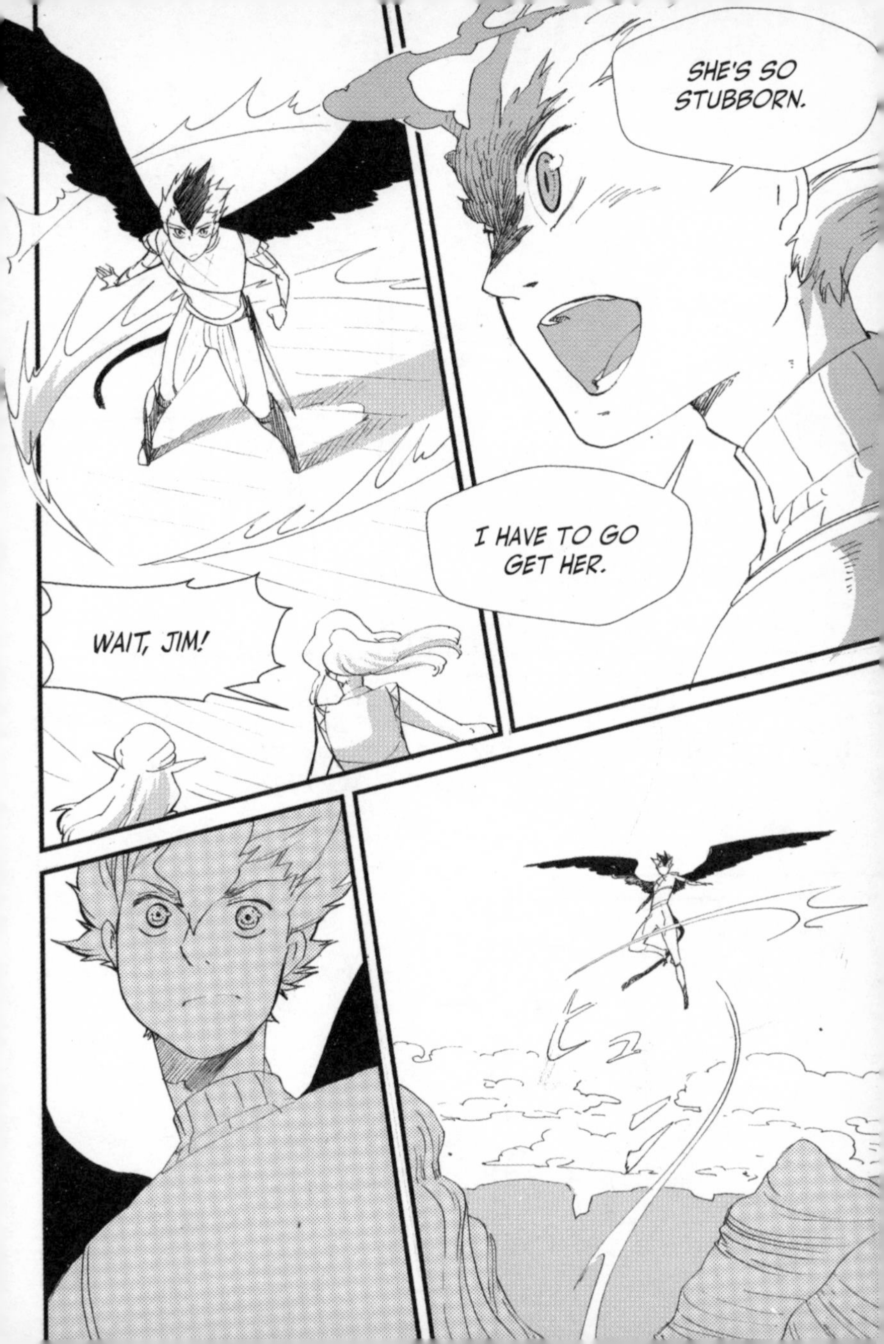
SHE'S SO STUBBORN.
I HAVE TO GO GET HER.
WAIT, JIM!
ヒュ

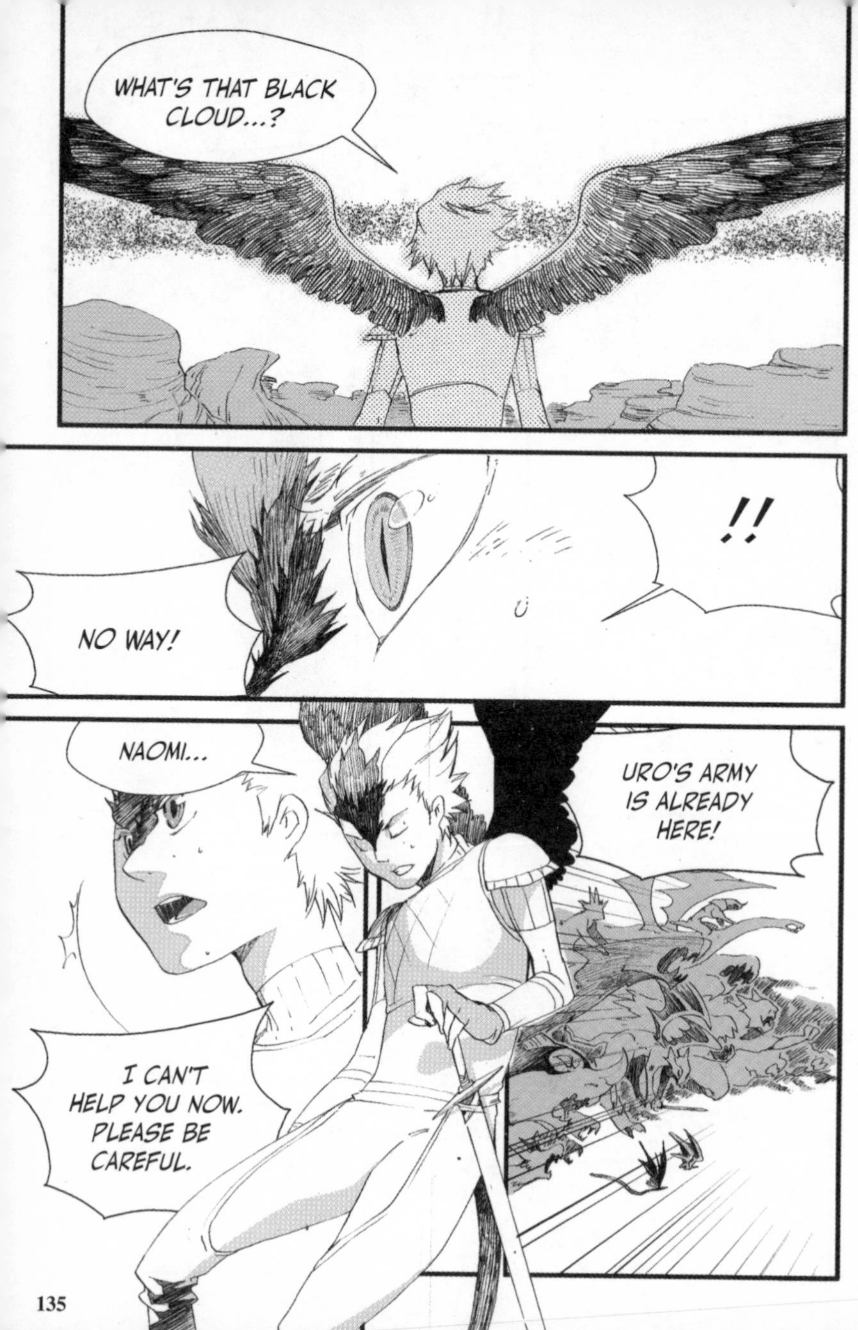
WHAT'S THAT BLACK CLOUD...?
!!
NO WAY!
URO'S ARMY IS ALREADY HERE!
NAOMI...
I CAN'T HELP YOU NOW. PLEASE BE CAREFUL.

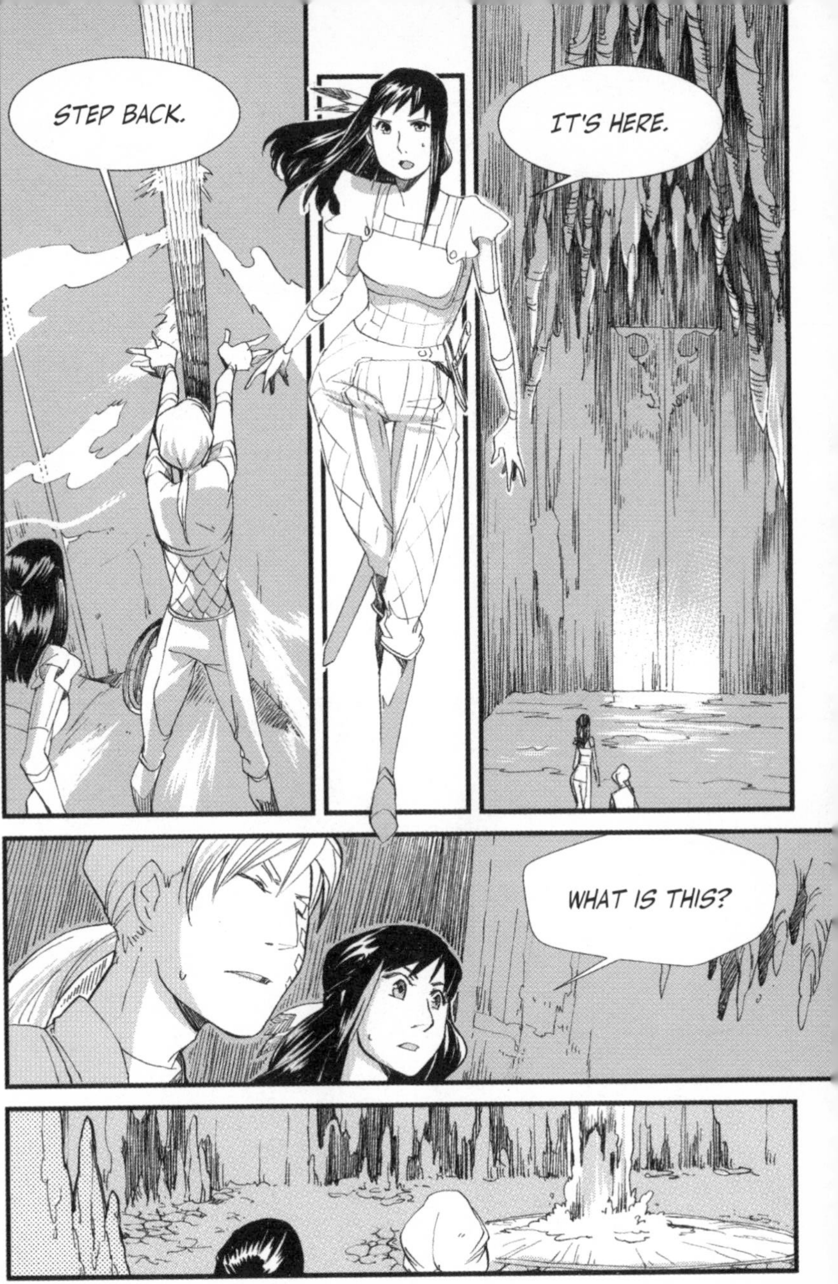
IT'S HERE.
STEP BACK.
WHAT IS THIS?

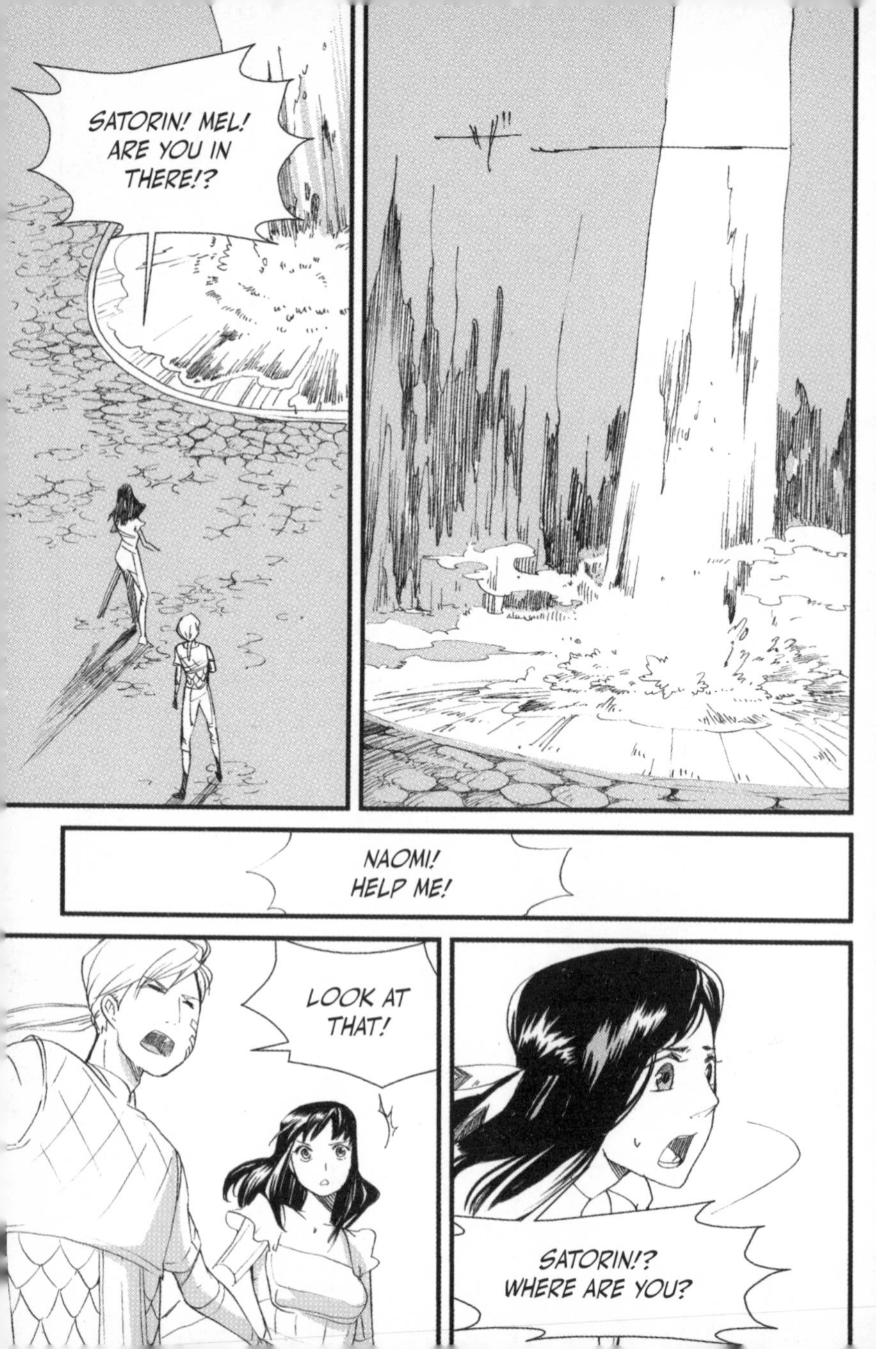
SATORIN! MEL! ARE YOU IN THERE!?
NAOMI! HELP ME!
SATORIN!? WHERE ARE YOU?
LOOK AT THAT!

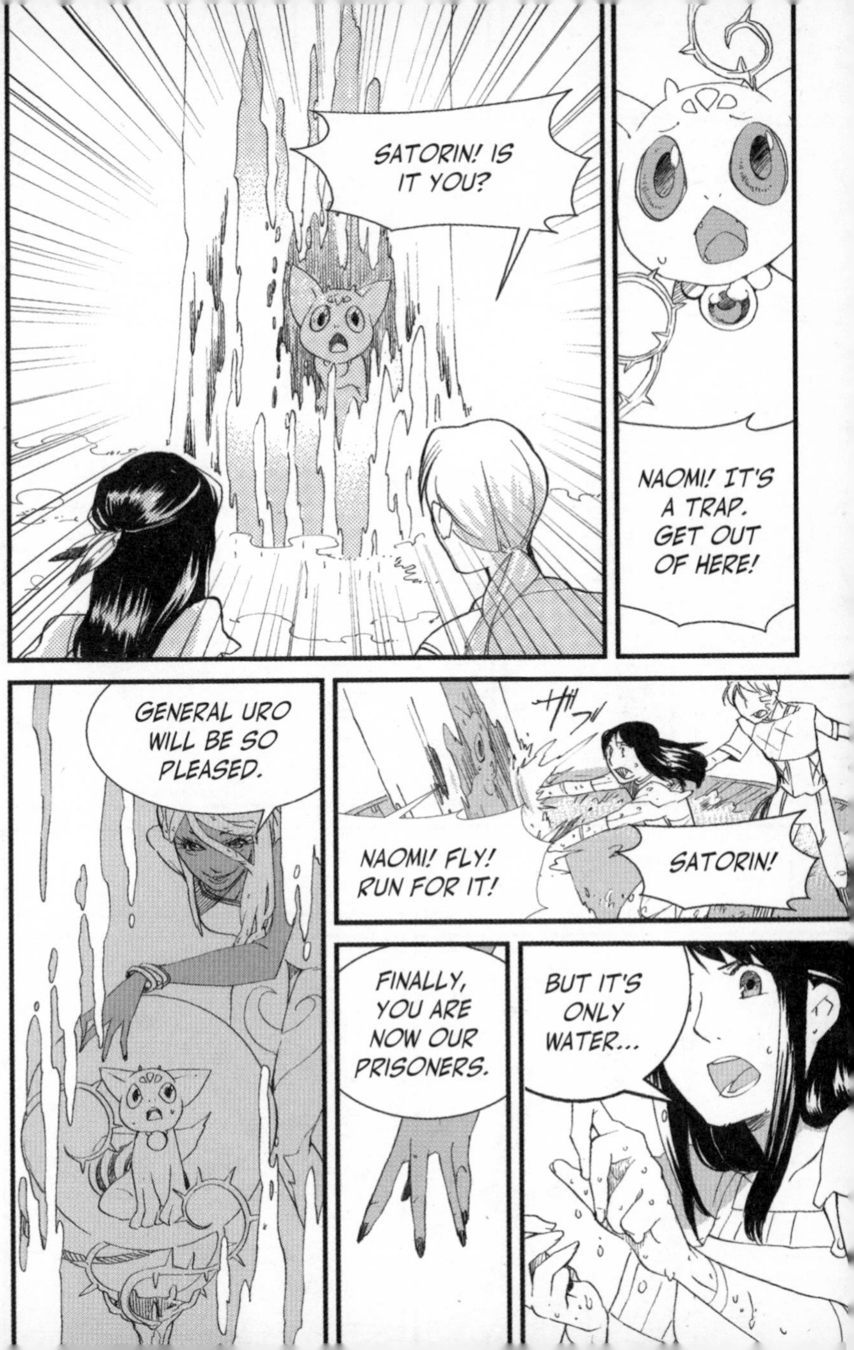
NAOMI! IT'S A TRAP. GET OUT OF HERE!
SATORIN! IS IT YOU?
SATORIN!
NAOMI! FLY! RUN FOR IT!
BUT IT'S ONLY WATER...
FINALLY, YOU ARE NOW OUR PRISONERS.
GENERAL URO WILL BE SO PLEASED.

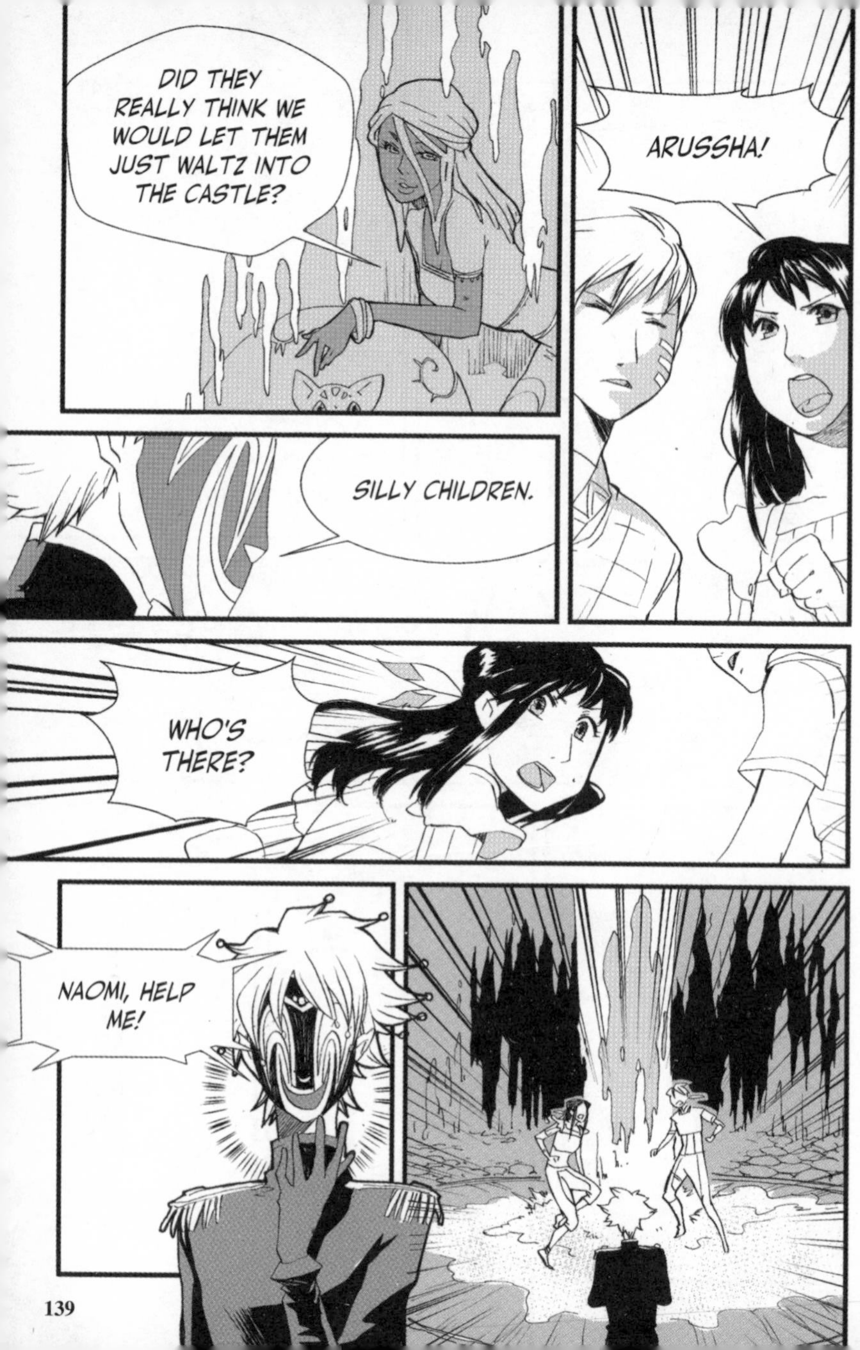
ARUSSHA!
DID THEY REALLY THINK WE WOULD LET THEM JUST WALTZ INTO THE CASTLE?
SILLY CHILDREN.
WHO'S THERE?
NAOMI, HELP ME!

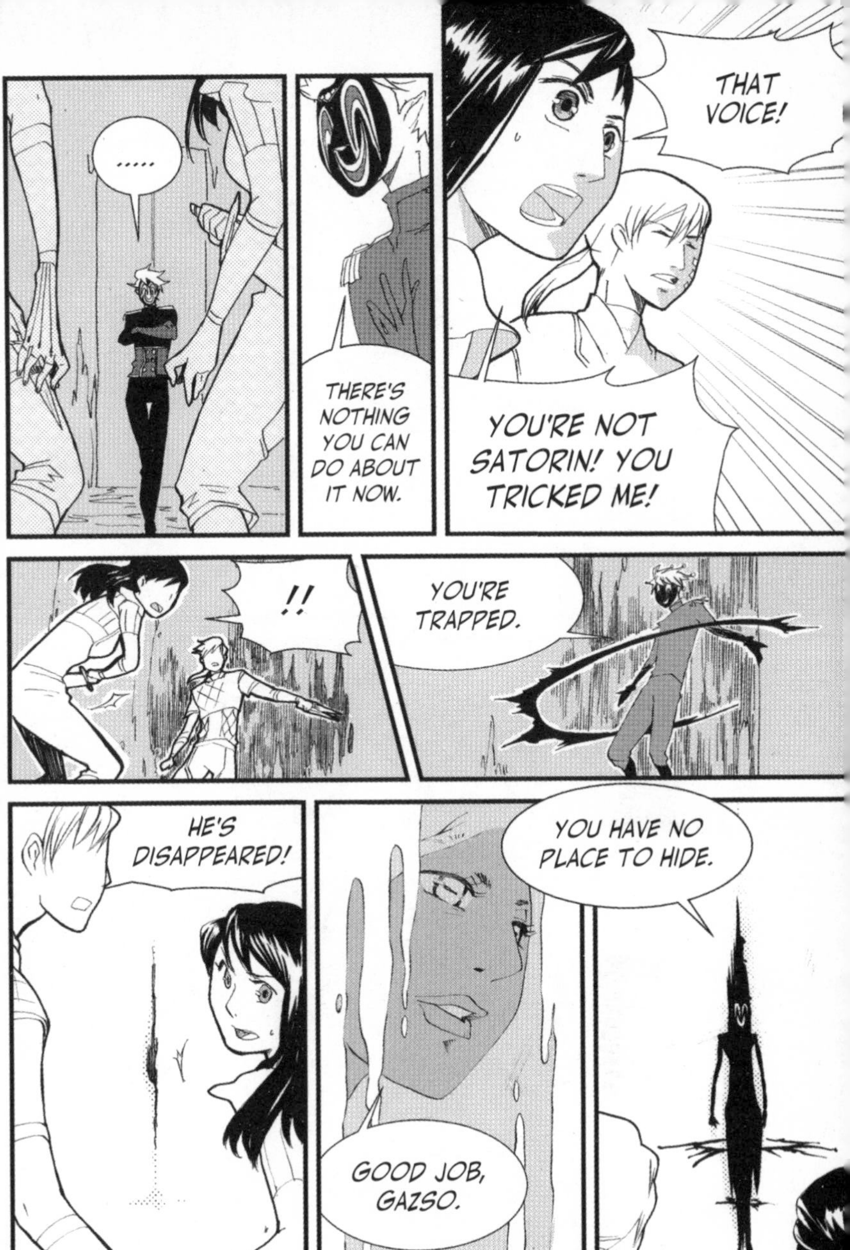
THAT VOICE!
YOU'RE NOT SATORIN! YOU TRICKED ME!
THERE'S NOTHING YOU CAN DO ABOUT IT NOW.
.....
YOU'RE TRAPPED.
!!
YOU HAVE NO PLACE TO HIDE.
GOOD JOB, GAZSO.
HE'S DISAPPEARED!

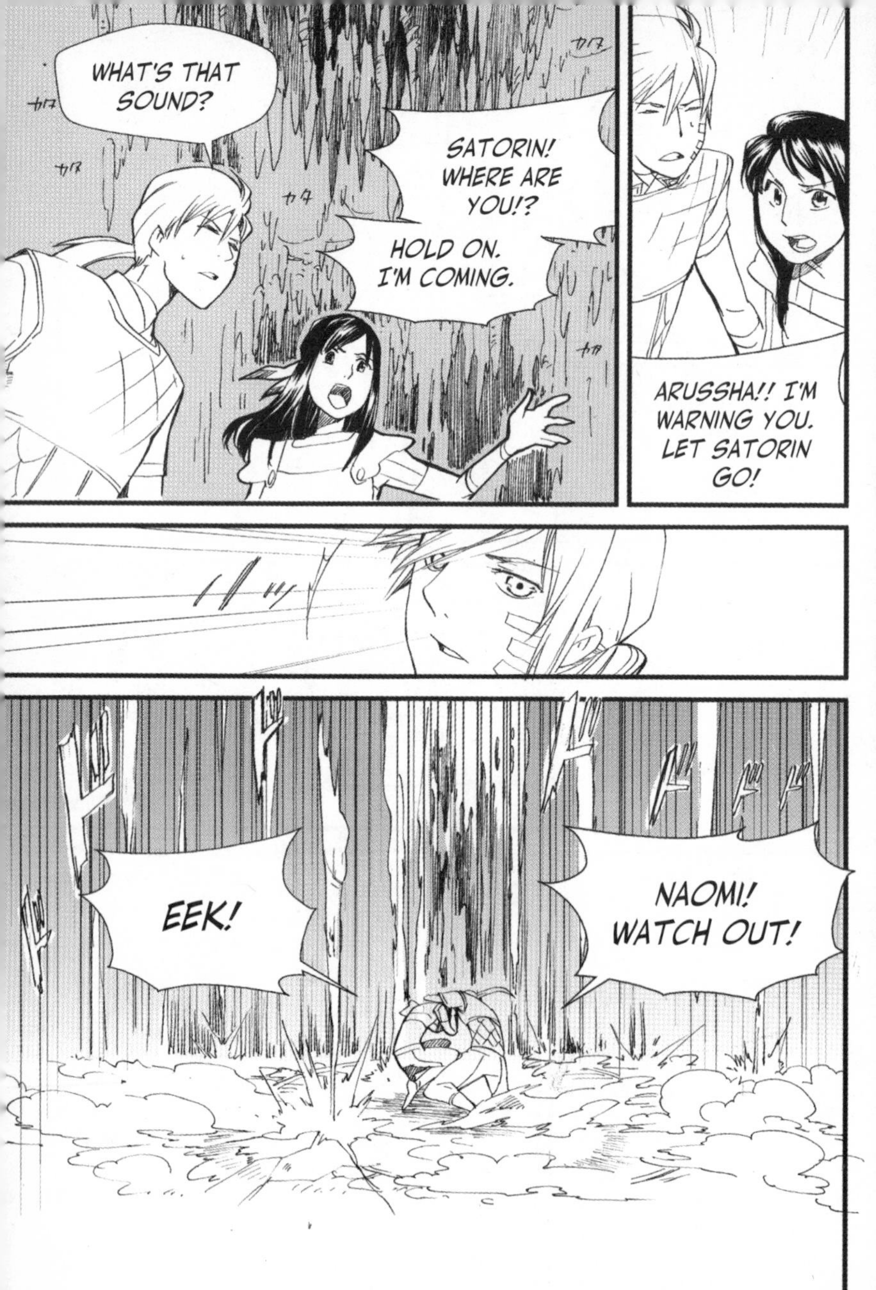
ARUSSHA!! I'M WARNING YOU. LET SATORIN GO!
WHAT'S THAT SOUND?
SATORIN! WHERE ARE YOU!?
HOLD ON. I'M COMING.
NAOMI! WATCH OUT!
EEK!

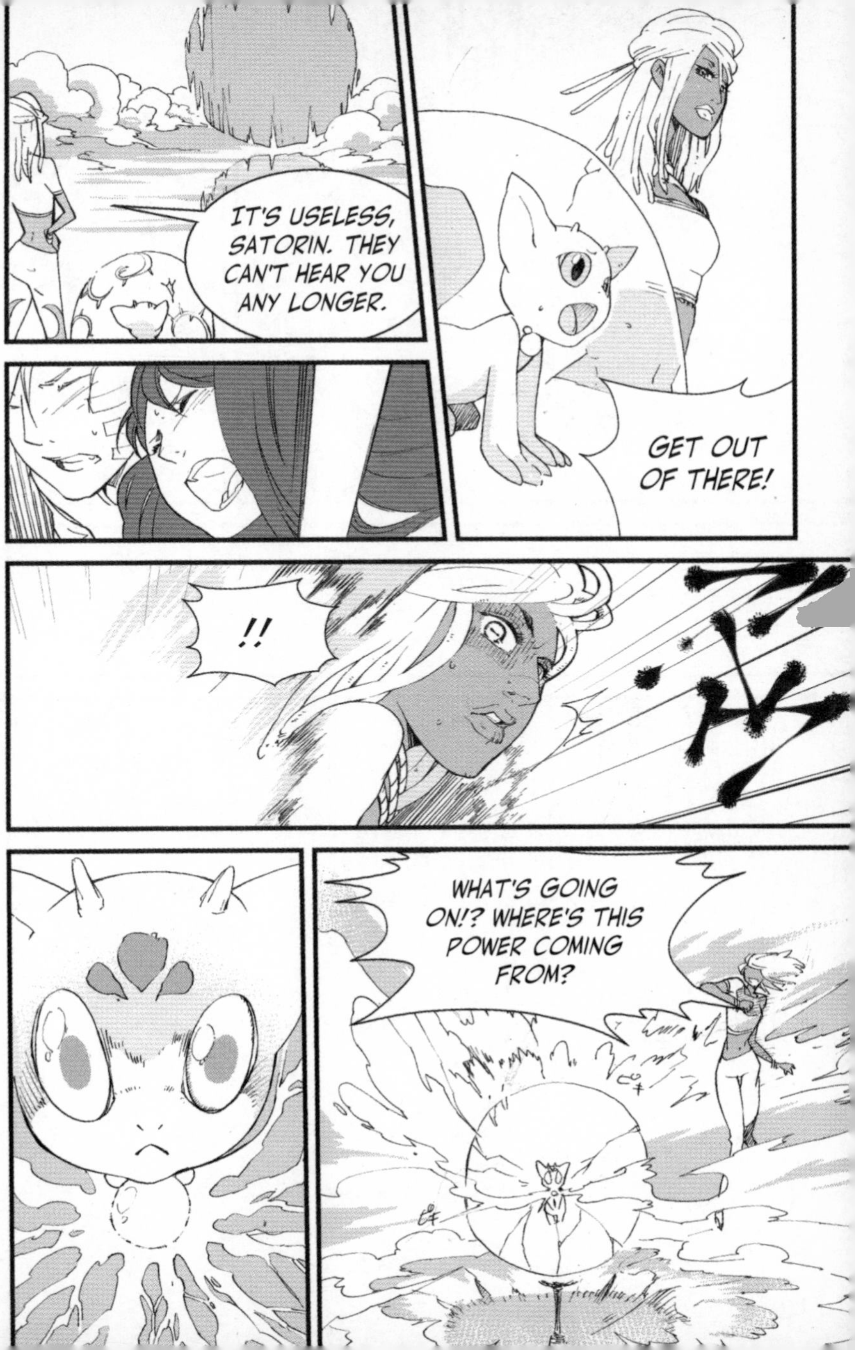
GET OUT OF THERE!
IT'S USELESS, SATORIN. THEY CAN'T HEAR YOU ANY LONGER.
!!
WHAT'S GOING ON!? WHERE'S THIS POWER COMING FROM?

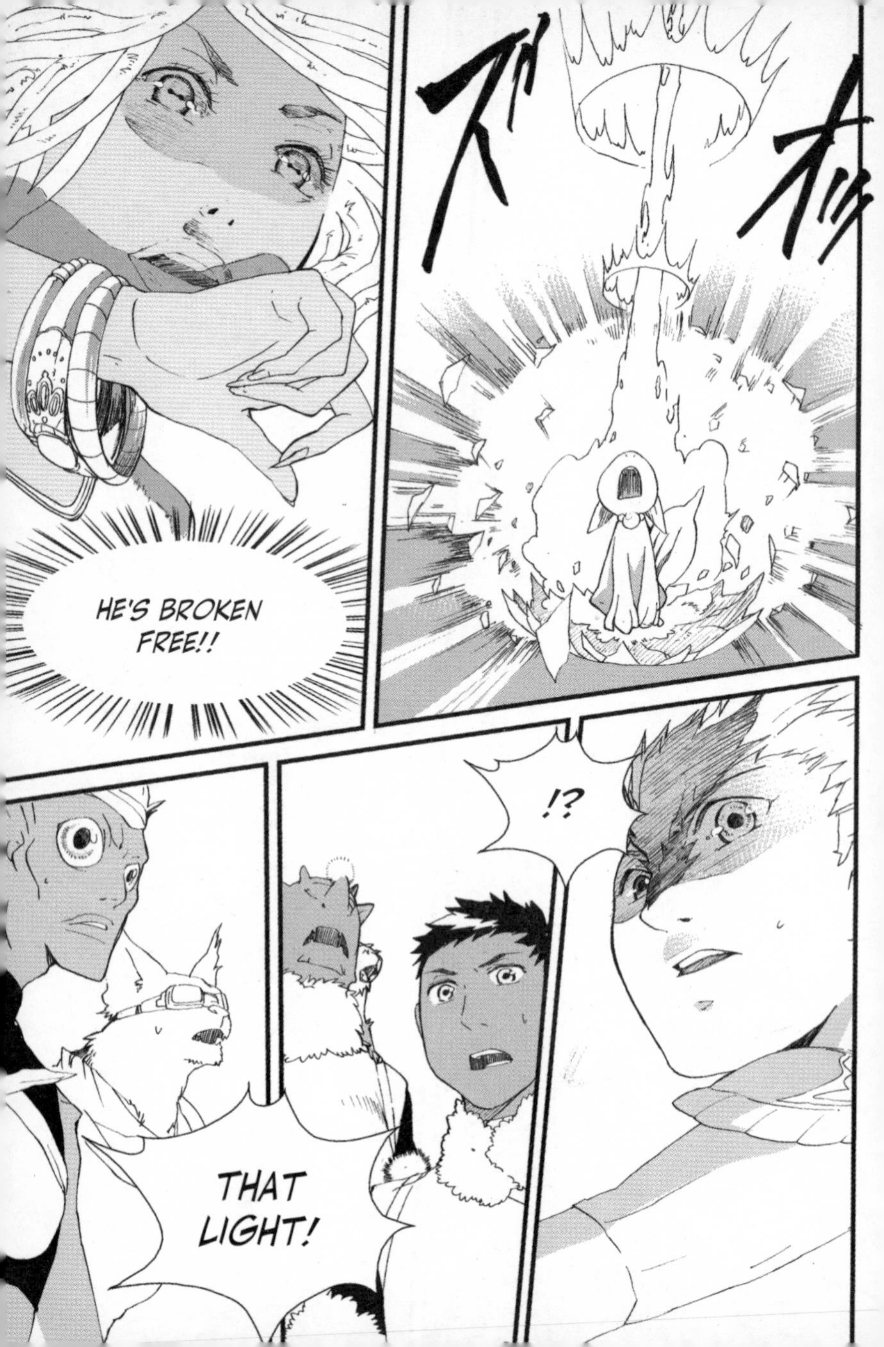
HE'S BROKEN FREE!!
!?
THAT LIGHT!

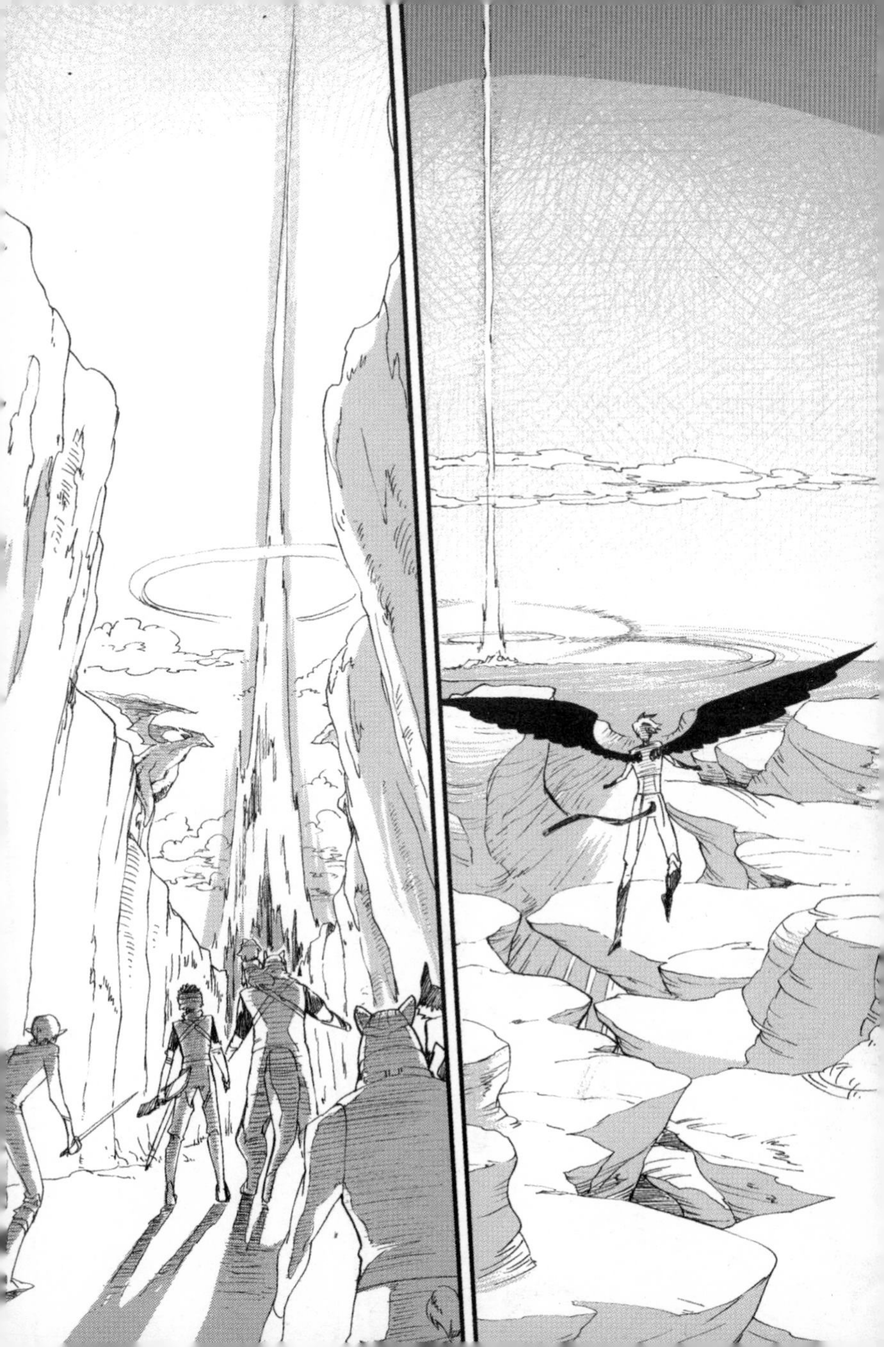

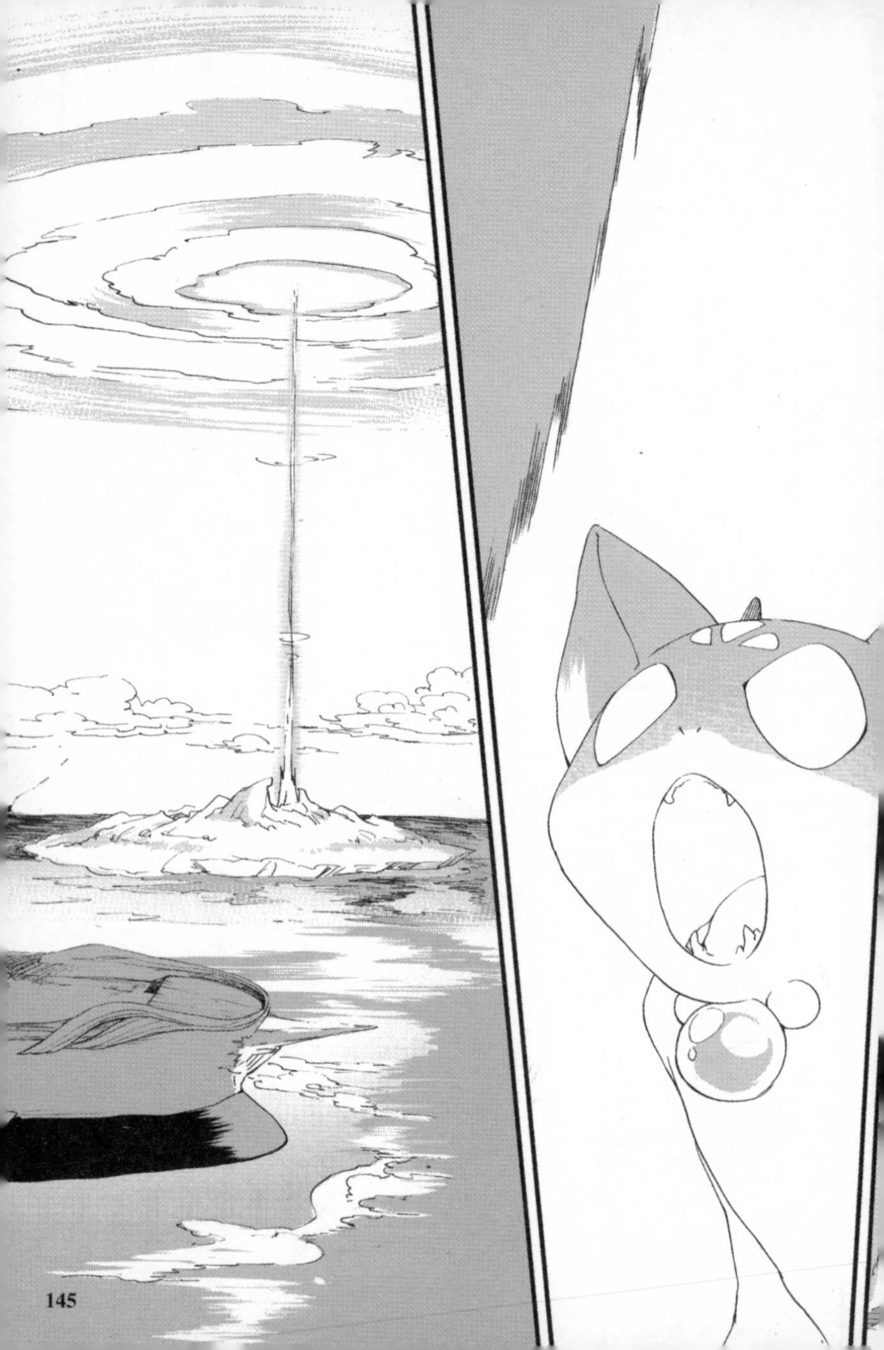

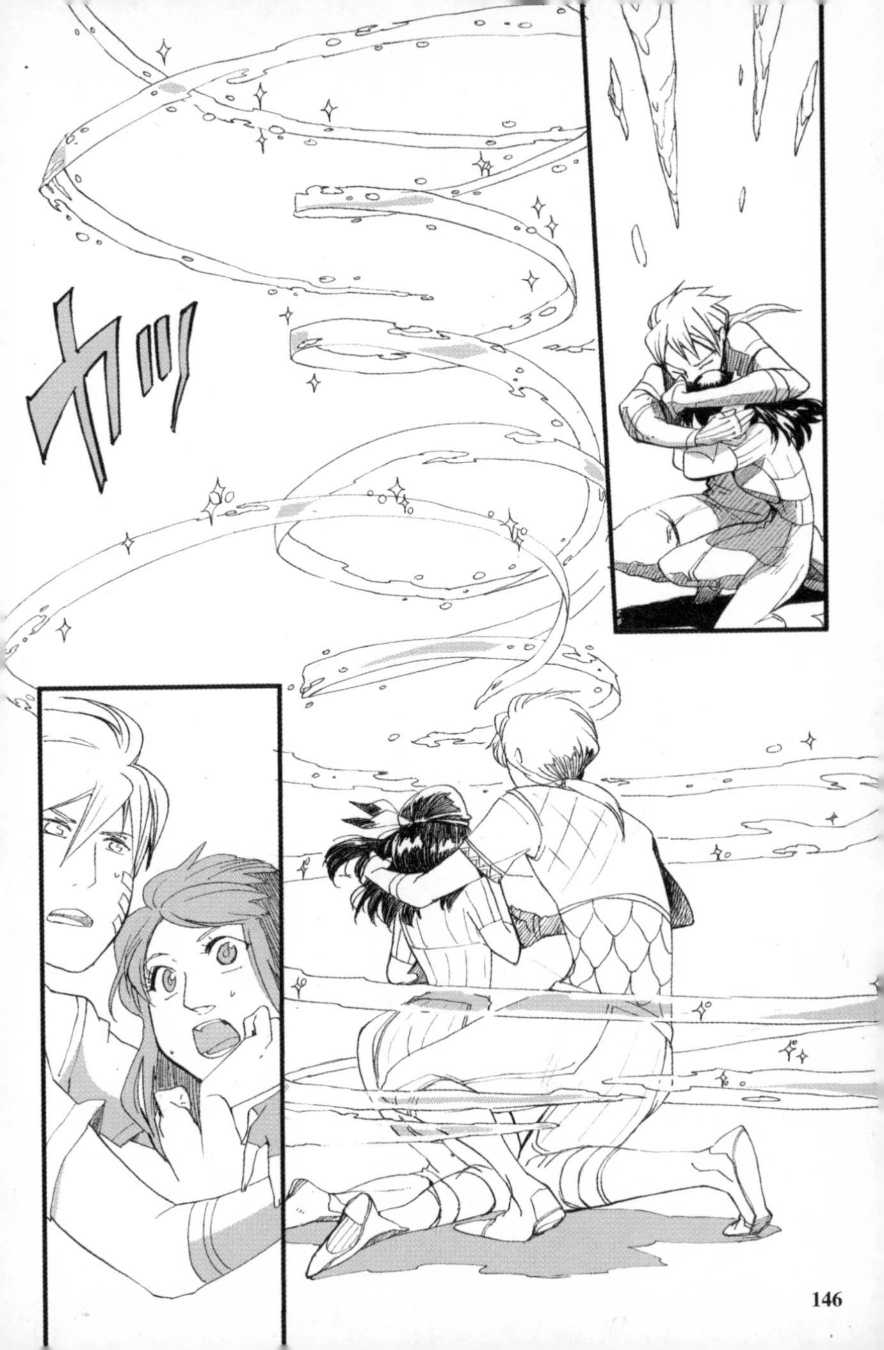
カッ

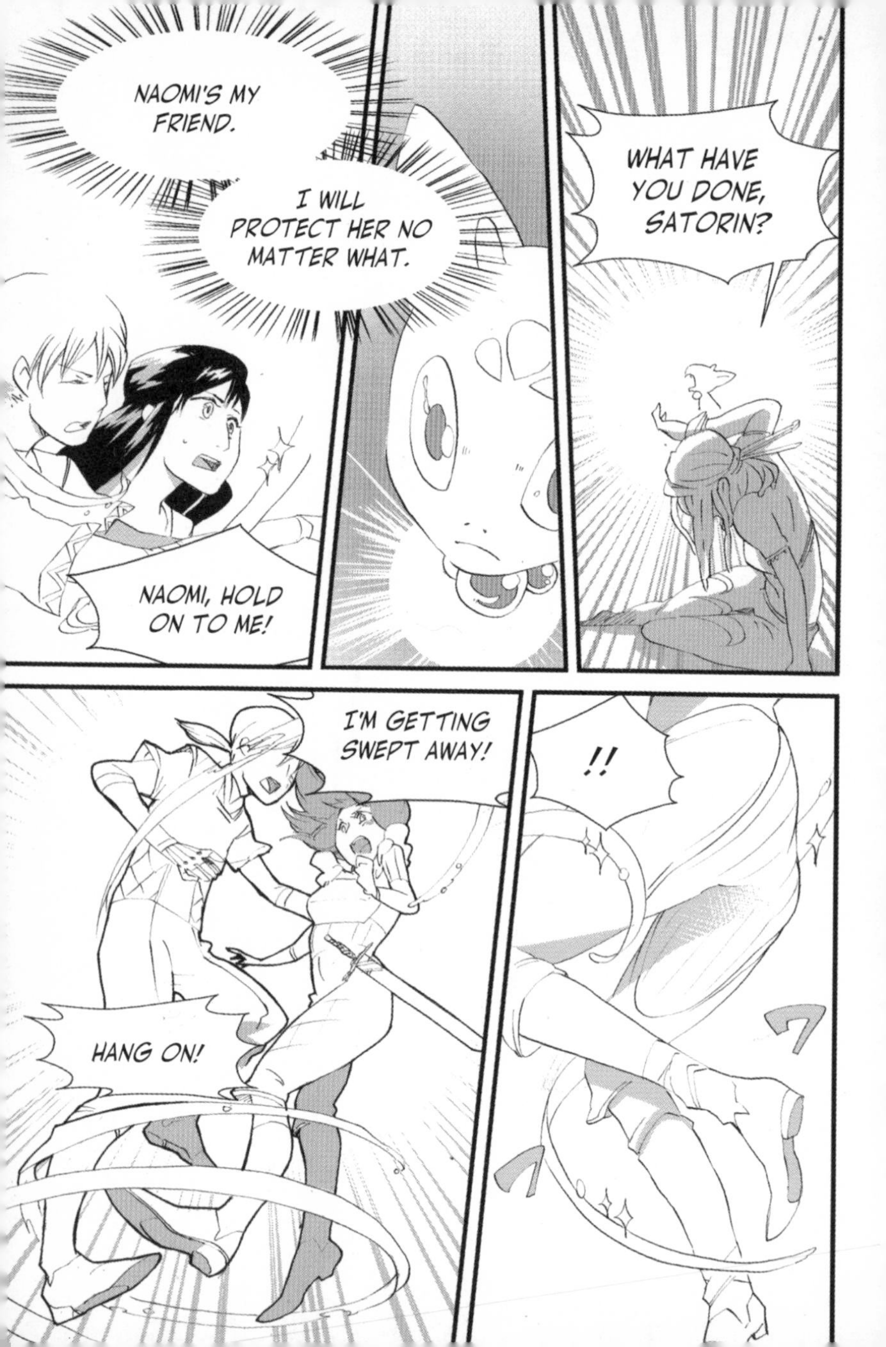
WHAT HAVE YOU DONE, SATORIN?
NAOMI'S MY FRIEND.
I WILL PROTECT HER NO MATTER WHAT.
NAOMI, HOLD ON TO ME!
!!
I'M GETTING SWEPT AWAY!
HANG ON!

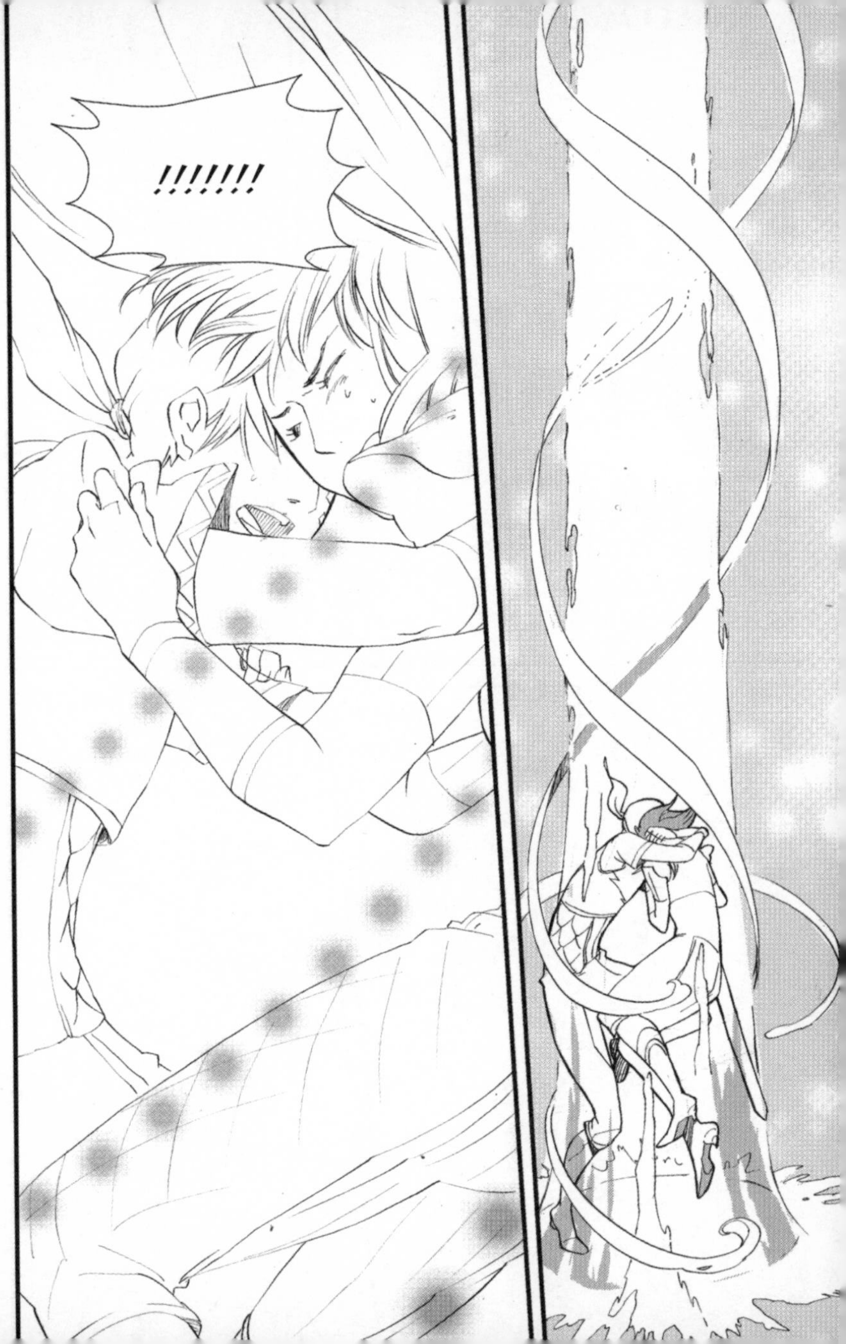
!!!!!!!

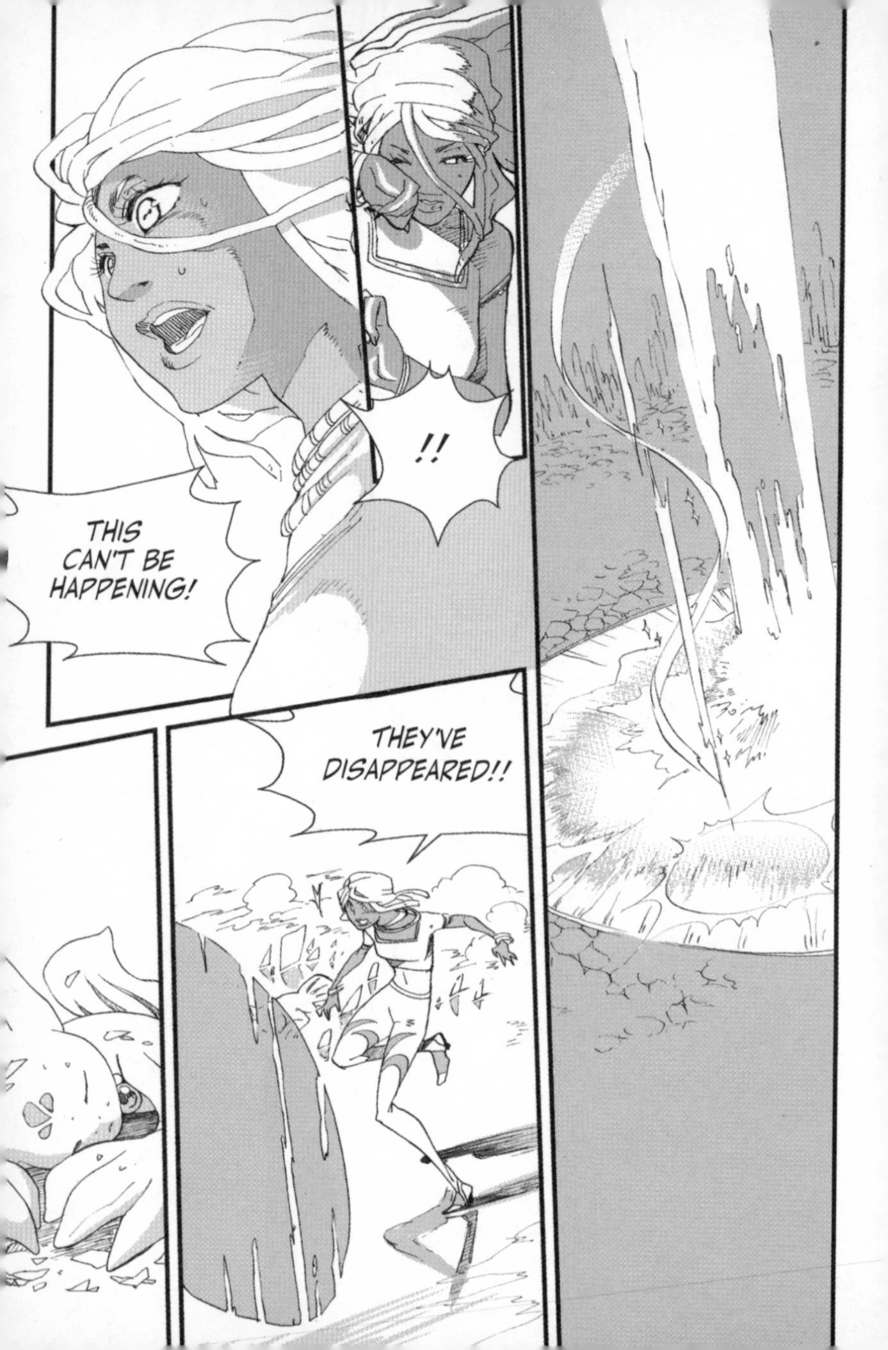
!!
THIS CAN'T BE HAPPENING!
THEY'VE DISAPPEARED!!

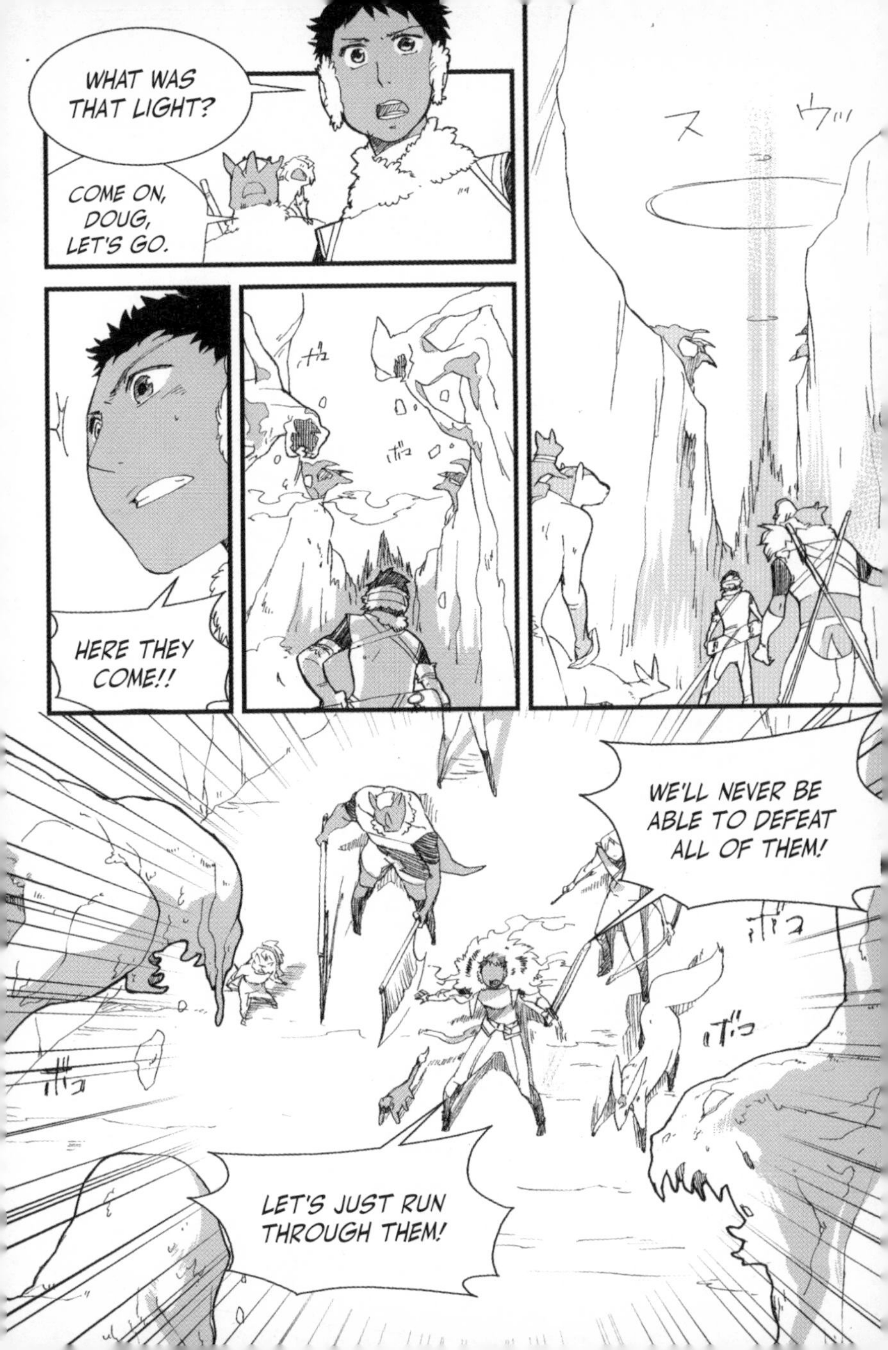
WHAT WAS THAT LIGHT?
COME ON, DOUG, LET'S GO.
HERE THEY COME!!
WE'LL NEVER BE ABLE TO DEFEAT ALL OF THEM!
LET'S JUST RUN THROUGH THEM!

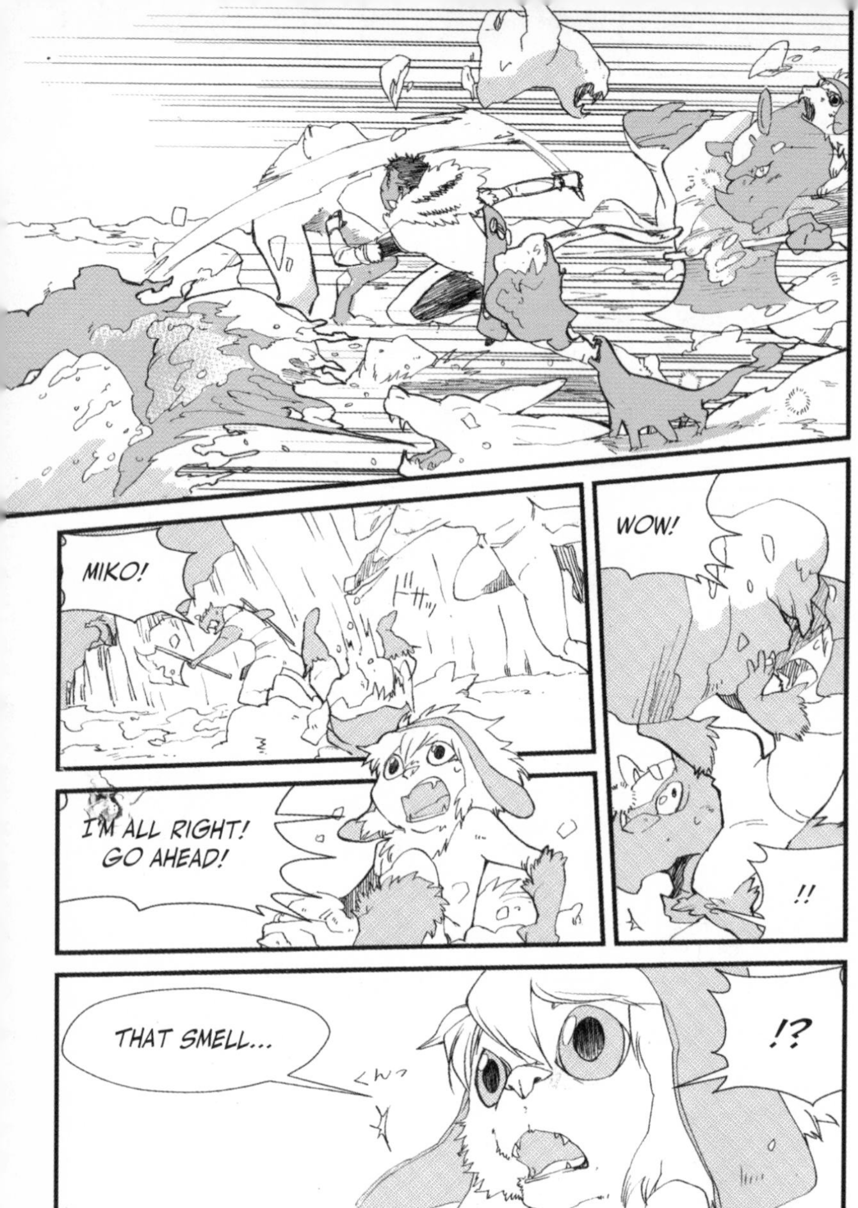
WOW!
!!
MIKO!
I'M ALL RIGHT! GO AHEAD!
!?
THAT SMELL...

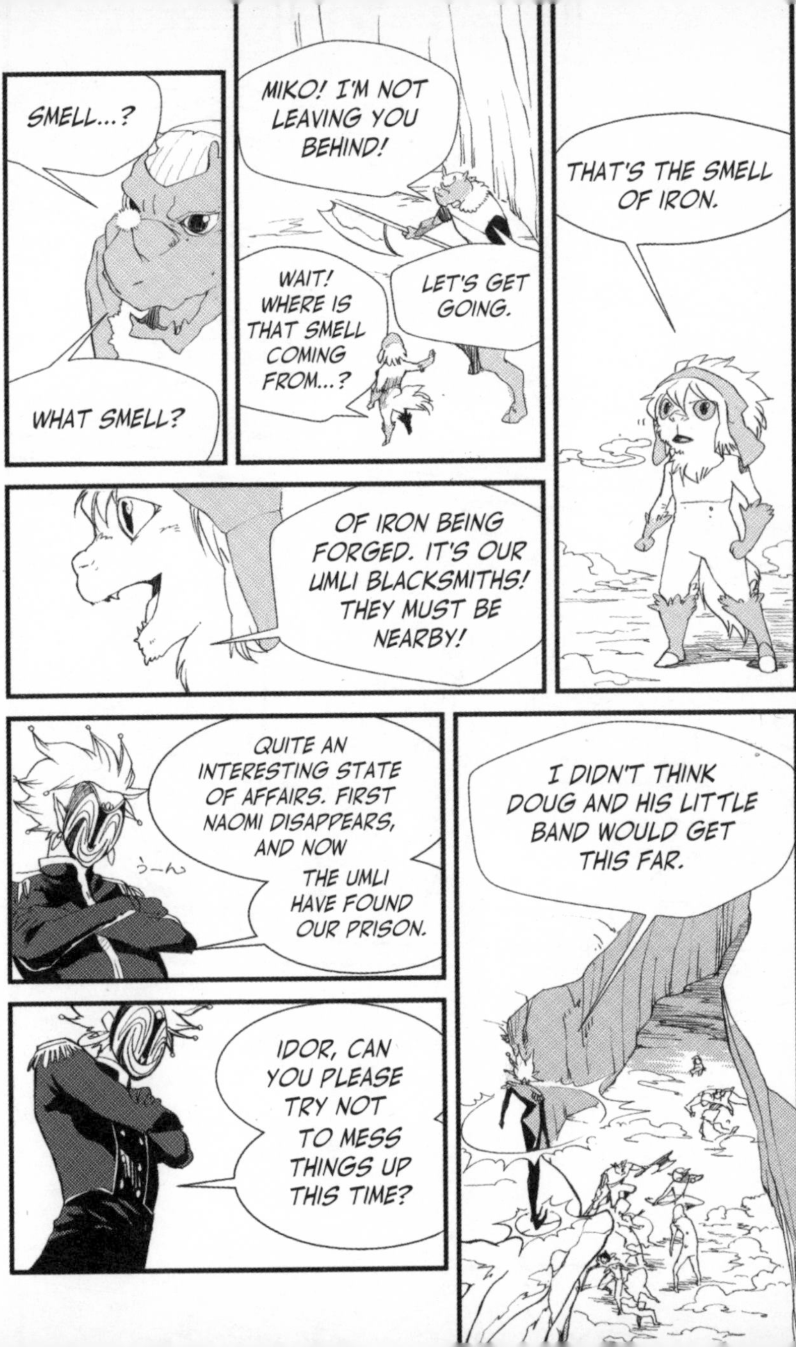
THAT'S THE SMELL OF IRON.
MIKO! I'M NOT LEAVING YOU BEHIND!
LET'S GET GOING.
WAIT! WHERE IS THAT SMELL COMING FROM...?
SMELL...?
WHAT SMELL?
OF IRON BEING FORGED. IT'S OUR UMLI BLACKSMITHS! THEY MUST BE NEARBY!
I DIDN'T THINK DOUG AND HIS LITTLE BAND WOULD GET THIS FAR.
QUITE AN INTERESTING STATE OF AFFAIRS. FIRST NAOMI DISAPPEARS, AND NOW
THE UMLI HAVE FOUND OUR PRISON.
うーん
IDOR, CAN YOU PLEASE TRY NOT TO MESS THINGS UP THIS TIME?

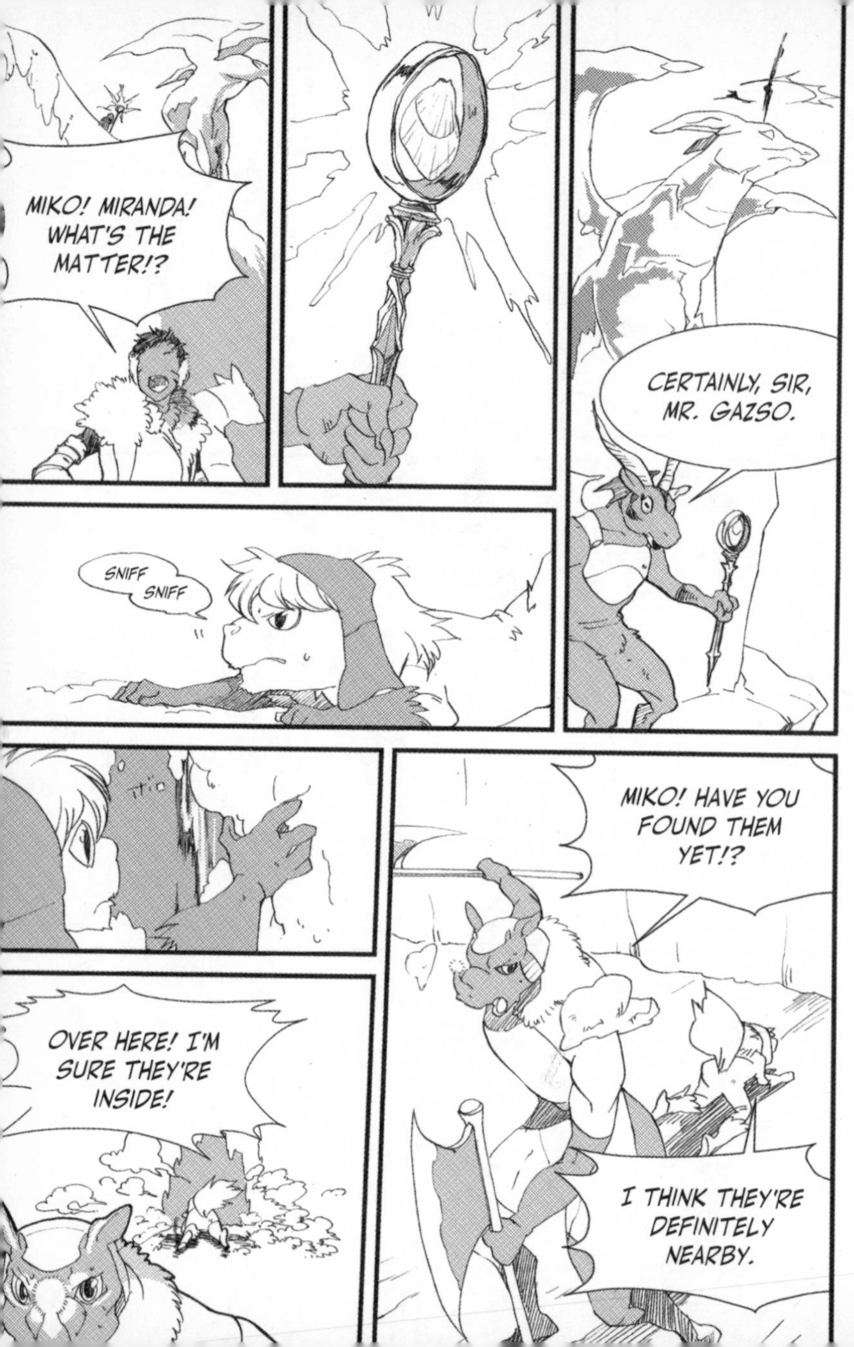
CERTAINLY, SIR, MR. GAZSO.
MIKO! MIRANDA! WHAT'S THE MATTER!?
SNIFF SNIFF
MIKO! HAVE YOU FOUND THEM YET!?
I THINK THEY'RE DEFINITELY NEARBY.
OVER HERE! I'M SURE THEY'RE INSIDE!

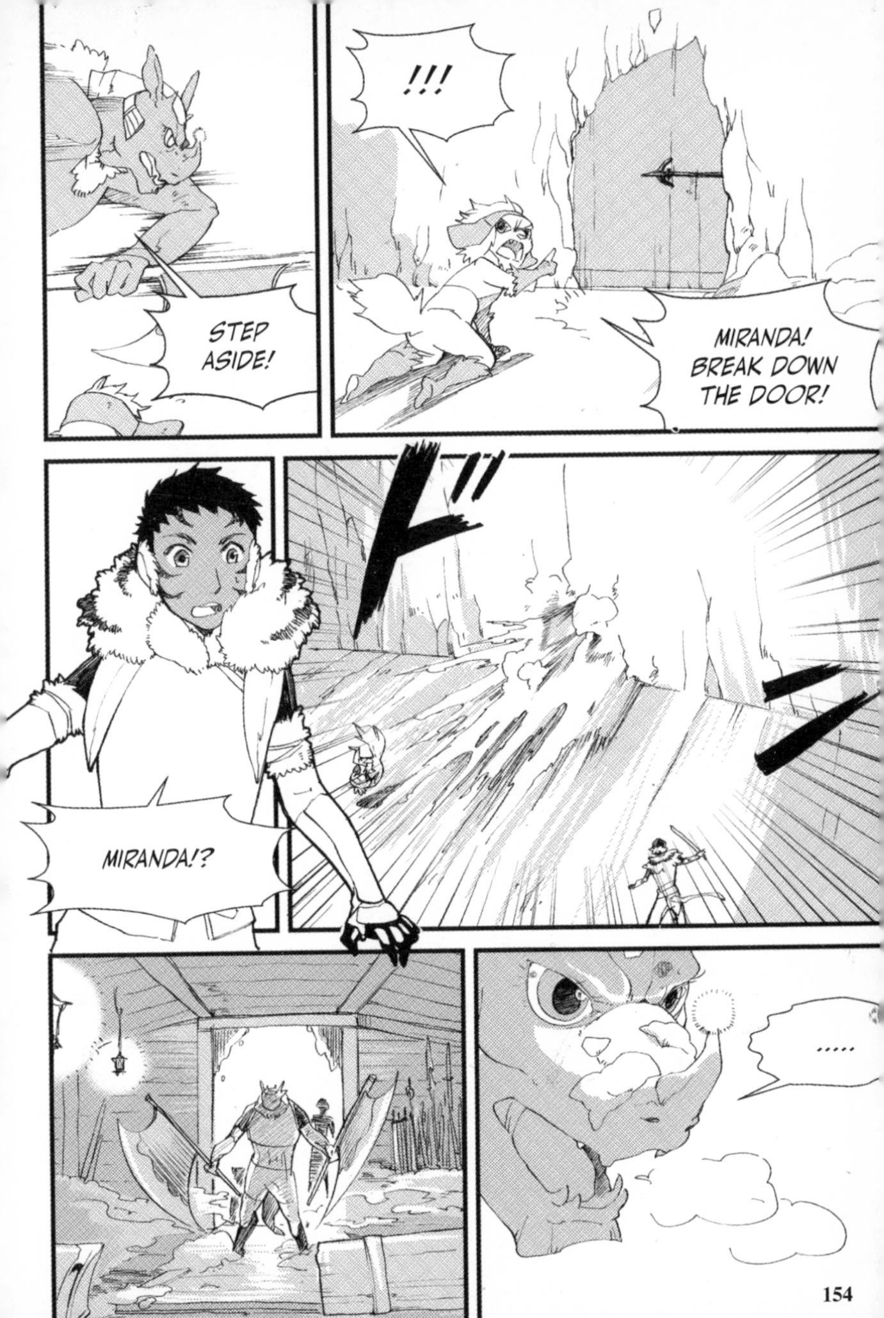
!!!
MIRANDA! BREAK DOWN THE DOOR!
STEP ASIDE!
MIRANDA!?
.....

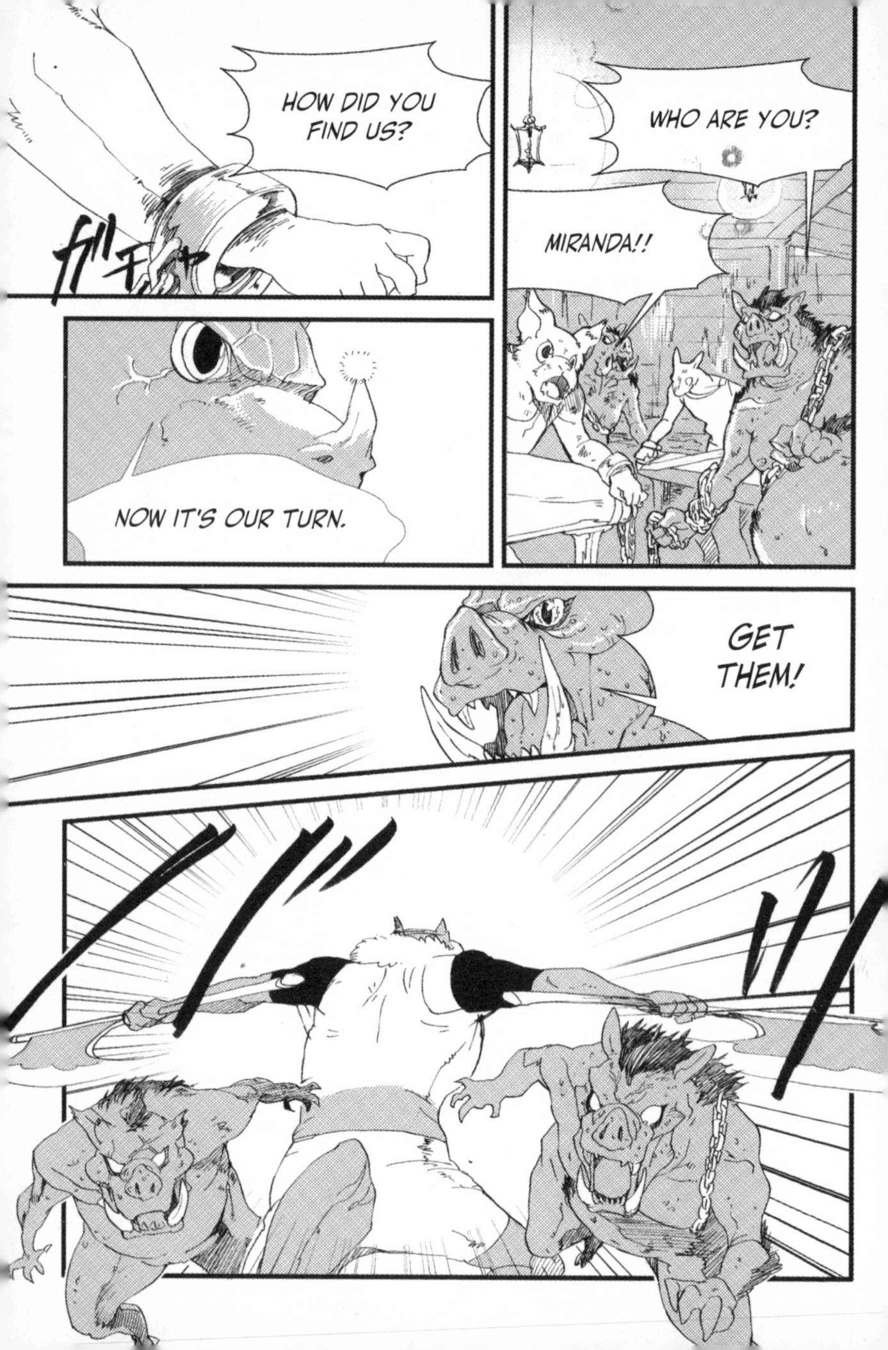
WHO ARE YOU?
MIRANDA!!
HOW DID YOU FIND US?
ガチャ
NOW IT'S OUR TURN.
GET THEM!

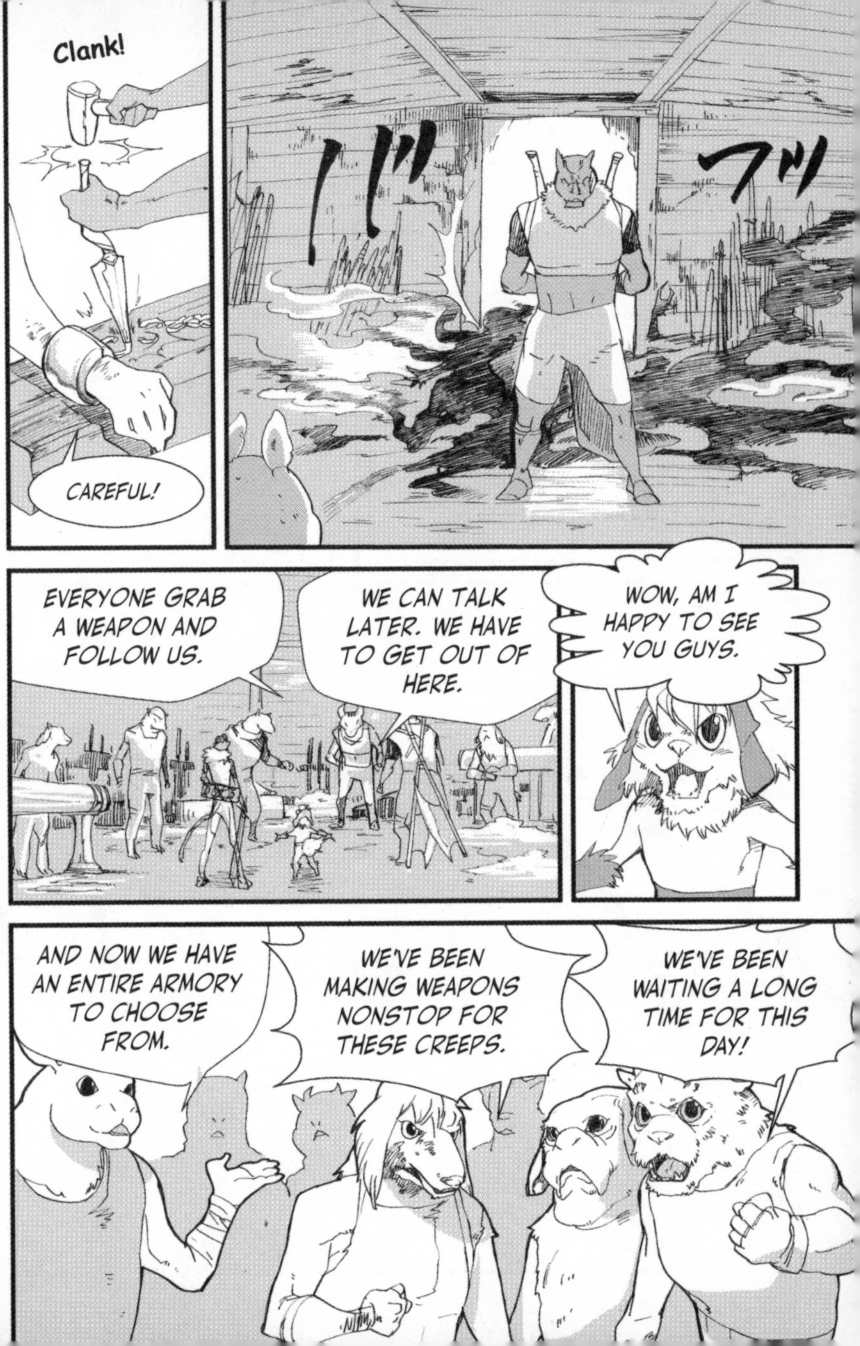
Clank!
CAREFUL!
WOW, AM I HAPPY TO SEE YOU GUYS.
WE CAN TALK LATER. WE HAVE TO GET OUT OF HERE.
EVERYONE GRAB A WEAPON AND FOLLOW US.
WE'VE BEEN WAITING A LONG TIME FOR THIS DAY!
WE'VE BEEN MAKING WEAPONS NONSTOP FOR THESE CREEPS.
AND NOW WE HAVE AN ENTIRE ARMORY TO CHOOSE FROM.

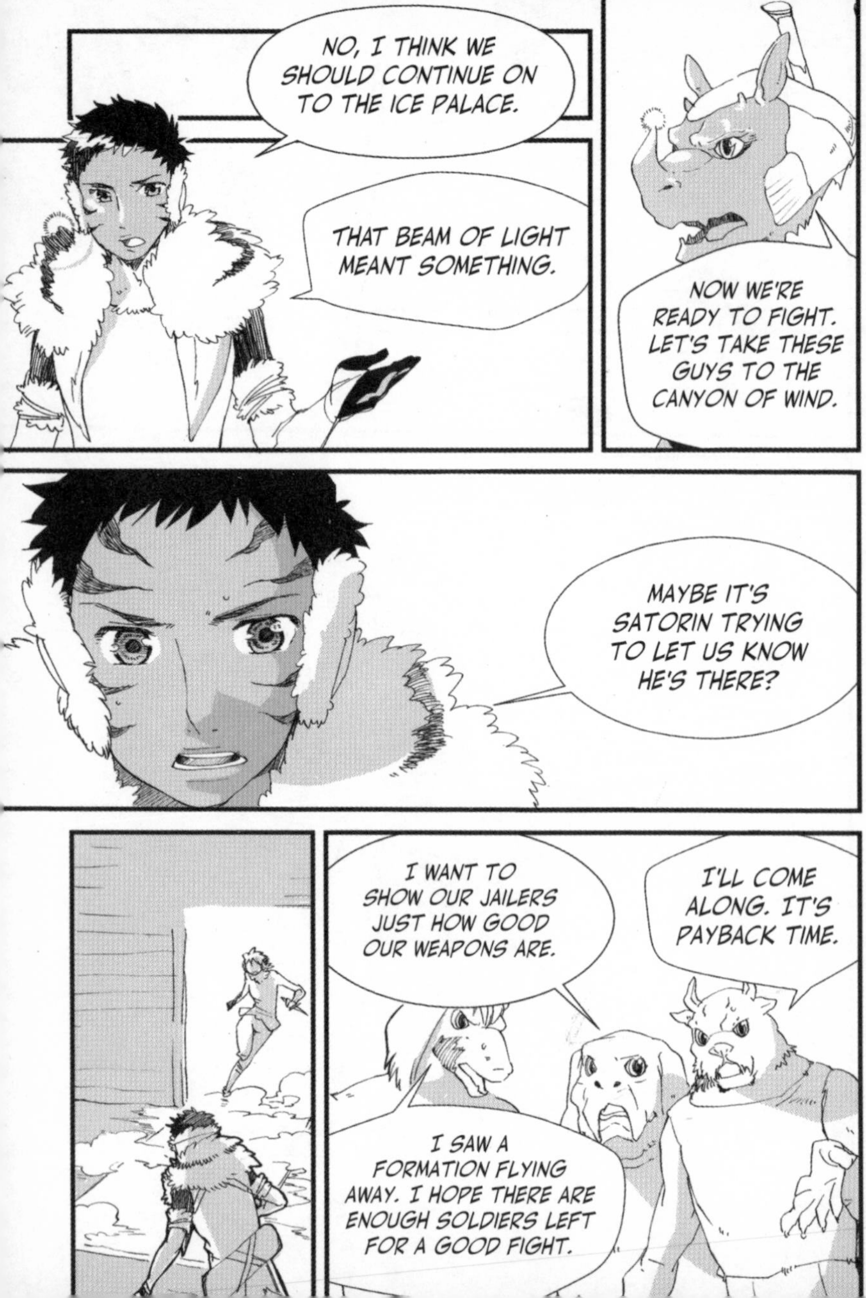
NOW WE'RE READY TO FIGHT. LET'S TAKE THESE GUYS TO THE CANYON OF WIND.
NO, I THINK WE SHOULD CONTINUE ON TO THE ICE PALACE.
THAT BEAM OF LIGHT MEANT SOMETHING.
MAYBE IT'S SATORIN TRYING TO LET US KNOW HE'S THERE?
I'LL COME ALONG. IT'S PAYBACK TIME.
I WANT TO SHOW OUR JAILERS JUST HOW GOOD OUR WEAPONS ARE.
I SAW A FORMATION FLYING AWAY. I HOPE THERE ARE ENOUGH SOLDIERS LEFT FOR A GOOD FIGHT.

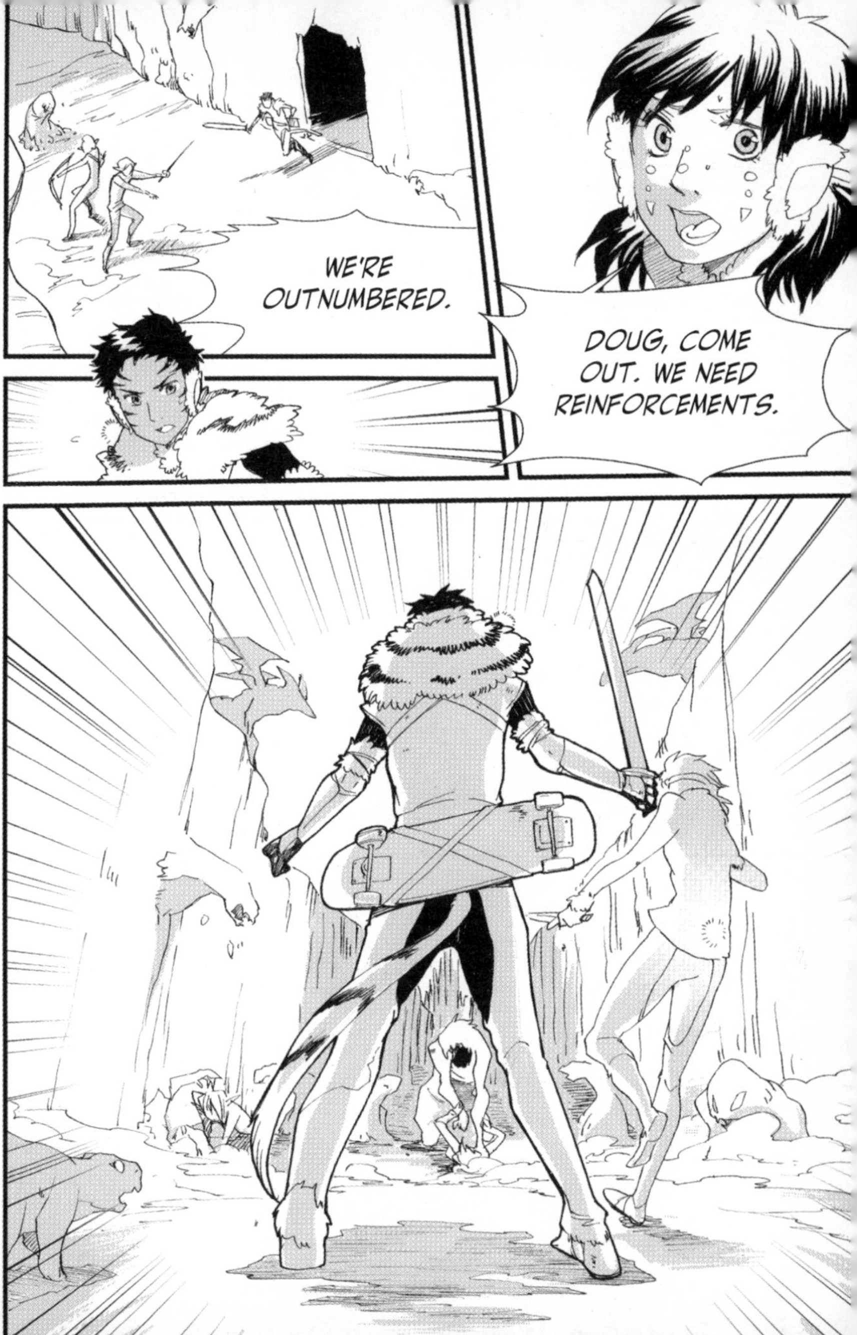
DOUG, COME OUT. WE NEED REINFORCEMENTS.
WE'RE OUTNUMBERED.

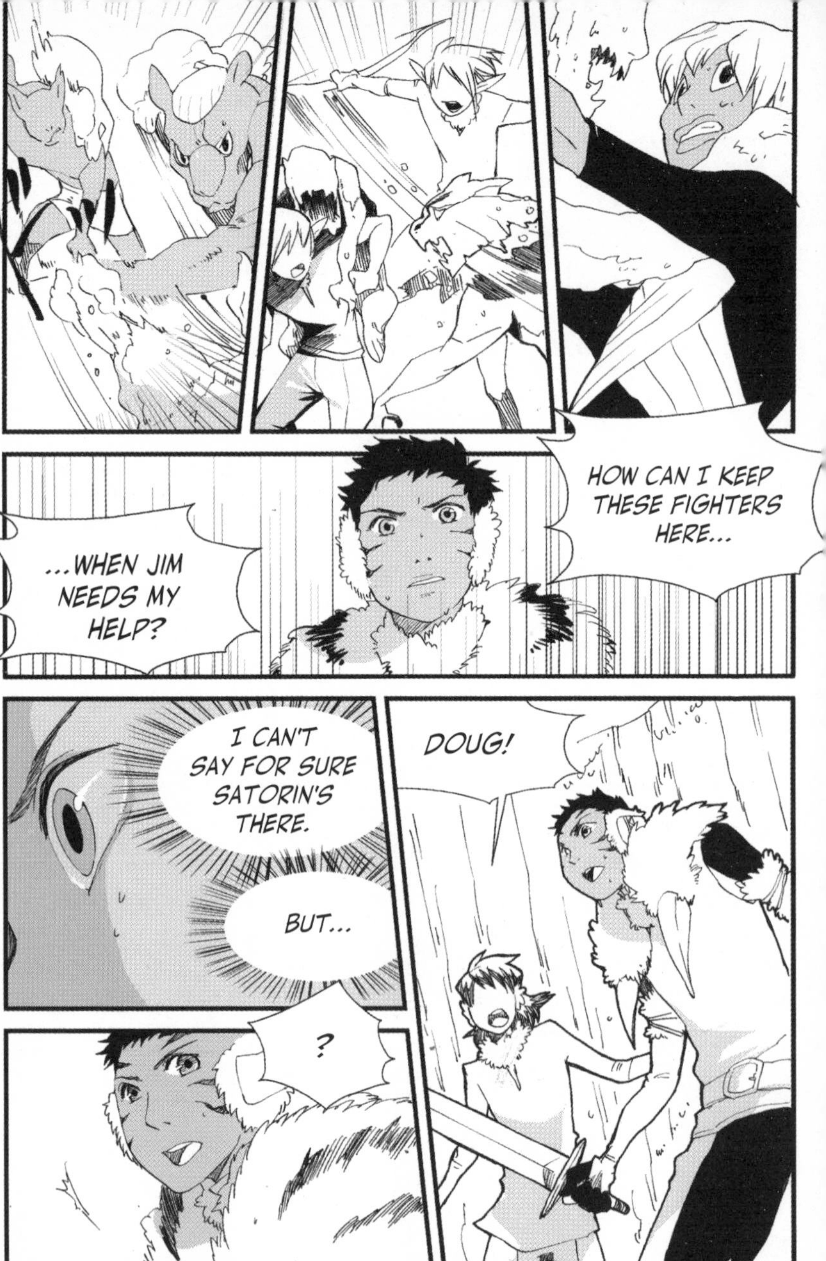
HOW CAN I KEEP THESE FIGHTERS HERE...
...WHEN JIM NEEDS MY HELP?
DOUG!
I CAN'T SAY FOR SURE SATORIN'S THERE.
BUT...
?

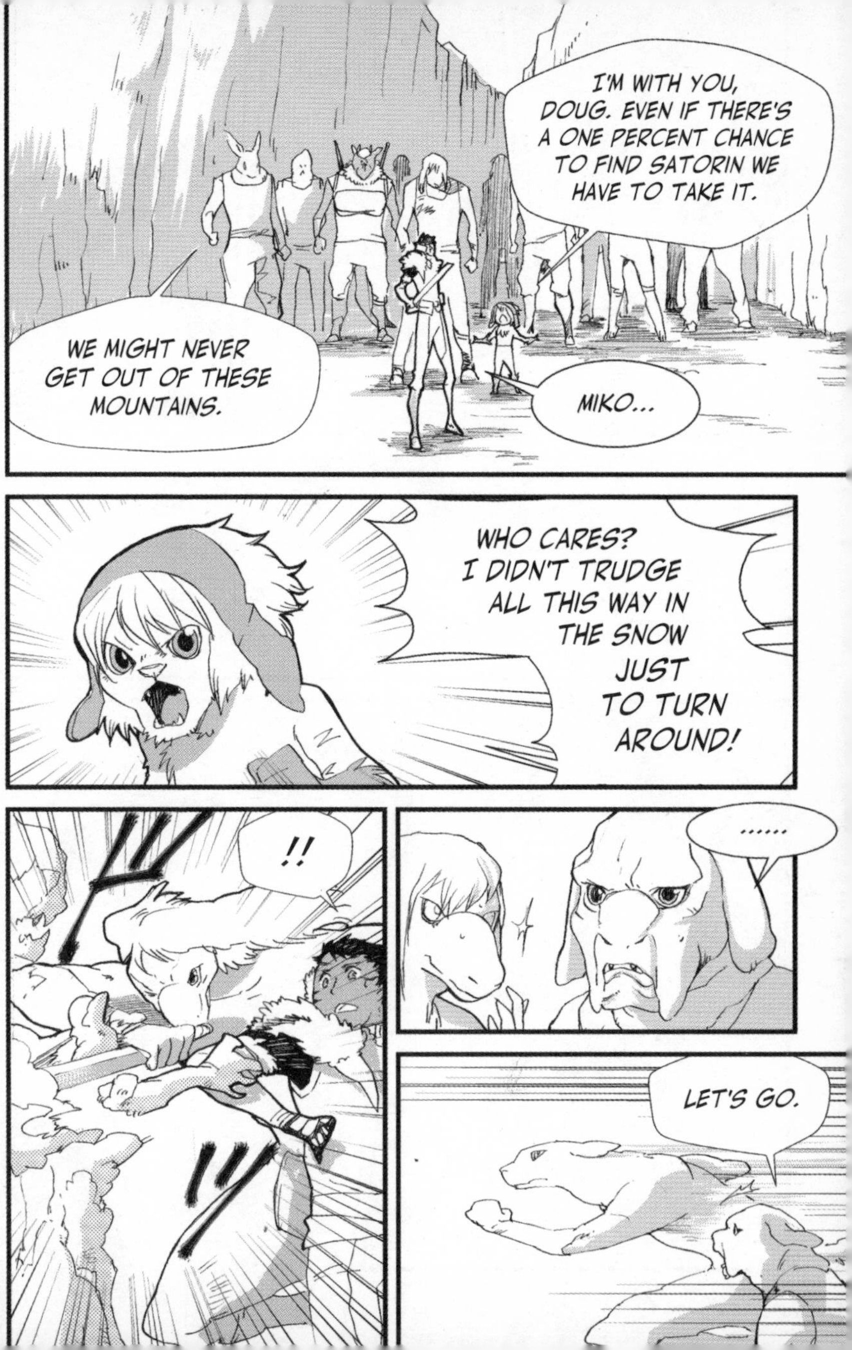
I'M WITH YOU, DOUG. EVEN IF THERE'S A ONE PERCENT CHANCE TO FIND SATORIN WE HAVE TO TAKE IT.
WE MIGHT NEVER GET OUT OF THESE MOUNTAINS.
MIKO...
WHO CARES? I DIDN'T TRUDGE ALL THIS WAY IN THE SNOW JUST TO TURN AROUND!
......
LET'S GO.
!!

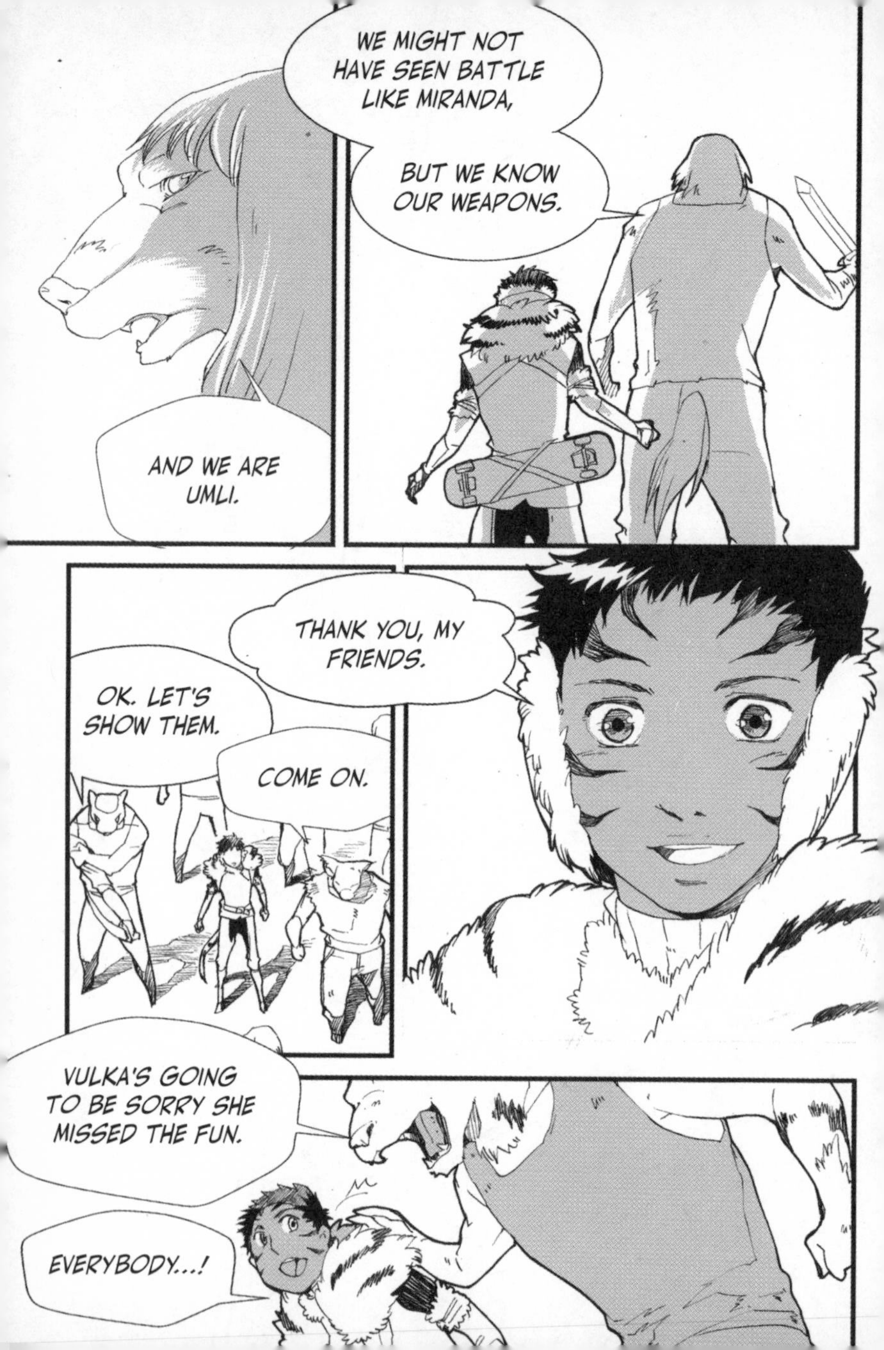
WE MIGHT NOT HAVE SEEN BATTLE LIKE MIRANDA,
BUT WE KNOW OUR WEAPONS.
AND WE ARE UMLI.
THANK YOU, MY FRIENDS.
OK. LET'S SHOW THEM.
COME ON.
VULKA'S GOING TO BE SORRY SHE MISSED THE FUN.
EVERYBODY...!

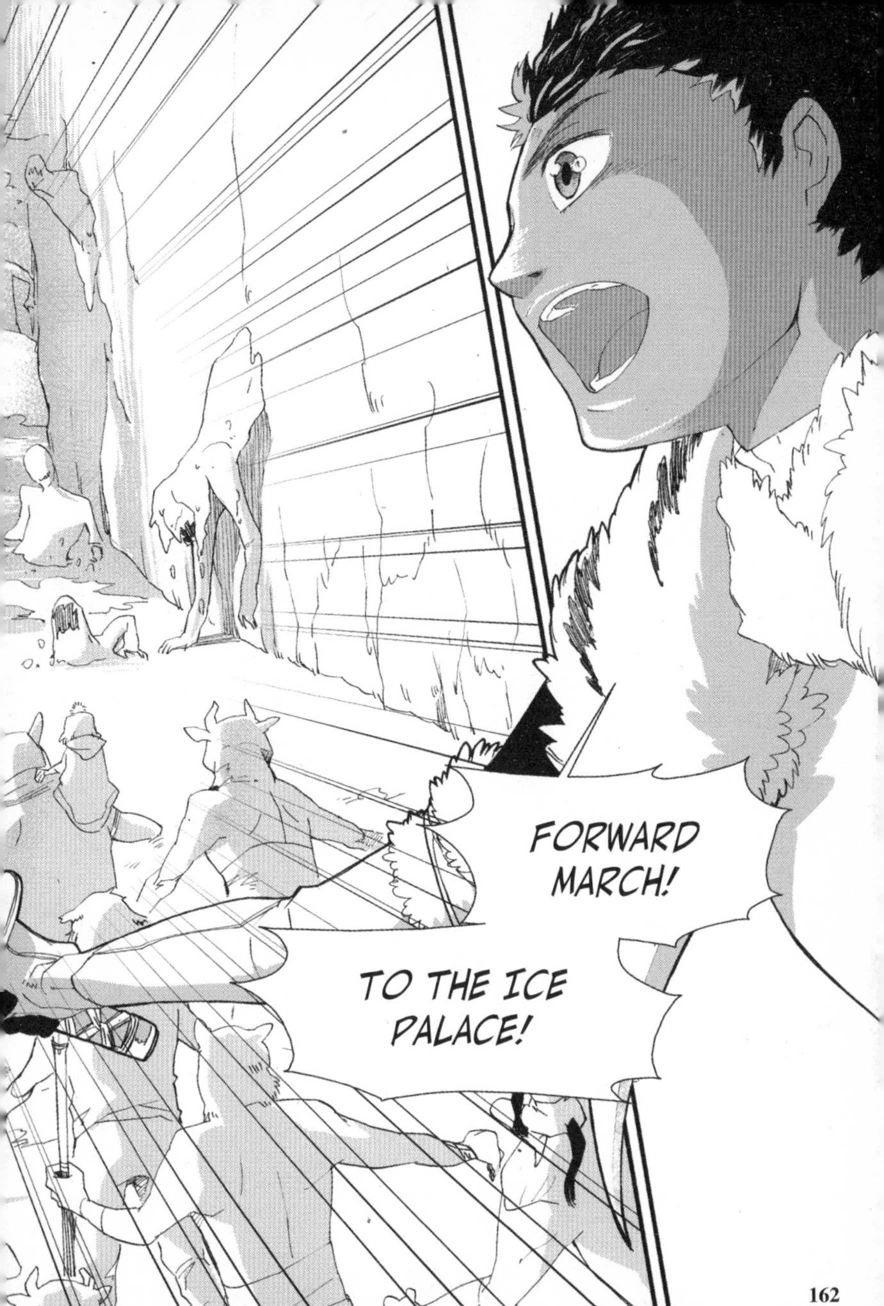
FORWARD MARCH!
TO THE ICE PALACE!

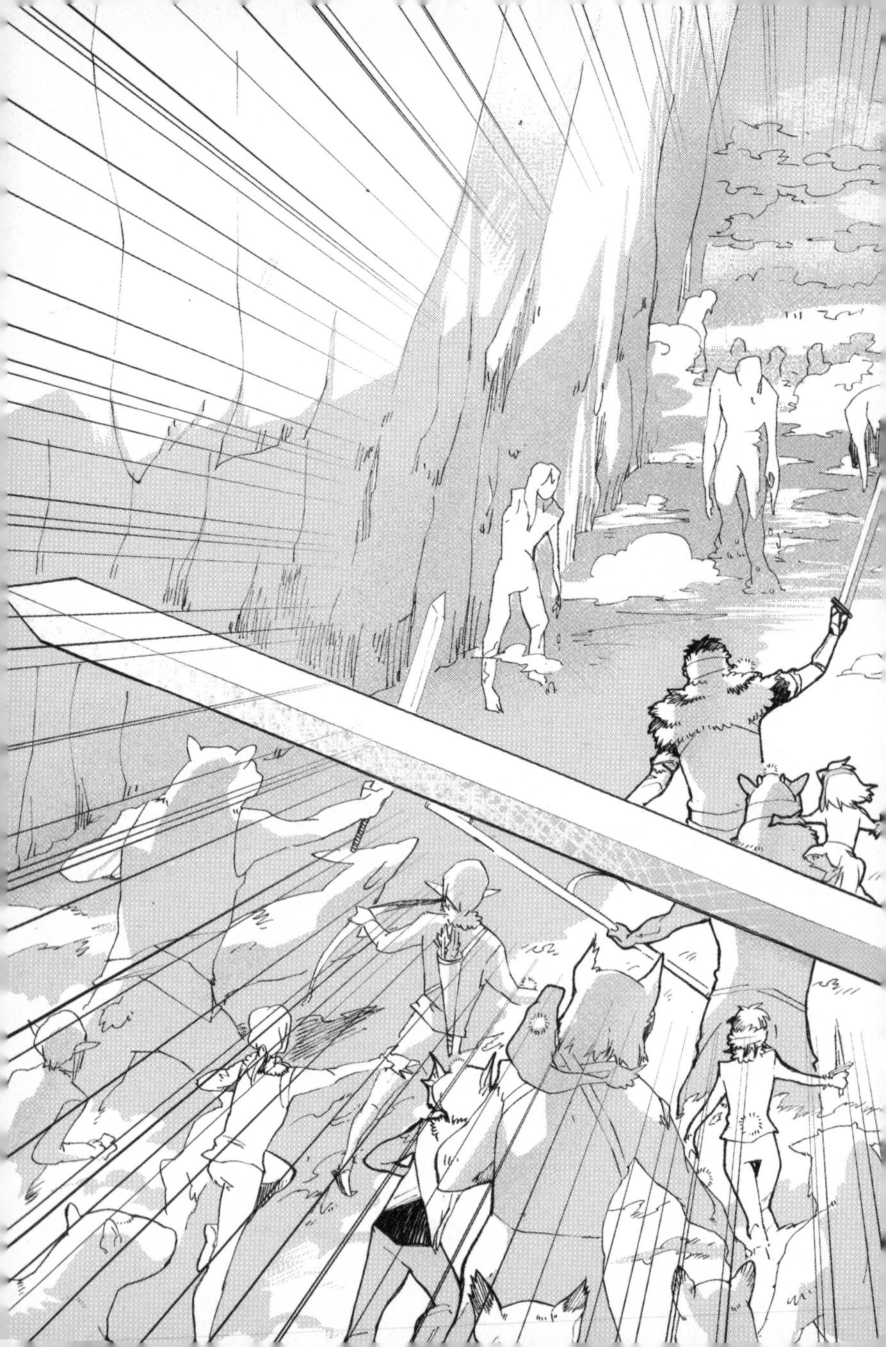

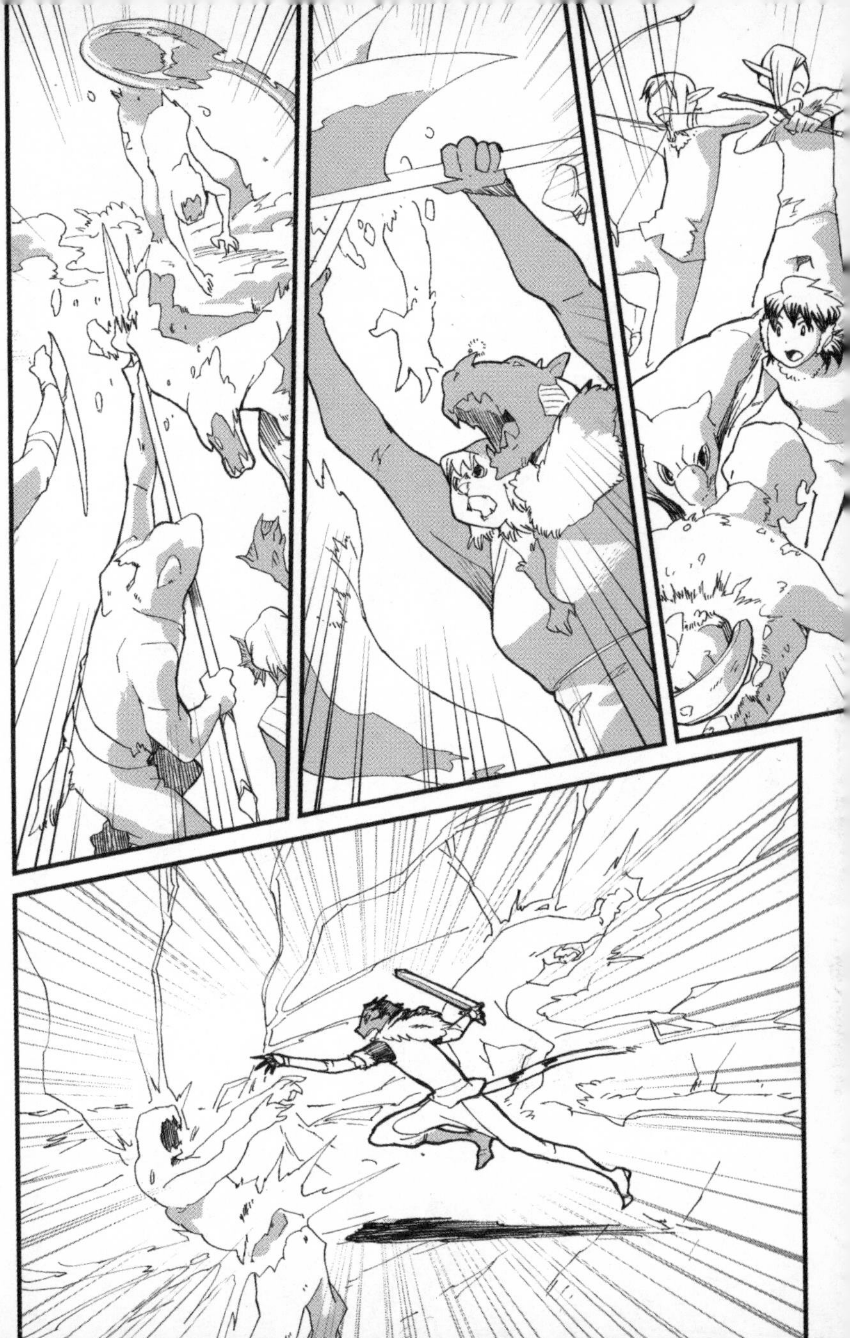

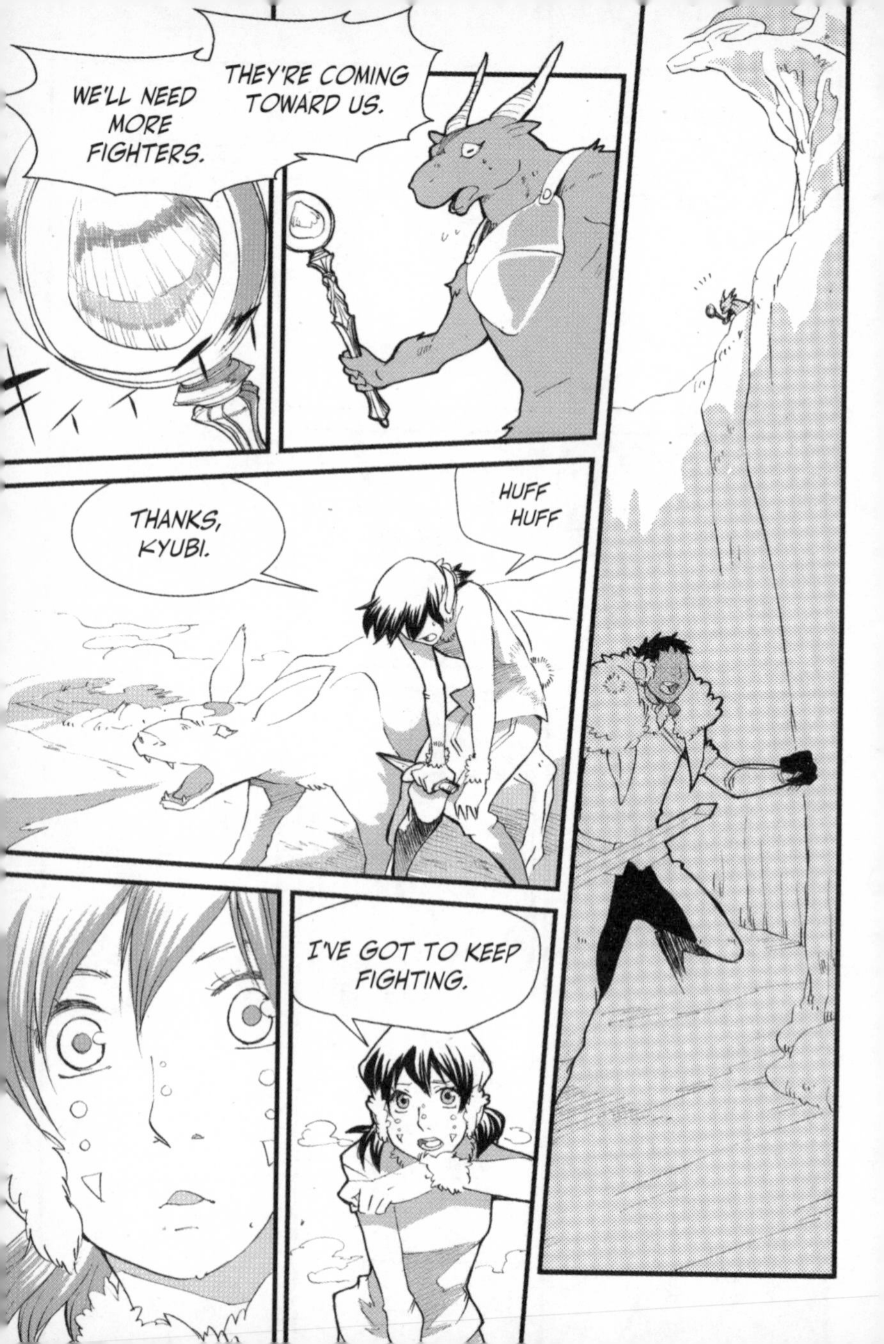
THEY'RE COMING TOWARD US.
WE'LL NEED MORE FIGHTERS.
HUFF HUFF
THANKS, KYUBI.
I'VE GOT TO KEEP FIGHTING.

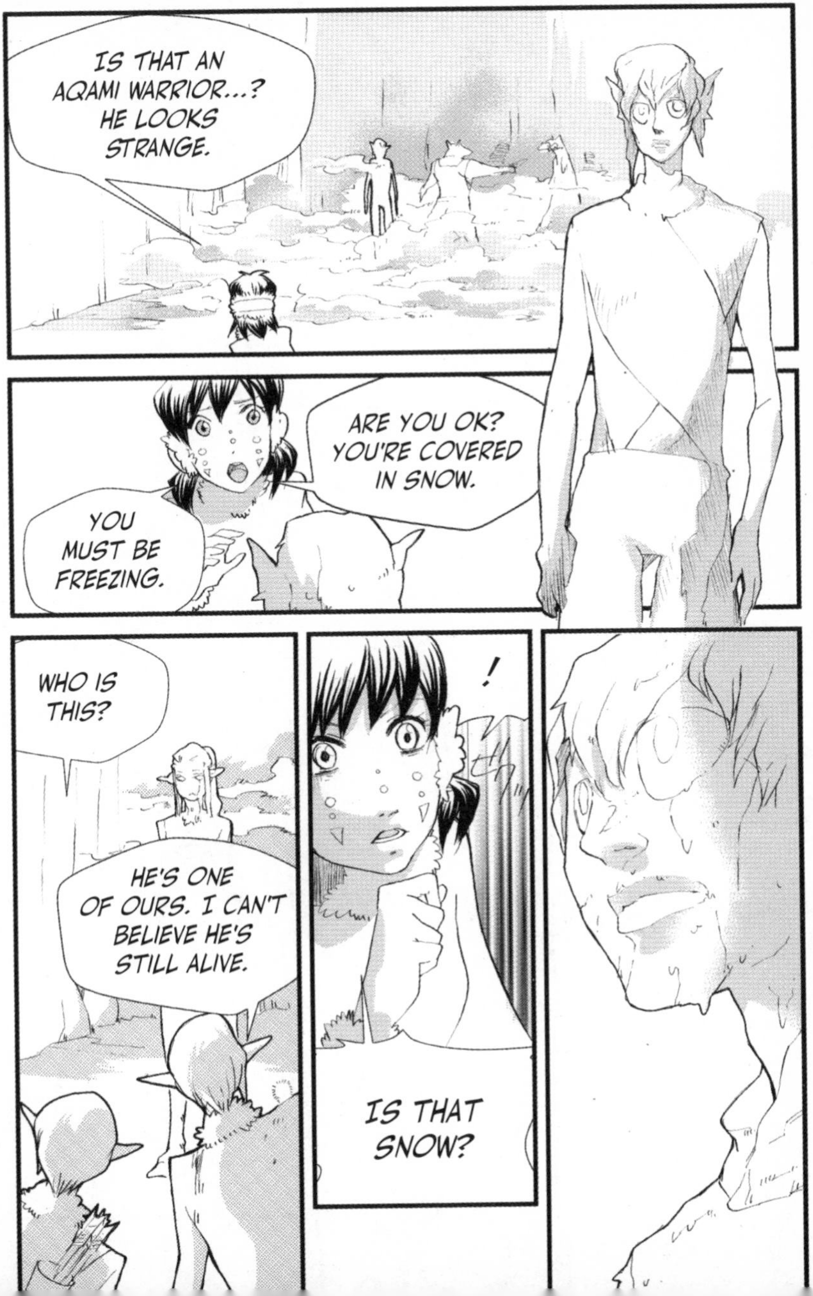
IS THAT AN AQAMI WARRIOR...? HE LOOKS STRANGE.
ARE YOU OK? YOU'RE COVERED IN SNOW.
YOU MUST BE FREEZING.
!
IS THAT SNOW?
WHO IS THIS?
HE'S ONE OF OURS. I CAN'T BELIEVE HE'S STILL ALIVE.

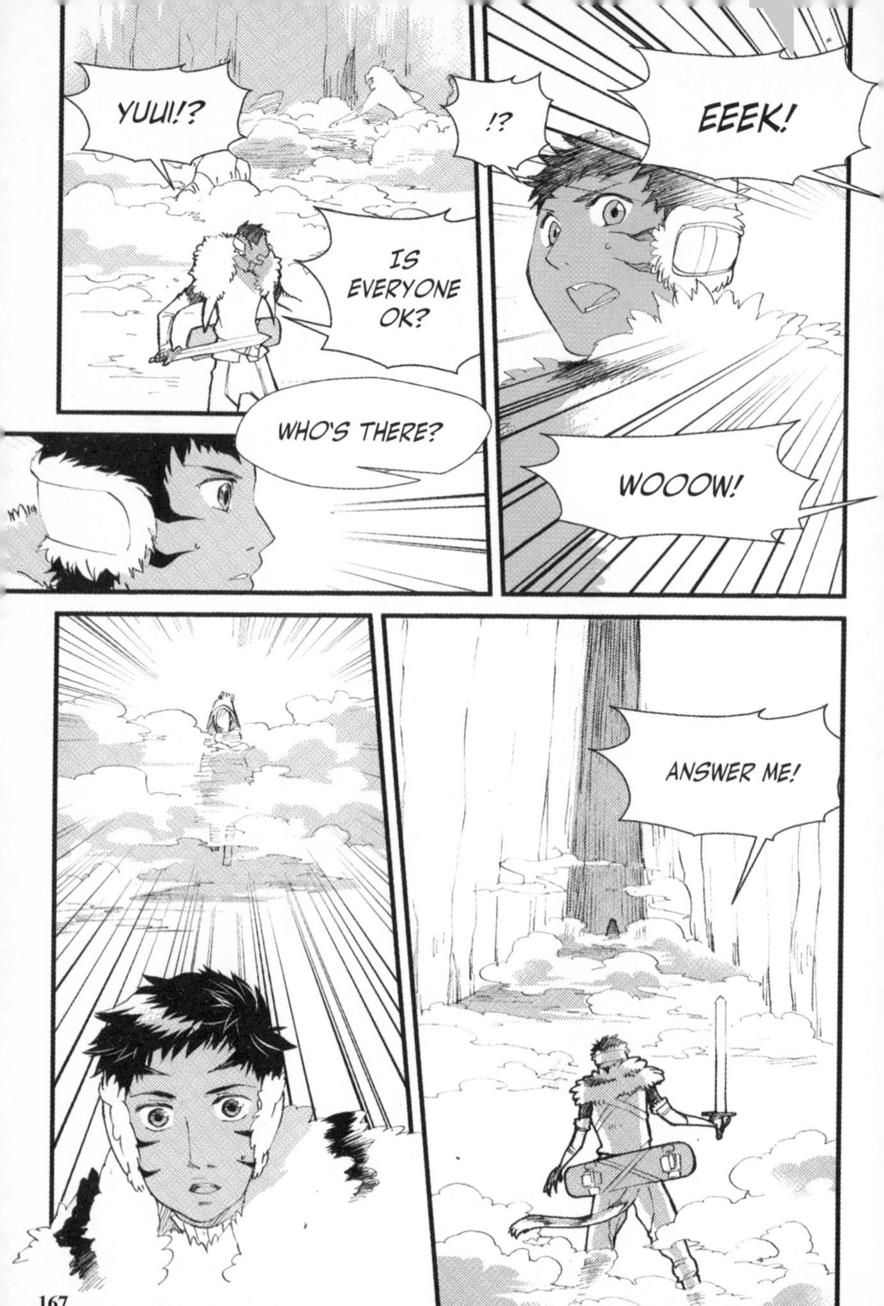
EEEK!
!?
WOOOW!
YUUI!?
IS EVERYONE OK?
WHO'S THERE?
ANSWER ME!

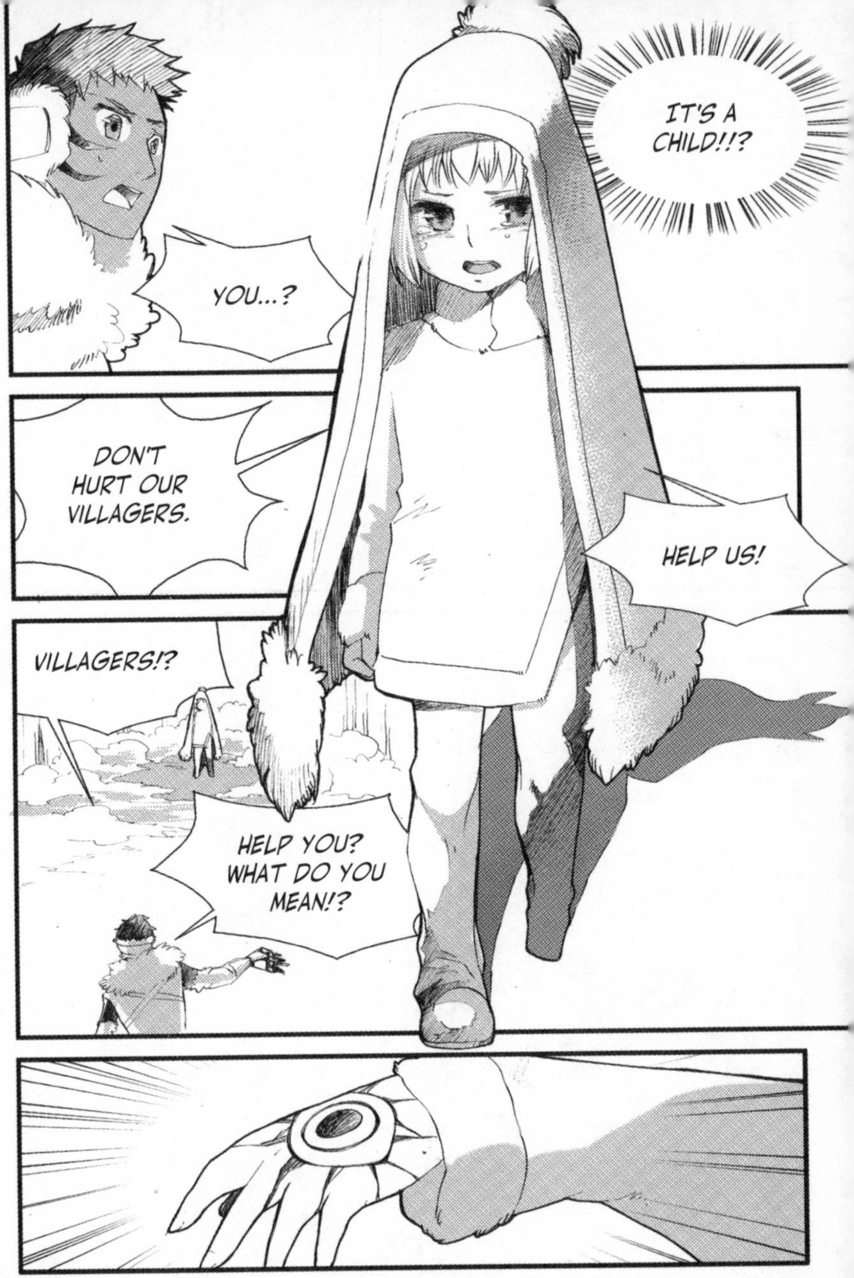
IT'S A CHILD!!?
YOU...?
DON'T HURT OUR VILLAGERS.
HELP US!
VILLAGERS!?
HELP YOU? WHAT DO YOU MEAN!?

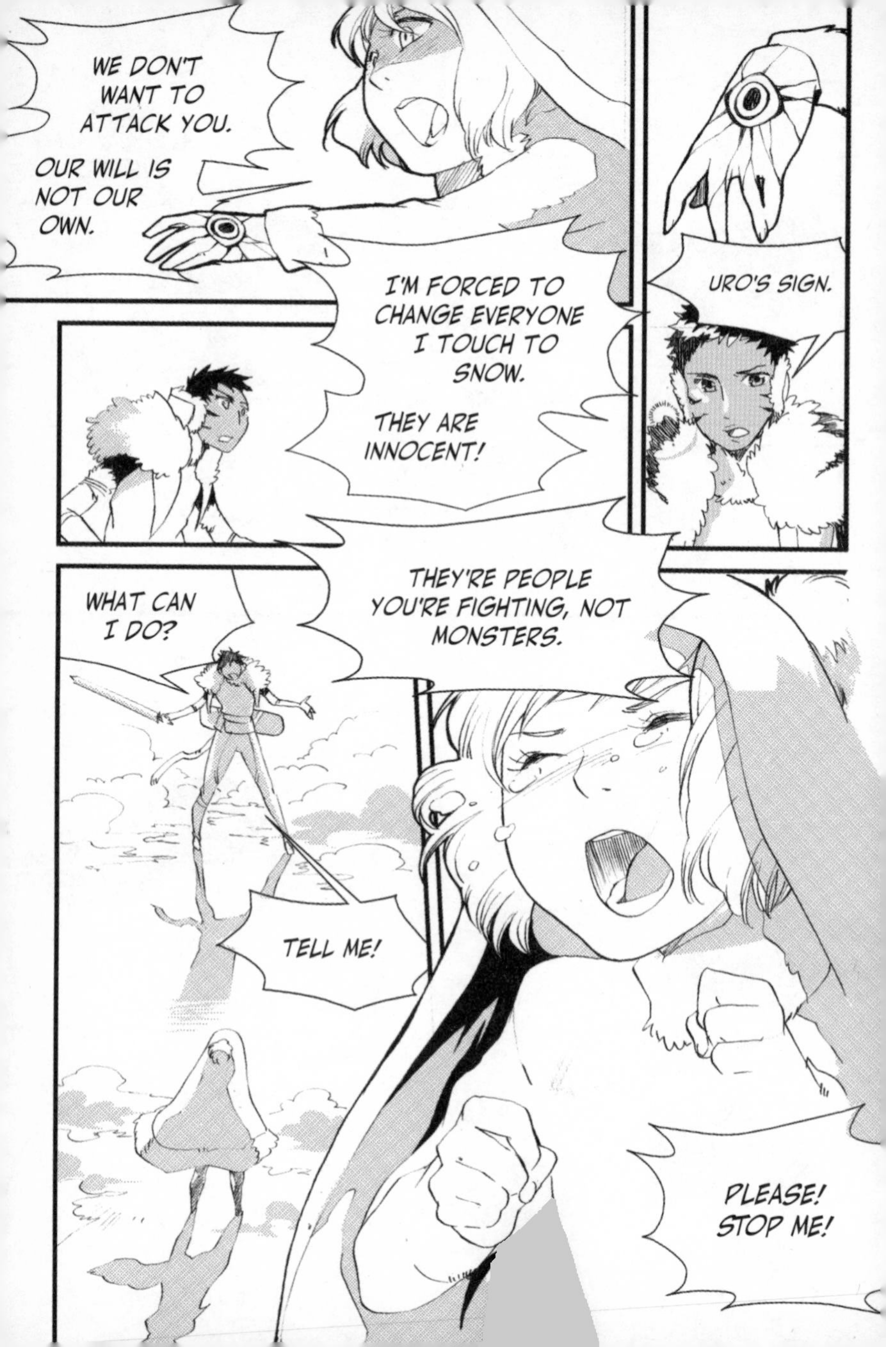
URO'S SIGN.
WE DON'T WANT TO ATTACK YOU.
OUR WILL IS NOT OUR OWN.
I'M FORCED TO CHANGE EVERYONE I TOUCH TO SNOW.
THEY ARE INNOCENT!
THEY'RE PEOPLE YOU'RE FIGHTING, NOT MONSTERS.
PLEASE! STOP ME!
WHAT CAN I DO?
TELL ME!

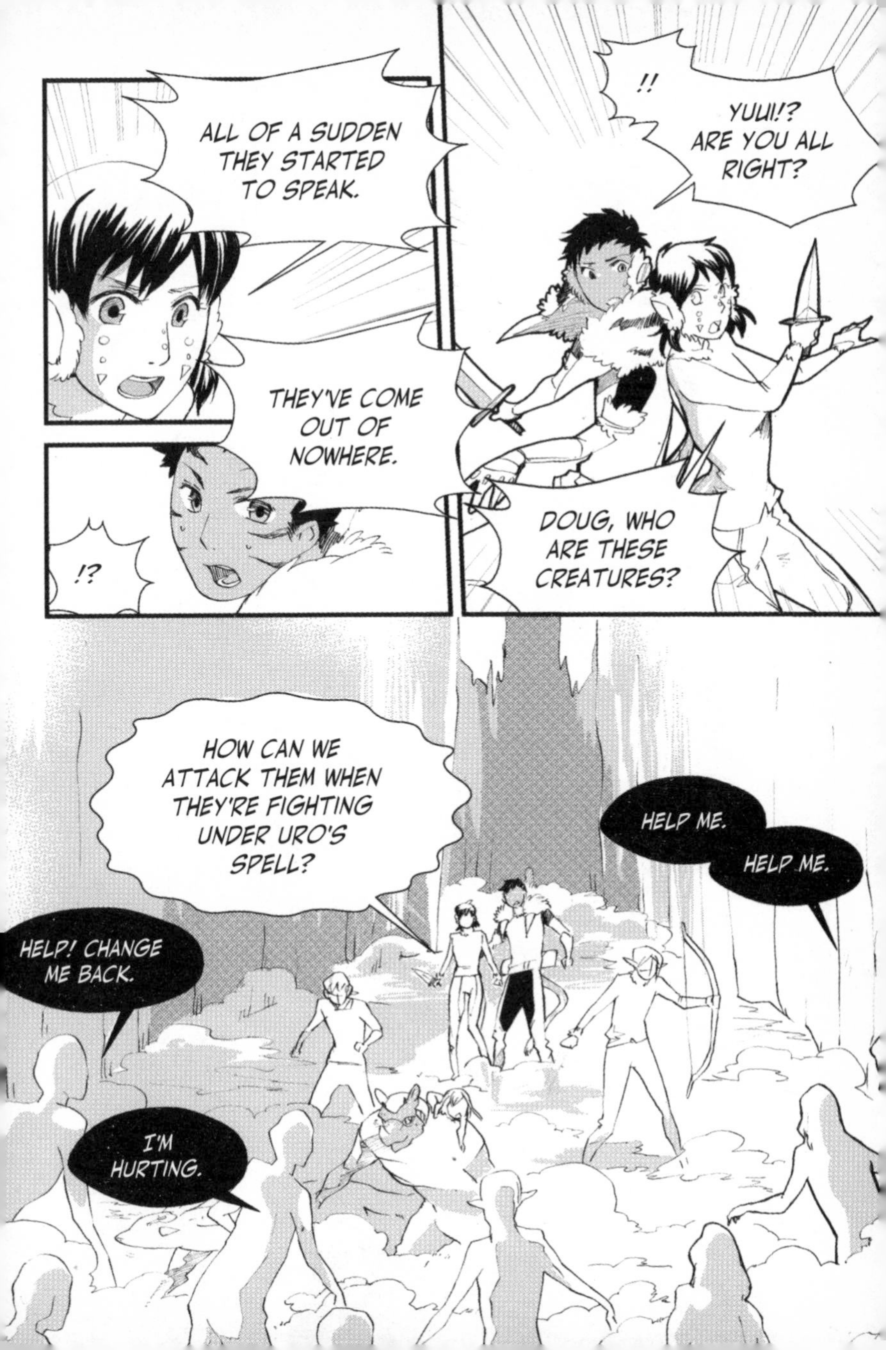
!!
YUUI!? ARE YOU ALL RIGHT?
DOUG, WHO ARE THESE CREATURES?
ALL OF A SUDDEN THEY STARTED TO SPEAK.
!?
THEY'VE COME OUT OF NOWHERE.
HELP ME.
HELP ME.
HOW CAN WE ATTACK THEM WHEN THEY'RE FIGHTING UNDER URO'S SPELL?
HELP! CHANGE ME BACK.
I'M HURTING.

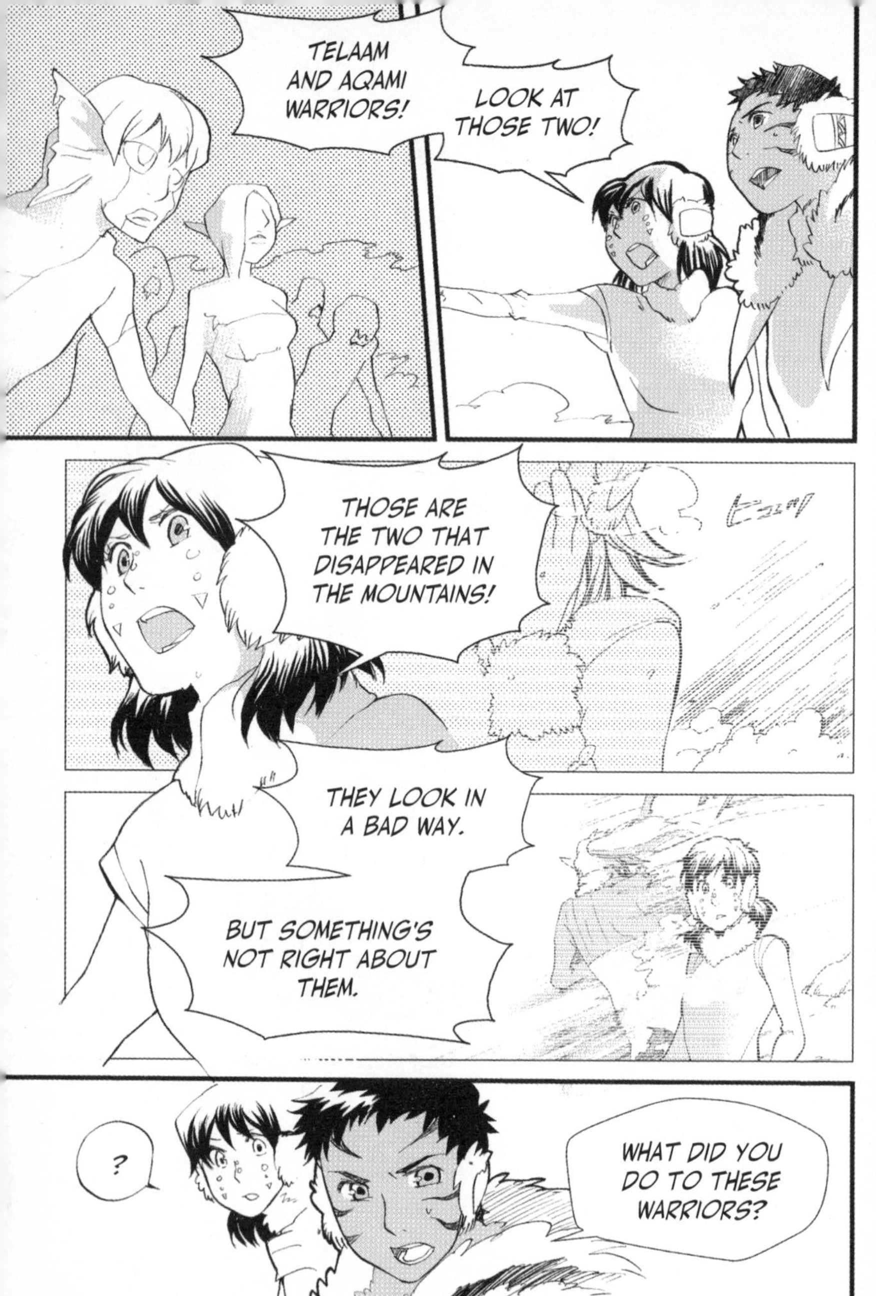
LOOK AT THOSE TWO!
TELAAM AND AQAMI WARRIORS!
THOSE ARE THE TWO THAT DISAPPEARED IN THE MOUNTAINS!
THEY LOOK IN A BAD WAY.
BUT SOMETHING'S NOT RIGHT ABOUT THEM.
WHAT DID YOU DO TO THESE WARRIORS?
?

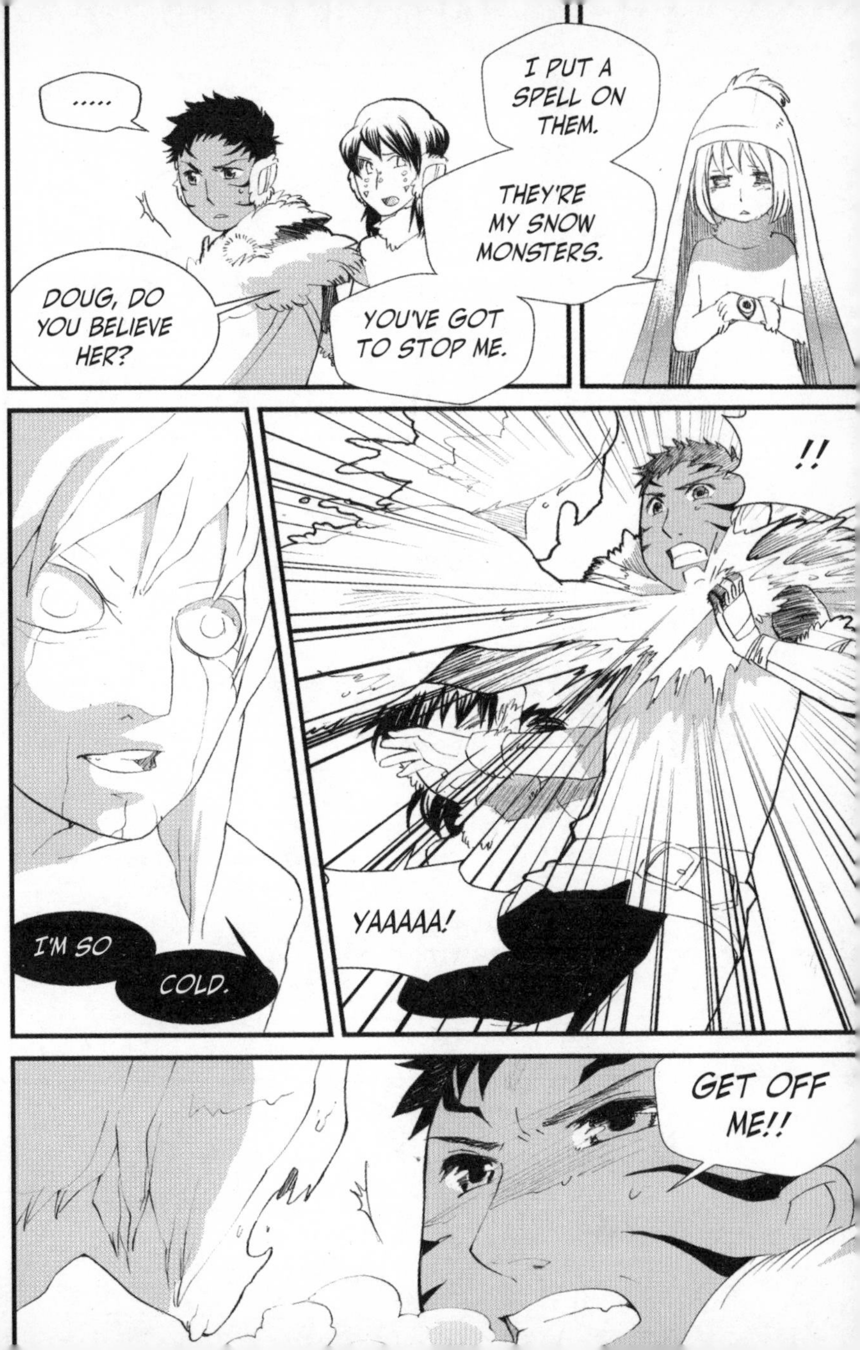
I PUT A SPELL ON THEM.
THEY'RE MY SNOW MONSTERS.
YOU'VE GOT TO STOP ME.
.....
DOUG, DO YOU BELIEVE HER?
!!
YAAAAA!
I'M SO COLD.
GET OFF ME!!

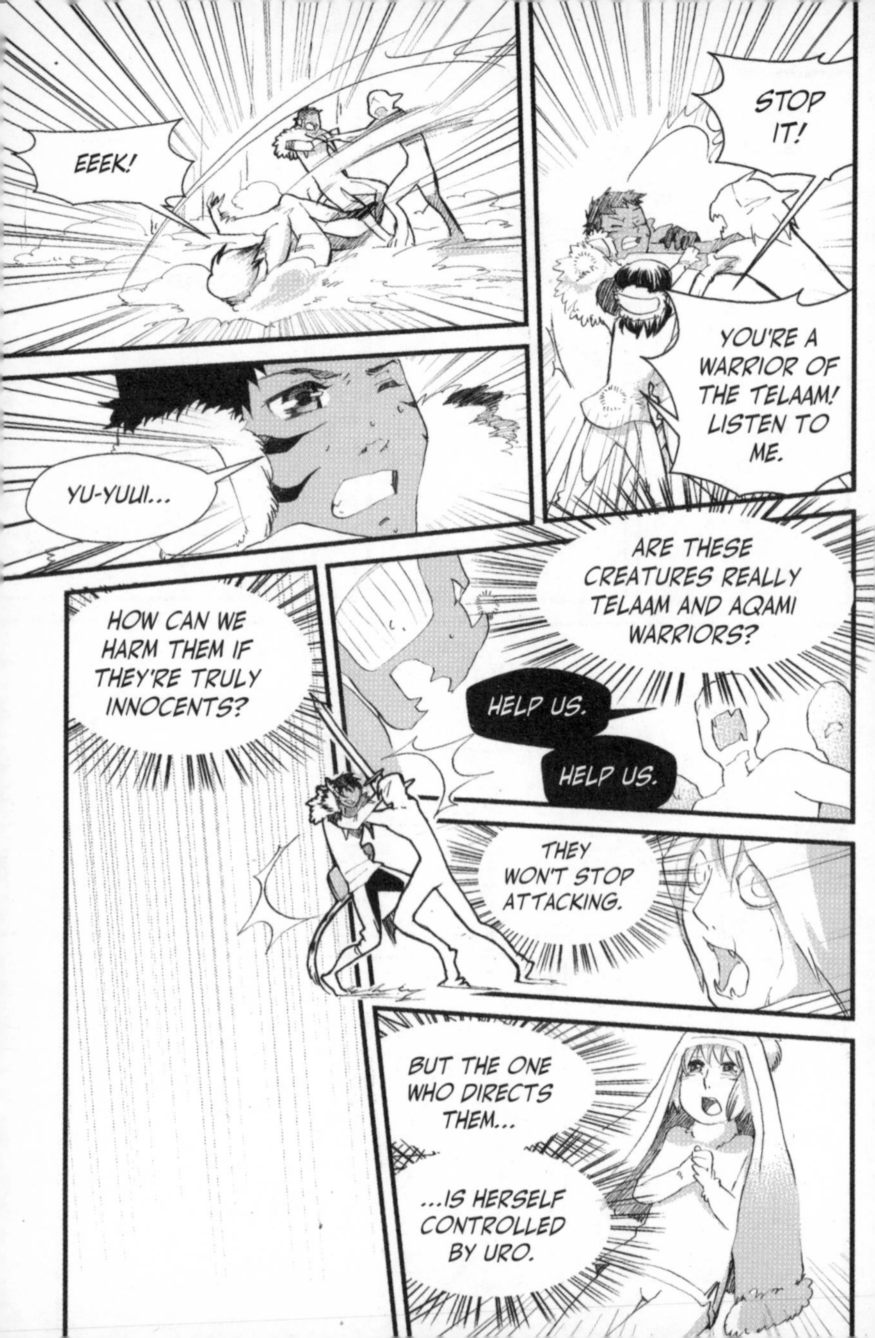
STOP IT!
YOU'RE A WARRIOR OF THE TELAAM! LISTEN TO ME.
EEEK!
YU-YUUI...
ARE THESE CREATURES REALLY TELAAM AND AQAMI WARRIORS?
HELP US.
HELP US.
THEY WON'T STOP ATTACKING.
BUT THE ONE WHO DIRECTS THEM...
...IS HERSELF CONTROLLED BY URO.
HOW CAN WE HARM THEM IF THEY'RE TRULY INNOCENTS?

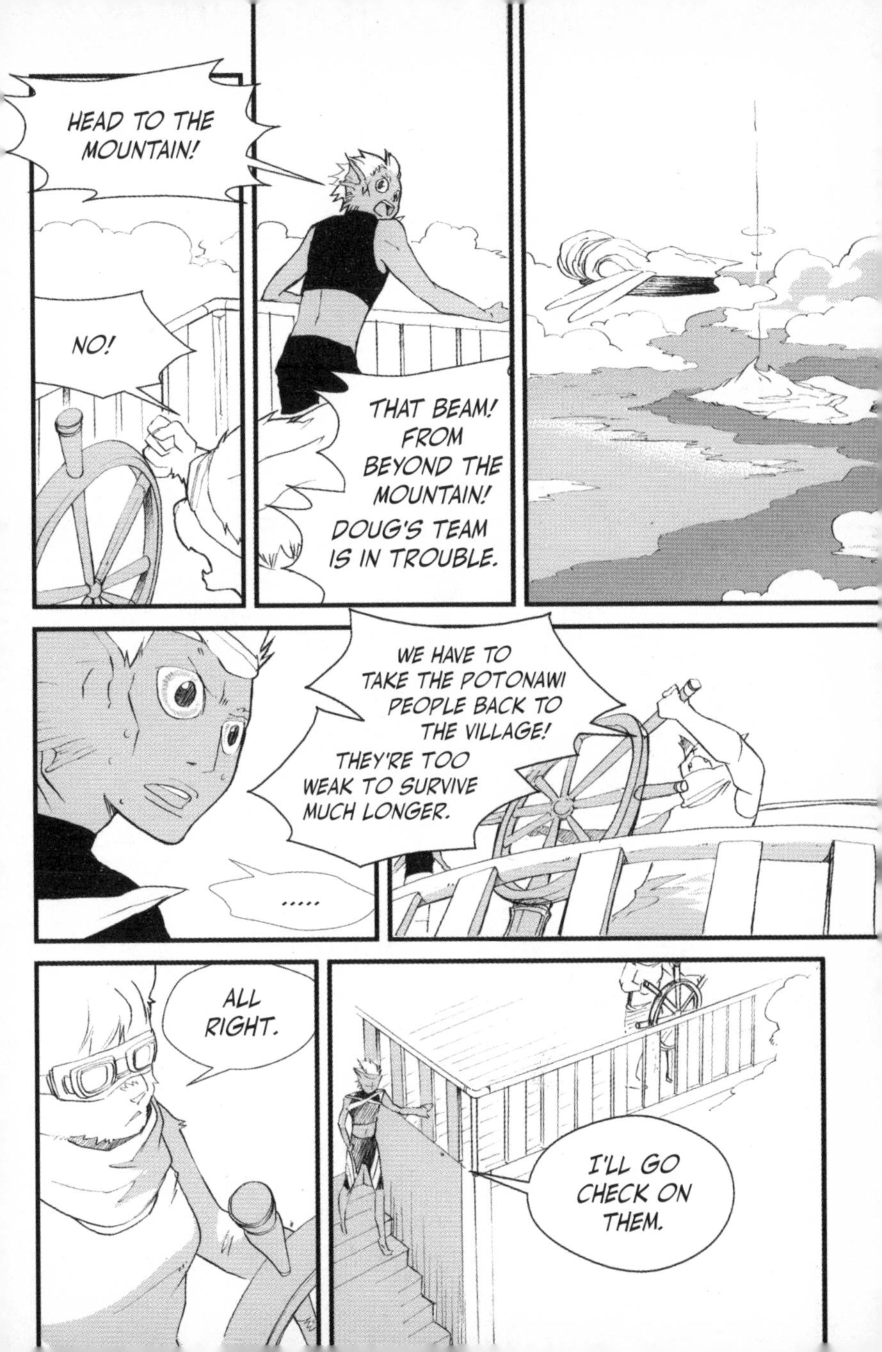
THAT BEAM! FROM BEYOND THE MOUNTAIN!
DOUG'S TEAM IS IN TROUBLE.
HEAD TO THE MOUNTAIN!
NO!
WE HAVE TO TAKE THE POTONAWI PEOPLE BACK TO THE VILLAGE!
THEY'RE TOO WEAK TO SURVIVE MUCH LONGER.
.....
I'LL GO CHECK ON THEM.
ALL RIGHT.

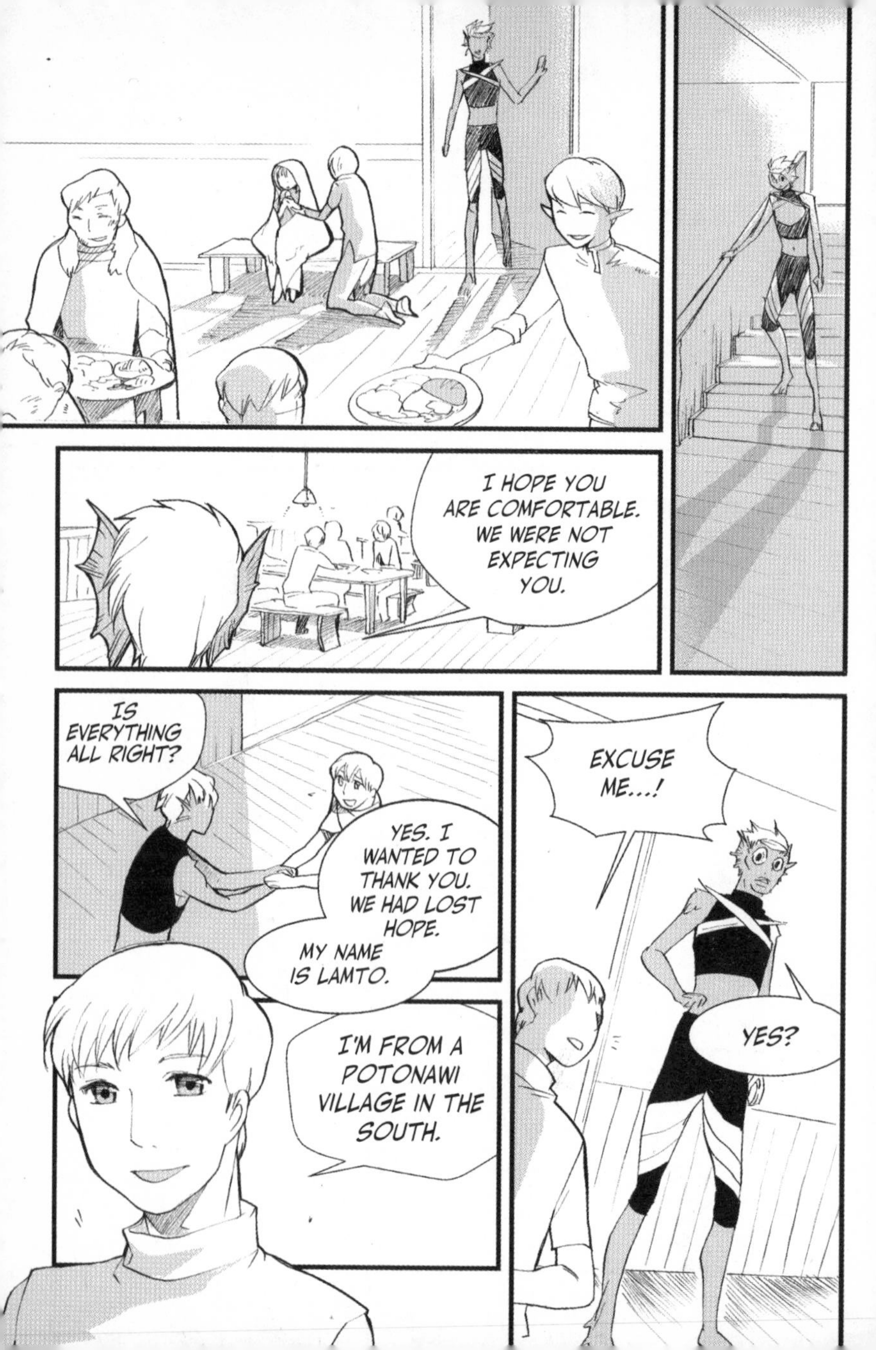
I HOPE YOU ARE COMFORTABLE. WE WERE NOT EXPECTING YOU.
EXCUSE ME...!
YES?
IS EVERYTHING ALL RIGHT?
YES. I WANTED TO THANK YOU. WE HAD LOST HOPE.
MY NAME IS LAMTO.
I'M FROM A POTONAWI VILLAGE IN THE SOUTH.

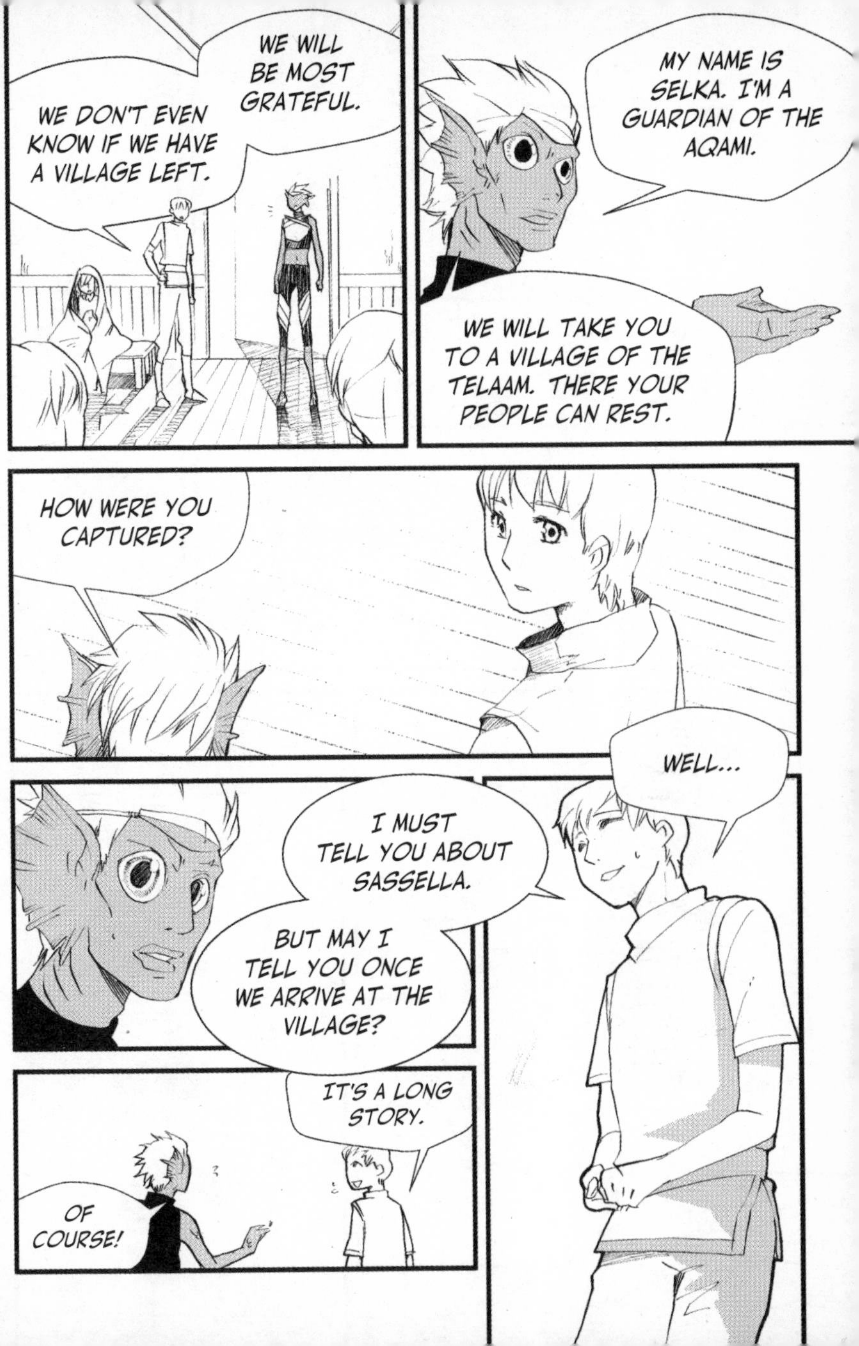
MY NAME IS SELKA. I'M A GUARDIAN OF THE AQAMI.
WE WILL TAKE YOU TO A VILLAGE OF THE TELAAM. THERE YOUR PEOPLE CAN REST.
WE WILL BE MOST GRATEFUL.
WE DON'T EVEN KNOW IF WE HAVE A VILLAGE LEFT.
HOW WERE YOU CAPTURED?
WELL...
I MUST TELL YOU ABOUT SASSELLA.
BUT MAY I TELL YOU ONCE WE ARRIVE AT THE VILLAGE?
IT'S A LONG STORY.
OF COURSE!

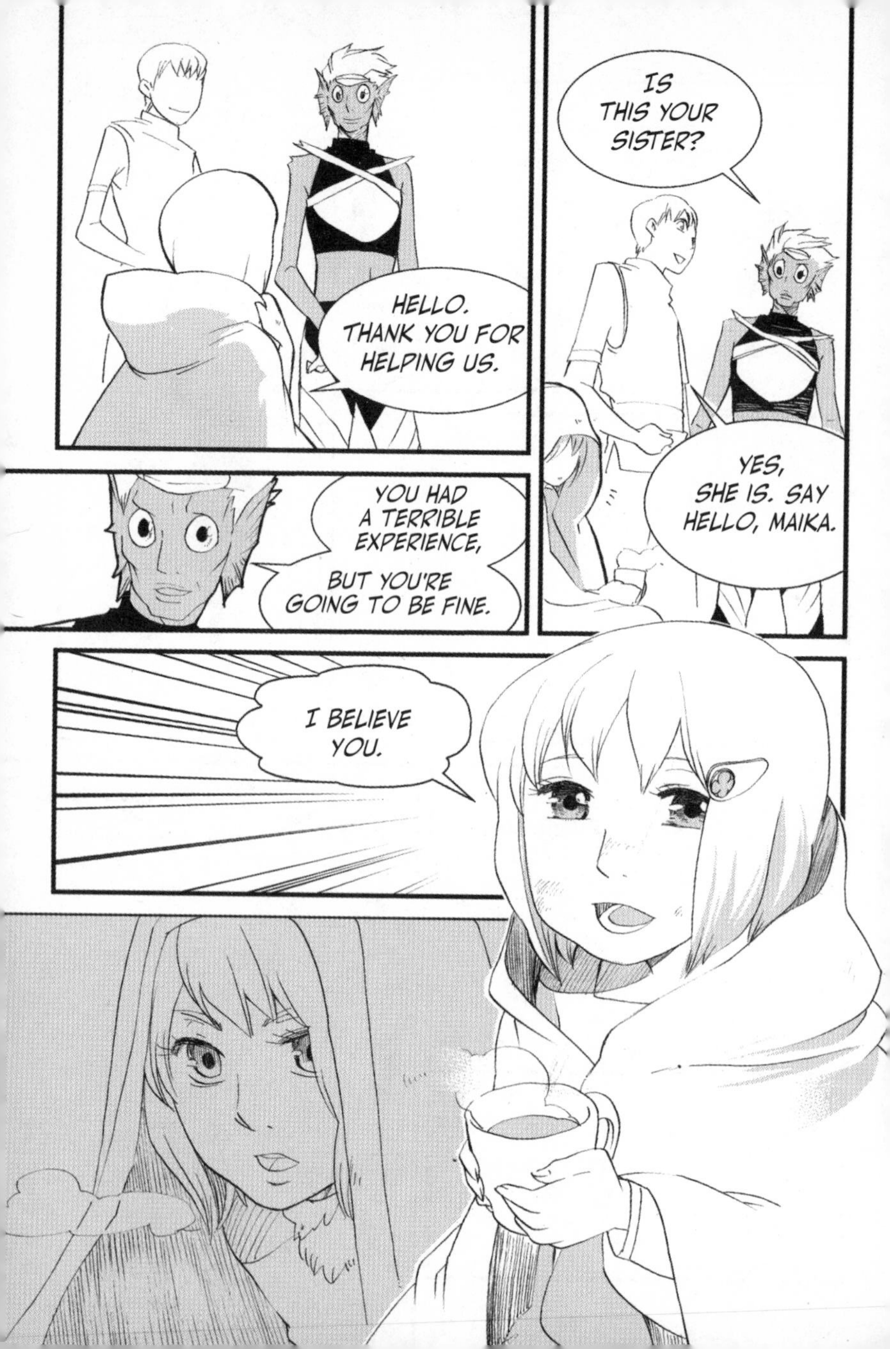
IS THIS YOUR SISTER?
YES, SHE IS. SAY HELLO, MAIKA.
HELLO. THANK YOU FOR HELPING US.
YOU HAD A TERRIBLE EXPERIENCE,
BUT YOU'RE GOING TO BE FINE.
I BELIEVE YOU.

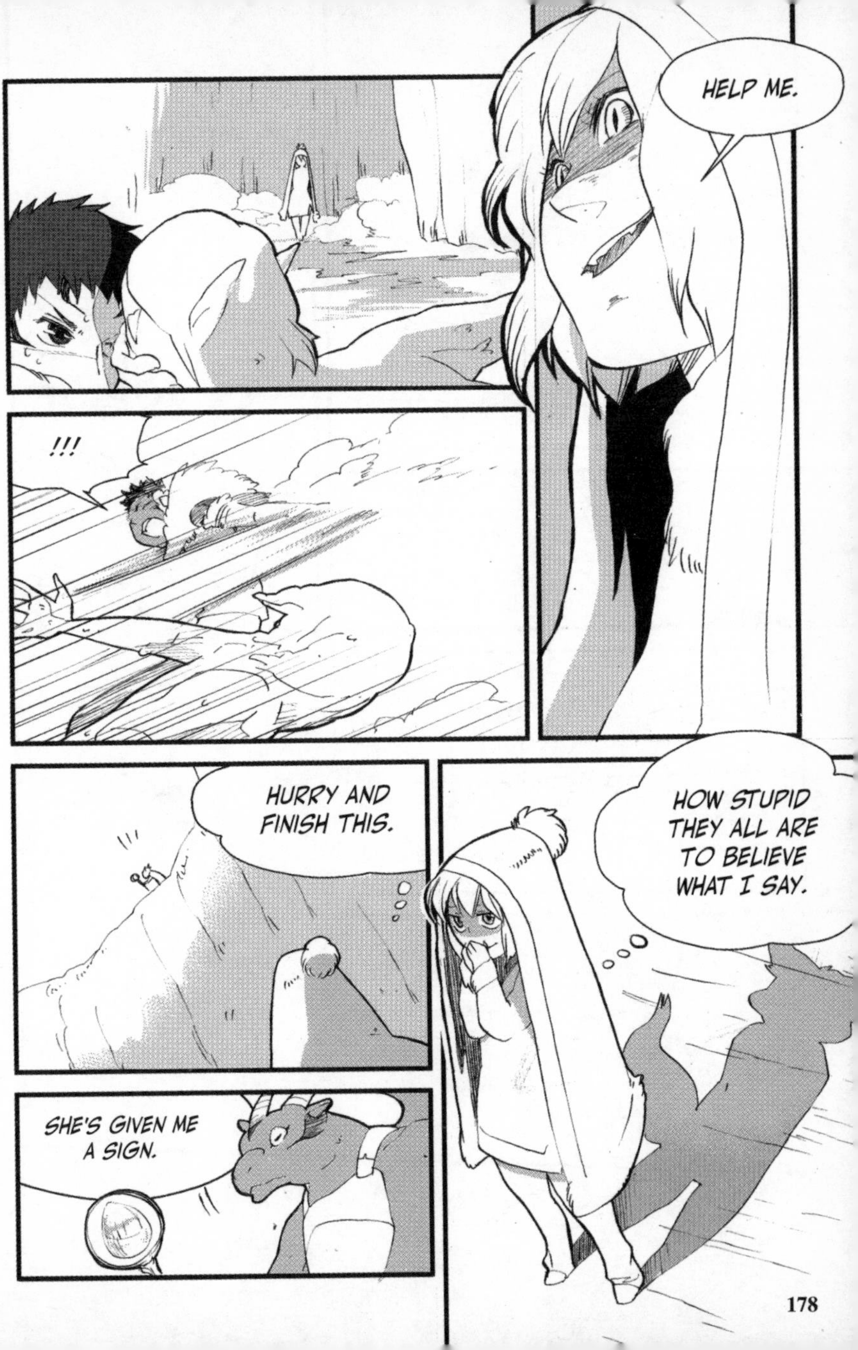
HELP ME.
!!!
HOW STUPID THEY ALL ARE TO BELIEVE WHAT I SAY.
HURRY AND FINISH THIS.
SHE'S GIVEN ME A SIGN.

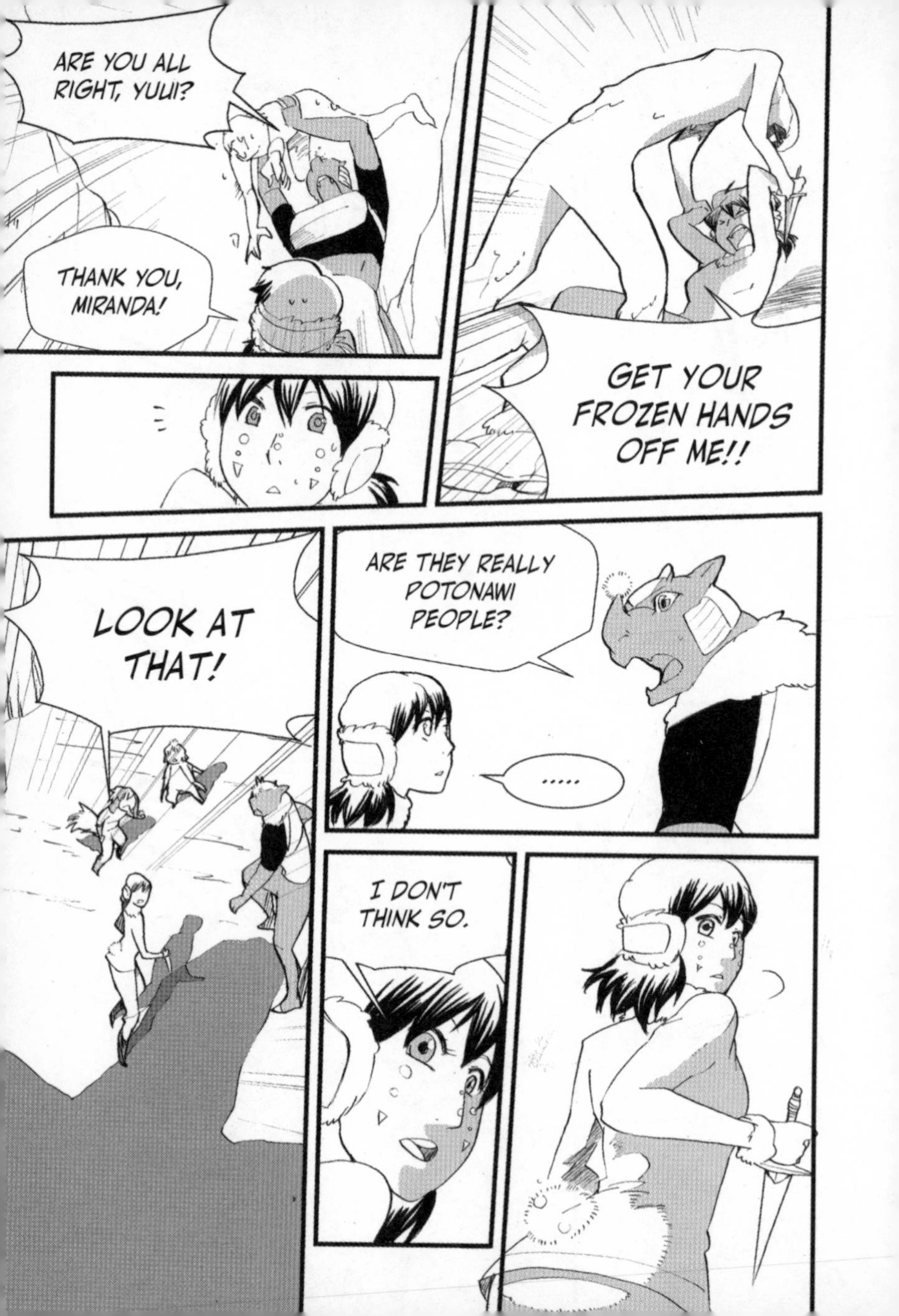
GET YOUR FROZEN HANDS OFF ME!!
ARE YOU ALL RIGHT, YUUI?
THANK YOU, MIRANDA!
ARE THEY REALLY POTONAWI PEOPLE?
.....
I DON'T THINK SO.
LOOK AT THAT!

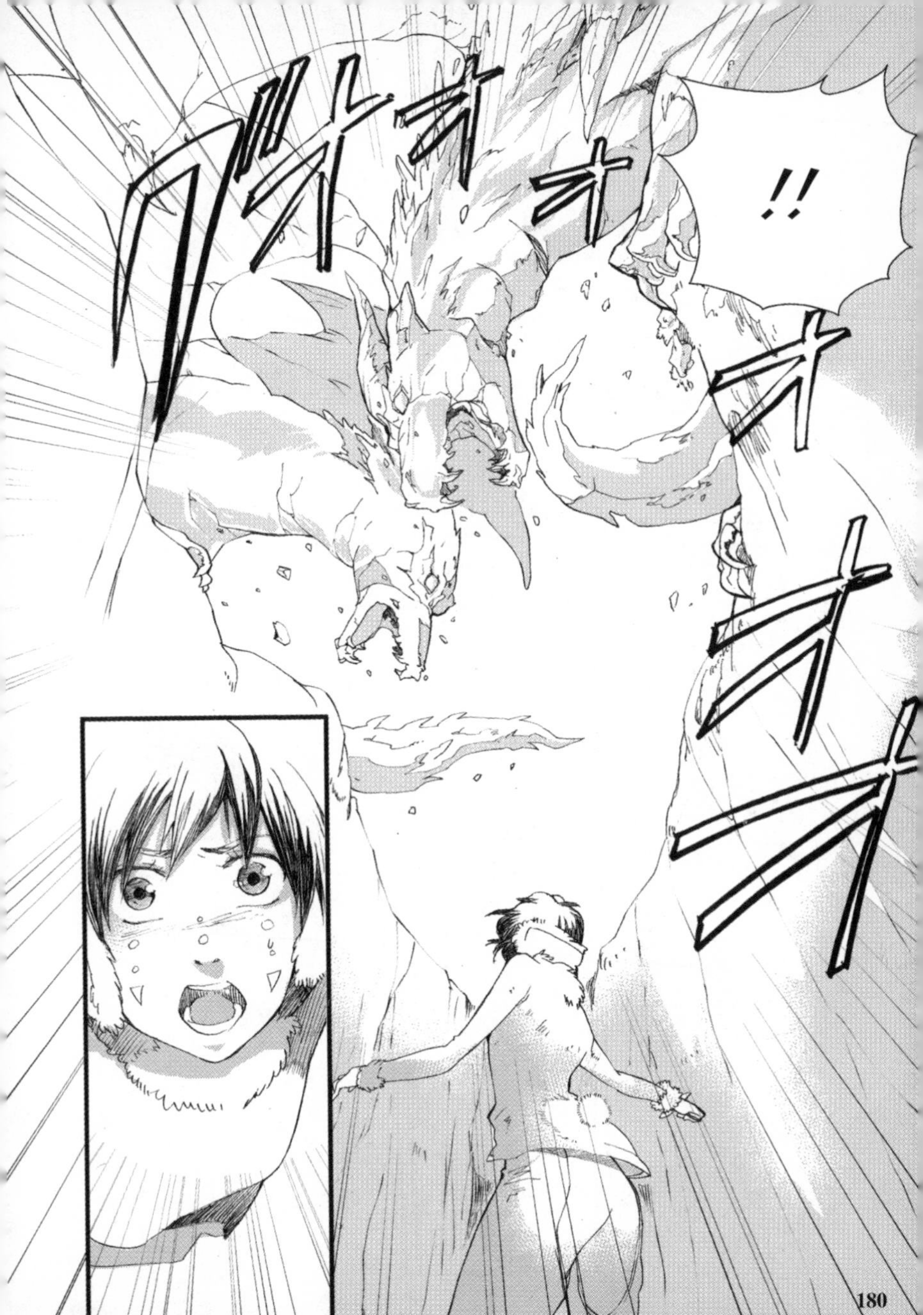
!!

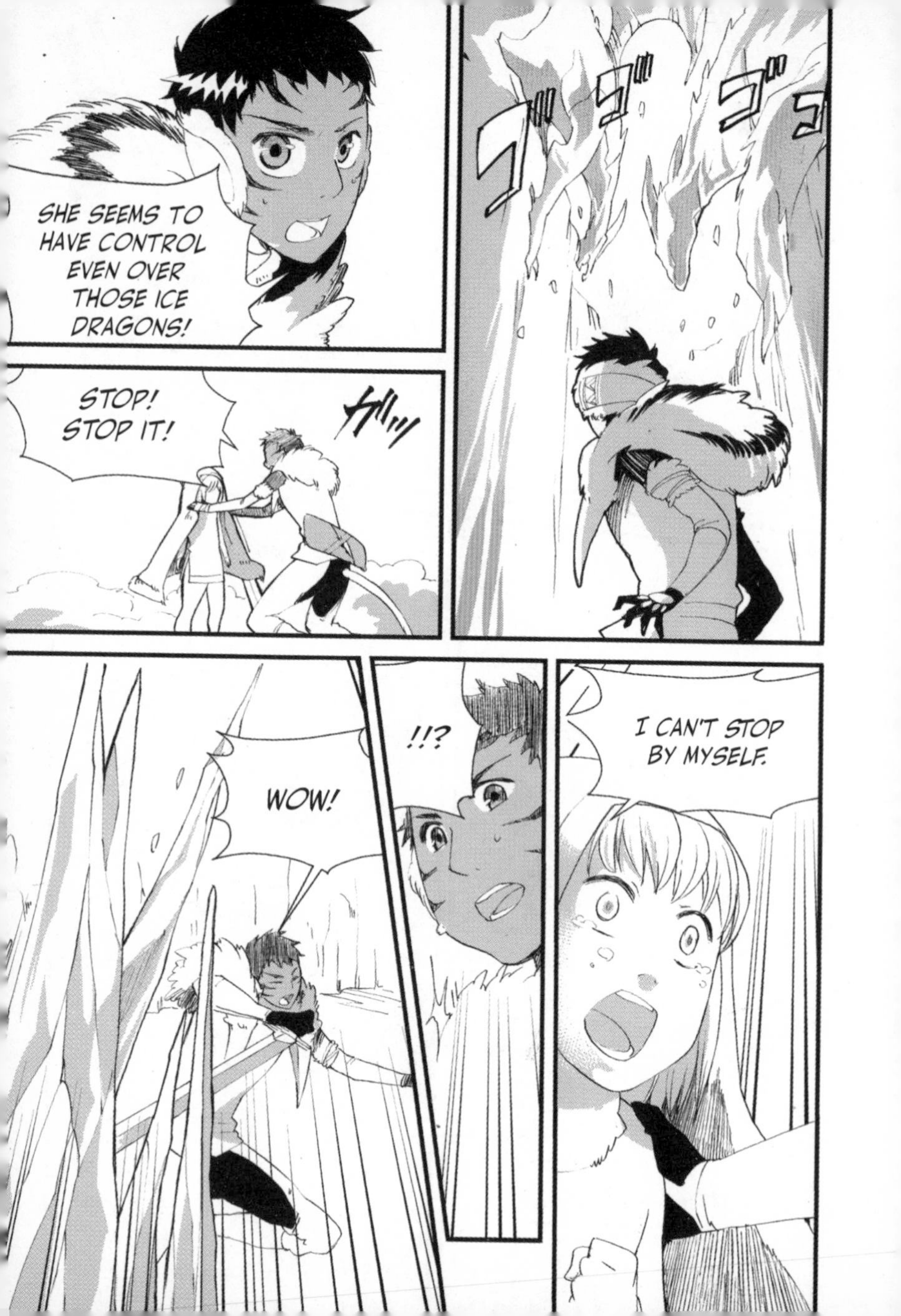
ゴゴゴゴ
SHE SEEMS TO HAVE CONTROL EVEN OVER THOSE ICE DRAGONS!
STOP! STOP IT!
I CAN'T STOP BY MYSELF.
!!?
WOW!

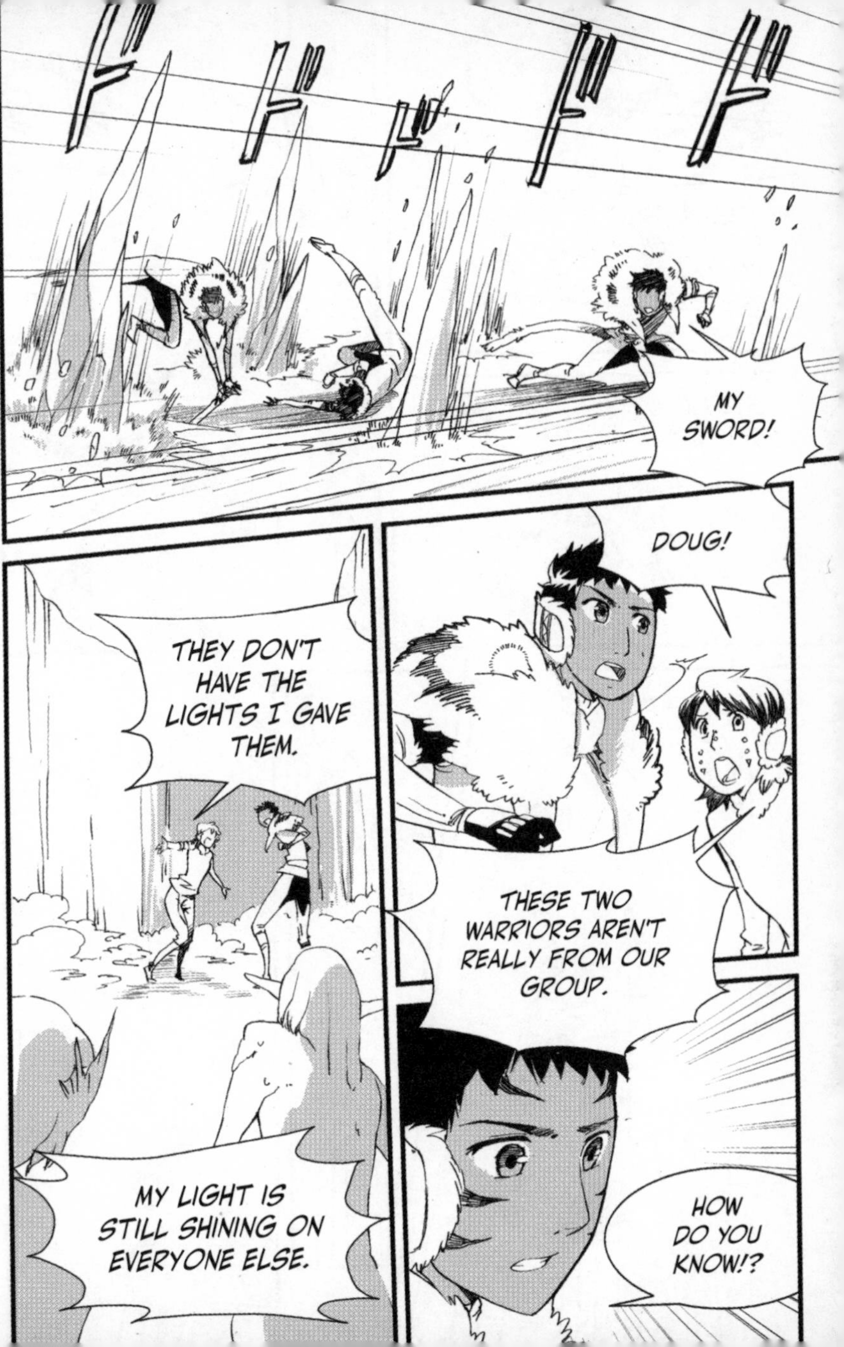
MY SWORD!
DOUG!
THESE TWO WARRIORS AREN'T REALLY FROM OUR GROUP.
HOW DO YOU KNOW!?
THEY DON'T HAVE THE LIGHTS I GAVE THEM.
MY LIGHT IS STILL SHINING ON EVERYONE ELSE.

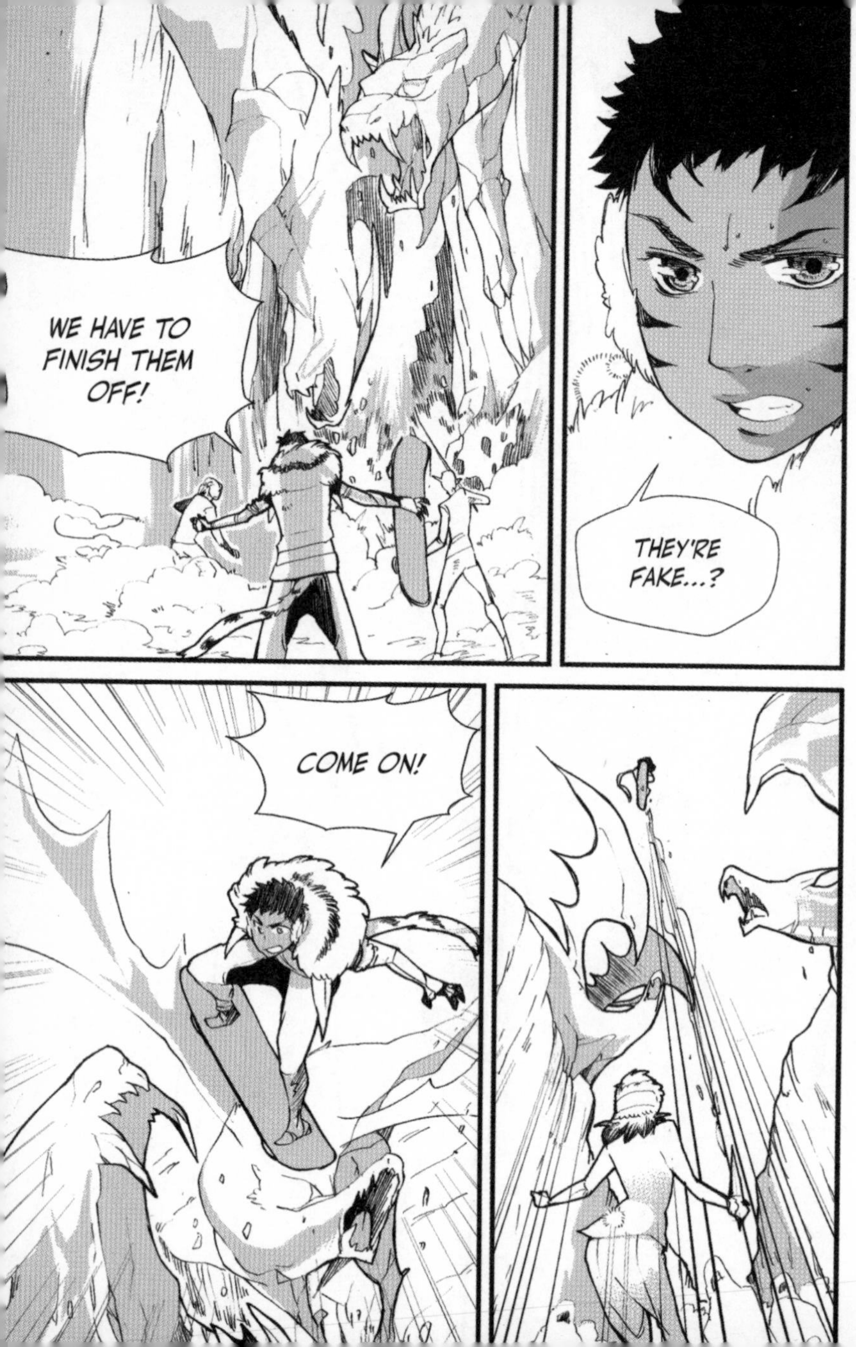
THEY'RE FAKE...?
WE HAVE TO FINISH THEM OFF!
COME ON!

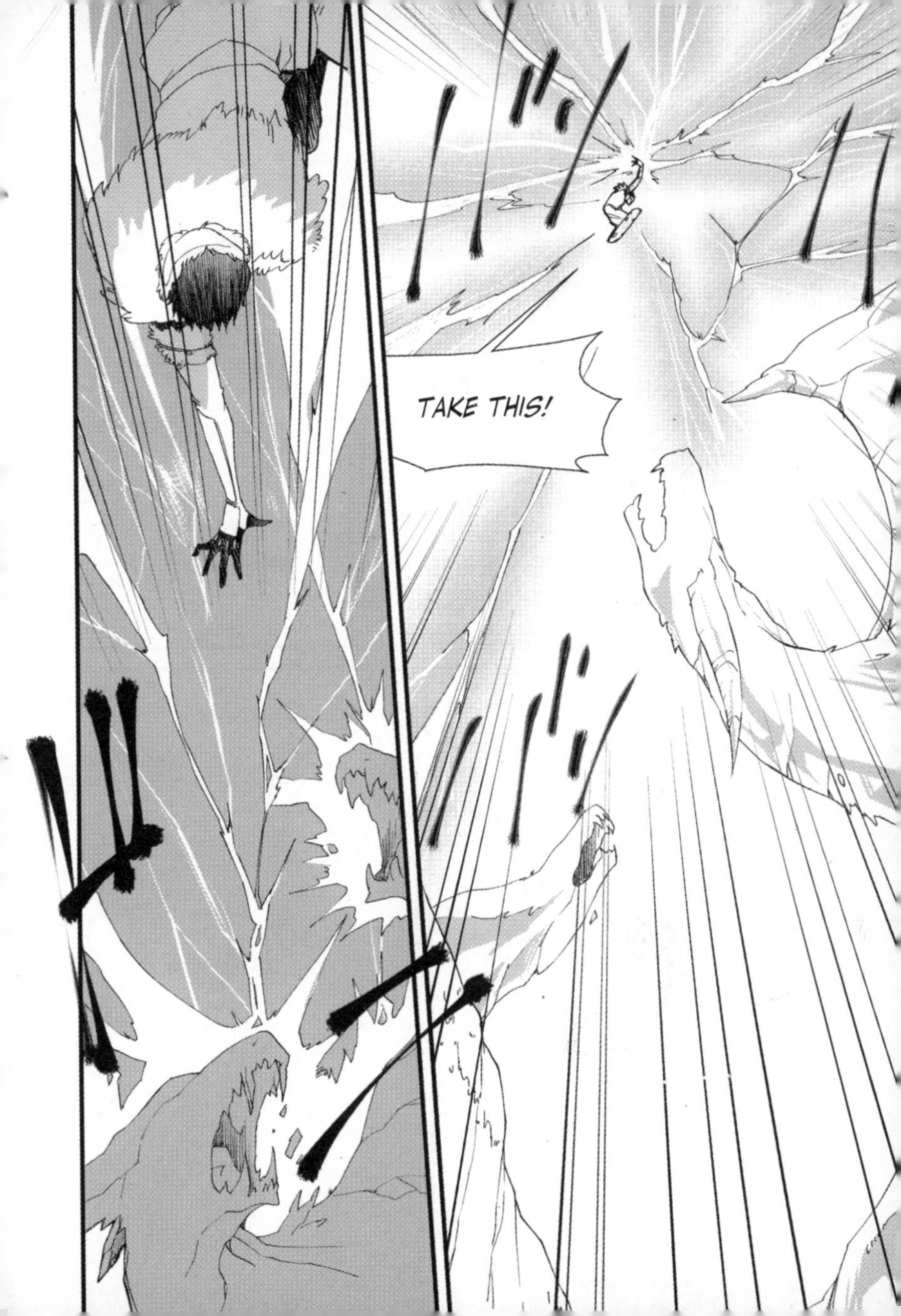
TAKE THIS!

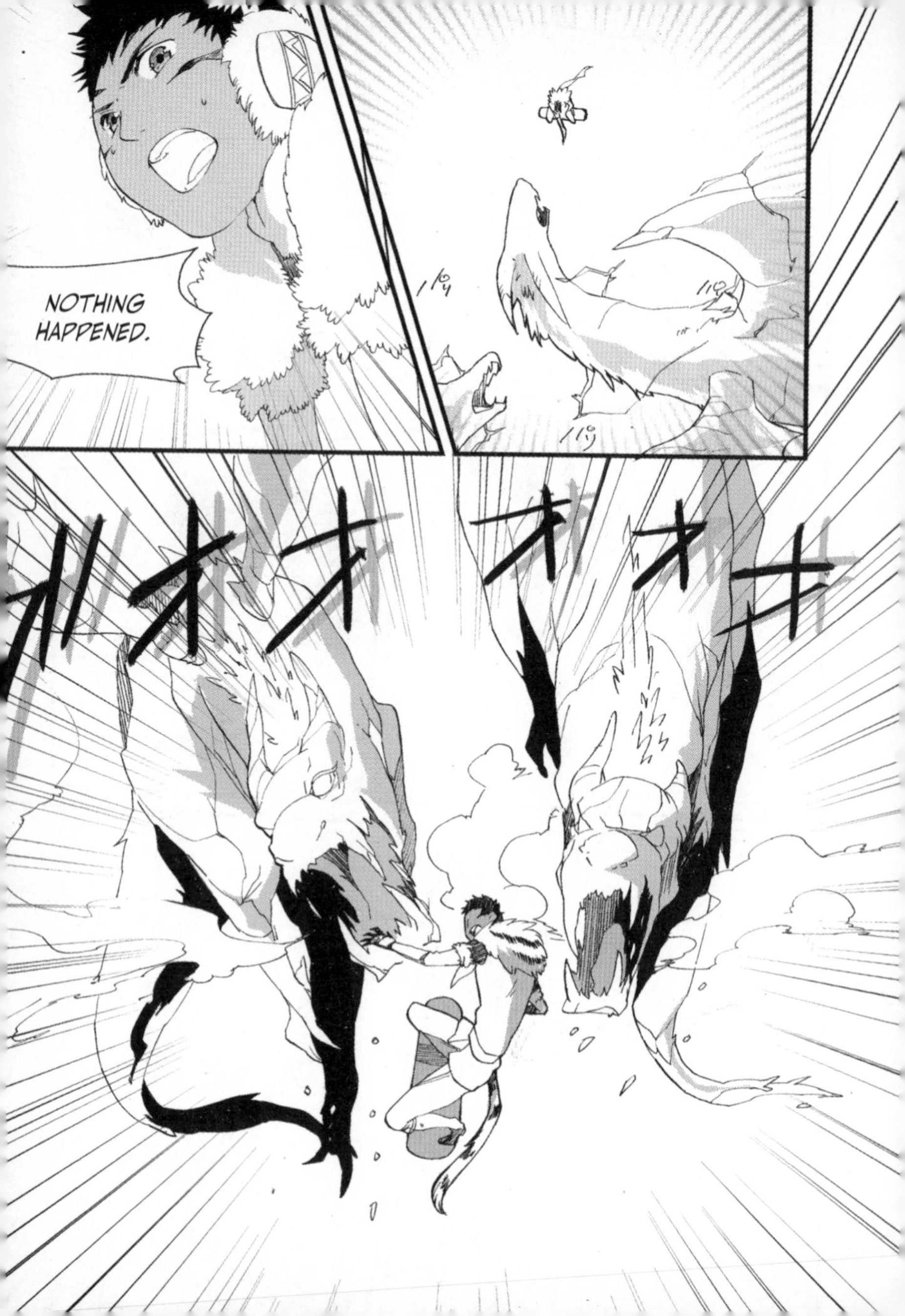
パ
パ
パ
NOTHING HAPPENED.
オオオオ

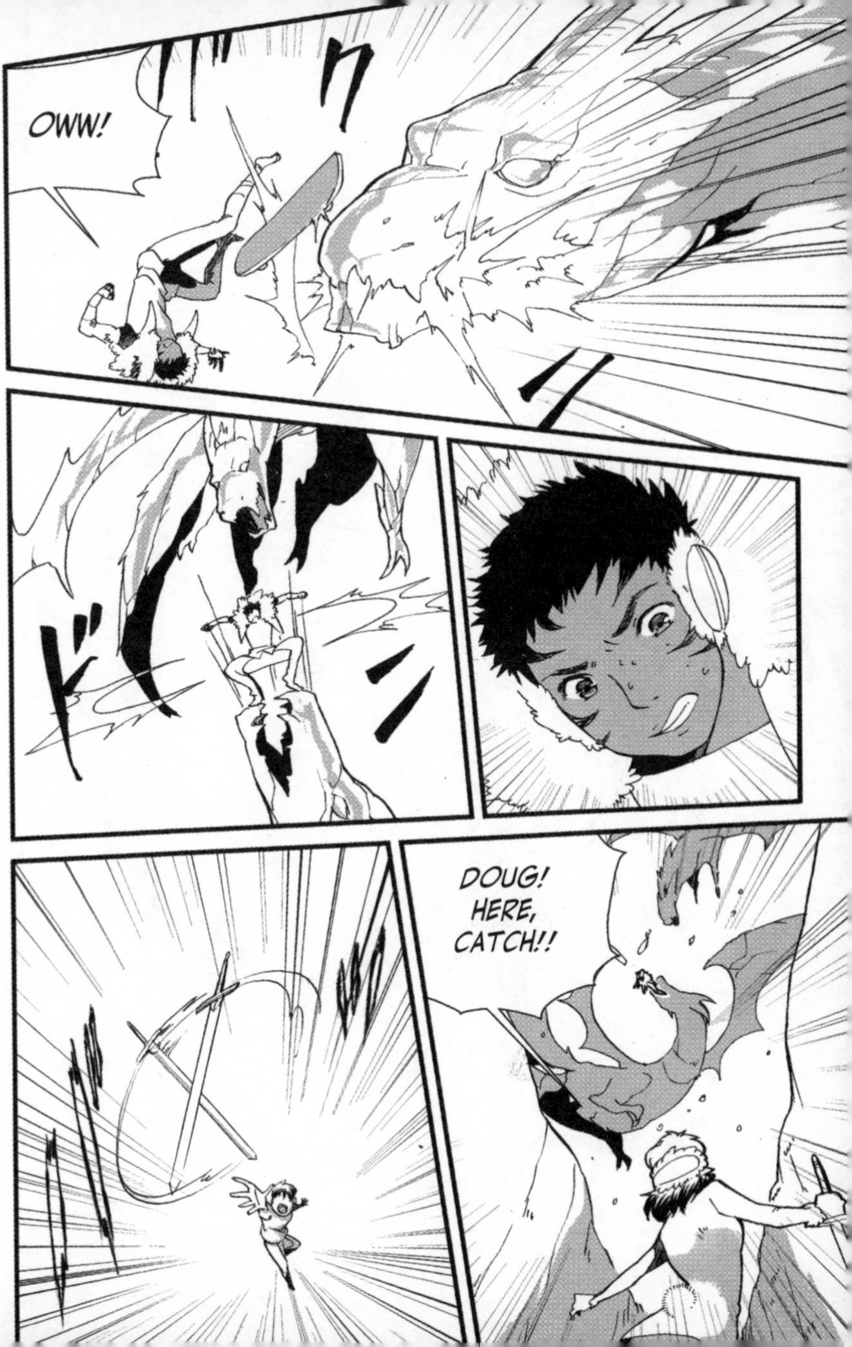
OWW!
DOUG! HERE, CATCH!!

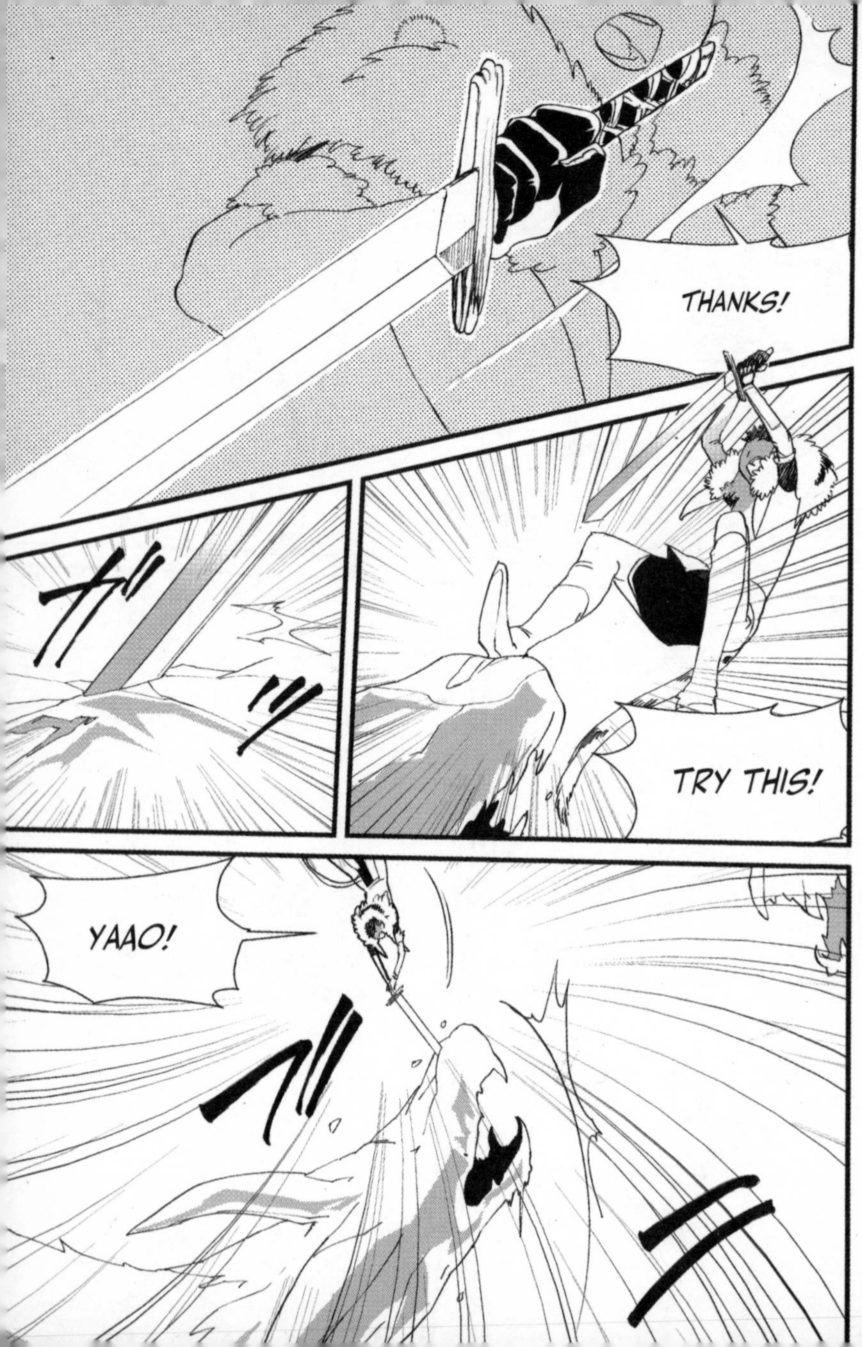
THANKS!
TRY THIS!
YAAO!

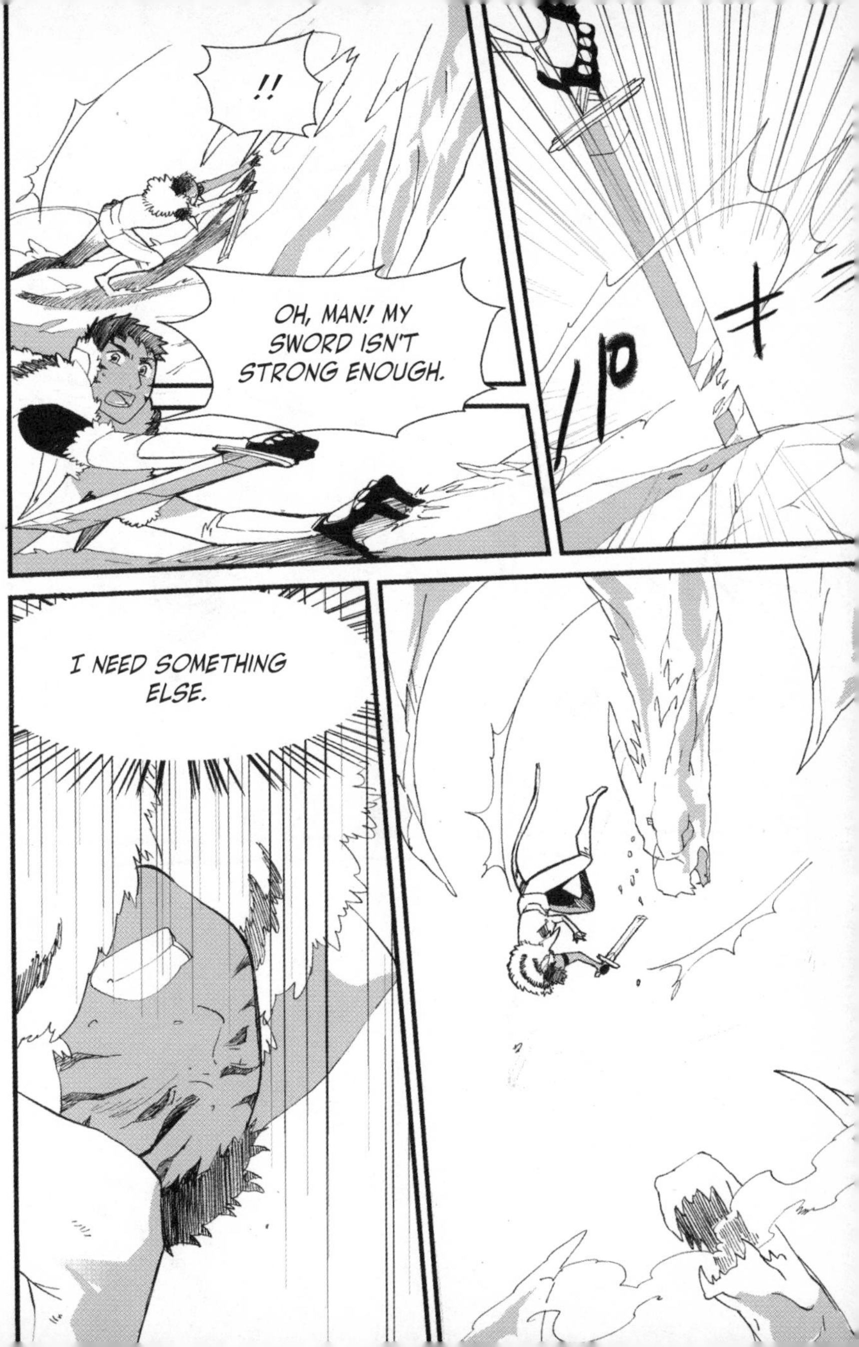
!!
OH, MAN! MY SWORD ISN'T STRONG ENOUGH.
I NEED SOMETHING ELSE.

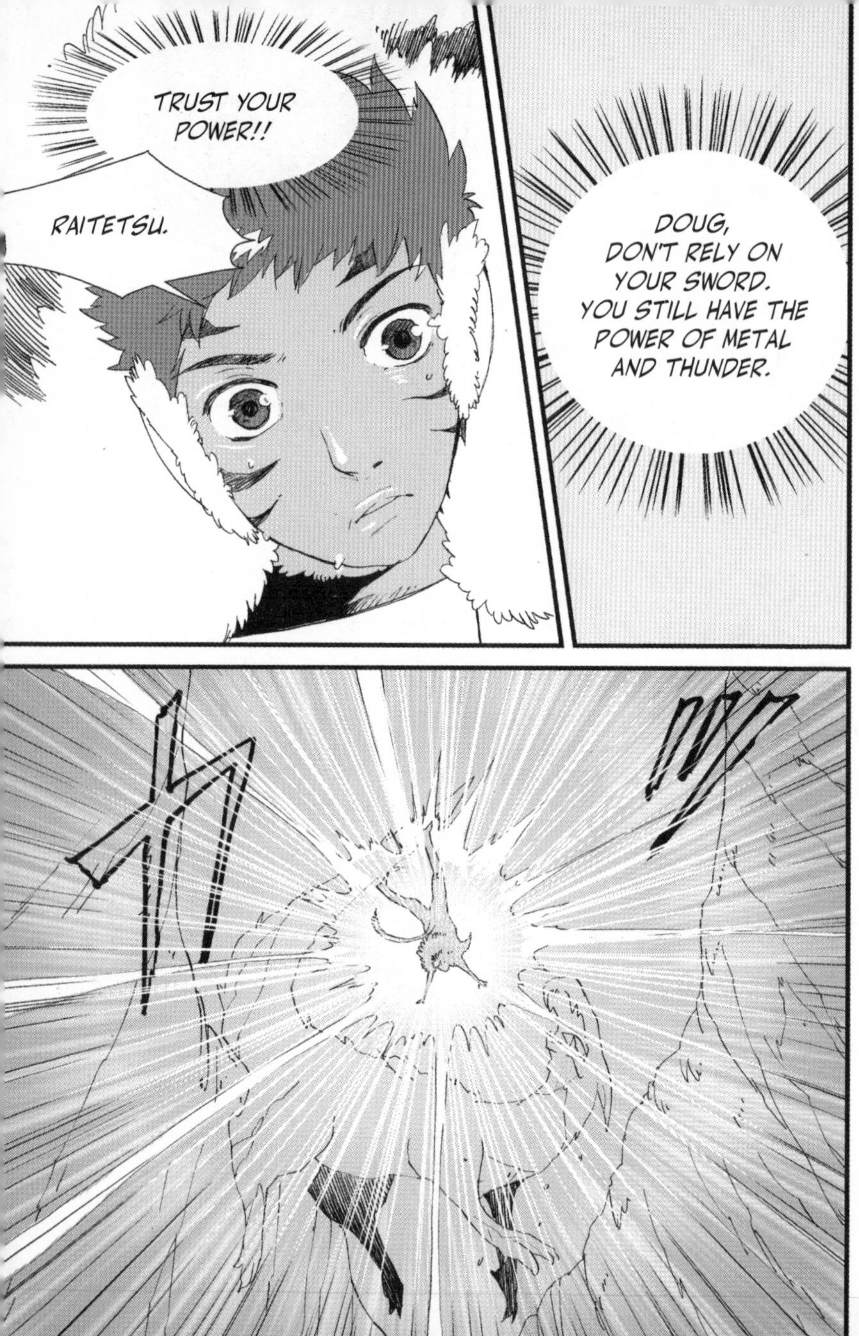
DOUG, DON'T RELY ON YOUR SWORD. YOU STILL HAVE THE POWER OF METAL AND THUNDER.
TRUST YOUR POWER!!
RAITETSU.

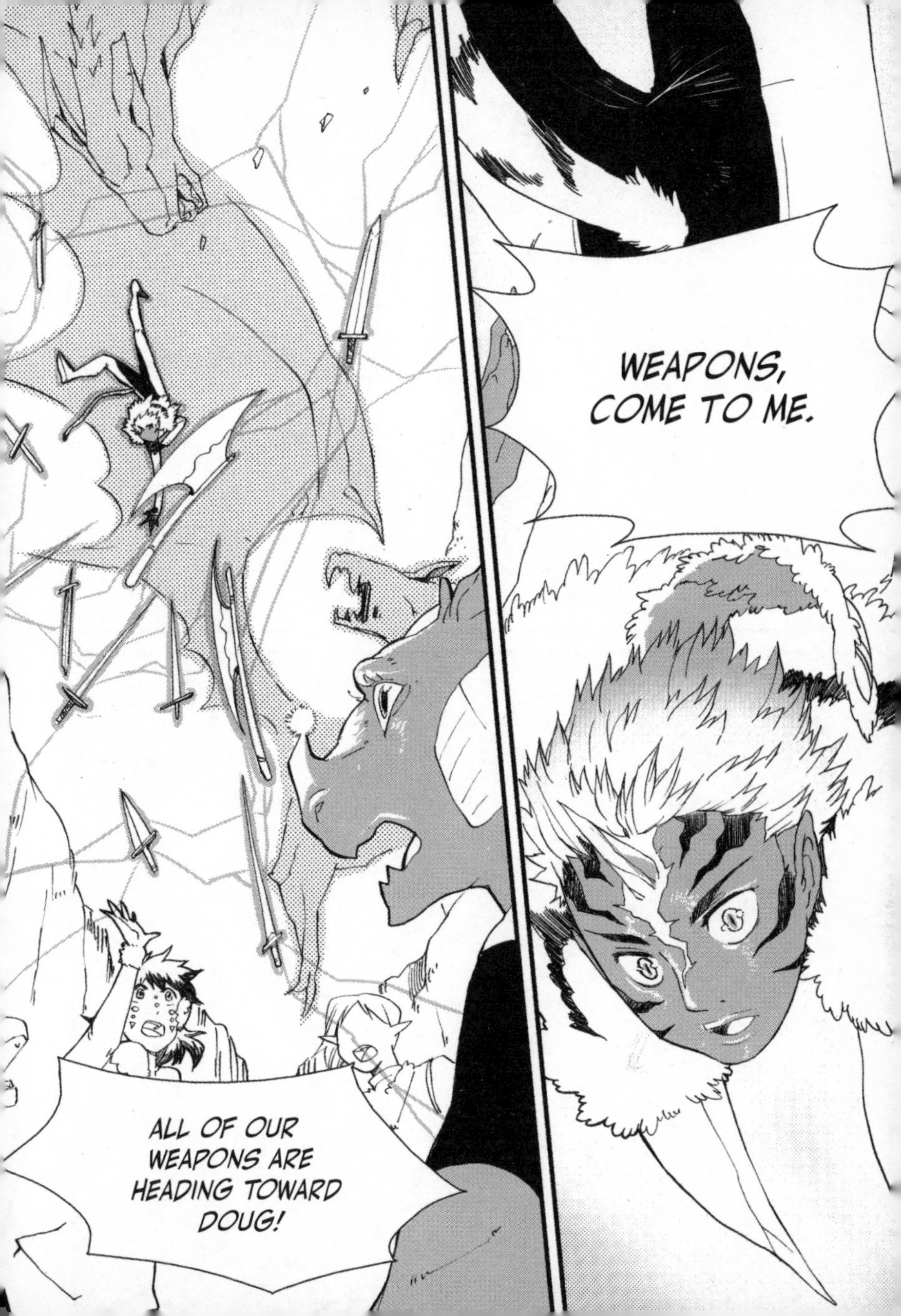
WEAPONS, COME TO ME.
ALL OF OUR WEAPONS ARE HEADING TOWARD DOUG!

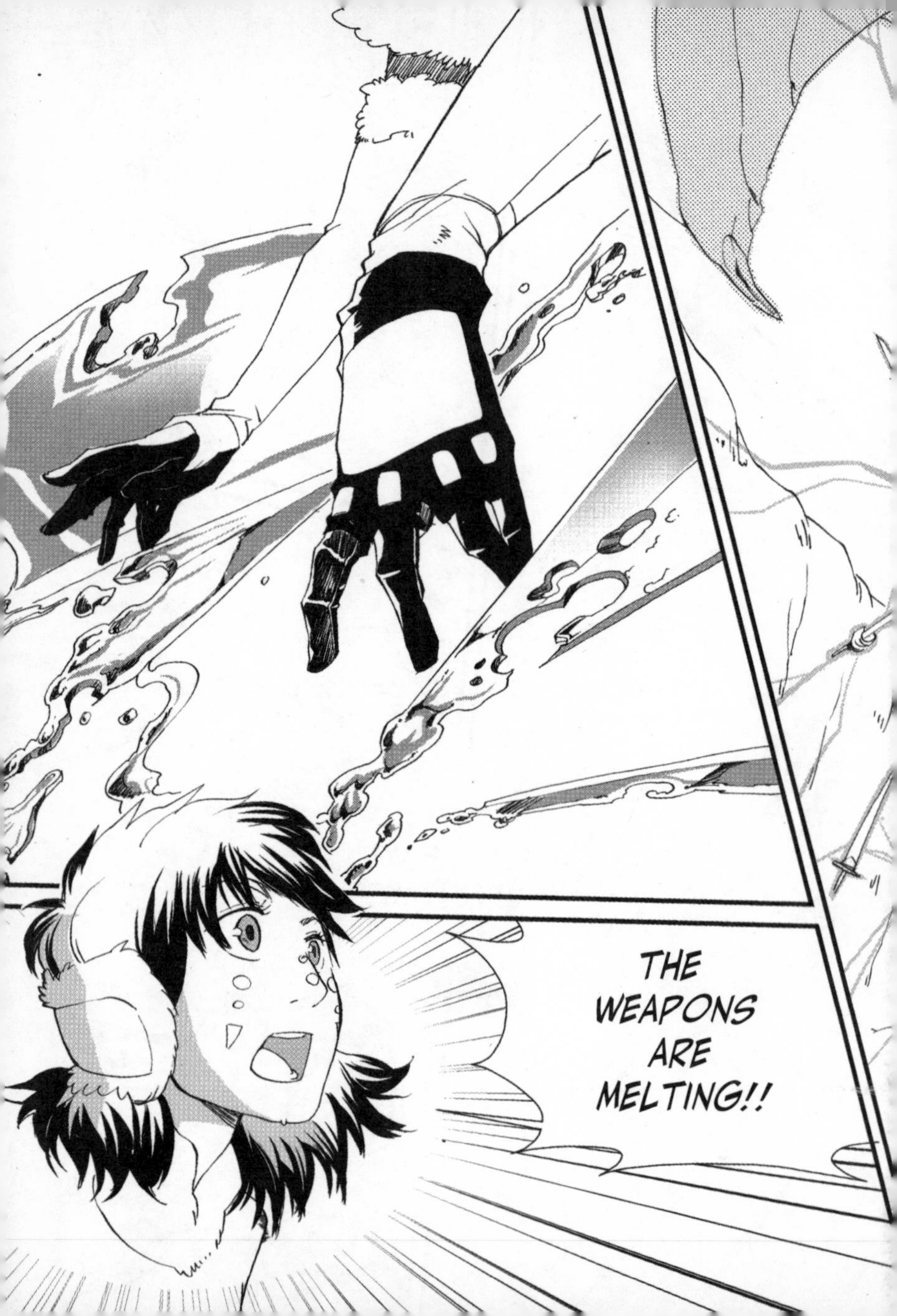
THE WEAPONS ARE MELTING!!

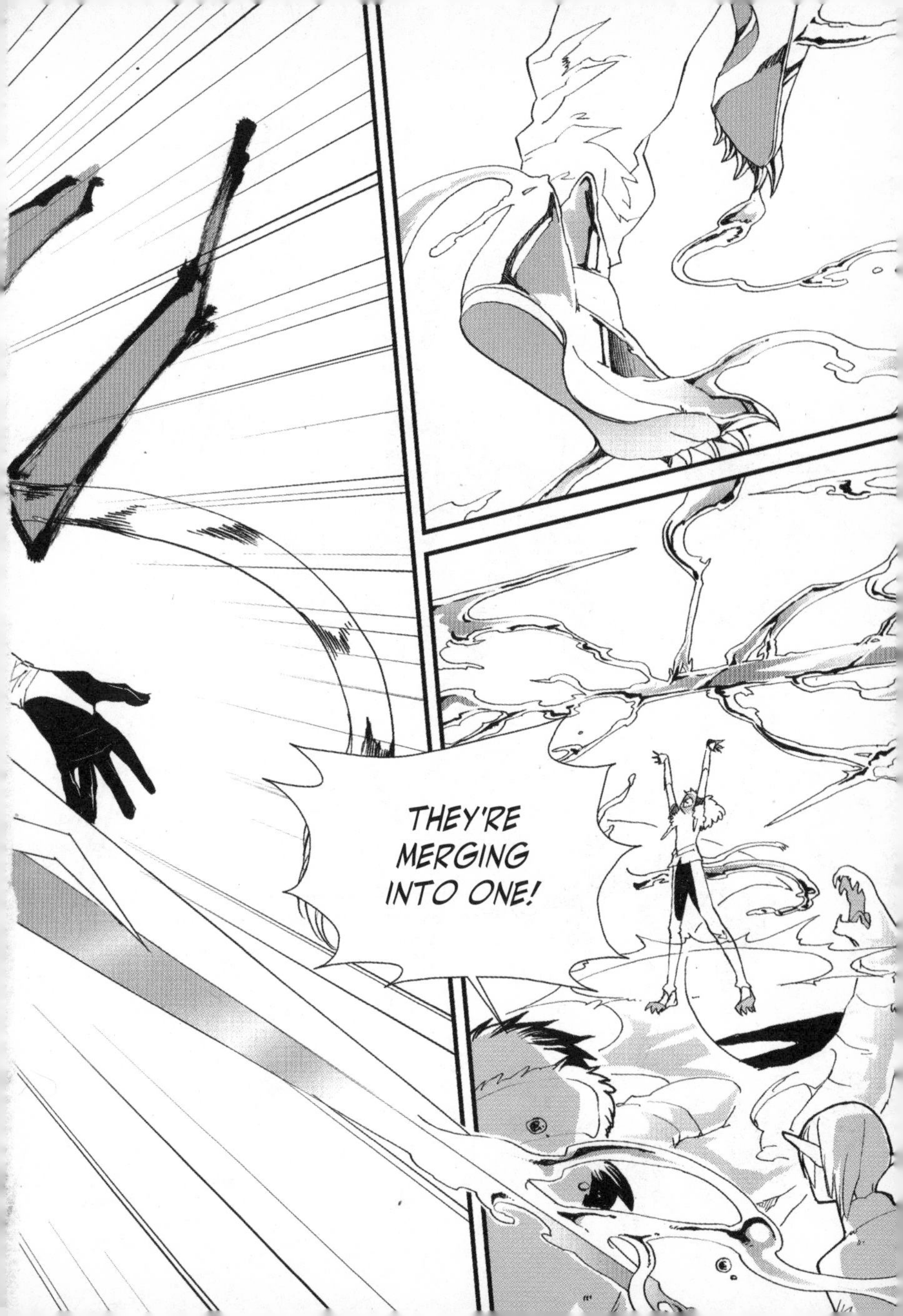
THEY'RE MERGING INTO ONE!

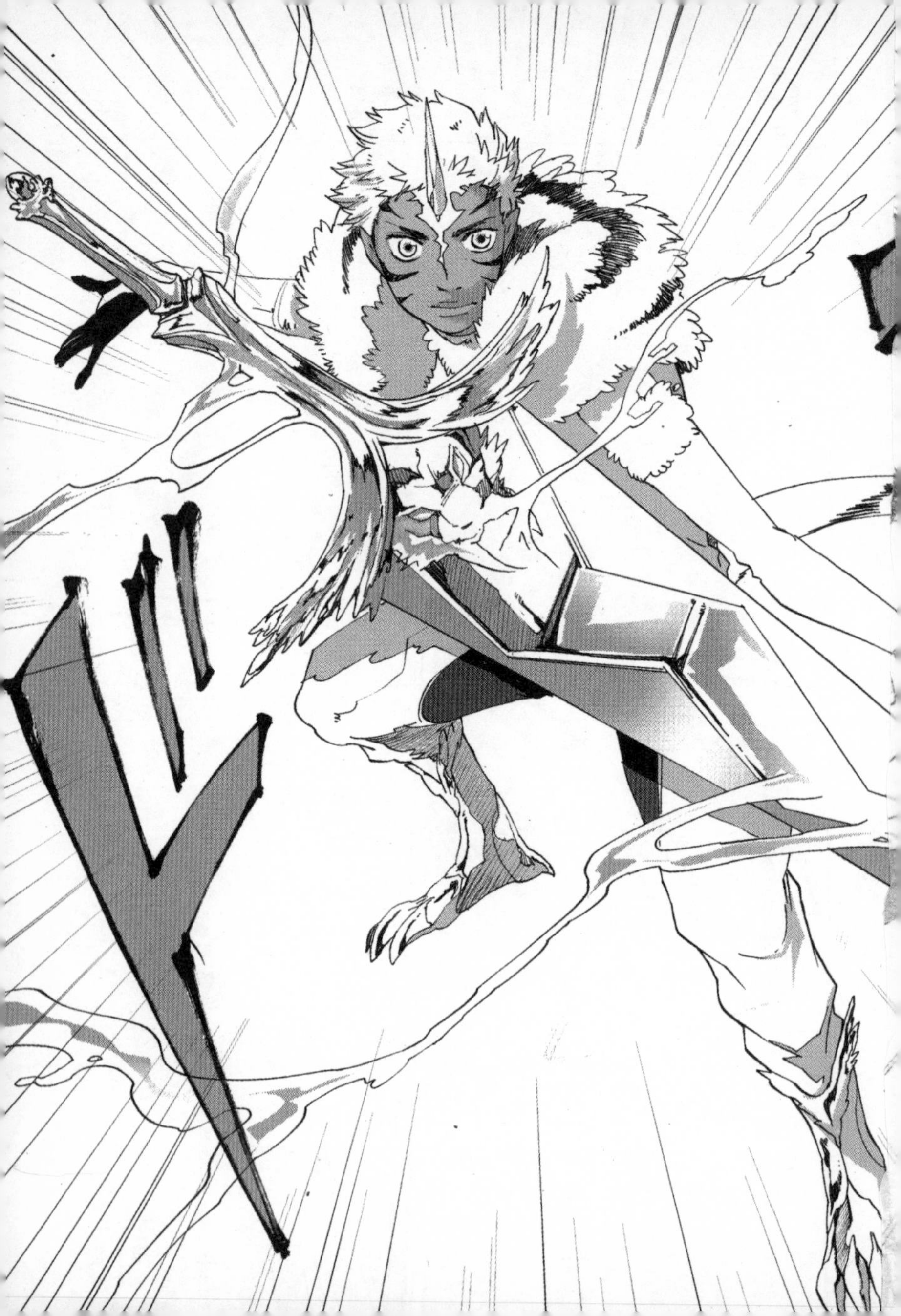

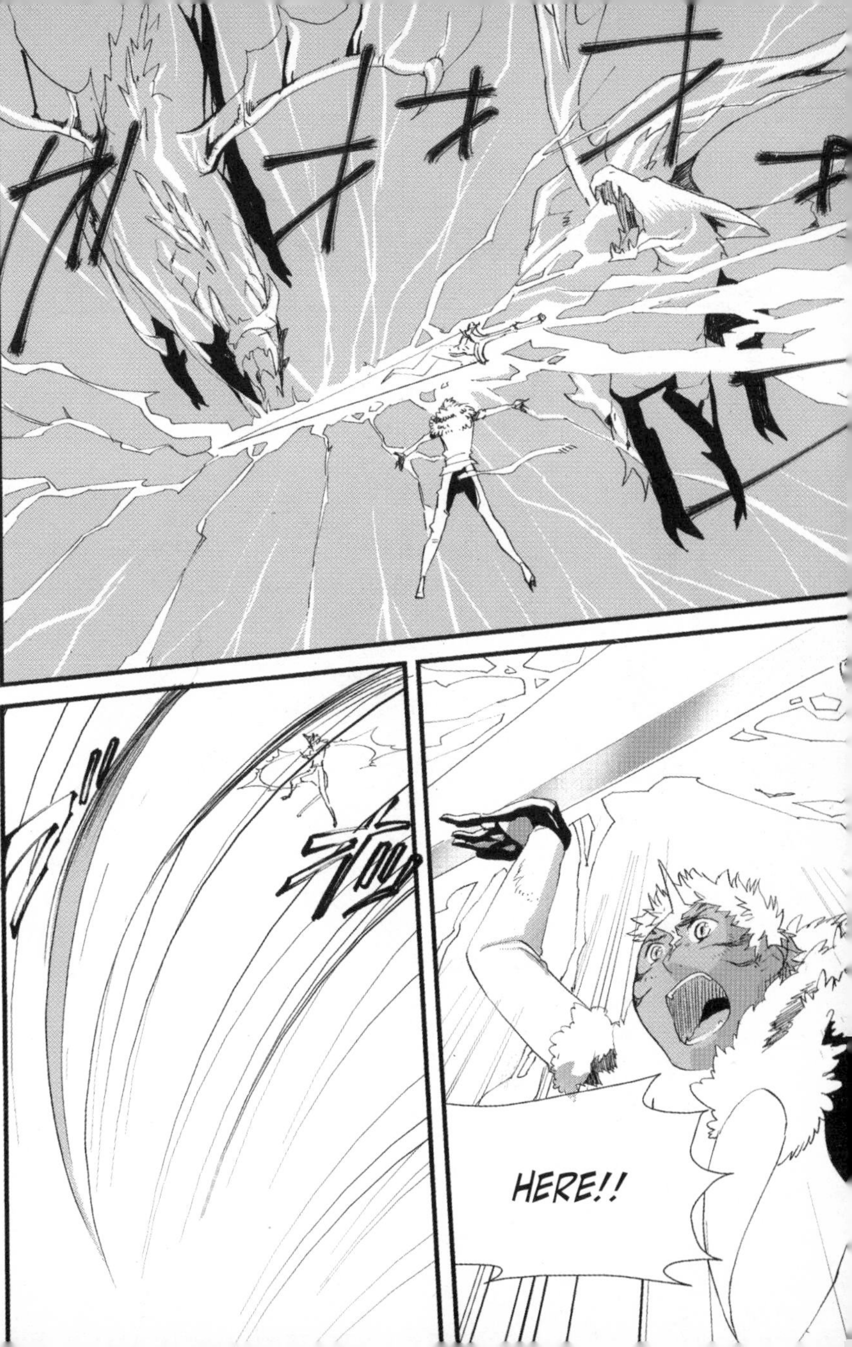
HERE!!

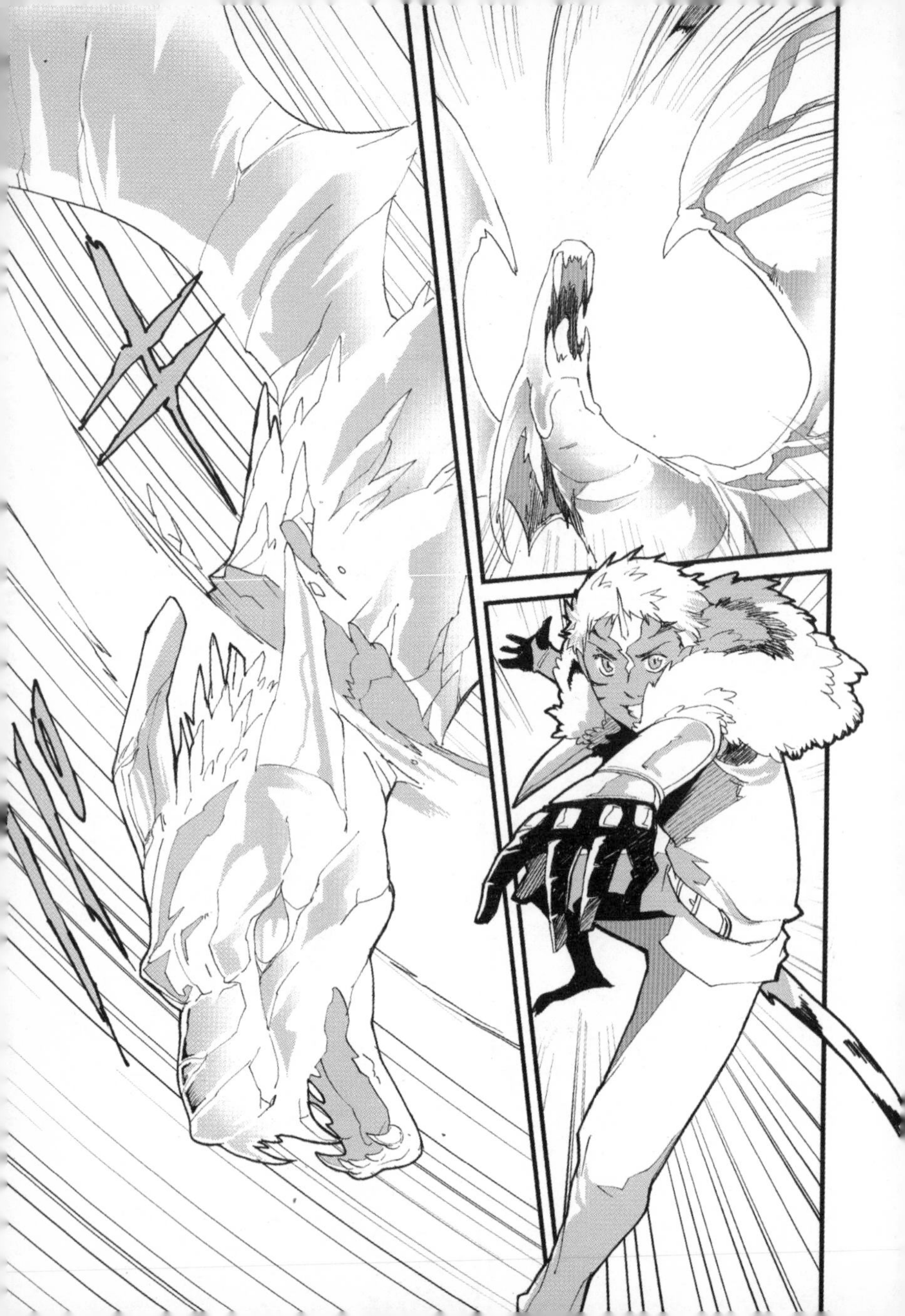

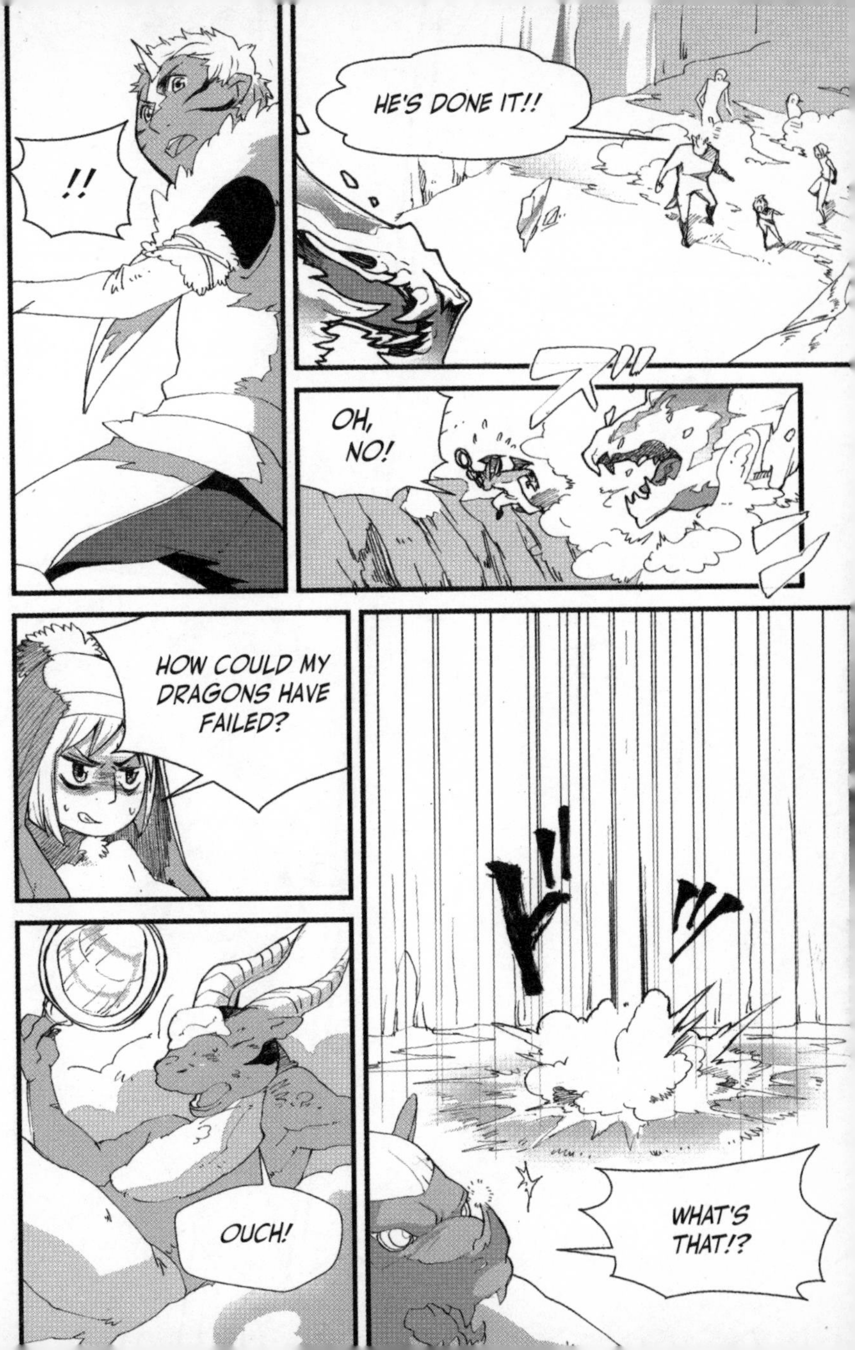
HE'S DONE IT!!
OH, NO!
!!
WHAT'S THAT!?
HOW COULD MY DRAGONS HAVE FAILED?
OUCH!

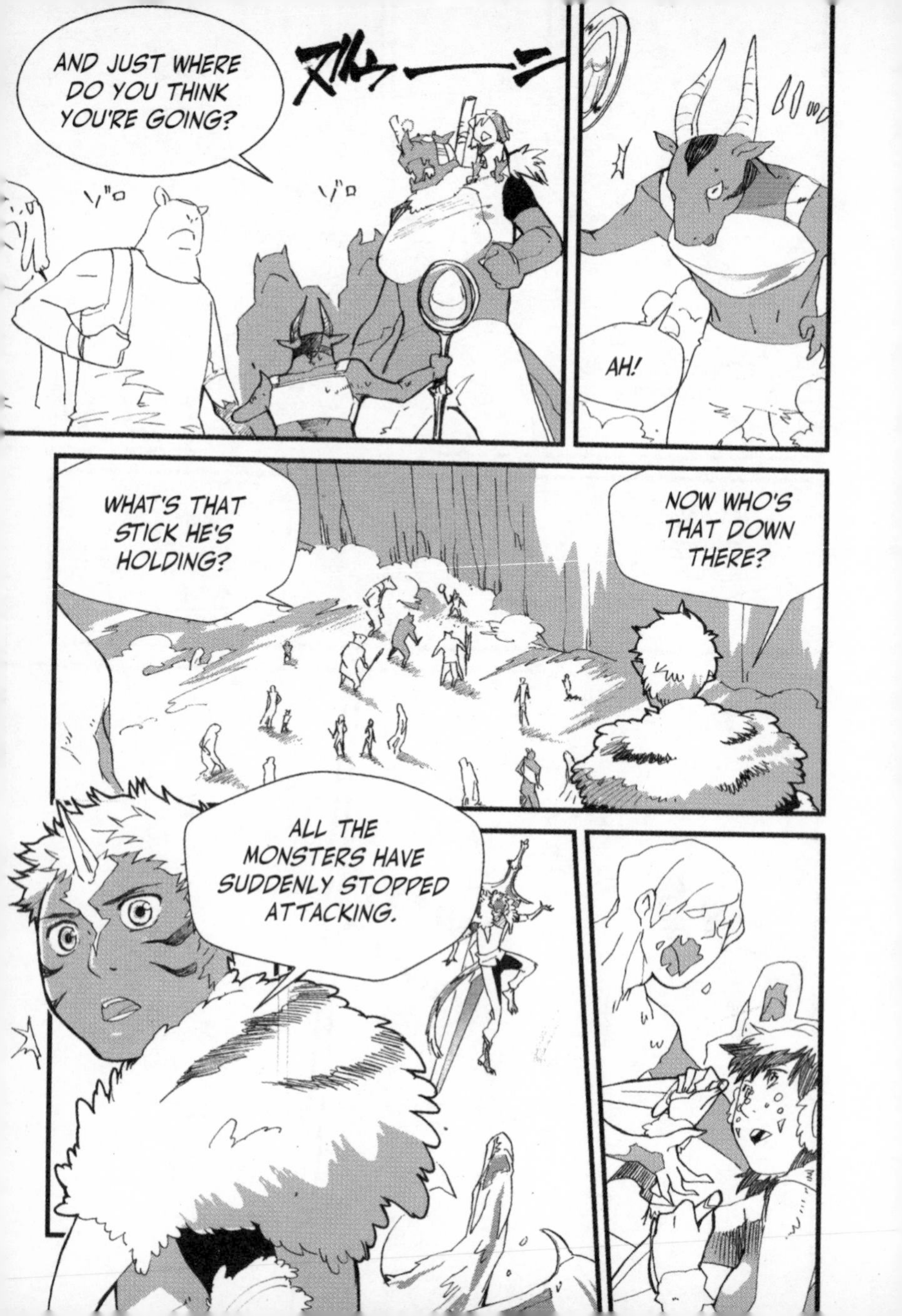
AH!
AND JUST WHERE DO YOU THINK YOU'RE GOING?
NOW WHO'S THAT DOWN THERE?
WHAT'S THAT STICK HE'S HOLDING?
ALL THE MONSTERS HAVE SUDDENLY STOPPED ATTACKING.

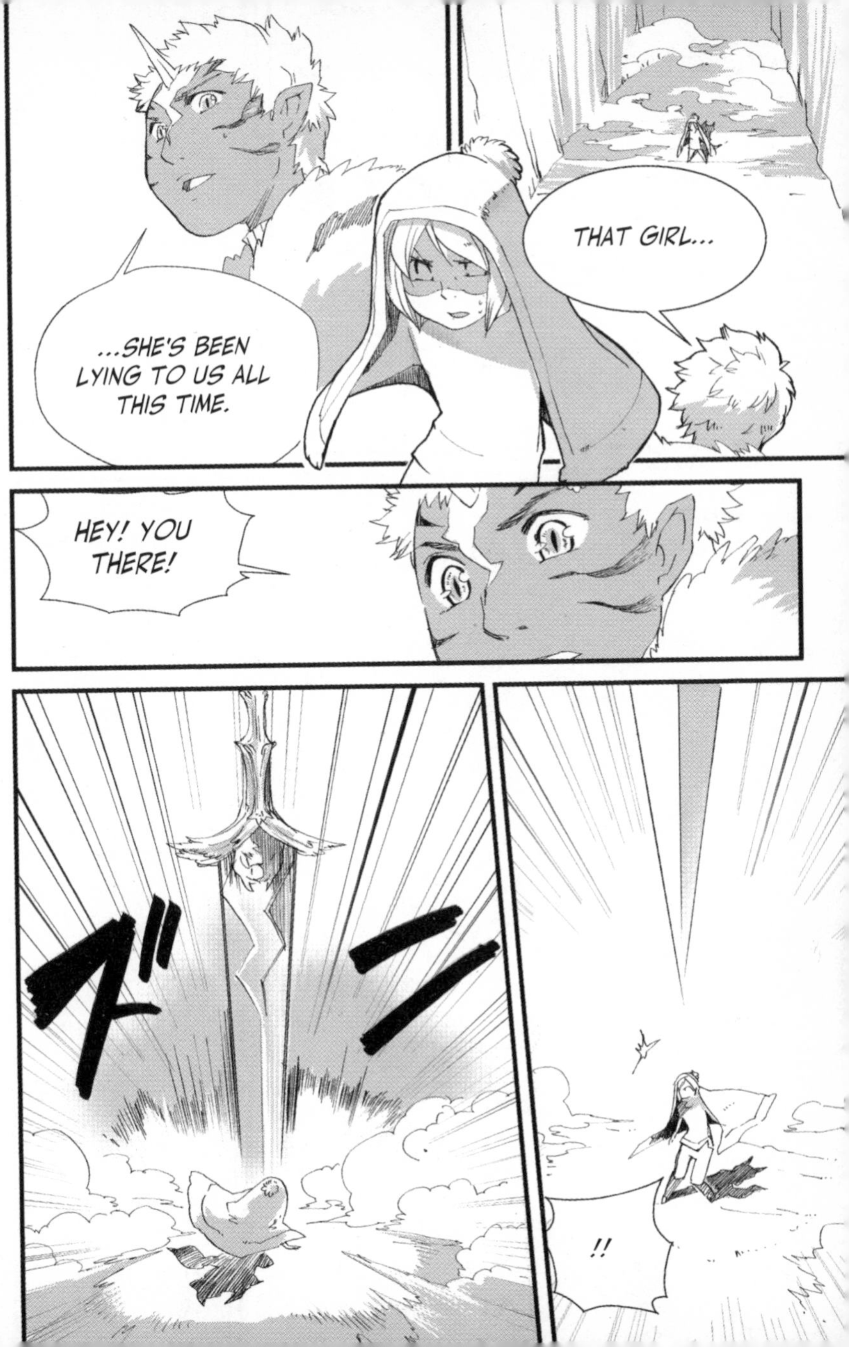
THAT GIRL...
...SHE'S BEEN LYING TO US ALL THIS TIME.
HEY! YOU THERE!
!!
ズン

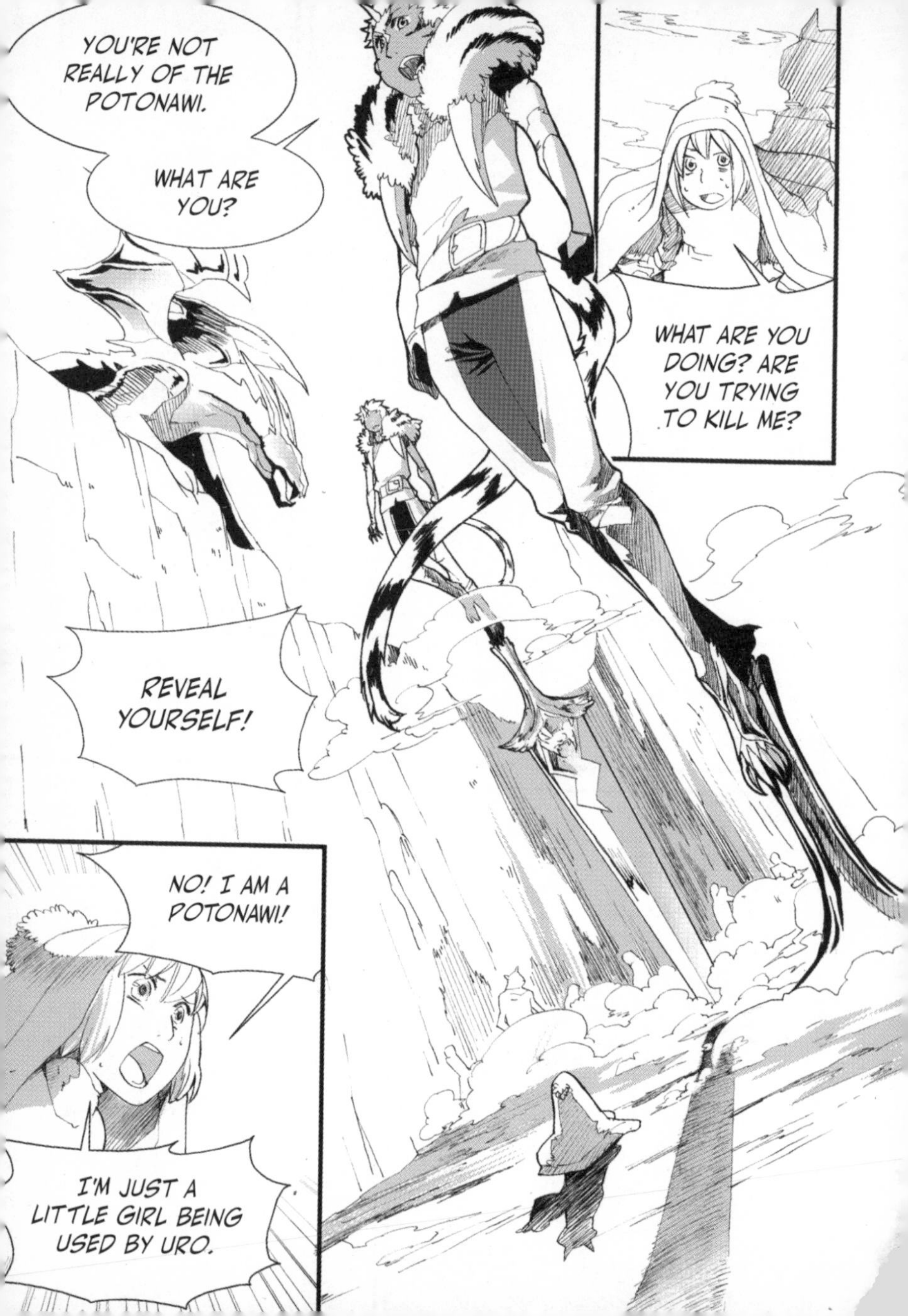
WHAT ARE YOU DOING? ARE YOU TRYING TO KILL ME?
YOU'RE NOT REALLY OF THE POTONAWI.
WHAT ARE YOU?
REVEAL YOURSELF!
NO! I AM A POTONAWI!
I'M JUST A LITTLE GIRL BEING USED BY URO.

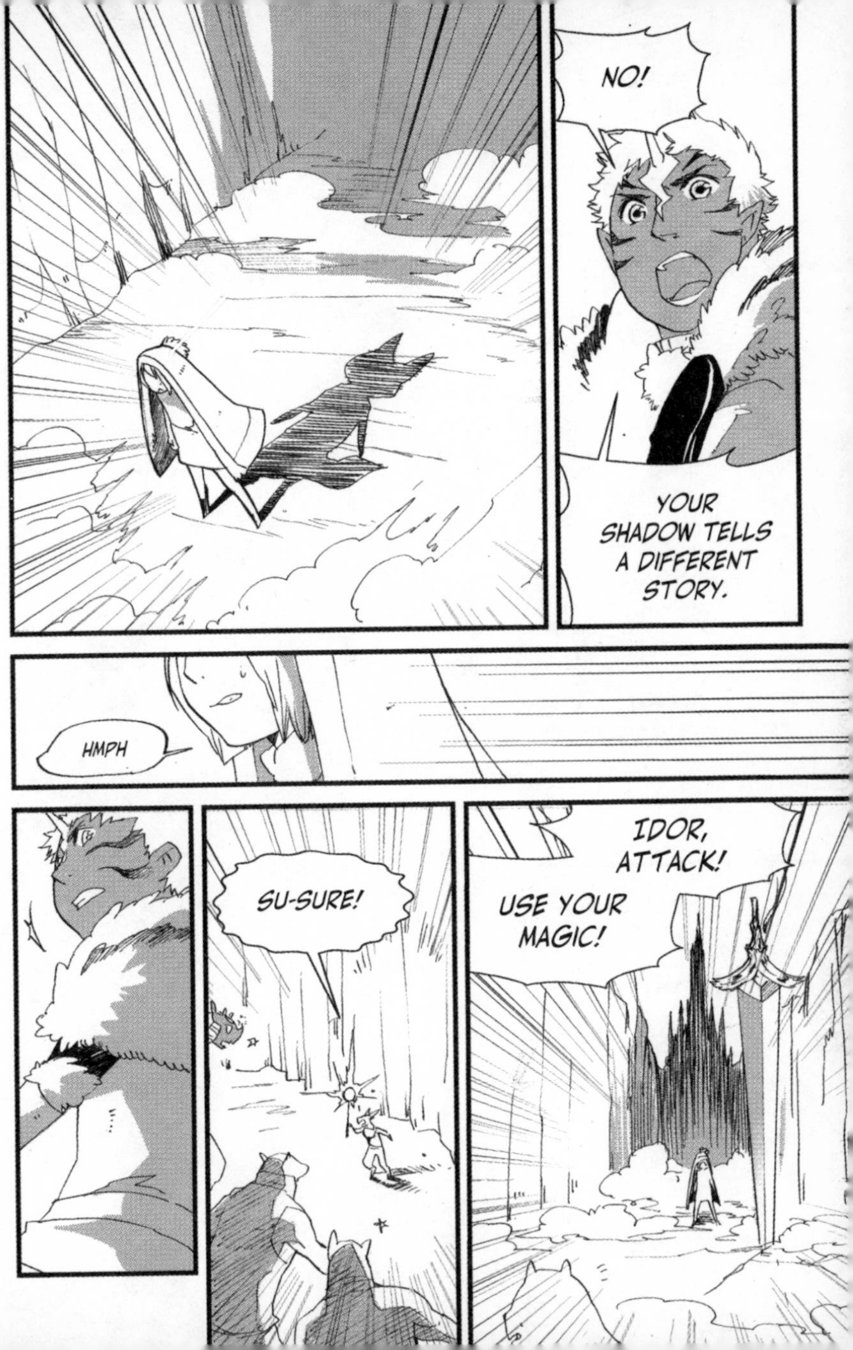
NO!
YOUR SHADOW TELLS A DIFFERENT STORY.
HMPH
IDOR, ATTACK!
USE YOUR MAGIC!
SU-SURE!
...

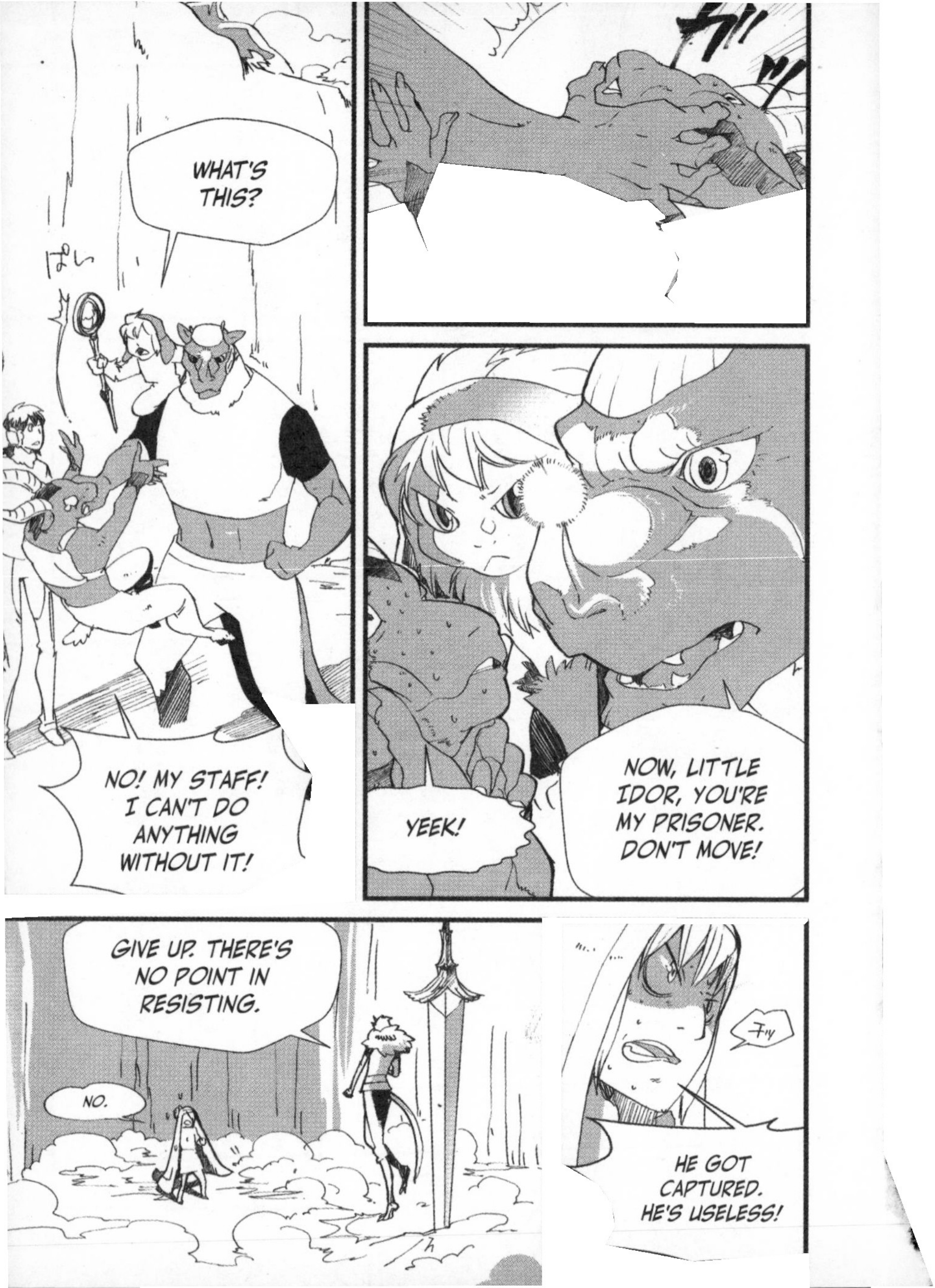
NOW, LITTLE IDOR, YOU'RE MY PRISONER. DON'T MOVE!
YEEK!
WHAT'S THIS?
NO! MY STAFF! I CAN'T DO ANYTHING WITHOUT IT!
チッ
HE GOT CAPTURED. HE'S USELESS!
GIVE UP. THERE'S NO POINT IN RESISTING.
NO.

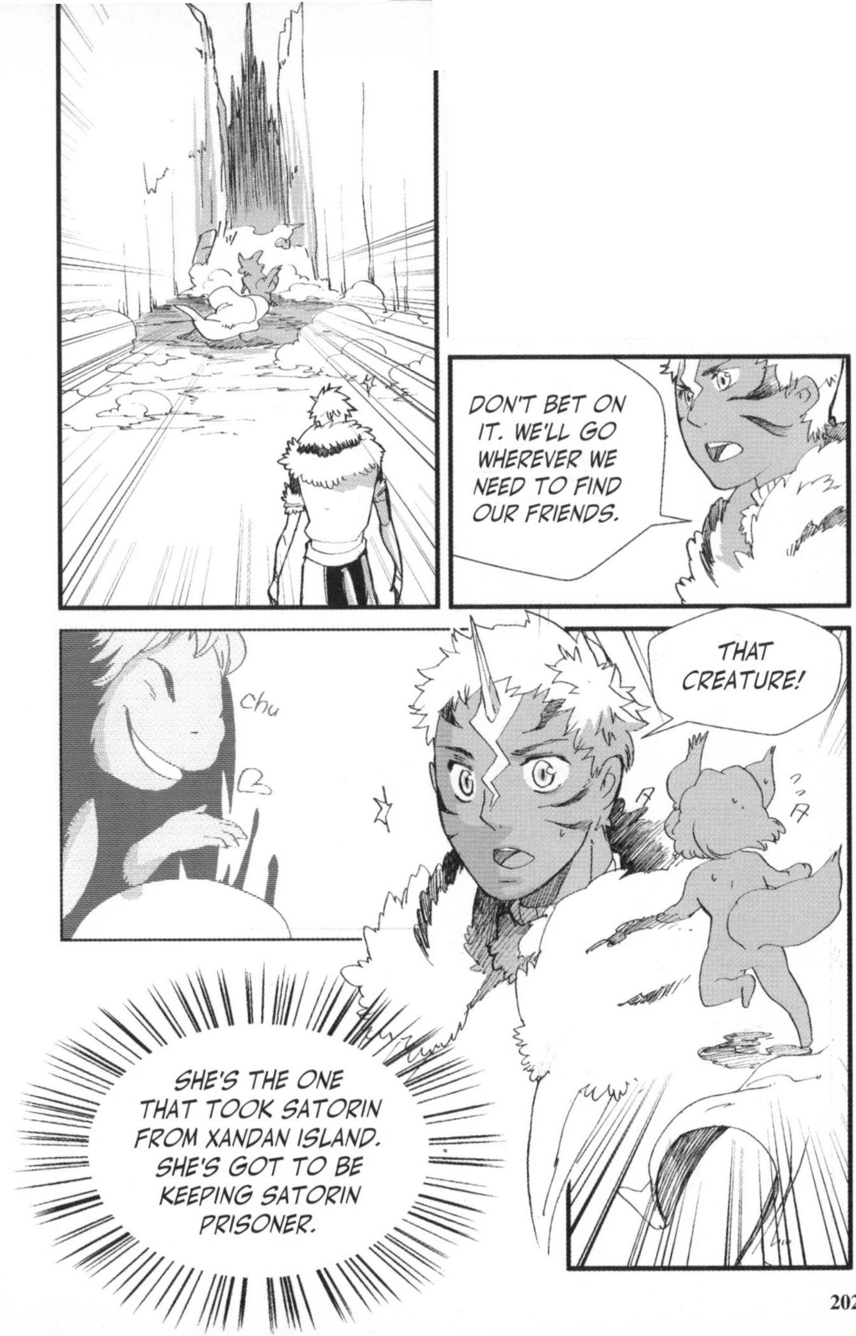
DON'T BET ON IT. WE'LL GO WHEREVER WE NEED TO FIND OUR FRIENDS.
THAT CREATURE!
Chu
SHE'S THE ONE THAT TOOK SATORIN FROM XANDAN ISLAND. SHE'S GOT TO BE KEEPING SATORIN PRISONER.

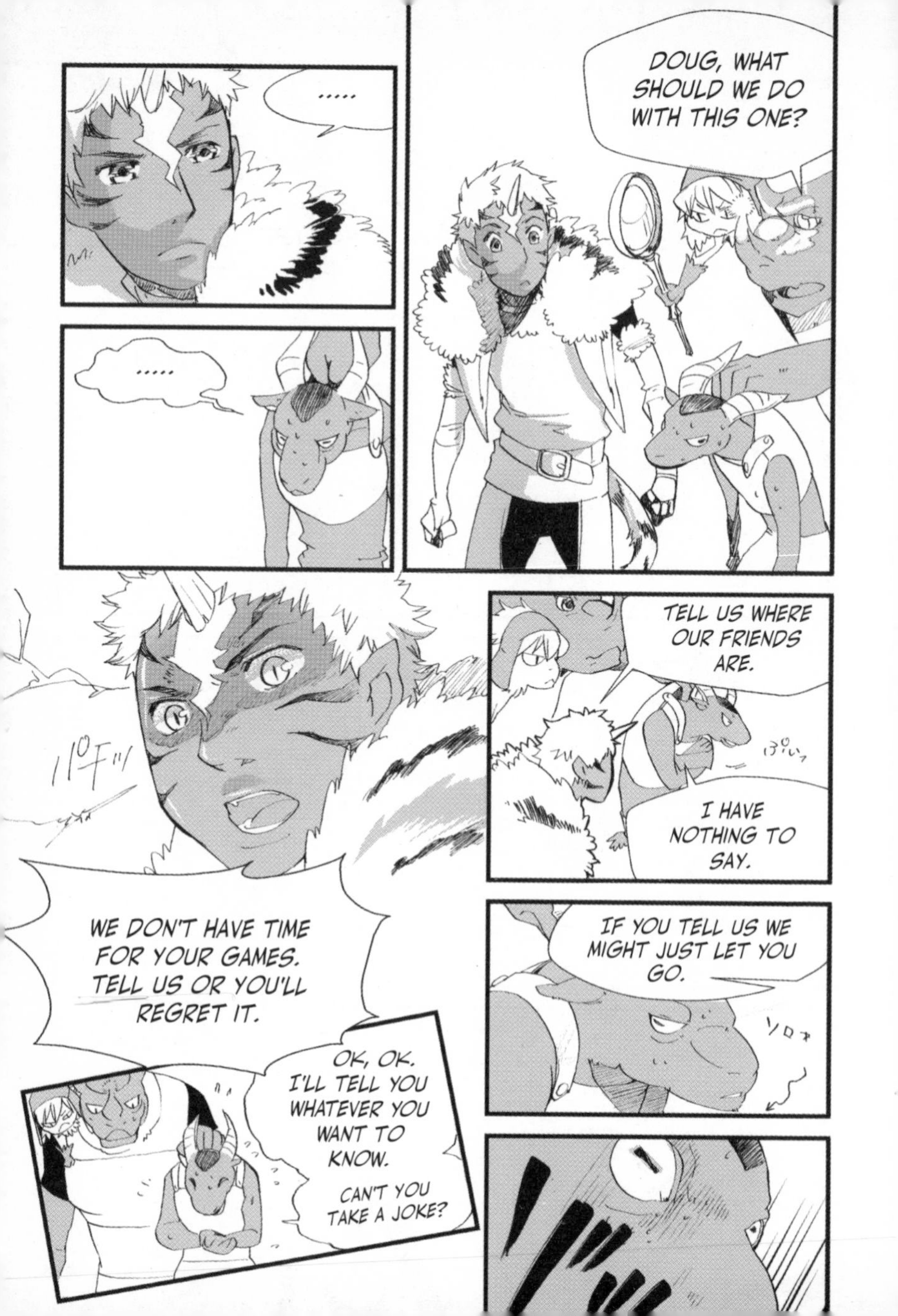
DOUG, WHAT SHOULD WE DO WITH THIS ONE?
......
......
TELL US WHERE OUR FRIENDS ARE.
ぷいっ
I HAVE NOTHING TO SAY.
パチッ
WE DON'T HAVE TIME FOR YOUR GAMES. TELL US OR YOU'LL REGRET IT.
IF YOU TELL US WE MIGHT JUST LET YOU GO.
OK, OK. I'LL TELL YOU WHATEVER YOU WANT TO KNOW.
CAN'T YOU TAKE A JOKE?

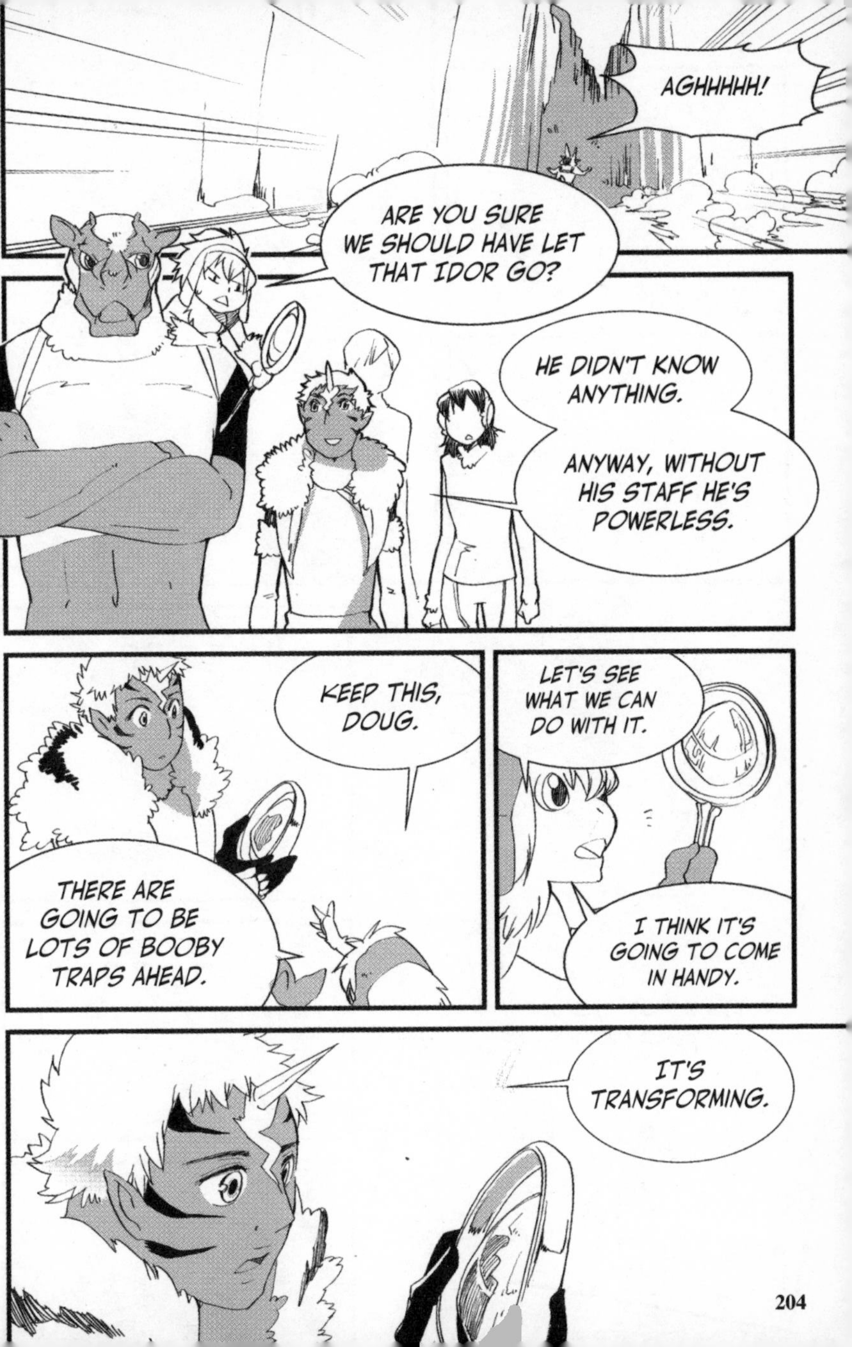
AGHHHHH!
ARE YOU SURE WE SHOULD HAVE LET THAT IDOR GO?
HE DIDN'T KNOW ANYTHING.
ANYWAY, WITHOUT HIS STAFF HE'S POWERLESS.
LET'S SEE WHAT WE CAN DO WITH IT.
I THINK IT'S GOING TO COME IN HANDY.
KEEP THIS, DOUG.
THERE ARE GOING TO BE LOTS OF BOOBY TRAPS AHEAD.
IT'S TRANSFORMING.

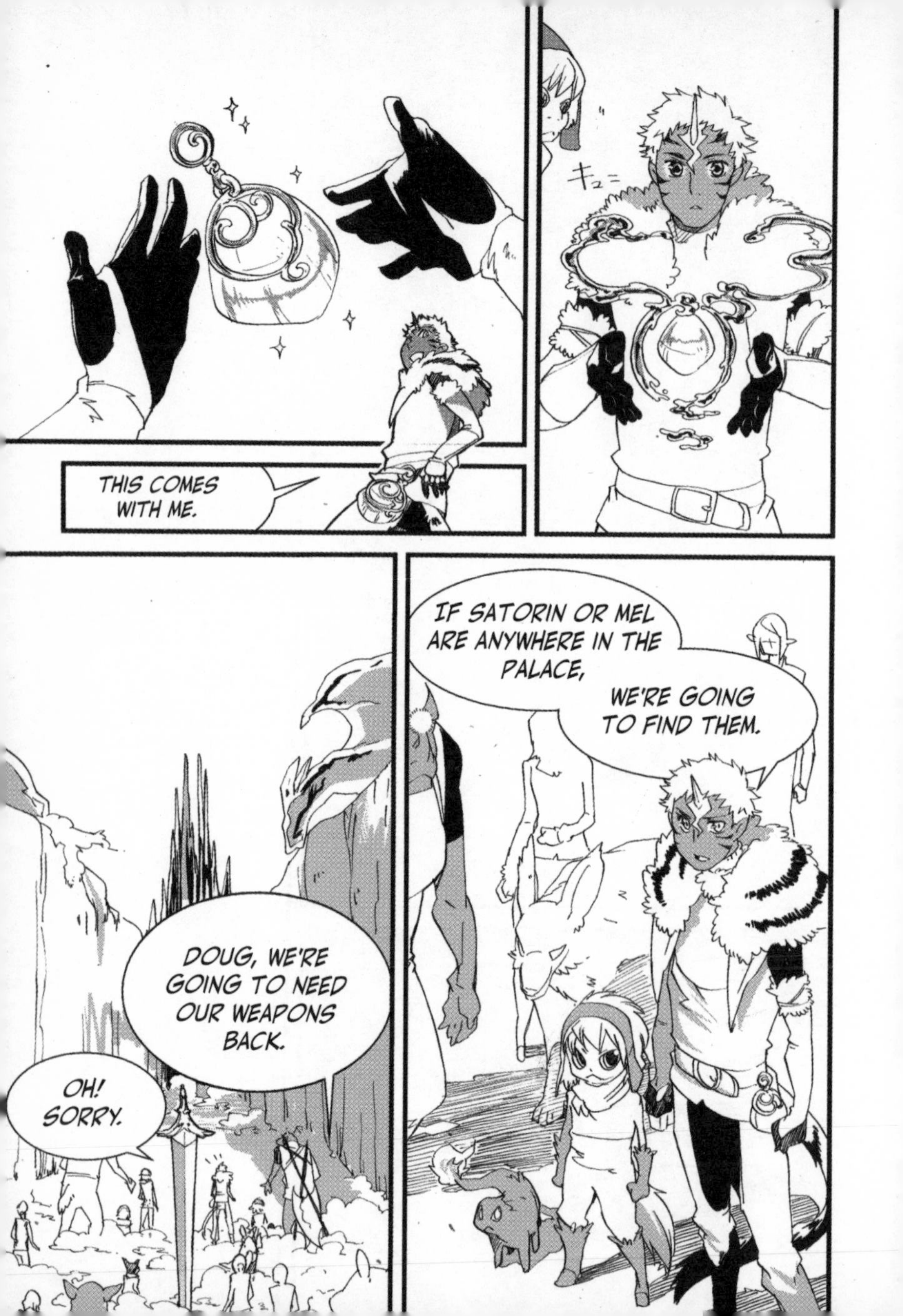
キュニ
THIS COMES WITH ME.
IF SATORIN OR MEL ARE ANYWHERE IN THE PALACE,
WE'RE GOING TO FIND THEM.
DOUG, WE'RE GOING TO NEED OUR WEAPONS BACK.
OH! SORRY.

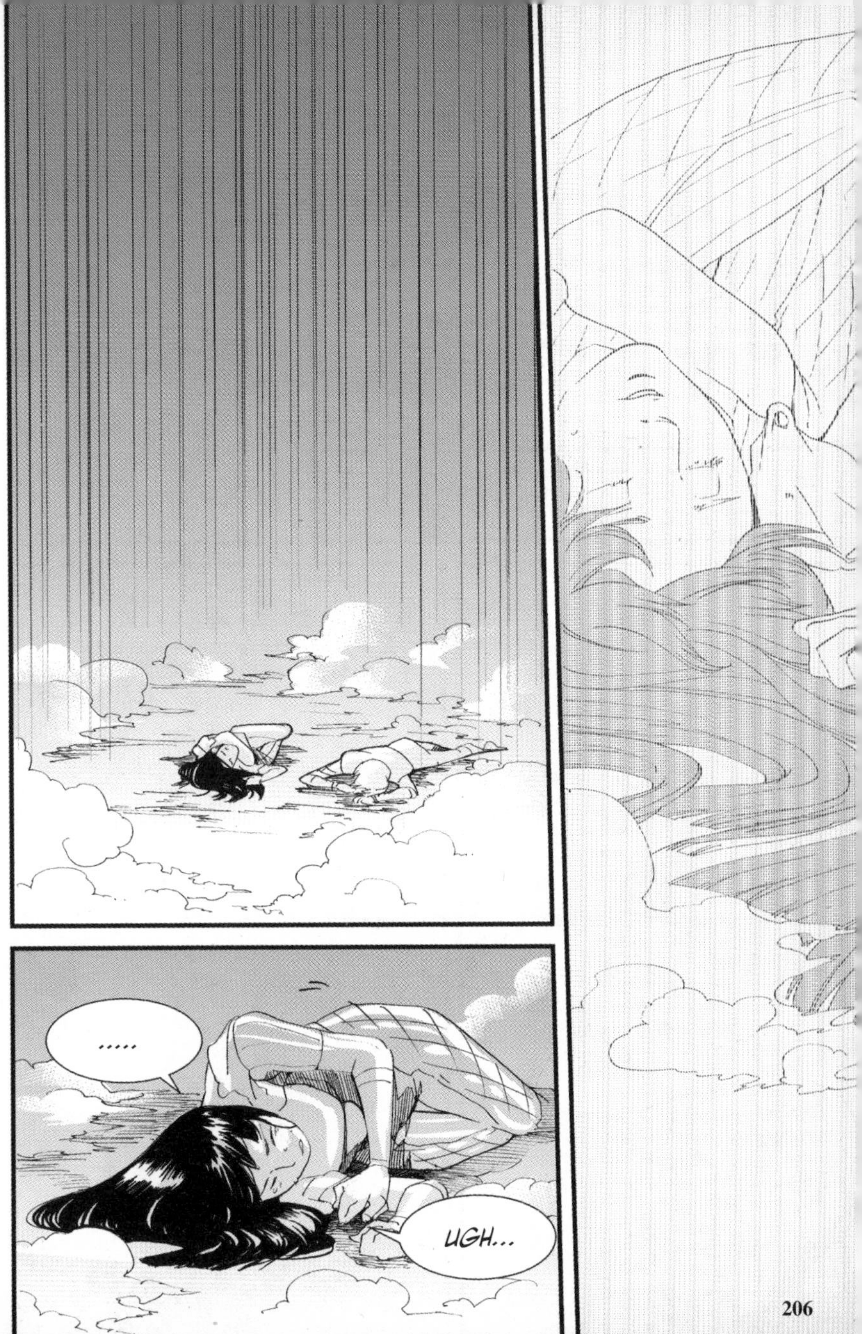
......
UGH...

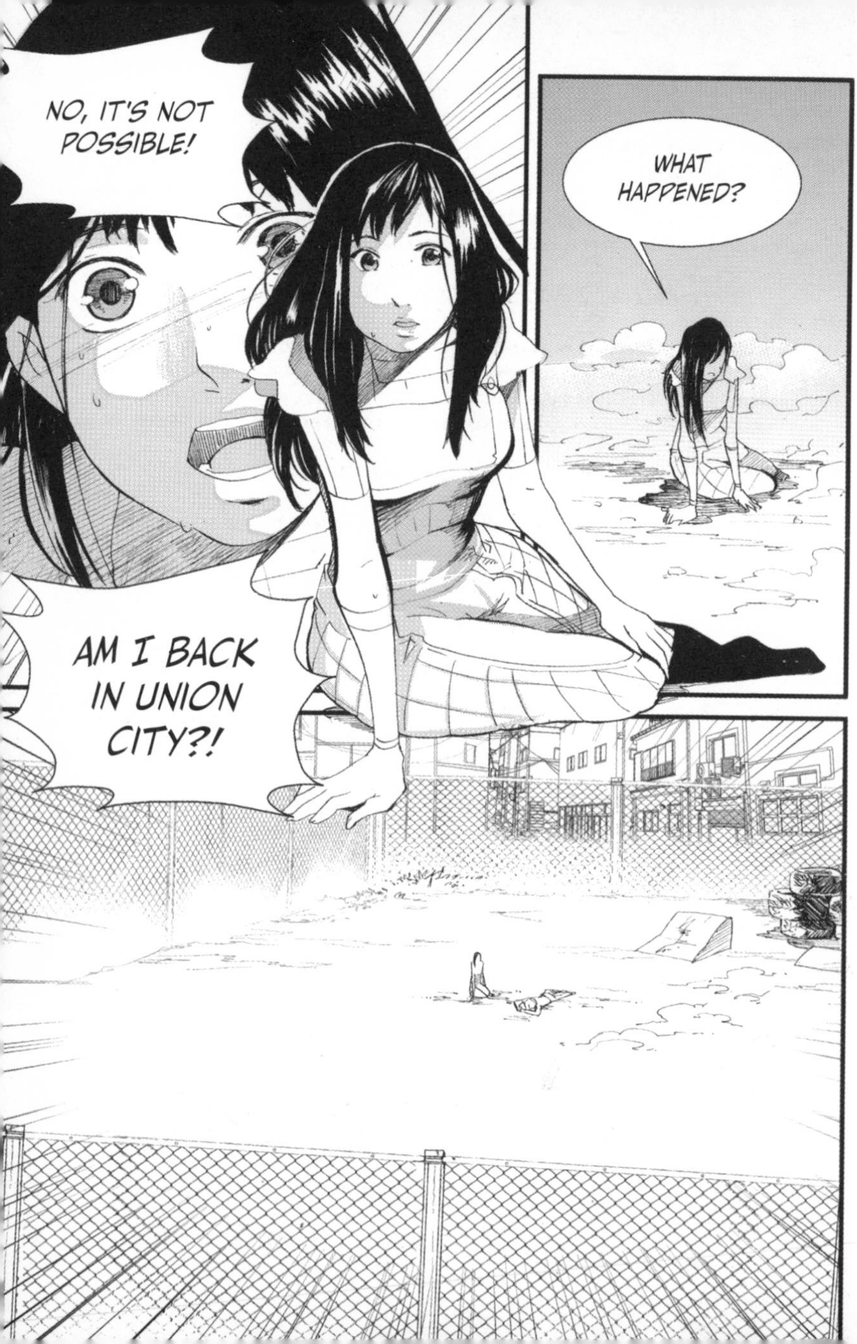
WHAT HAPPENED?
NO, IT'S NOT POSSIBLE!
AM I BACK IN UNION CITY?!

FIRST U.S. EDITION 2012

LIBRARY OF CONGRESS CATALOGING-IN-PUBLICATION DATA IS AVAILABLE.
LIBRARY OF CONGRESS CATALOG CARD NUMBER PENDING
ISBN 978-0-7636-5917-2

12 13 14 15 16 17 SCP 10 9 8 7 6 5 4 3 2 1
PRINTED IN HUMEN, DONGGUAN, CHINA

THIS BOOK WAS TYPESET IN CCLADRONN ITALIC.

CANDLEWICK PRESS
99 DOVER STREET
SOMERVILLE, MASSACHUSETTS 02144

VISIT US AT WWW.CANDLEWICK.COM

WWW.VERMONIA.COM

Coming soon . . .